Mystic Highland Legend

Daniel Thompson

PublishAmerica
Baltimore

© 2010 by Daniel Thompson.
All rights reserved. No part of this book may be reproduced, stored in a retrieval system or transmitted in any form or by any means without the prior written permission of the publishers, except by a reviewer who may quote brief passages in a review to be printed in a newspaper, magazine or journal.

First printing

All characters in this book are fictitious, and any resemblance to real persons, living or dead, is coincidental.

PublishAmerica has allowed this work to remain exactly as the author intended, verbatim, without editorial input.

Hardcover 978-1-4512-1285-3
Softcover 978-1-4512-1386-7
PUBLISHED BY PUBLISHAMERICA, LLLP
www.publishamerica.com
Baltimore

Printed in the United States of America

To Jo
Best Wishes
Paul Williams

Chapter I

Driving rain swept down and the violent sky cracked as three shallow draft war ships drove up on the dark rocky shore of our remote island. A large fir tree exploded in smoke and flames from a direct strike while the busied Vikings went about their duties. With their mind on the business of securing their ships, they paid little attention to the explosion a few meters away.

Gretchen and I watched from our rock near the natural harbor inlet of this Isle, located in the stormy North Irish Sea between Northwestern Scotland and Ulster, Ireland.

The high pitched screech of wood scraping on beach rocks echoed off of the high cliffs above the shore and onto my sensitive ears. Crews of thirty, war clad warriors jumped over the sides into chest deep surf with practiced ease. The hustle with which the group performed their tasks reflected years of experience at sea and adept skill in beaching their light weight warships far from their native, Scandinavian village.

With heavy lines tethered to the bow, below the ship's towering serpentine head, ten crewmen formed a tow line and pulled each vessel onto shore and secured them from the reach of the pulsing surf. No man tried to speak above the roar from nearby lightening strikes nor the driving wind as they went about their well practiced routine of flipping the ships on their sides. They would be used as shelter against the downpour. The frenzied beach activity washed with sea foam as the storm bashed against the high walls above the shore.

Each lethal, leather vested warrior was enlivened by the prospect of new exploration of these unfamiliar shores of the Irish Sea and the uncharted land within. The urgency of making camp this first night peaked as another strike from the violent sky struck in their midst.

Like stage hands between scenes of a Viking longhouse victory celebration, the movement was sure handed, quiet and efficient. New urgency was brought on by another bolt of lightning that lit up the sky and the figure of their mighty Chieftain standing firmly on the shore in the middle of the activity, his massive arms crossed over a mighty chest.

Within a few moments of landing, the three overturned ships protected meager supplies, stowed under the makeshift canopy. A few hide bound portions of mead, a satchel of hard biscuits and a bundle of dried fish were placed next to the colorful array of ceremonial shields that came ashore attached to the sides of the three ships. They had been proudly displayed adjacent to their owners rowing position, as a mark of the man who carried it into battle.

Prince Rollo, of the Vysteinssen clan, the mighty Viking Chieftain of this band looked inland towards the western fading light. The outline of the rock strewn hills above the shore and a few of the details of the shoreline were still visible in the strained light of dusk and the fast moving storm that bought Rollo's crew to the relative safety of the shore. The hill top and rocky cliff face appeared momentarily as the last few bolts of lightning from the passing storm lit up the landscape to the west.

I knew Rollo must know that he was on the eastern side of the biggest isle of the *Sudrys, The Southern Isles*, as they were known by Scandinavians but the dim light of dusk hid the details of his surroundings and exact position.

My daughter Gretchen, sat at my side on the storm washed rocks that protected the inlet as we watched Rollo and the crew make camp. Gretchen was being entertained by the seals that played around her graceful fluke, excited by the light show around them and the driving surge bashing onto our rocky perch. The seals barked and yawned while they swam near Gretchen, darting in one direction and another, trying to entice her to join them in their folly around the rocks.

The passing war ships had given the seals as much energy as the beach landing gave a young shipmate among Rollo's crew, named Knut. Gretchen showed little interest in the seal's play. She was occupied, as I was, watching the crews make camp. We were trying to learn as much as we could about Rollo and the mission that had taken he and his crews so far from home and away from their normal hunting and raiding sea routes on the opposite side of Britannia. Ventures off of the western shore were quite rare in these times, unlike the busy eastern shore and the islands of Orkney and The Shetlands.

"Aren't these uncharted seas for Nordic crews?" Gretchen asked. "I thought that they were more interested in monasteries and villages along the eastward side of Britannia."

"That is true, Gretchen," I said. "This is a new land for them. This isle sits between Britannia's western shore and the Isle of Hibernia of the old Kingdom of *Dal Riata*. They must be on an important mission as Grandmother suspected."

I am Esther, the first daughter of Sarah, Princess among Maidens of the Seas of Britannia, Hibernia and the Isles of The Hebrides. We were sent to watch Prince Rollo from the rocks off shore. I do not like high winds brought in by night storms, but I should be used to it though I dread the seas on the west side of Britannia. I prefer the leeward side where we can bask in the sun without being walloped around like baitfish in a fisherman's wooden bucket. I have spent every day of my seven centuries among these sparse, rock strewn islands and violent shores. I just prefer the more peaceful waters of the leeward side.

My daughter Gretchen comes from the line of the first King of the mighty, founding people of the highlands. They were known as, "The Pict." Like the Vikings, the Pict are a hardy people who scrape out a living during these difficult times in lands where their work in the fields bring few rewards. The inland soils are not suited for farming crops other than grains for small farming villages and family strongholds. They have learned to mix what they can grow in small garden patches with morsels that they take from the shoreline. The people of the highlands are a hardy breed who have little that is not made from highland stone. This sturdy, independent breed are as steadfast as the twisted, snarly tree trunks on the shores of these isles that resist bending with the wind and they, like their Norse neighbors, are proud and stingy with the few treasures that they gather in their difficult existence.

The unwavering, independent determination of these stoic people is both their greatest gift and their haunting, worst enemy. Gretchen's Father was such a man. The blood of a strong, determined and heroically brave man runs through her veins along with the traits of centuries of Irish Sea Maidens, known to the Celtic people as *Mur'uchs*.

The Viking Prince who Scandinavians called "Rollo," is a big man. Quite a handsome man, I thought. From the top of his broad brass and leather helmet and leather clad chest, to his high laced seal skin boots, he stood dominant among his crew. They scurried around the camp site finishing their duties on the shore that Rollo selected for tonight's camp with practiced rhythm of a well disciplined and experienced crew.

Rollo's tree trunk like legs were firmly planted on the rocky shore, spread wide to proclaim this island, his own, with lightening cracking all around him, Rollo stood out in the open watching his crew prepare fires under the canopy of his ships, tipped on their sides with oars acting as piers holding the ship from the rocky shore. There was no doubt of who was in charge of this group, though neither direction nor gesture came from the man in the center of the frenzied activity.

As they finished their last preparations Rollo duct under the ship's canopy and took the brass and fur clad helmet from his unruly crop of red-brown hair that hung, braided, down his back in twin tails.

Young Knut, Rollo's thirteen year old camp boy, had come over the side of the ship moments before with a sling used for collecting fire wood and half of the agility of the other crew members who landed on the beach with a manly and certain thud.

"Where are we Prince Rollo?" the boy asked. "What are we going to do here?" he persisted in unrestrained excitement brought on by the activity of his fellow crewmen who scampered across the pebbled surface.

"Gather the wood, Knut" Rollo growled. "I will answer your questions later. For now, we need to get settled, fires lit and our gear stowed away from this infernal storm."

"Yes Prince," Knut mumbled. "But, I just wanted to know where we are, what we are doing here and has anyone ever been here before?" he said apologetically.

"Ha!" Rollo roared, his voice echoed through the ship's inverted interior. "Is that all that you need to know? I am surprised that there is not much more, young mate."

The other crew members looked back at Rollo and Knut in appreciation of the patience that their Captain had for his young shipmate. There was a noticeable bond between the big crew chief and his young charge. The familiarity that Rollo allowed the young crewmate revealed a special place for the boy dressed in tattered cloth held together with wide sashes and hide strings. Knut enjoyed far more leeway with Rollo's famous temper and though they recognized that fact, they allowed the boy his special place in Rollo's presence.

"Viking crews are 'no-nonsense' people who take the lead of a man who has earned their allegiance and respect brought through his leadership, his warring skills and the bounty of loot from raids along the eastern shores of Britannia that he rewards them with. He provides for them and they return his care with unquestioned loyalty," I told Gretchen.

"He is a different kind of Chieftain, Mother," Gretchen said. "He is strong and yet kind to his young shipman."

"Rollo is a different breed of Viking Chieftain, indeed," I answered.

"Most would not allow a camp boy to question a crew chief, especially in a driving storm that threatened to soak their supply of grain, mead bags and dried meats. This Rollo is different. In the midst of this, he found time to chide his young crew mate," I said. "He is bound for a special destiny, it seems."

"We are on the biggest of the Sudry Isles, west of Caledonia," I heard Rollo pronounce to his young mate. We are here to explore this island as a possible settlement for our people, and, no, as far as I know, no one has ever settled here before. Now go get the firewood before I plant my boot on your boney arse!" Rollo growled.

The rest of the crew laughed at Rollo's jesting with their young camp boy.

"Ha!" Rollo's graveled voice roared. His words echoed off of the looming, high cliffs above the shore as he stepped out into the downpour and watched young Knut scurry off for more firewood.

Rollo showed at least some of the same excitement of his half litre camp boy as his laughter filled the camp.

I could see that Rollo was especially fond of the boy. The growl spoken out by the giant Captain did not upset the boy, cause him to cower or deny his curiosity. I saw appreciation for the youth's excitement for doing what Norsemen do. They explore.

The boy was too enlivened to think about settling down for the night. He had just stepped onto a big, broad, unknown island after many days on the ship. The days of anticipation before coming upon this unknown island, far from home, had the boy's interest captured in his head, under his three sided, woolen cap.

Understandably, the boy's curiosity peaked at the wrong time of day. His energy was poorly timed, given the time of night, but such were the lives of Viking explorers. They spent the lion's share of their lives on a ship traveling north, south and west from their native Norway.

The global reach of Norwegian ships extended in every direction except east into the Baltic where Danish crews patrolled the shores of Prussia.

Most likely, Knut had rested on the sail across the Irish Sea from the ancient settlement in Dumbarton, in the Strathclyde Province of Scotland. The prospect of seeing a new island lifted the boy's spirits and driven his natural curiosity for new lands and exploration.

Chapter II

Rollo and his fellow explorers were several days away from their home village in the far north of Scandinavia on a small tidal isle. They began this important mission more than a month ago. Rollo had been pressed by his father, the great sea captain, Rognvald Vysteinssen, to locate a settlement site. He had proposed this isle, in part, because he believed that it was uninhabited. That alone held promise for new farm lands for his homeland villagers.

The neighboring seas were thought to be as productive as the virgin farm land. With no one around to challenge their claim, this isle held the promise of a bounty that had long disappeared from their homeland.

That was promising indeed, for his instructions were to lay claim to a settlement site without a fight. "There will be no need to strip it away from an owner," Rollo's Father promised. "Find a virgin land, far from another settlement and claim it as our own. We need to settle in peace with the promise of a productive land. Our homeland is can no longer support our numbers. Make haste, son."

Vikings had no issue with stealing. However, their patron intended to claim a territory upon which they could build productive villages with the prospect of much improved living conditions.

I had learned Rollo's history from my Grandmother. She told me about Rollo many years ago. His home village is in Norway. Rollo is the son of Rognvald Vysteinsson, The Earl of Moor. I understood that the man called Rollo, sometimes Hrolf, by his fellow Norwegians, was also the one who many called "Hrolf, The Walker." His huge frame prevented him from mounting a horse. He walked, instead.

Gretchen and I mused that we needed to help him find one of those big horses used by armored knights of Britannia or maybe one of the others, used in France to pull huge logs from the forest. Perhaps one of those could hold this big bruiser off of the ground. He was not just taller than his crewmen, his mass was nearly twice the others who scurried around on the rocky shore.

Little fat added to this man's bulk. He was big! Big boned and broad chested, he stood two heads over his crewmen. His arms and legs were thick with muscle and sturdy bone worked by years of a hard life on the sea.

Mother Sarah sent me to see where Rollo's band intended to settle. The islands that Norsemen called the Sudrys were largely uninhabited, just as they had predicted. The Isle would make a great home for a new Nordic settlement. Rollo's Father had been wise in his choice. They had done quite well.

"Rollo fell out of favor with King Haraldr of Norway," Grandmother said. Being relegated to a lower distinction as a Jarl, or Earl, he fled Norway to settle out of the reach of his alienated King. Grandmother had told me about Rollo's Father. She said that he was the leader of the Vikings in the Norwegian outpost that became known as Iceland. Like Rollo, Rognvald cared for his people. He was obligated to find a better life for them.

Rollo's fall from favor with his king did not affect the grace and solid assurance with which the big warrior carried himself, nor the respect that his crews held for him. They followed his orders without question or hesitance. In the wise words of Grandmother Estella, "there can be but one captain on a Viking crew."

Rollo's camp faced east, towards the gentle shore on the opposite side of Britannia in a land that Romans called 'Caledonia' where the high fortress of Lindisfarne stood prominently upon the stone mount in the center of the small, coastal isle. I had seen the dark stone fortress that rose from the tiny isle. It was a structure built to impress its subjects with all of its pomp and grandeur. There was nothing humble about the dark stone walls and tower that pointed upward, toward the skies as if to pronounce the future of its pompous inhabitants in heaven.

As Mother instructed, I was on the beach when they came ashore to raid Lindisfarne a month ago. They came to pillage the rich monastery for coins of silver and gold and supplies from the hoard known to be kept for the exclusive use of the fat churchmen who resided over starving peasants.

Rollo needed to renew supplies before he set off to explore the west coast of Caledonia and the outlying Sudrys.

Lindisfarne was on Holy Island, just off shore of the northern border between Britannia, of the south and Caledonia in the north. Britannia had been seized long ago by the Romans as part of their vast empire and let go when they were unable to capture the loyalty of native highlanders.

We watched Rollo's crew preparing camp for night watch. They started a fire under with the wood that Knut provided and gathered under their portable cover. They collected grasses to cushion the cold, rocky surface for sleeping and they broke out a supply of dried meat and biscuits which would serve as supper.

Over the noise of Gretchen's playmates, I heard Knut say, "not like home, Prince Rollo." He ran off for yet another load of wood, "we have lots of fire wood here," Knut yelled. Knut's enthusiasm drove the completion of his chores. He disappeared into the flickering, orange light of their first fire on the isle. The crackle and pop of the fire added to Knut's excitement as he darted off to claim more wood before it all became soaked in the persistent rain.

Unlike their homeland, the Sudrys, as Nordic crews called them, are covered with trees. Rollo must have seen this from his camp. The great, high cliffs blocked his view inland, towards the west but the outline of a tree lined shore to the south looked promising. The tidal isles of his homeland had been denuded of trees from the fragile forest that survived the conditions of the Nordic North.

Strategically, this camp site would make a great base for their explorations to the south of Britannia and the land that they call "Wales." Knowing that Vikings chose their settlement sites to improve the shipping lanes for gathering goods and loot in lands further to the south, this site was an ideal location for a stop off to the south western shores of Britannia as well as the western reach of the kingdom of Dal Riata.

Rollo's Father had finally won a struggle with Hibernian natives near the mouth of the River Poddle and a small settlement that he called 'Dublinh.'

Gretchen and I watched the activity on shore as Mother instructed. Sarah, Queen of the Mur'uchs of the Irish Sea and the shores of the Britannia was not to be trifled with. She and our kind are known by some in these times, as "Mermaids." The Irish call us "Mur'uchs," (Mur-ooks) in their Celtic legends and lore of supernatural creatures of the sea.

Like mermaids of other cultures, we have the upper bodies of mortal women. We have human-like arms, except for the green scales on our wrists and webbed hands. Our lower body is similar to a porpoise, with a powerful fluked tail that propels our bodies through the water. We can swim for great distances, like a porpoise, but we prefer to lay claim to an island or mainland shoreline where we take possession of rocks off shore and watch over the villages and settlements of our human subjects.

Our ability to adapt our physical appearance to meet a man's personal preference is a skill used in luring a man and take from him whatever we desire, the seed of their loins. Mur'uchs outside of Mother's realm often take their suitors to a merciless death in the depths of their domain. We choose to take the seed of the most powerful among them to improve our own bloodlines

Tales of Mur'uchs of our realm tell of fishermen and sailors who capture us and take us ashore as their mortal wives after they take the source of our power, our red, seal skin hat. We stay with our captor and even care for our children for as long as they keep it hidden from us. We will leave him and the children and return to our water world if we find our hat.

Our vision is much like a human's, being no stronger or weaker than theirs. We depend more upon our accute hearing. It is several times stronger than a human's, especially while submerged. So much so, that loud noises cause severe discomfort. We try to avoid areas where there are frequent loud noises. If a mortal really wanted to keep a mermaid away, all that they would have to do was expose us to banging and screeching noises. They affect our hearing and our sensory organ that receives vibration and disturbance in the water.

The sound of Rollo's ships driving up onto the rocky shore put chills down my spine. I wanted to submerge, below the rock where we sat watching the camp. We cannot function in a noisy environment.

Estella is my Grandmother. She is the Queen of the shores of Scandinavian settlements on Norwegian, Swedish and Danish shores. She warned Mother that a crew of three ships left the ancient port of Oslo on a mission that would take them west. She said that they were packed for a long expedition.

"See where they go, Sarah," Grandmother had ordered. "Have them followed and tell me where they put ashore," Estella said.

"The Norse people have become restless. Their King is driving them away from my realm and I must know where they intend to make their new home," she told Mother.

"The raid on Lindisfarne had been a fortunate first stop in Rollo's mission," I told Gretchen. "They intended to collect enough loot to trade with the Nordic outpost in the Orkney Islands, just off of the far northern coast of Caledonia. The Orkney isles are part of a group of the Inner Hebrides Islands. They are home to Nordic trading settlements and ports, much as this settlement will function once they have erected homes, a longhouse, pier and storage buildings for supplies."

"Once fully supplied, they planned to sail down the west coast of Caledonia, towards the mouth of the big river that the Anglos called, 'The Clyde.' Rollo and his crew needed grain, dried meat and fish for the remainder of the voyage and the first few months of their camp. They would get those supplies on Orkney once they had funds to trade with."

Chapter III

Grandmother had advised us that Viking settlements and villages on the tidal islands of Scandinavia had become overcrowded in recent times. The land no longer supported the family groups that built settlements on Nordic coast lines as far east as Gotland, off shore from the land of the Swedes.

The riches that they took from churchmen in Lindisfarne and other monasteries would supply them for months to come. They used loot from such raids to finance their explorations and to reward their ship crews for their loyalty.

Rollo and Rognvald favored Lindisfarne for the first raid. It was believed to hold the largest hoard of valuables of all of the monasteries in Britannia.

At Lindisfarne, the three *drakkars* came ashore before mid day. The immense rock mound in the center of the small, tidal isle kept a high fortress and monastery at its peak. Rollo expected to find riches of gold and silver that were known to be hidden within the high stone walls.

I watched the raid begin as I stood on the shore of Lindisfarne, disguised in the clothes of a peasant girl. Mother wanted me to witness Rollo's business, where ever he put ashore. I stood by at a good vantage point to see Rollo's crews ram their ships ashore in a manner that brought attention to their arrival. The landing was loud but sure. The crunching and scraping noises made by the wooden ships as they glided over shore rocks were disturbing to my senses. I tried not to flinch at the intentional disruption on the peaceful shore.

Rollo intended to have local villagers see and hear the approach of the dreaded, serpent headed ships and run for cover, leaving the monks to fend for themselves. As I had learned from previous raids, Rollo had no quarrel with the peasants who worked around such big fortresses. He had no intention to see them harmed. He only wanted the loot from the high fortress that loomed over the small peasant village at its base.

The noise of the ships ramming over the rocky beach insured that civilians would not get in the way of his crews. Before the Vikings arrived, I watched as men and women of the village rummaged around the grounds like chickens living off of the crumbs of the wealthy.

With their swords and shields raised high, the crew ran by me on their way to the high fortress, making all of the noise that they could muster. I lowered my head to avoid being seen by Rollo as he raced by me.

I was concerned for the village fishermen and shore scavengers as they scattered in every direction screaming crewmen, but no harm came to them. They were allowed to flee and take shelter. Rollo was not on Lindisfarne to kill peasants. He was after gold coins, silver and gold challises and ceremonial ornaments that churchmen used to hold their subjects in awe of their power. Only God like creatures could possibly possess such riches and power.

Finally, I heard the sound of splitting wood and crashing iron hinges coming from the entrance of the monastery. The monks were in Morning Prayer as Rollo's crew split the door open with a makeshift log ram. I ran up the hill to the huge stone structure that sat at the top of a high outcropping of black rock.

The sanctity of Lindisfarne's retreat disappeared forever as the heavy wooden door crashed to the stone floor. Rollo and his band had an obvious and certain disdain for monks and their mighty fortresses. That was easy to see from my vantage on the steps to the grand entrance.

The absence of light momentarily halted the charge. The small high set windows let in little natural light. When their eyes finally adjusted, the crew charged the monks who were gathered around a large table. The Abbot and his monks jumped up from their bench seats in shock at the intrusion.

Rollo grabbed the priest at the head of the table and drew his dagger. The blade rested on the old Abbott's throat. As the knife drew a trickle of blood, the crew swiftly dispatched the other monks. Crewmen rejoined their Chieftain and the old Abbott, held silent with the certain prospect of losing his head.

"Where are your riches, you fat, old tyrant?" Rollo demanded.

"Where have you hidden your supplies?"

"I swear, I will bring this sword to the crown of your arrogant scalp and do these peasants a great favor if you do not show me to your treasures and stores," Rollo yelled. "You miserable, old tyrant, I will feed you to the crows!"

Rollo could not have expected an answer. The old Abbott had little knowledge of Rollo's Germanic tongue and Rollo did not speak the language of Anglos. I saw Rollo press the knife with more force against the Abbott's throat when he did not attempt to offer his valuables and food supplies.

The crew collected a few shiny challises, crosses and plates left out in the open and packed them in their loot bags. Those items were easy pickings. There was little else to be found in the open.

It would take more effort to find what the crews were looking for. They intended to take all of the time that they needed.

I knew that in these times, monasteries were not protected by the church's army. There would be no rescue or protection of the inhabitants or the wealth of this once peaceful religious retreat.

"Look in every room. We are not leaving until we find their hoard of treasures," I heard him say as I stood by the doorway. "I want to leave nothing unturned until we find the silver and gold that this place holds," He said

"These walls and heavy doors are intended to separate the peasants from the riches held within. There would otherwise be no need for them."

The only means of communicating with the old monk was through pressure of the blade at his throat and the fist full of the monk's hair fringe around his ears. Rollo had a lethal hold of the old man's hair. He pulled on it so hard, I thought that he would lift it from his scalp.

Rollo pressed the blade with more force, causing the old Abbott to choke and gasp. He finally pointed towards a corner room in the big sanctuary.

"Here they are, Rollo," a crewman yelled from the other side of the hall.

He was immediately joined by his comrades. They knocked the store room door down. A room with shelves and wine barrels, bread, dried fish and meats lined the walls and covered the floor, came into view with candle light carried in by the crew.

There were pork legs and dried fish. Several deer carcasses hung from a rack in the corner. All were covered in salt and hung on iron hooks inside the cool, dark room.

"Take what we need for the voyage to Orkney," Rollo directed. "These monks have much more than they need to feed the few of them within these walls. Take what we need and leave the doors open for the village peasants."

"These churchmen hold far too many riches for such an obscure and remote place," a crewman named Ruud, said to his chief.

Rollo roared with each demand. It was plain to see that he had a deadly disrespect for the Anglo churchmen and their big, fancy fortress.

Later, I spoke with Knut on the shores of Orkney, I came to understand that his hatred of this place and their traditions was not one that came overnight. He had a deep seeded hatred for religious sanctimony. He believed that these fortresses were financed by peasants who had little enough money to feed themselves, while these fat monks sat on their arse's feeding themselves into obesity."

"It is their way," Rollo ranted.

"They show homage to their God by hoarding what no common believer could possibly own. They separate their God from common man with huge buildings and high walls. They perform strange ceremonies in a language that commoners do not understand."

"Take it all. They are fools."

"Odin never needed such riches and their God does not either. We will make better use of these things."

"I despise this place," Rollo ranted.

I watched him overturn tables and benches as he took his disgust on inanimate objects around the room. It was easy to see his certain disrespect for the monastery. Whether he was right or wrong in his accusations of the mortal's religion, he was certain in his beliefs.

"Odin has been celebrated for thousands of years," Rollo told his crew. "

"He requires nothing more than a quiet place to pray. Damn these people and their colossal churches mounted on the backs of their own peasants!"

I believe that the contempt that Rollo displayed helped him justify the carnage that came upon Lindisfarne that day. Other Christian monasteries fell over the next several years. That made that fact abundantly clear.

High taxes, levied on peasants were the reason that Rollo and his father left Norway. King Haraldr also placed a huge and unreasonable burden on his destitute public, just as the Church of Rome and the Bishops of Britannia.

The senior Vysteinsson had seen enough of this arrogance in his adopted settlement in Iceland, with the expansion of Christianity on the mainland and Scandinavia. Christians had been around for almost eight-hundred years. It was no longer new and the ways of its church officers were well established.

Vysteinssen believed that the leaders of the Christian church in Rome enriched their lives and exist in privilege at the expense of commoners. Rollo had seen too much self-aggrandizing financed by the purses of a people held captive while supporting the opulence of church officers. Vysteinssen believed that the Christian church had forgotten the simple and peaceful message left by Christ and his disciples who traveled throughout the Mediterranean, teaching the way of their messiah.

We had all seen the misery of commoner's lives in Britannia. These raids should not have come as a surprise to anyone. The message of their messiah was good, and even humble, but the celebration of his life in languages that common man could not understand was where it failed when compared to the old, humble, pagan traditions of Normans. Vysteinsson became a Christian himself, but he had no respect for the pomp of organized religion. His views estranged him from many of his peers in Scandinavia, including the King.

Over the decades of watching Norsemen in this region, I had seen the simple, Pagan ways in which they showed appreciation for the few blessings that their difficult existence provided. They are a humble people and no fortune came without thanks to Odin, the Norse God of the north.

There were many Christian converts in the settlement in Iceland. There, the savior's message was celebrated in its simplest form. In Britannia, however, Vysteinssen believed that God was kept from the poor with layers of rich churchmen who insisted on keeping Christ's message to themselves, while feeding the public with self gratifying interpretation when they saw fit. Rollo's views were common among his countrymen. Grandmother told us of the growing disrespect that Chieftain's and governor's of Britannia held for the organized church and the self indulgence that its leaders gave themselves.

"They do not practice what they preach," as Rollo always said. "Let them live as true believers live."

"Now I see why they need the heavy doors and walls of fortresses. They hoard riches from their own people," Ruud said. "Doors like these are made to keep riches away from those on the other side."

"Look at the high stone walls of the big room. This is a fortress. This is not a place of worship," he said. "Wherever there is a heavy door, there is treasure to be found on the other side of it. Without treasures, why would such heavy doors be needed? The natives of this village toiled for years to build such a place. They pay taxes to support the arrogant fools who live within these walls," Rollo reasoned.

"Ahhh! Damn these fools!" he roared.

Rollo and his warriors took what they needed and left the doors open for the village to take the rest. The head priest was hoisted onto a hook on the door of the store room. When they filed out through the open doorway on their way out, the hood of the fat Abbott's brown smock, suspended him above the floor. He was left to age with the remaining provisions.

The crew led Rollo through the door, still ranting and raving about his hatred of those who kept their God from common people.

"This way," Ruud said. "This way Prince. We have all that we can carry."

I lowered my head as the crew ran past me. I looked up as they led Rollo through the doorway and out onto the steps. Rollo momentarily halted his escorts as he approached me.

Rollo stood near me and looked into my eyes. He said nothing. His crew led him towards their ships, but the fleeting expression on his face as he saw me made me realize that he recognized my origin. He tried to stop his crew as he passed. He was only able to look backwards as they led him down the wide steps of the monastery. I returned his smile. I was sure that our courses would cross again.

"By the spear of Odin, I want to burn this damned place down," Rollo growled, still protesting his removal from the fortress. With the goal securely in hand, the crew led Rollo out of the retreat and down the hill towards their ships secured on the beach."

Chapter IV

When the crew ushered Rollo onto his ship and left Lindisfarne, they sailed north to the Inner Hebrides and the islands of Orkney. Norsemen and the Pictish people lived peacefully among each other on the heavily used isles off of the far northern shores of Caledonia. Vikings established a settlement and a jumping off point for their wide travels to the south or the west. I followed behind them, as Mother had instructed.

Orkney held a small, but booming port village with twenty or more huts of sod and stone. Single room dwellings helped villagers escape the cold, damp climate of these northern islands. There were no trees remaining on Orkney to use for rafters or wall supports, nor was there wood for fires. Dried peat blocks and body heat were the only fuels to be had.

The faces and bodies of many of the Pictish inhabitants of these huts were adorned with symbols of their native Celtic culture. Similar symbols were carved into freestanding rocks and monoliths around their village and on the high on the bluffs overlooking the sea.

The old Celtic people that the Romans called Picts, called themselves Cruithne, or Pryten. In the early times of their inhabitance on these isles, it was said that they were short, stocky and often had a crop of fire red hair. Since then, they had intermarried with Norsemen and many of those traits have been bred away.

Rollo had his ships put ashore near an Orkney village and secured for the night. After resting tonight, they would begin the important task of exploring the western seas for a settlement site.

"Knut," Rollo said, "set watch over the ships through the night. I will be in the village longhouse," I heard him tell the boy.

Knut humbly did as his master instructed. I was sure that he would rather have followed Rollo to the village tavern and the reception that his Chieftain would receive, but he did as he was told and stayed by his master's small fleet of ships.

Rollo walked towards the village to join a small crowd in the sod covered longhouse. There was a fire pit in the center and a few rustic tables and benches along the walls where other crewmen sat and took their evening meal. Rollo joined them for a cup of mead to warm his belly.

I could easily hear the crowd in the tavern as I listened from behind the tavern. It was a boisterous crowd, typical for a gathering of Viking crews. After long stints at sea, these men were ready for the flow of mead, heather ale and highland whiskey as well as a visit with a few tavern winches supplied by the local inn keeper.

I watched the young crewman take Rollo's command in silence. He obediently laid his shield, bow and arrow quiver against one of the ships and found a comfortable seat for the night. He covered himself against the cold night wind with a fur cape that he had worn around his shoulders on the voyage north from Lindisfarne.

I decided to find out more about Rollo and his dislike for the Monks of Lindisfarne from the young seaman.

I dressed myself in peasant cloth. My human form would not alert the boy or cause him alarm. He did not see me swim ashore from the rock where I had witnessed Rollo and his crew beach their drakkars, nor did he see me change my form and take the appearance of a village peasant girl.

I walked towards Knut. I hoped that he would tell me more about the raid and Rollo's plans.

Knut stood as I approached. I sensed his concern. "Who is it?" he yelled out.

"Just a peasant girl," I lied.

When I came into view, Knut stood and looked me over. I sensed that he took his master's task seriously. I did not want to cause the young man concern, so I stood still as he challenged me.

"What do you want?" he asked.

"Just company on a cold night," I said.

Knut was tall and lean. He stood proudly as I approached, protecting his master's ships from an intruder. He notched an arrow in his bow as I came out of the dark.

"I mean no harm, Knut," I said. "I saw your Captain walk towards the village and I hoped that I could share your blanket."

Knut did not answer. Instead, he asked, "How do you know my name?"

"I heard your captain call you by name. You have nothing to fear from me, Knut. I only want some company tonight and hoped that you would share your blanket with me," I said. "I have no blanket or shelter."

He remained standing while I sat near his bow and shield. He rose and moved them from my reach before he hesitantly took a seat beside me.

"I am Esther," I said. "I live in the village. I saw your ships come ashore and wanted to see who it was," I lied.

I heard the tavern chatter rise as Rollo entered the sod covered stone building in the village, high on the hill above the port. His arrival brought new purpose and creditability to the Viking captains and crewmen gathered in the tavern. I heard many rise from their seats and greet him as he walked through the door.

"Prince Rollo," one called out. "Come, sit and take a cup of this dump's infamous grog that the inn keeper passes off for mead." The crowd roared with laughter as the crowd continued chastising the innkeeper.

Rollo would soon be telling the story of the raid on Lindisfarne. His description of the valuables that he claimed from Lindisfarne's Abbey would travel widely among Norse crews after tonight.

The reach of ships like Rollo's would be expanded as they cruised the shores of Scotland and Ireland, France and Britannia looking for opportunities like Rollo took advantage of at Lindisfarne. Travel to such places and more would be common if Rollo was successful in building a settlement on the Sudrys. The western base would allow Nordic crews to go on to the settlement on the River Poddle and on to Wales.

I wanted to hear it all. I sat near Knut and tuned my attention to the noises of the tavern.

As I expected, I heard Rollo detailing the riches that he took from Lindisfarne's Abbey to the crowd. His voice roared and his tankard crashed against those hoisted by others, celebrating his success. Rollo listed the loot from the monastery and the ease with which he took it from the unsuspecting Abbott.

The crowd cheered as Rollo explained how they came ashore and broke the door down like a pile of sticks. "The massive room could have held a crowd of thousands, yet was occupied with a few fat priests sitting around a table sipping mead and eating from loaves of sweet bread," he said.

"The door crashed to the floor as we rammed it down, making a terrible noise that caught the priests unaware. The jumped to their feet and tried to flee the chamber, but it was far too late for an escape," Rollo went on. "We finally found their stores in a corner room. It was full of hanging venison, wild boar and game hens. The shelves held sacks of wheat and barley, probably taken from their subjects as taxes. We relieved the old tyrant of his goods," Rollo bragged.

"Did they put up a fight?" I heard one ask.

"No," Rollo answered. They had no weapons and made no attempt at stopping us. Ruud broke the door down with the ram, while they sat at their table, praying. I wanted to take the old tyrant's head off for the riches that we found, but my crewmen stopped the swing of the sword," he said.

"It was the richest hoard that I have seen in one monastery," he bragged.

"Father said that we would find riches beyond our imagination there. Father said 'the bigger the church, the bigger the vault!'"

"So we took as much as we could carry and left the old monk hanging from a meat hook in his store room," I heard Rollo say. "There was venison, pork and salted fish hanging in their. Now there is a fattened monk hanging there as well."

Knut's voice took me away from Rollo's story in the longhouse and brought me back to the shore as he declared, "they are not my crews," he said.

"They are Rollo's crews. He is the Prince of the Nordic people of Norway," Knut corrected. "These are his ships and he left them with me to watch through the night."

"A Prince?" I asked, in mocked surprise.

"He is the son of Rognvald Vysteinssen, leader of Nordic people of Norway and Iceland," Knut boasted. "Our village settlement is led by Rollo and his father. He is a mighty warrior and the Captain of these crews."

"And, are you his son?" I asked.

"No. You ask too many questions," Knut objected.

I heard Rollo listing the loot from Lindisfarne. His voice carried a great distance to my ears. "There were silver platters and plates, cups and candle holders. The old man had enough gold around his scrawny neck to buy half of this village," he jested.

The crowd carried on for Rollo, making promises to raid a few monasteries of their own. "We'll strike out in the morning if you think that there may be more hanging there than the monk," one jested. "I am tired of my people trying to scratch a living off of the land in Norway. What little they gather is taken from them in taxes by the tyrant who is our King," he went on.

"Sure, help your self," Rollo answered. "We have enough to last us a few months."

"I only want to learn more about you and your captain. You are a handsome young man and I am only interested in getting to know you while we sit together. Your captain has left you with great responsibility. You must be important to him," I said, when I turned my attention back to Knut, hoping to prompt the young man to relax his guard.

"My Father and Mother died of the coughing sickness," he said.

"Many people of our village took to the coughing sickness last season. There was sickness in every house of our settlement," Knut said.

He began to loosen his guard and hesitance to speak as he told me about his village. I detected his eagerness to speak with authority about

Norway, Rollo and the reason for their expedition. The importance of the raid on Lindisfarne would not be recognized by the youngster. His concentration was firmly planted on protecting his master's ships which he had been left in charge.

"We live in a small settlement that Rollo and his father started many years ago. Other families joined them because they both care for their people, but we have outgrown it. We need to find a place for a new settlement where we can farm, fish and hunt," Knut said.

I knew from Grandmother's words that life was difficult on the tidal isles of the Norwegian coast. Viking crew had just begun to travel widely with an aim to find new settlement sites for their villagers. Survival during the winters in Norway required vast stores of grain and salted meats and fish. Without room to grow grain, stores fell short and winter die off of the old and very young hit their villages. Children were often adopted by other families, increasing the burden during hard times.

"Tomorrow, we begin our expedition," Knut said, as his voice brought me back to the young man's words of concern.

"We will probably go south and see if we can find a settlement site," he said. "Our island is overcrowded. We have no room to grow," Knut said.

The gravity of their mission was clear to young Knut. I could see the seriousness of his commitment to the important task before them. His young brow, below a crop of red brown hair tucked into his wool cap wrinkled as he explained how they needed to find relief from the misery and poverty of their home island.

"Rollo took me in after my parents died. My father was a crewman on one of his ships," Knut said. "Rollo watches over me out of respect for my Father."

"May I share your cover?" I asked. "It is cold tonight and I did not bring my cape."

Knut pulled the cover over our shoulders and we leaned back against the ship. The blanket was not big enough to maintain the distance Knut intended to keep between us. I decided to take the initiative and move closer to him. He leaned away from me, still unsure of my intentions. I am sure that he had never sat with a woman and he was not sure of himself or this encounter with me. His eyes stayed on me for the first few moments as we sat back against the hull.

As he told me about his master and how he was treated as his son, the space between us gradually narrowed. He enjoyed talking about Rollo, so I let him tell me what he wanted me to know, while he relaxed with me. I could see that he was a serious young man. He was honest and straightforward in his unrelenting support of Rollo.

I began to enjoy his company as we relaxed under the stars that lit the night sky over Shetland. He looked at my face and into my eyes when I spoke. I was sure that this was a new encounter for young Knut.

"Where have you come from, on your voyage?" I asked.

"We came from an isle off shore in Britannia, named Lindisfarne," he told me.

I did not interrupt him or let him know that I witnessed the raid.

"What did you do there?" I asked.

"We raided the big monastery there," he said. "Rollo and the crew took what we needed from the Abbott and his monks. We needed treasure and goods for trade here on Orkney. We took what we needed and left the remainder for the peasants."

"Are you going to trade for goods, here?" I asked.

"Yes. Rollo will get grain, knife blades, axes and other things while we are here," he answered. "The rest of the loot will be divided up among Rollo's crewmen. Our crews are loyal to Rollo and his father. They take care to reward us with a share of the loot that we take from monasteries like Lindisfarne. Loyalty is important to Rollo. Without it, Rollo could not help them find a new settlement," young Knut told me.

I moved closer and he leaned into the warmth of my body. He looked a bit uncomfortable with our closeness, but he went on to tell me more about the raid on Lindisfarne. I could feel the cold leave his body as he took my warmth and leaned against my chest and shoulders. His hesitance left his mind as he found the comfort of a woman's body consoling.

"Rollo despises the Anglo monks," Knut said.

"Our people are poor," he went on. "The more fortunate among us, like Rollo, share what they have with the village. No one lives better than the poorest among us," Knut said. "It is our way," he said proudly.

"Does Rollo have a wife in his village?" I asked.

"No," Knut answered, hesitantly. "She died during the last winter season,....with my Mother."

"Our village is poor and winter seasons bring struggle and death to our people. Our land is overcrowded and our forests have been used up. We have little firewood and no place to hunt for game, without traveling to foreign shores. All Norwegians face the same problem. We need to find a place for a new settlement," he repeated.

"We left our home village to find a place where we can plant crops and hunt the forest. Too many die each winter. We have seen people from other lands who do not suffer as we do," Knut explained.

The furrow of his brow showed his genuine concern. His eyes opened wide as he talked about the issues that were so important to him.

"Rollo is respected by all Nordic people," Knut said. "He and his Father have always looked after us. Now our King has raised taxes in our village when he knows that we can not pay," he said, looking into my eyes. He touched my arm, wrapped around his shoulder while we shared our warmth under the cover.

Knut leaned in against my chest and as if he wanted to ensure himself that I was a young woman as I had presented myself. When his shoulder found the side of my breast, he moved his arm to investigate its soft, fullness. I smiled to myself with the young man's subtle attempt at testing my womanhood. My young friend was more mature than I had thought. I pulled his shoulder in to my chest and squeezed him. He found my soft flesh pleasing and settled in against me. I was amused with the young sailor and was happy to provide him with the comfort of a woman's embrace.

He looked into my eyes and touched his fingers to the skin on my arm and hands with a bit of an inquisitive look on his face as if he had a question in his mind that he did not have words for.

Someday, I will join Rollo's crew as a warrior and hold my sword to the throats of English churchmen like Rollo did," Knut boasted.

"Our King is only interested in his own wealth," Knut continued. "We want a place where we can live without King Haraldr or his taxes. Rollo will find that place. I know that he will because he always does what he promises," Knut said.

I watched over Knut during the night. He continued to pour his heart out with his admiration for the man who intended to find a better life for his fellow Norsemen. Knut laid his cheek under my chin and found the security of warmth against the cold night air.

Knut finally relaxed, completely, as he told me more about his village. I kept my arm over his shoulder as a cold breeze rose across the shore and my young friend found comfort in my embrace.

Knut refused to fall asleep. He knew his responsibilities and he resisted letting his master down and he was probably too entertained by our closeness to fall asleep anyway.

I was sure that he had never felt the warmth of a woman. Knut was young and inexperienced. I felt the uncertainty of his mind as he adjusted his head on my shoulder. I had no intentions of taking him from his innocence or to take advantage of his uncertainty as others of my kind would certainly have done if given this opportunity.

I would fulfill my needs and my Mother's plan at a different time in a different manner with an adult male of the human kind.

"Do you have a man?" he asked.

"No," I said. "I have not found a man to take me in."

"How old are you?" he asked.

"I am twenty, or so," I answered. "My mother and I live together after my Father left us."

"What happened to him?" Knut asked.

"He left one day. We never saw him again," I lied.

"Now look who's asking all of the questions," I chided. He looked up from my shoulder and smiled. "Can you stay with Rollo and me, forever?" he asked.

"I do not know what the future will bring. Perhaps we will meet again and then we will see what is in store for us," I said.

The sounds of merriment had long settled down in the village. I was sure that Rollo and his crews were turned in for the night. As I sat beside Knut, listening to his story, I first heard foot steps coming from the far side of the ship. Knut did not hear the sound. I placed my finger over my lips as a sign to be silent and rose from my place next to Knut.

"Shhh. I said.

"What is it?" Knut asked.

"Shhh. We have a visitor," I whispered.

"Stay put for a minute and let me see what it is," I said.

When I walked around the back of the ship I saw a man approach and prepare to board the ship.

I had wondered what might come from Rollo speaking so openly in the tavern about the treasures that sat in his ships. Apparently, not all of his audience were honest enough to bypass their temptation of relieving Rollo of some of his ships' burden.

I thought that Knut would stay in the safety of the other side of the ship, but I heard him rise and start around the bow. I saw him kneeling below the serpent head as I took an oar and brought it across the head of the thief. He fell to the rocks without a noise. I turned around when I heard footsteps approaching. It was a second thief coming to the aide of his companion.

"Whack!" I heard an oar crack.

Knut hid along the inside wall of the ship from where he downed the second man with a swift blow to the head, as I had done.

"Got him!" Knut proclaimed.

We tied the two unconscious men together to await Rollo's arrival. Knut was so proud of his conquest. I decided that I would let him tell his master the story when he arrived in the morning.

I stayed with Knut through the night. We laughed at the two would-be robbers, trying to escape. They were lashed together with a single rope, that Knut draped over the bow's figurehead and connected the bound pair behind their backs.

"Where did you learn that trick?" I asked Knut.

"It is one of my master's ways. If they misbehave we will raise the line until they are suspended from the ground with their hands tied behind their back's, as Rollo does," Knut explained

We began to arise as Rollo approached. I wondered if he would remember me from the steps on Lindisfarne.

As he came upon us, he said, "What does Rollo do?" he asked.

"I showed her how you tie robbers from the figurehead," Knut explained.

"Oh, I see," Rollo said.

"Who might you be?" the big, handsome warrior asked.

"I am Esther. I am an orphan from the village. I came to share a blanket with your faithful crewman. I meant no harm," I said.

He placed his heavy hand on my head and rubbed my scalp in dismissal of my concern. He then extended his hand to help me stand. It was heavy and strong and his touch was firm.

Rollo held my hand in his big open palm as he inspected it. I did not resist nor interfere with his inspection.

"No harm done," he said. "I am sure that Knut enjoyed your company."

I let him hold my hand in his. His thumb tested the softness of my skin. I sensed his curiosity and perhaps some appreciation.

He lifted my hand to his lips and lightly brushed his lips across the top of it while he looked deep into my dark eyes. He let the moment linger, feeling the smoothness of my skin with his lips. I allowed his touch and even felt a stir from his presence. He acted as if he was holding the hand of a princess. I supposed that he was no stranger to gatherings of royalty in his native Nordic land.

"You are a beautiful young creature, my lady," he said. "Knut was a lucky young man to have found such a beautiful maiden to share a blanket. Few men meet the fortune of such an opportunity to sit with such a beautiful creature."

I noticed a hesitation in his voice that was surely caused by his inability to rest his mind with what I had told him. I knew that I was about to be discovered. He had called me a creature several times but I sensed no threat from the big Chieftain.

He reached out and gently lifted my chin with his wide, rough hand and looked me in my eyes once more. I knew at that moment that the big warrior recognized my kind. A broad smile crossed his lips. He looked at me and shook his head, ever so slightly as if in amazement of finding out a secret that others might have missed.

"From the village here, are you, now?" he asked with the broad smile still on his mouth.

He loomed over me with his mighty, leather sleeved arms crossed over his broad chest. He had the eyes that showed the confidence of a worldly man. I saw the knowing mind of a wise traveler and caregiver of his people. The sky blue tint of his gaze peered through my very core and made me wish that we had more time to spend together. I wondered if all Vikings would cause these deep stirrings of lust for these people.

The recognition of my kind did not cause him concern as it surely would have for a lesser man. He looked at me in a gentle, assured way that his knowledge of the legend of sea maidens brought to him and there was a calm assurance that I posed no threat to he or his young companion as a commoner would. He knew the power that our kind can bring down upon a human that has crossed our will our tried to harm one of us, but he somehow recognized that I was not here to cause harm as many of our kind would have.

There are those among us who would capture a man like Knut or Rollo and tear away their throats in the manner that we eat fish and take them to the depths of the sea to keep their corpses near the entrance to their lair as a trophy of power. That was not my purpose for being here and somehow Rollo recognized it.

As I looked, deeply into Rollo's eyes I saw the image of his preferences of the female form. The ideal image of a maiden kept deep within his mind matched the details of my form, face and figure in every way. I sensed an immodest desire in his eyes. The dark features of my eyes and the luster of my blue hewed, black hair that fell over my shoulders and onto my breasts were all within his preferences. I brushed my long hair from my chest and exposed the features of my form that he questioned in his mind. A smile of appreciation crossed his lips.

Perhaps like his young mate, Rollo would prefer the softness of fuller bodies to keep them warm at night but I knew that I was close Rollo's ideal image. He would not change my form in anyway and I found that unusual and strangely appealing. Perhaps I would have the opportunity at a later time to make adjustments to suit even his wildest, lustful fantasy.

For now, I knew that I had met his approval and that was all that I needed for now.

I mused over what Mother had once said about Viking's preference in women. "If we had to suit these rascals to their ideal we would walk bent over from the weight of our chests and we could never submerge again from their buoyancy." Mother had seen some of the larger framed women of their homeland who were built to hold heat under the fur covers during their brutally cold winters.

My animal instincts brought me to lust for the touch of his flesh against mine. I desired this big handsome warrior but I resisted. "We will meet again," I told myself.

"Rollo. Come see what we have done," Knut said. He led us to the opposite side of the ship where we found our two thieves lashed together. Knut had rags stuffed into their mouths to keep them quiet.

"Well, what do we have here?" Rollo asked?

"I whacked one and Esther whacked the other before they could get onto the ship. They must have been after your loot." Knut suggested.

"Well done, Knut," Rollo said, "and to you, young lady. I will have to turn these two over to the village chief and let him deal with them."

Rollo stood before me. I looked up at the handsome chief and our thoughts merged with the recognition between us and his confidence that I would not bring harm to he or his young mate. I was sure that he knew that I would seek him out at another time.

Rollo surely knew that I could wreck him, his ship and his young charge if provoked. I had seen my Mother bring havoc on dozens of men. I had defended myself on only a few rare occasions myself. Instead, there was a sweet sense of peace between us. He appreciated my assistance to his young shipmate and I appreciated the calm manner that he showed me.

Rollo wore a moss green sash that crossed over his shoulder and his chest, where it came down to his hip and a sword scabbard. His face was weathered behind the red beard. He had the gentle demeanor of a confident and well respected leader. I knew that I had not fooled him with my transparent ruse.

The big man smiled down at me as if waiting for me to offer a new explanation for my presence with Knut. I had never experienced this kind of peaceful encounter with a mortal man. I knew that he did not believe that a peasant girl would bring down two Nordic seamen. It was time to come straight with him.

"I am Esther, grand daughter of Estella of your native Scandinavian shores," I said. "I mean no harm to you or your loyal ship mate," I said.

He brushed his coarse hand across my cheek and continued his knowing stare into my eyes. The back of his hand lingered on my cheek and then moved down to brush a few hair strands away from my shoulders.

I sensed the anxiety of isolation from a woman's care that was part of his life at sea. I took his hand in both of mine and raise it to my lips for a soft kiss across the coarse hide that covered this kind hearted man's hand. My lips touched his coarse skin as my lips lingered. My coarse tongue touched his palm as I turned his hand over and kissed the other side. Rollo smiled and looked toward the sky as if to find relief for the agony of delay that was causing him to endure. We knew that we were toying with each other's minds.

His lack of concern of harm that I might bring to he and his young crewman struck me strangely, but also brought out the kindness that this big man carried for young people. His eyes were kind and appreciative of me and my kind.

I sensed an assurance and familiarity with all creatures of the sea. He carried no intention to capture me or try to take advantage of me as many humans might. Instead, his mind turned to taking me away for a sensual encounter in a peaceful place of his choosing. As Mother taught me many years ago, our kind selects the strongest men among mortals and allows them to take us away to mate and allow them pleasures of the flesh in exchange for their seed. I would have been pleased to do so with this big chieftain had I not set my intentions on a later encounter with him.

"Did we not meet on the steps of the fortress at Lindisfarne only a few days ago?" he asked.

"Yes," I said. There was no denying his memory of the brief moment when he looked into my eyes on Lindisfarne as they left the abbey.

"You are truly a beautiful, Esther. You have improved on your Mother's famed beauty. I have only seen her once and that was many years ago. She was the most beautiful of all Mur'uchs of these isles. I must say that you are at least her equal and I am pleased to find young Knut in your care."

He bent down and brought his lips to my cheek. I felt the softness of his lips through the stubble of his coarse beard as he moved his lips to mine and kissed me. He took in the sweet sea fragrance that Mur'uchs are known for. His fingers lifted my chin before he sighed a deep breath and withdrew.

"Oh my," he said as he shook his head in mock concern. "You and your Mother are made to be heart breakers," he teased. "And now you come to Knut's rescue."

I knew that he wanted more from our encounter and I would have gladly obliged this big gentle man under different circumstances. Somehow I found the confidence that we would meet again and would not be inhibited by the presence of a young man, too inexperienced in such matters.

I sighed with him. He was just as handsome as Mother said and a lot more gentle than some of his lust driven sea mates that Mother and I had come across before.

"I recalled your beauty from the brief time that I saw you a few days ago. I thought that you were likely a Sea Maiden then. You did not look like one of the weather beaten women of the village. You reminded me of the vision of your Mother that I have held in my mind for many years. You are much too beautiful, and her image has just been replaced by yours," he went on. I was a little surprised by his soft spoken compliments.

"I knew the instant that I saw you and kissed your hand, that you were not a mere orphan of the village. Mur'uchs have ageless skin. It is much different from that of our own women. There is a radiance about you that only comes from your kind," Rollo continued. "There is no mistaking it. Weather and difficult lives in the north bring age to them before their time," he explained.

"Yes. Grandmother has told us about the difficult times in the north and of your quest to find a better home for your people," I said. "You are a wise and gentle man, Prince Rollo. This young man is most fortunate that his captain cares for him the way that you do," I offered.

"May you live among the peaceful, Esther," he said. "I would enjoy the opportunity to meet you again. We are on an important mission and I do not have time to explore my own pleasures or selfish interest in getting to know you better. Perhaps we will meet again. I would enjoy your company just as my friend Knut has. Of course, I would have to try to steal you away from my young ship mate. I suspect that he would not relinquish his claim on you so easily," he teased.

"I truly hope that you will allow me to meet you again one day. I hunger for the comfort of your company," Rollo said. "Goodbye for now, sweet Esther," he said.

Rollo turned and started to walk away with young Knut at his side.

"And, I would enjoy the companionship of such a proud and worthy man," I said.

Rollo stopped and looked back at me. Then, perhaps we will meet again. Mother and Grandmother Estella, have much interest in your quest."

Rollo and Knut turned and walked towards one of their ships.

"Do you really know Esther, her Mother and her Grandmother as well?" I heard Knut ask.

"How do you know Esther's Mother?" Knut persisted. The same curiosity came to Knut as he had shown on the Sudry Isle where Gretchen and I watched them came ashore. He walked in quick strides beside Rollo, trying to keep pace, stumbling on the rocky shore, his eyes turned up to his master.

"Where did you meet Esther's Mother, Prince Rollo? Is she really as pretty as Esther?" Knut persisted.

"Yes, I met Esther's Mother. She is the daughter of a famous lady named Sarah. My Father knew Sarah and her Mother, Estella a long time ago in Norway," Rollo said. He answered only half of the questions that Knut asked in quick succession as he stumbled along the shore.

"And, she is every bit as pretty as her Mother, and her Grandmother, like you said?" Knut went on.

Knut peppered his captain with a line of questions that could not have been answered without interrupting the emotionally charged youth. I laughed at the scene of the two of them, walking along beside each other. Knut would not let up.

"Hold it, son!" I heard Rollo say. "You have remarkably good taste for your age," I heard the big man tell Knut. "I am very proud of you. You sure can pick the pretty ones, but ease up, boy."

Rollo turned and looked at me one more time before he walked off. He placed his fist over his heart as a sign of hope for our future encounter. Then he laid his broad arm over Knut's shoulder and boarded his ship. I knew that I would possibly enjoy another encounter with Rollo and Knut and I sincerely looked forward to it.

I needed a mate at this time in my life. Rollo fit my needs perfectly. I knew that we would meet again. We prepared, in our own way to make our way to the Sudrys.

After the village sheriff was summoned and arrived to take the pair of would-be thieves away, Rollo's course was set to follow the western shoreline down towards the Clyde River and the village of Dumbarton on the western shores.

"It is time to do Odin's work," Rollo roared from his position at the bow of his ship.

"He would have us expand our reach into new lands. By the watchful eye of Odin, we will find a home for our people and grow our own crops," I heard him say as he walked young Knut towards their ship.

"We may even stop stealing from these foreign dogs. We will celebrate the teachings of Odin's great Queen, the Maiden Frigg as well as the beautiful beings of the supernatural world of these Celtic natives. We will populate a new land with her people," he growled, his clinched fist raised in the air as his ship was rowed through the harbor with the others following his lead. The mainsails were raised and the ships disappeared onto the open sea.

"What is the supernatural world, Rollo?" I heard Knut ask.

"I will tell you someday soon, son. For now, we have Odin's work to do."

The crews rowed the three ships into the harbor and out to the open sea.

I followed Rollo's small fleet as they set sail for the south. The day remained uneventful as they sailed within sight of the shores near the Scottish Highlands.

The Pict people of these highlands were well known to Norsemen and to our kind. They had long accepted Norse crews into their villages and had benefited from their ways.

Rollo's ancestors launched raids against the painted people of these lands many years ago. After years of fighting Romans, the Pict no longer had the numbers to hold off Norsemen and gave in to their relentless raids on their settlements. They eventually abandoned their independent ways and let the Vikings settle in their villages where they inter-married locals and became a corner stone for a strong and independent minded Scotland.

Pict settlements had once been overwhelmed with Nordic invasions. Viking crews were absorbed into the mixed blood of the people of Caledonia. The early Scottish people benefited greatly from both large and small improvements in their lives brought by Vikings. Norsemen built better ships and their ways in war were superior because of their fierce warring skills and superior weapons

The coastal soils of Caledonia were almost as poor as that on their own tidal islands in Scandinavia. The shallow wind swept soils of the highlands would support nothing but grass and grains, like barley. They were much better suited for grazing animals.

Highlanders found the waters between the islands of the Hebrides and Hibernia were much better fishing grounds than they had seen in Scandinavia. The fishing along the western shores made up for that shortcoming.

Rollo knew about the village at the mouth of the Clyde River. This was the home base of the kingdom of Dal Riata, and part of the domain that I inherited from Mother and Grand Mother. The kingdom reached across the narrow passage between the Big monolith at the mouth of the River Clyde and the northeastern shores of Hibernia.

Rollo's people had settled in with the native inhabitants of this area many years ago. The massive rock at the mouth of the Clyde stood prominent over the nearby shores and the village at its base. The massive rock could be seen for miles around. Even in the dimmest light, the sentinel rock could be seen as it stood at the entrance to the harbor like a towering giant, protecting the harbor and the people who depended on it.

The Strathclyde Kings used the rock as a fortress against attacks from Roman invaders and later, Viking raiding parties, by scaling its nearly vertical face and escaping the assault from below. Once they made their way to the peak, villagers defended their position by dropping rocks down on their foe.

Not wanting to establish a camp in Caledonia, Rollo turned his progress south and west towards the biggest island in the Sudrys. It was situated near the old kingdom of Dal Riata and the ancient *Scotti* people who came across the North Irish Sea.

"Perhaps we can make camp there and see what it has to offer," Rollo said. "Rognvald said that the big isle would suit our needs. We will see."

Knut picked up on his Captain's interest and began to pellet him with questions. "How far is it, Rollo? How long will it take us?" he went on.

"Keep an eye out, son," Rollo told him. "Stay near the bow and let us know when you see it."

Once they landed on the isle, Gretchen and I saw them post a watch and settled in for the night in the peace of the leeward side of the isle. I sat with Gretchen and watched as Rollo directed his people in building their new village.

Chapter V

Dawn arrived in the camp and the dense fog was set in on the Sudrys. It covered the shore, the sea and the hills in every direction from Rollo's camp. The storm had passed over night and Rollo's crews had risen from under the shelter of their ships.

One by one, the crew relieved the oars of the ships burden and returned them to the upright position. Knut helped them replace the masts to their positions at mid-ship.

I could now see the tall figureheads on the bows of their ships were carved into serpent creatures. I often wondered the origin of the serpents and dragons on their bows. I suppose they were installed, along with the upturned tail like stern to add to the freight that must be caused to peasants as they came crashing ashore on one of their raids.

As Gretchen and I watched from our vantage point, the crew ate their morning meal of wheat cakes and dried meat before Rollo sent them off in all directions. He sent a hunting crew inland. They needed fresh meat to go bread and root vegetables that they found near the shore.

Being strangers on this island, they must have felt ill at ease without a clear view of danger that might approach from the sea. Their backs were against a wall of unknown height. Rollo must have suspected that they would not be able to scale it, if they needed to retreat from a potential invader from the sea. Perhaps when the sun cleared the fog, Rollo's guard might be relieved when he could see the real nature of the hill behind him. Until then, he would have his defensive skills peaked.

The crews moved warily while exploring the island and its shores. Rollo reminded them that the isle was unknown. "Step lightly and lively, boys," he called to them.

Late morning lifted the surrounding fog and unveiled the gentle slope from the hills above to the shallow shore where the crew had made camp. Crews began to return with the requested information for their captain. By midday Rollo held the knowledge of a suitable, shallow harbor, a short distance south.

Gretchen and I trailed behind as Rollo followed the shore line south. There, he entered the natural harbor that his crew spoke of. It was inset deeper than he had pictured from the description that his crewmen gave. The arbor held ample space and a gentle slope to the water. Rocks protected the harbor from the wind and rough seas.

"This is good," he said.

He sent a crew further south to see how far they were from the southern end of the island. When they returned, he learned that they were quite close the southern end. It was marked with a smaller island, just off of the tip.

"The north shore is not promising, Prince," Eric reported. "The land is much flatter and there are few places to avoid the strong winds blowing over the isle from the west," he reported.

"This is good," Rollo said.

"By Odin's spear, this is good and he will be pleased!" Rollo announced.

He sent a crew to return to the old village on Gotland to tell the people about the new settlement site.

"Return with families to begin building homes and shops," he said.

"We have found a good site for a village. We have much to do before winter. Return with them as soon as possible," Rollo commanded.

Later, hunters began to return with goat carcasses from the hills on the southern end of the isle. Fishermen brought in a fresh catch, as well.

Another crew circled the isle in their ship while another walked over the top to see the expanse of the island.

As the ship of messengers left the new harbor, on its journey back to Oslo, it passed by Gretchen and I. We sat on the wave washed rocks off shore. The seals frolicked around us, barking and growling with renewed excitement. The sailors could not see us. If they could, they would have stopped and taken a better look. We were probably a sight to the unaccustomed eyes of youthful sailors.

The Viking chieftain had recognized my resemblance to Mother when he met me on Orkney. Most Norsemen would. Their travels and life at sea made them wise beyond their years. Our appearance would never be mistaken by a seasoned sailor's eyes. Had the crewmen seen us as they went by, they would have investigated our presence and probably not shown me the appreciation and respect that Rollo did when he found me with Knut on the shore.

As Rollo knew, all Mur'uchs have black shinny eyes. They were surely part of the reason that my attempt at posing as a villager on Orkney failed. We have been told that our eyes are one of our dominant features. It is sometimes said that they are almost too large for our faces. They are always solid black and appear to weep like a seal pup's eyes.

Neither Norseman nor others can tell our true age. Our bodies never age beyond our twentieth season. Our appearance as young maidens belie the potential centuries of our immortal existence. Rollo knew about this trait. When he said that we were different from women of the far north coastal regions, I understood what he meant.

Mortal skin shows the wear of exposure to the weather and their difficult existence, just as Rollo said. Normally, we have dark, shiny hair that extends down our backs. It carries luster that no mortal from this region could posses, given the wear of the climate and lack of time to care for one's appearance.

The truth is, I was just as taken with the big Norseman as he was with me. When it comes to beauty, we are unsurpassed and irresistible to all men. It is our craft and trade and part of the lore and legend among Celtic and Nordic people. As a seasoned sailor, Rollo had taken notice of my nature and found promise in it.

We watched with interest, as the crew stowed their oars and hoisted the sail, bound for Scandinavia. I followed them from the old village of Dumbarton, at the mouth of the Clyde River several days ago as Mother had directed. She said that she needed to know if Rollo intended to build a new settlement or move on to another island. Grandmother had become alarmed by the sudden abandonment of Nordic settlements on Scandinavia's shores. She needed to determine their intentions. Her realm was at risk.

Like all Mur'uchs, Mother is possessive of all things of her realm. She insists on knowing all developments involving people relocating in her domain where she holds all things as her own.

Mother is also fiercely protective of me. When I was young she never let me out of her sight. Even when I played with my cousins, the Selkies, around the rocks with the Selkies near the shores of the land of the ancient Pict people, she kept me within sight. She trusted nothing around her first born.

Mother understood the Nordic languages. I was pressed to learn the languages of the old *Cruithne* and *Scotti* natives of the Dal Riata Kingdom. Now I needed to learn the Germanic languages as well.

It was through Romans, Viking Chieftains and Scottish Kings that Mother planned the continuation of her line of Sea Maidens. If the mighty Vikings intended to build a new settlement in her domain, she wanted to know about it.

When I returned to the rocks, off shore from Edinburgh to update Mother on Rollo's plans, she said, "It is as I thought. They are looking for new land outside of their homeland in the north," she said. "The old northern isles can no longer support their numbers and their foolish and ruthless King has chased them from his realm."

"They will undoubtedly return with villagers from the north to populate their new settlement," Mother said. "The interior of the Sudry Isle can be farmed. That is what they are after. We will take the southern shore and the small island off of the tip. You will find a suitable mate among them," Mother predicted.

I did not tell her that I already had one in mind. I found that it was usually best to let Mother think that all such things are in her control. I was seriously taken by the big Norse Chieftain, as he apparently was with me, but I had no intention of telling Mother about him until it was absolutely necessary.

Chapter VI

In Mother's time, she had lived among powerful war lords and Kings of Dal Riata from the lands of, "Hibernia and Caledonia." She had lived as the mate of the mighty during the centuries of her immortal existence in Britannia and the highlands. As the Celtic legend of Mur'uchs and Merrows said, she lured men to approach as they neared her rocky shore, tempted to lay their eyes upon her beauty.

Mother had long ago perfected her skills in attracting men. No man, even the wisest and most powerful could resist her beauty or escape the powers that she used to capture and dominate them.

They did not know her purpose but she harbored no intention of harming her victims as many mortals feared. She only wanted the seed of their loins to propagate the shores of Caledonia with beautiful daughters with the traits of their mighty sires and her own ancient bloodline. She had no intention to kill them or take them under as some Mur'uchs are said to do in the lore of our kind. She simply wanted to be "captured" by her chosen suitor and live with his people while she let them sire her young.

She took only the most powerful among the natives of Caledonia and those who came to rule over them, like the Romans did in the early days of the first century, or Viking Chieftains like Rollo and his Father Rognvald who were beginning to settle in with natives after they came to raid their shores. It was with these mortal men that she schemed to have my sisters and I sired. We would all eventually set out to find our own domains off shore from castles and settlements of her realm and continue her plan.

She used her beauty and haunting voice in song to lure her chosen to her rocky perch. She never allowed any man to take her unless it suited her purpose. This was her way as taught to her by her Mother, who ruled the shores of Scandinavia. Grand Mother carried out her own scheme with Norwegian and Danish Kings.

Grandmother Estella was the original Irish Mur'uch. She sat on the rocky shores near Oslo, in these times, still luring sailors and fishermen with her alluring beauty. Sailors from Norway, Sweden and the Island of Gotland, Iceland and the Danish shores knew of Grandmother's beauty and the skills she perfected to capture them and take their seed to produce Mother and her many sisters who now sat near the harbors in the Baltic, Estonia and the City of St. Peter. Their ports and harbors were jealously guarded by Mother's beautiful sisters.

Many centuries ago, Estella sent Mother to increase their numbers near the shores of eastern Scotland, the Hebrides Islands of Orkney and Shetland, the Scottish Highlands, Western Scotland and Ireland. She would begin with my Father, the Roman General of Britannia, in the most Western reach of the Roman Empire.

After I returned from watching Rollo and his crew, I sat with Mother one fine day, on the shore near where she first met my Father many centuries before. I loved to hear her tell about her exploits in seducing my Father while she worked to undermine his activities being carried out for his Emperor. While she allowed him to sire her first born, she took advantage of her control over him to disrupt the Roman defenses against attacks by our native people, "The Pict," or "The Pryten," as we prefer to call them.

Mother was never shy about the details of her adventures and times with the cultures of Caledonia beginning in the first century. She enjoyed talking about the control she held over the most powerful men of these isles.

It was a beautiful, sunny day. The warm summer sun drenched our rock perch. Our cousins, the *selkies* swam around the rocks near us. I fed them bits of fish that I dismembered and cast out towards them, watching them dive to fetch my treats.

I sat back and prepared to spend my day listening to Mother talk about her fascinating life. I hoped to tell these stories to my own young someday. I wanted to make sure that I had heard them all, although, looking back, I don't honestly know what the hurry was. Mother was already seven or eight hundred years old and she would be around to tell my young about her exploits herself.

"Oh well," I thought.

"Tell me about the times of the Romans, Mother," I said.

"I love to hear about your days with Father and the Romans who came to claim our people and our lands for their empire. I love to hear you tell about my Father."

"Merrows, as you know, are our male counterparts. They are despised by all of us, even in my Mother's generation," she added. "They are unable to even produce their own offspring, and their slovenly existence is hopeless," Mother explained.

"They are to be avoided at all costs. Estella's plan insured that we only produced female young. She had perfected a system to exclude Merrows from our descendants that I used with you girls," she began.

"Does she always have to begin with this every time?" I wondered.

"Merrows are just eunuchs, Mother," I interrupted. "We are not as judgmental of their kind as you have been in the past, Mother. They are harmless. They just sit on the rocks near the shore of fishing villages waiting for whisky hand-outs. They drink and sing old Celtic ballads in their drunkenness, but I never believed that they ever really hurt anything," I said.

"Well, you will have to learn to deal with them in your own way," Mother said, dismissively.

"As for my generation, we never talk about such things. They are disgusting. They are kept like pets, from a vague belief that they might bring good luck during fishing season," she went on.

"That is all that I need to know about them," she declared.

"From my viewpoint," Mother asserted, "Mermen just do not fit into the scheme of things. I want my daughters to expand my empire by mating with leaders of the mortal world, not a bunch of stinky, drunken 'he-fish,'" Mother went on.

Her voice rose with determination as she replanted her narrow views hoping that they would take this time. She spoke of a creature that had just about been bred out of existence anyway.

"If she would just let it go, they would be gone soon, anyway," I reasoned in my mind.

"So," she continued, "in order to reduce the possibility of bring mermen into our world, I drained my mates of their seed as often as possible."

"I took their seed several times a day along with every drop of their strength while they were young. I kept them in my bed for hours at a time. That is the basis for Grandmother's system for eliminating mermen from our world," Mother declared.

"After I received what I wanted from these mortals, I left them and returned to the sea with my daughters to begin a new generation. You, my dearest, were my first prize and the very reason for my existence," Mother said.

"I was so proud of you. You were the first baby mermaid that I ever saw," she declared.

"Mother Estella's system," she went on, "is based on natural science, you see. The male seed is faster than their female counterparts. However, males are not as plentiful nor as resilient as female seeds. Females have much better staying power. So, if frequently released, female seeds surround the egg and keep the males from breaking through the barrier and fertilizing the egg. Simple, but brilliant, actually," she said. "It works quite well, once he has been depleted the first time."

"I passed the knowledge of Mother's system on to you and your sisters. Since your birth, my other daughters have ruled the shores of the mainland, the Iberian Peninsula, Gibraltar, the French coast, Italy and all of the way to the Greek Islands," she bragged. "We are not to be denied in this world and our legend has been passed down from generation to generation the people of those lands. We exist in all of their legends and culture."

"Your father was my first," she finally said, as she began telling about the part I liked to hear about.

"He was such a big, strapping man. I simply had to have him. Despite the human frailties that I exposed during my time with him, he was a magnificent man and I was anxious to try out my new skills on him."

Mother was right of course. We all learned from her wisdom on this matter of selective breeding. Aside from her narrow minded bigotry towards the male counterparts of our kind, her system has proven quite effective. Today, I have sisters who rule the shores in all of those places, as Mother says.

"Continue, Mother. Tell me about my Father when he was young," I said.

I sat back against the rocks and got myself comfortable for a long day of listening to Mother tell about the men who she captivated over the many years of her life.

"Well," she began, "I took my first mortal husband, your Father, hundreds of years ago. I put the powers that I inherited from Estella to work on him. I have learned since then that I may have overburdened the poor man. Your Father was a mighty Roman General in Emperor Haden's army, but he was no match for me," Mother said.

"Tall, dark and handsome, he led his special auxiliary of conscripted workers to construct Emperor Haden's wall. Detestable and impotent as it is, your Father built it. The poor dear tried his hardest to keep our unruly natives of the highlands away from the preferred subjects of their empire in the south. What a waste. It was such a lame job for such a magnificent man."

"When I look back on those days, sometimes I regret some of the things that I did to defeat the poor dear. He was a reasonably good man. He was just a bit of an elitist," she said.

"Oh my," I thought. "Imagine my Mother calling some one else an elitist. Oh my!"

"I knew that his silly wall would never repel our native people of the northern highlands. Nor, would it hold them away from their targets in the south. The entire idea was a hopeless cause from the beginning."

"Hadrian was frustrated by the independent nature of the people who lived in small settlements in the highlands. He tried to will the completion of his silly wall from his pompous seat in Rome. He had no idea what he had charged your Father to complete. Hadrian had no knowledge, what so ever, about our native Pict people of the highlands. He never understood how hopeless this project was or what he had charged your Father with completing," Mother said.

"I watched for your Father for quite a while before I made my move. Then, I saw him watching me from the shore. I called him to my rock. I planned to allow him to approach me and take my purple and seal skin hat, like Mother told me to do."

"As you know, a mortal man can only take us as his captive mate if he takes the source of our power and keeps it from us, our hats," Mother explained, unnecessarily.

"Yes Mother, I know that your hat is the source of your magic," I said, impatiently.

I was already revealing my annoyance for her to get on with the story, and she was only just beginning. She always took too long with her self indulgent details of her fool proof baby making system, before she got on with the stuff that I liked to hear.

"All right, then," she said. "As you know," she continued," a man can have us follow him ashore and be taken as his mate. They need us to bear their children and raise them with the love and affection that we are known for," she explained.

"She is so full of herself," I thought. I always ask her to tell me about her early times and it normally takes a blink of an octopus eye to become perturbed over her self glorifying details. Sometimes I can forgive her for it, but sometimes she gets under my scales.

"Mermaids, like myself, and you of course," she admitted with a trace of reluctance, "are loving and possessive care givers to our men and our young."

"Men, my fluke!" I thought. "She nearly killed my Father and eventually interfered with him to the point that he was sent back to Rome in disgrace."

Mother was still upset with me because my first child with a Pictish war lord was my son, Robb. She still does not let a day pass without criticizing me for my 'indiscretion,' as she puts it.

"Indiscretion," I thought. "After hearing about all of the men from the old Roman camp who she drug into the sack, she should accuse my indiscretions?"

"We are also dedicated mates. The legend says, if we ever reclaim our hat, we would leave him to return to our own world in the sea," Mother explained for the umpteenth time.

"Yes, Mother. I do know that too," I said, impatiently.

"Well, we have lived among the Pictish people and been part of the lore and lives of the people of Scotland and Ireland for many, many centuries," she said. "We are part of their culture and they are our charge. They need us to explain the forces of the sea and life in their often harsh land. Our presence helps give closure to widowed wives of fishermen and sailors who fail to return home from the sea," she said. "That is the reason for our existence."

Mother was right of course. The island's harsh conditions often took the young before their time, especially in the olden days when she first began her tradition along the shores of Caledonia. Women died during childbirth and children died of exposure or starvation during the difficult winter season. Our Pictish people were hardy beyond a doubt but even they fell to the difficult conditions of the highlands and the shores of the Hebrides Isles.

Like the children of Scandinavian villages in the north, the children of old Caledonia did not really have a childhood. Due to the harsh conditions of their lands, the endless wars and fights with their enemies, they often died before their fifteenth season. As Mother said, the legends of Mur'uchs, Merrows and Selkies and other forces of the supernatural world helped explain much of the agony that ended their meager lives. Mother did not list the many other forces of the supernatural world of Celtic Faeries and Witches that plied their powers on land and sea. There are many.

In order to make sense of their hardships, locals followed the signs of traditional pagan gods in all matters of life. *Sidhe Lena Gig* is dominant among those forces. She is an ancient power who is at the center of many of their prayers and blessings. She is the matron goddess of all things female. The image of her short, vulgar figure, displaying her female reproductive parts is recognized as the center of the matrilineal clans that inhabited the lands of the highlands and Hebrides isles. Mother did not include *Sidhe Lena Gig* in her story, but she knew the forces of our omnipresent matron goddess.

The world of the Pict people was one of the few places, out side of the supernatural where the female was the center of society. This is the place of origin of *Sidhe Lena Gig*.

A king's right to ascend to the Pict throne came through the lineage of his mother. *Sidhe Lena Gig* was the force behind the head mistress of the village who ruled in all earthly endeavors.

Most old Caledonian households had an icon of *Sidhe Lena Gig* in their settlement. All matters that could not otherwise be understood were the center of *Sidhe Lena Gig's* domain.

"Mother, please go on. I love to hear the story about you and Father in the Roman camp," I pleaded. "I already know all about our lore among the Scot-Irish people."

"Well," Mother continued, "I placed my magic hat on the rock where your Father would find it. Thinking that he was daring enough to take my hat and convince me into joining him ashore as his woman, he would fall prey into my web of trickery," she said with obvious self delight.

"I wanted your Father's seed," Mother continued. "Even though he worked against the welfare of our native people, I intended to have him put his seed in me. The lust that I had for him still puts a smile on my face. His politics were put aside while I went after him like a shark on a seal pup.
"

"Bad imagery, Mother," I said.

"Well, while I lived in his camp, I enjoyed causing all of the havoc that I could bring down on those arrogant, imperialist Romans," Mother went on.

"Even Roman Generals could not escape my powers," she said. "My beauty separated me from human females in those times. Even the women in the courts of Rome, that your father was so fond of recalling, were not as beautiful as I."

"Of course not Mother," I said while managing a half lip smile.

"Being taken out of the lap of luxury in Rome and placed on a rocky, remote and hostile island was not intended as a promotion for your Father. I am sure of it. I never heard the reason that your Father was sent here," she explained, "but, it must have been some kind of trial or test. Who knows?" Mother said.

"Your Father was a big powerful man in stature and authority. Despite his rather remote assignment in Britannia, I could see that he was a man of some consequence. I thought that he would make a good beginning to my dynasty," she said.

Grandmother was proud of her for landing this "big fish," as she was fond of saying about my first encounter with mortal men.

"Your Father had seen me sitting in this very place," Mother said. His camp was over there," she pointed beyond the shore, to the broad expanse of the meadow.

"The Romans had been in Britannia for quite a while before your Father was brought in to build the wall. The Romans tried for years to tame the Pict as they had the tamer, native people of southern Britannia. The Pict resisted with all of their might, right down to the last one of them. They would not be subservient to the Romans, as the Britons from the south had become."

"The Pict of the north were inexhaustibly independent. As you know, their refusal to come together as a united people, would cause them great losses on their way to frustrating the Romans and causing them to abandon their hold on our people. That independent streak is what eventually frustrated Hadrian and caused him to recall his army back to Rome," she went on.

"Tell me more about Father," I said.

"Your Father could not believe his eyes as he approached me," Mother continued. "I sat with my purple and seal skin hat on my head and sang ballads of Rome while sunning upon the rocks. I acted as if I did not see him approaching. I looked off in a different direction, combing my hair and giving him a good silhouette of my figure.

"He must have been terribly set on taking me back to shore for he came straight at me and never looked back. If you would have seen some of the poor women who hung around his camp, you would understand what a sight for sore eyes that I must have been."

"When he first laid his eyes upon me, he saw a young, blonde maiden with hair the color of winter wheat," Mother recalled.

Mother loved to describe herself with such natural, wholesome and poetic metaphors. It must help her repel thoughts of some of the terrible things that she did in the Roman camp.

"It fell down over my naked shoulders," she continued, "and on to my waist and plump little backside."

"Plump little backside," rang unbearably through my ocean depth equipped inner ears. "Oh my! Ouch!"

"The pale pink of my skin transitioned to a light green enticingly placed, just below my hips," Mother continued, avoiding my rolling, black eyeballs. "I watched him stare at me as he caught a good view of my hips and tummy where my skin transitioned to our green Mur'uch scales. My hands were still green and scaled, with talons that extended from my webbed fingers," Mother continued.

"Come to me soldier," I ordered, when I first acknowledged his presence. What do you seek? I asked," Mother went on with her story.

"Your Father was totally speechless and unable to express his thoughts. He tried to respond but all that he could do was take in my beauty. The power of my hold on him, kept me in control of his mind and coordination of his body and voice. He could neither speak nor move. I held his mind like a vise holds a sculptor's marble while he forms the creation of his mind. I refused to release him until I discovered what his mind held in its deepest places," Mother explained.

"I gathered my hair behind my head, as I was practiced at doing and I lifted it from my shoulders, so that he could feast his eyes on me," Mother explained.

"Your father was still unable to speak. His mind could only take in the perfection of my form. I was learning how to display my body. I watched him react to the display of my form," she went on.

"As Mother had years before me, I was able to read his mind from the very beginning. Your Father was a man who had entertained many women in Rome and he had an appreciation of a woman's finer traits, especially the curves of our round, soft and sensuous bottoms," Mother continued in her less than humble recollection of how Father was out of control in the presence of her……dainty butt.

"I held your Father's eyes, and his mind. I wanted to record the last of his mental image of an ideal female beauty. Our skill at meeting a man's personal and ideal image of female perfection is among our many powers over mortal men," as you probably know."

Mother had actually trained me well in the skills of a mentalist. Grandmother, herself, had often taken on the appearance of a dark headed and olive skinned beauty that the sailors of the north lusted for. After seeing women of the Mediterranean while on their lengthy expeditions, Vikings had fond memories of sultry, dark maidens with black hair and warm olive skin. Nordic taste for earthy, Latin women is quite notorious. Their own women are usually quite light skinned and therefore have small nipples, along with light colored hair and light blue eyes. Latin women are known among Nordic crews as romantic and free to uncover their tanned skin for their lovers.

"What appearance did you take, when you first met Father?" I asked.

"Yes, I was getting to that part, Esther," Mother said, impatiently.

"As your Father stood near me, I continued to adapt my details in subtle ways as I learned his preferences. The image of a fair skinned, flaxen haired woman came clear in his mind. My hair lightened to meet his preference. My waist narrowed and my belly tightened as I focused further on his inner vision."

"My breasts lifted and separated like field flowers reaching for the radiance of the spring time sun until they fully developed, and matched perfectly to his mind's demand," Mother claimed.

"Oh Brother," I thought. "No humility here. If spring lifted them, fall must have let them drop."

I had to find some relief from her self indulging reflections of her beauty. Comedy was as good as any, I thought.

"I held onto his gaze, not allowing him to look away. I was not quite finished," she continued. "I held your Father's face towards my eyes. He could not move nor escape my control," she continued. "At last, I saw that I was his vision of a spring nymph."

"Oh, brother, here we go with the nature metaphors again," I thought.

"Finally, when I was sure that I was perfect, I released him. To finish my transformation, I lost the green tint of my skin and the form of my scaled fluke and began to develop my tummy, legs and feet. He preferred long slim legs and petite feet.

"The soft, pink skin of my legs extended from my belly, over my hips and butt, across my lap and down to my feet," she continued. "He noticed every detail of it.

"He sat down beside me and looked deep into my eyes. They were dark and shining, 'like those of a seal pup' as he used to say. My lips had changed from the tight and stretched mouth, like a fish, to soft, pink and perky, like a young woman's. He reached out to touch me, unable to control his passion any longer," Mother continued.

"My arms were absent the green scale that had covered them when he first saw me, but the talons on the ends of my webbed fingers remained menacing, and foreign to his eyes. He was not sure what to make of them but I was reluctant to give my weapons up until I saw that he intended no harm. Some men like it rough. I was not sure about your Father yet."

"He later said that my talons alarmed him in the beginning, but then he realized that the most beautiful and delicate flowers of the world required careful handling to avoid being stuck by the thorns that protect them," she said, with yet more of her nature metaphors.

"I was radiant in the summer sun. I was fully prepared to ply my skills on the handsome General. He kissed me and tasted the fresh, sweet of sea scallops when he put his mouth to mine. He told me that later," she explained.

"He touched the smooth, soft mounds of my chest as they sat plump in his palm, cupped on his hands. They were smooth and still wet from sea water. Like I said, your Father was a breast man. His mind was always on them and I learned quickly how to use them to manipulate him and the other men in camp.

"At last, your Father saw my hat on the rock and put it in his pocket and out of sight. Realizing the relationship between my hat and the finalization of my transformation, he tucked it even deeper into the leather chest and back plate of his uniform," Mother explained.

"Was Father satisfied with every detail of your transformation?" I asked, as if I did not know what her answer might be. I loved to hear her tell about Father and his feeble attempts at trying to be manly around her.

"Right down to my new belly button," she said. "Strange things, belly buttons," I thought. Men like them on women, even mermaids. But he insisted," Mother explained.

"I thought the same of my new nipples. I thought that Mermaids did not need those either. That, I realized, was wrong. You came along and you were a hungry and anxious little feeder. I soon learned what they were for. I should have realized this from watching other mammals of the sea, like our cousins, the Selkies."

"Anyway," Mother went on. "My transformation changed my exterior to the smooth, unmarked skin of a pampered temple priestess in Rome. I believed that the visions of court maidens from home must have influenced your father's vision. I was perfection in his eyes. He could think of nothing to perfect my appeal. My skin was now like priestesses and concubines of Rome who softened themselves with oils and mountain water that came down from the hills into their baths."

"Your Father would not release me after my transformation. He held me in his arms and felt the soft, smoothness of my skin. My powerful tail disappeared. My feet were small and pink and my legs separated, no longer bundled in the form of my tail. Your Father loved my thighs. They were soft and supple to his touch. My flat belly was smooth and soft, with a light, almost undetectable cover of fine, blonde fuzz. I moaned for him when he placed his hand on my belly. He lifted me into his powerful arms and carried me to his skiff as we prepared to go ashore."

Chapter VII

My Father's name was Constans. He had no wife in camp and he had tired of the concubines who were rounded up and supplied to the officers at camp. These Pict slave women were foreign and unattractive to Father. His taste for women was based on what was available to him in Rome. There, fine concubines were oiled after their baths and prepared for the entertainment of nobles.

Later in life I learned that Roman concubines and slaves came from the expanse of the Roman Empire. From Britannia to the lands of the Greek gods and the northern shores of the African continent, they were light skinned from the north, black skinned from Nubian lands, black headed and blonde, long legged or petite. All of the concubines were selected and maintained for the purpose of entertainment and enjoyment of Roman nobles.

Romans were advanced in hedonistic pursuits. No one could match their dependence on leisure and the public pursuit of pleasure of the flesh. They were the masters of group orgies and they made no apologies for their public appreciation of beautiful women of all kinds. The sign of a wealthy nobleman of Rome was a stable of fine horses and beautiful slaves from around the empire.

Their appreciation for beauty was shown all around the city. Greek and Roman statues were everywhere. They adorned themselves in robes and uniforms denoting their station in Roman life. Their horses were fitted out in silver and gold and the facades of their buildings were gilded and covered with statuary and relief carvings in Roman marble.

I also learned from Mother, that Father had a favorite among the concubines found in Roman baths. She was from the Euro continent in the land of Francs, a young maiden named, Anne.

Anne was said to be a woman in her late teens with light brown hair and soft, tanned skin. He was never able converse with her, for she spoke only the language of Saxony. However, Father must have enjoyed her company. Despite being abruptly taken from her family, she was light hearted and appreciated the kind attention that Father gave to her. Father dressed her in loose, flowing silk robes that highlighted her young figure. Father kept Anne in his villa. Attendants prepared her everyday for Father.

Anne was said to be tall and slim, her face round and youthful. She had perky, soft lips and hazel brown eyes. Mother said that he missed the private moments that they had in Rome where they lay on a soft bed, surrounded by a silk and nearly transparent canopy that gently moved with the breeze from the open court of Father's villa. Mother said that this was something that he enjoyed later with her. In Rome, they reclined upon silken sheets and he taught Anne the subtleties of lovemaking while she taught him the reward of patience.

She was attended to by maidens who bathed and oiled her skin before dressing her in the sheer gowns that Father bought for her. Rome was a center for trade goods. Fabrics, gold and spices came from the vast expanse of their empire and China, India and other points in Asia. Anne was gifted with all of these fine goods. The spices, oils and silks were used to keep her fresh and available to Father.

Mother said that Father may have married Anne, but he thought better of it when he came to his senses. She was a common concubine. She was prepared like a fine noble woman, but her origins were much more common and it would have been poorly looked upon by Father's superiors.

It seems that he could have Anne as his own and enjoy her, but he could not lower himself to marry her. Father's assignment in Britannia took him away from Anne and his preoccupation with her. I always wondered whether Father was sent away because of Anne and the issues that she confused him over.

"In contrast to Anne, Pict slaves captured from villages of the highland north, wore little to cover their bodies. Their skin weathered from constant exposure to weather elements of the Highlands. Both men and women carried sheaths for their weapons and ornaments in their hair or around their bare necks. In the old times, it is said that many were short in stature and not soft in appearance like the pampered slave women and concubines of Rome that your Father was fond of bedding," Mother explained.

"Their faces and bodies were covered with tattoos and paint markings. The Romans gave them the name "Picts," meaning, painted people. They braided their wild, reddish brown hair with wooden and stone artifacts. They showed none of the benefits of attention and care of the fine women who served the members of the Roman Senate," Mother explained.

"In Rome, women spent time every day being attended to in communal baths and were never seen until they had been fully prepared for their audience. With the experienced care that centuries of carnal indulgence had taught them," each concubine received care for her hair and skin. They were adorned in silk and aerie, thin flowing robes that displayed their fine care. No such leisure would ever be afforded the women of Pict land," Mother said.

"Tell me more about Rome, Mother," I pleaded.

"Well, your Father spent his early years as a young officer in Rome. He attended affairs with senior officers and often accompanied them to lavish dinners held in Senator's homes around the city. These affairs were hidden from the eyes and imaginations of common peasants. Your Father's life in Rome could not be imagined in the minds of commoners.

Roman wives stayed away from these affairs. They were replaced by female fancies from all corners of the empire. They were brought in to lie with court nobles on silken benches, set around a warm pool where court women bathed nude and made themselves available to a courtier's fancy. On padded benches or in the warm embracing waters of the pools, they spent hours in prelude to serving themselves for the pleasure of nobles," Mother explained.

"These orgies were conducted by house slaves, servants and concubines," Mother continued. "Your Father learned to enjoy the finer things and had no intention of taking a naked, painted, heathen warlock to his bed at the risk of having his eyes clawed out."

. I knew that the skin of the Pictish people of Caledonia bore the effects of sun, household insects, rain as well as the harsh winds of the northern isles. With the Romans at their southern border, their lives were sometimes as brutal as the wind swept land that they lived on. The Pictish people were pacifists by nature, but they had learned to fight for the land that they held sacred.

My Father needed a woman but he had no intention of keeping one who had every reason to strangle him while he slept. The conflict over Father erecting the wall in the southern territory of the Pict had brought vengeance upon them from the beginning. The Romans intended to protect everything south of the wall as part of the Roman Empire.

The Pict were stubborn, independent and fearsome as they faced outsiders intending to split their land with the arbitrary placement of a wall. They knew that the simple wall would never keep them from roaming their native land but it was an invasion that they deeply resented. The Pict had enjoyed the freedom of roaming their lands from the north and south and greatly resented foreigners placing a barrier from sea to sea. This wall was seen as an impotent attempt of containing them."

"The freedom of movement for the purpose of relocating from summer camps to winter villages and for hunting and fishing were prized by the Pict. They had no intention of allowing the foreigners to dictate restriction in their travel. The problem was that the Pict were outnumbered a hundred to one. In your Father's time, there were ten thousand Roman legions and auxiliary in the main camp and along the wall," Mother explained.

"Tell me more, Mother," I said.

"Your Father yearned for a soft, young maiden. His preferences were women with lighter hair, plump bottoms and shapely bosoms. There were few of that description in this region and even fewer with a temperament that a man would like to wake up to," Mother said.

"So, your Father was determined to follow the lore of one of Caledonia's better known legends. He intended to collect a woman more to his fancy from the legend of the Mur'uch from his host culture."

"Facing me on my rock, he found himself satisfied with my appearance. He had been told of the legends of Merrows, Mur'uchs and Selkies and thought that he had prepared himself for this encounter. He intended to test the Celtic legends of sea maidens for his own. He learned in the beginning of the encounter with me that he would not come by one without risk," Mother explained.

"I am not sure that he was prepared for the invasion of his mind or his privacy that I would bring with me," she proclaimed with satisfaction.

"I was certainly much more beautiful than the poor, tattered, women who were kept around camp. He knew nothing of my character or what to expect from a she creature with my kind of powers. I am sure that he was determined to see this through, before he really knew what he was dealing with. In Rome, concubines are submissive and pliant. I am neither," Mother boasted.

"Yeah. No kidding!"

"Once he took me to the camp and his quarters, I laid back on the bed and pulled him onto me. We joined for the first time on the cool sumptuous sheets of his bed."

I was on my way to meet the world, and Father's new concubine, suited his station in the Roman army and in his camp.

Chapter VIII

"The Pict's fight to remain independent from the influence and containment of the Roman Empire in Britannia came at a high price in the ongoing conflict over the wall. The Pict were fierce and relentless enemies for the Romans, who refused to allow the Romans to domesticate their culture. Romans learned that dominating the natives of southern Britannia was a lot easier than taming the natives of the north. They would not be taken, settled with or beaten into submission. Your father was unaware of the difficult task that lay in his future," Mother began.

"His assignment had been to continue the effort to tame the natives of this part of northern Caledonia, while building the middle section of Emperor Hadrian's wall. It had been much more difficult than he had anticipated," Mother told me later.

She explained, "The Pict attacked the fortresses and guard houses, at will. Pict warriors came down upon the Romans in small raiding parties, disguised by the night and the dark markings on the bodies. They introduced the fear of night in his auxiliary force. The auxiliary workers were not Roman legions, trained in warfare. They were laborers and masons conscripted to complete the wall that Hadrian hoped would separate his tame subjects of the south from the inexhaustibly fierce warriors of the north."

"I consorted with a Captain named Quintus. He told me that the Pict adapted their guerrilla tactics in order to instill and maintain fear among the auxiliary. They not only attacked the workers and their guards housed along the wall at night, but they began coming into camp, killing his soldiers while they slept in their tents," Mother said.

"At first, the haunting sound of drums coming through the valleys and over the rocky heights around the wall kept them from sleeping."

"Beginning far out into the distant night, the drums sounded through the rock covered valleys and off of the hills as they approached the camp. Gradually, the rhythm could be heard as it approached closer and closer until it finally ceased. It sounded as if the Pict had advanced to the wall before they quit beating the drums and playing their mournful sounding pipes.

"Quintus and the other Roman officers were unable to stop the attacks. No one had seen or captured a Pict warrior or put a face to the terror that resonated through the hills in the night. 'Once the drums and pipes sounded, we anticipated that an attack was eminent,' Quintus explained. Panic among the auxiliary and our legions spread like wildfire fed by winds coming from the highlands."

"Quintus told me that the uncertainty created by the drums and pipes fed the panic that eventually ravaged the camp. He said that once we learned that the drums and pipes foretold an attack, we told the legions to prepare for an attack. That failed to prepare the camp. The Pict would change their tactic," Mother recalled. "We could not adapt to the Pict's changing guerilla tactics."

"Quintus said, 'We listened in the night for the sounds of the advance and planned a defensive response. We conditioned the legions to listen for the sounds and leap from their beds, ready to fight.'"

"The Pict adapted their ways to keep us off guard,' Quintus explained. 'One night, we arose from our beds in response to the sounds of an eminent attack. We made ready to defend ourselves against the night fighters. Then, we found that the Picts had already been in camp and killed dozens of men and left them in their beds, with spears and stakes driven into their hearts,' Quintus told me," Mother recalled.

"Quintus said that the scene of left behind a Pict attack had lasting affects on our legion. The victims were not simply killed and left where they fell. They were slaughtered and staged to show the torture that they endured. Their heads were often taken away and displayed separately from the body. Eyes were removed and tongues extended and pierced with all manner of devices to demonstrate the horror that these men faced," Mother went on.

"The rhythm of the drum and the sorrowful, mourning tone of the pipes brought a sense of doom through the camp' Mother recalled Quintus saying. 'Our men were trained to face their enemies in traditional ways. They had never seen fighters as fierce as Pict warriors and they had no experience in dealing with guerrilla tactics being used by the natives of Caledonia,' Quintus told me."

"Our soldiers are veterans of many battles and have never shown fear before they met the devastation and torture that the Pict brought to them,' Quintus told me."

"I took Quintus as my lover so that I might learn more about our fight against the foreigners. I lay beside him in the Officer's tent and stroked the poor man's brow. It was clear that he was facing dismissal for his inability to protect Constan's auxiliary. Quintus had not slept for many nights. 'The ways of the 'evil enemy' brought panic, doom and uncertainty to Officers and legends alike," Mother recalled Quintus explaining.

"Quintus said, rumors soon spread about the mystic, monstrous creatures that came undetected in the night, bringing slaughter to those who dared close their eyes to sleep. The unrelenting sense of doom soon spread through the camp until every night was met with dread and anticipation of death being dealt among them,' Quintus told me."

"Not able to stop the attack or to rise in time to defend themselves, your Father's legions soon found their situation hopeless," Mother went on, "Quintus told me that officers began to question why they should give their lives and the lives of their soldiers to a violent and senseless death at the hands of people who they did not know, and had never seen."

"Our soldiers had no history with these people,' Quintus explained. 'We were months from home, fighting a people we had never seen.

Perhaps these enraged savages have reason to repel us,' they said. 'We have no reason to fight these people,' he explained," Mother related.

"The Pict warriors began to harass and kill the workers along the wall," Mother said. "They were masons and laborers taken from their homes from all over the empire. They were not professional soldiers. They were simple workers who depended on the professionals to keep them safe while they performed their work in erecting a wall.

"Why are we building a wall, miles from civilization?' they asked, Mother recalled."

"At night in the worse weather a Roman ever imagined, hardened killers came out of the night to slaughter every Roman in sight. It did not matter whether they were soldiers or laborers. They killed them all, without hesitation or reason. It is as if they possessed an unholy power of one of Caledonia's many supernatural forces," Mother recalled.

"The attacks were swift and brutal. From the very beginning of their assault on the wall and the camp, the intensity of their attacks took the Romans by surprise. Killing them was not enough. The enraged assailants that Roman soldiers were calling *guerriero della spirito notte*, ghost fighters of the night, mutilated Quintus's soldiers and workers. The bodies were displayed in a manner that put the fear of the unholy into them," she went on.

"The night attacks continued. Quintus was unable to kill or capture even one of the Pict fighters. He desperately needed to show his men that their enemy was neither ghost nor devil. Without taking even one of the enemy, he could not deliver the promise that he made to his men. 'These are not ghosts' he told them. 'They are skin and flesh and bone, just as you are,' he promised. 'Do not cower from these people. Their weapons are crude and they do not have training and discipline that we have. Rise up! Kill them in their tracks and see that they are flesh and bone, not ghosts," Quintus told them.

"Quintus said that he and a small band of legion hid in waiting one night. They were certain an attack would come. Three of Quintus' best soldiers finally found their opportunity when a dark feature came along the wall and passed them. He did not see Quintus and his men in the shadows. One of the legions jumped the warrior and tried to wrestle him to the ground."

"A cry came from the Pict as he rose from the legion's hold to escape his captor. Several soldiers joined the fight. They were finally able to subdue him by penning him to the ground. They drove a spear deep into the warrior's chest. Impaled with the spear, he attempted to rise and fight off his attackers. With blood running profusely from his wounds, the warrior finally collapsed with a groan and ungodly howl that was heard across the camp. The warrior's eyes carried the rage from within the scarred and painted body as it lay lifeless. His haunting dismissal of the people who brought death to him had deep meaning to our legion.

Quintus called his soldiers to his side as he examined the Pict fighter. He said that it was difficult to make out his features in the dark of night or color of his ornamented skin," Quintus told me later.

"Quintus had the body carried to the camp and placed near a fire. He intended all to see that their enemy was a mortal man. He was neither ghost nor devil," Mother recalled. "I remember looking at the Pict after they laid him out near the Officer's quarters. They left him there while they gathered others to see the remains."

"As I started to walk away from the poor soul, a group of three Pict warriors came through the dark and around the back of the tent. When they saw me, they stood back and looked me over. I made a gesture to take the fallen fighter away. They kept their eyes on me as they lifted the man and carried him off into the night. I quickly left the scene. I did not want it to appear that I had anything to do with the body's disappearance," Mother said.

"When Quintus returned with a group of soldiers, I watched as they were shocked by the disappearance."

"Quintus saw me walking away, and called to me. 'Sarah, did you see what happened here?'

"No, I said. What are you talking about? 'The Pict fighter has disappeared,' he said. What happened to him?" he asked. "I don't know. What do you mean?" Mother recalled. The confusion and terror of that moment fell on the faces of the group that Quintus brought to inspect the body. The look in their eyes showed the result of having their worst suspicions confirmed. They were ghosts," Mother said.

"They executed their night attacks with eerie silence. Now they possessed the reputation of the unholy, the undead and the spirits with natural and ghostly stealth. Their attacks against the wall continued. Naked and seemingly impervious to the wicked weather conditions that the northern highlands are known for, they kept Quintus and his fellow officers on the edge. Like silence before lightening, strikes from the Pryten people came during storms of the northern seas," she said.

"I beckoned *Sidhe Lena Gig* for the worst weather she could devise to help cover the attack of our native people. As the Mother of all things female in the pagan belief of the Pict, she was the force that we called upon to bring further disorder to the Roman camp," Mother said.

"Hidden by the dark of night and the driving rain of the rugged countryside, the natives struck with ungodly accuracy with their spears, throwing axes and arrows. They showed no military sophistication of the trained legions of Constan's army," Mother explained, "but they were experts in their own style and tactics and they were unrelenting and merciless in their attacks."

"Like an uncoordinated surge of a pack of jackals charging towards wounded prey, the Pict continued their surge upon Roman auxiliaries. The masons and laborers had become as frightened as disserted sheep."

"The Pict lost few of their fellow fighters. Their guerrilla tactics were disastrous for the disciplined professional soldiers from Rome. Some said that the Pict were the fiercest warriors that they had ever faced. The Romans were prepared to face an enemy in a head-on confrontation of open field battle. The Pict had no intention to give them that advantage."

"After the Pict broke through sections of the wall, they set off havoc in every direction. They traveled south, pillaging, killing and collecting whatever they needed from the frightened villagers of Britannia. Those were very difficult times for your Father," Mother said.

"The Pict ignored the purpose of the wall and continued their attacks to the south. They raided farms and villages, stole and looted goods and supplies. The complaints from the lowland population of Britannia fell on

Rome's district governors who soon found themselves unable to offer promise of protection," Mother said.

"Young women of age were taken from lowland families and taken to Pictish settlements in the highlands to be *handfasted* with men within their clans. Pict clans were remote from sister clans. They needed fresh bloodlines to mate with young males and they had no hesitance to supply them from the south. These kidnappings had disastrous affects on the lowland subjects of the Roman Empire.

"What did the Britons do about it," I asked.

"They did little of anything. They were afraid of the Pict. They looked to the Romans to keep them safe. Their livestock disappeared over night as farms were raided by bands of naked warriors who descended upon them from territories in the north," Mother related. "Taking young maidens away was a tragic development for them. Quintus said that they complained to the Regional Roman Government. In the end they were helpless to stop the invasions."

"The Romans were unprepared to fight the Pict or to stop raids to the south of the wall. The Pict did not fight like their traditional enemies. The Empire did not foresee problems with the northern natives and did not originally plan on having to defend construction crews from attack," Mother said.

"Local Britons were concerned that the wall would never be completed before all of them were killed. Others worried that even a six meter wall would not stop the combatants who flew over the wall like locusts. It was a bad time for the pacifist of Britannia in the early days," she said.

"The Britons had given in to Hadrian years before your Father arrived," Mother said. "They were much more inclined to accept Roman leadership in the early times of the south as Rome installed province governors as administrators of Roman law. Until the Pict showed that the Roman wall would not stop their incursions, they were lulled into confidence as their governor promised their safety."

"What of the Pict's early history? Mother," I asked. "Where did they come from?"

"The earliest settlers of the northern territories are said to have come from the Iberian Peninsula. Many believe that they lived for a time among the Basque culture between the northern shores of Iberia and the land of the Francs. The stone monoliths that the Romans found in the north reminded them of some that they had seen in the old Gaelic lands of the Iberian Peninsula. That would make them descendants of sons of Mil Espa'ine or Milesians as they called them."

"The old timers told tales of the people who called themselves the Cruithne. They were said to have escaped the advance of raiders coming from the east of the Indo-Euro lands. They escaped by running west. They were forced to build boats on the coast of the Iberian Peninsula and sail away from danger," Mother said.

"They were not sailors. They were driven to escape from Mongol hoards. They arrived in a land where they found tall, rocky bluffs and a friendly tribe of Scotti people," Mother said.

"During the voyage, these peace loving people lost many of their children and women. When they came ashore, they took lands that provided adequate farms and forests to hunt. Over generations, the Cruithne split among the sons of a prominent woman and formed ten tribes which spread throughout the Caledonia region," Mother explained.

"The border war between the Pict and Roman invaders began when Romans tried to hold northern highlands as part of their empire. The Romans gave them their name, painted people, "Picti," for the tattoos and markings on their bodies and faces. Their ability to ignore foul weather added to the terror that plagued your Father's legions," she said.

"After years of fighting, the Romans finally realized that the Picts would not be tamed. Attempts to gain treaties never brought peace. Emperor Hadrian ordered a wall erected to protect the more obedient south from incursions from the unruly north. His reasoning must have been 'if I can not tame them or defeat them, I will wall them off and forget them.' Even that logic fell short," Mother said.

After years of Pict warriors breaching the wall, the Romans decided that the wall, alone, was not enough. They began to erect guard houses and fortresses that they called milecastles. These garrison sized fortresses were built along the wall's entire length, one every Roman mile, from coast to coast. As defensive battles continued, milecastles were manned with garrisons of Roman soldiers.

Other fortifications along the wall acted as defensive turrets, placed every Roman mile along its length. In the end, nothing that the Romans tried would keep the vengeance of the Pict from bringing havoc to the wall and the legions who were to defend it."

"Mother, the Picts did not have a united army like the Romans, did they?" I asked.

"No. They had no single leader in those times. They were a loosely formed confederation of tribes that lived nearly independently from each other. Pict settlements existed in isolation, making negotiations impossible and frustrating for the Romans who were always interested in a truce," she said.

"Your Father said that in the early days, truces were reached at great expense in goods and weapons given to the Pict. They became frustrated when other Pict clans ignored agreements and continued the attacks," Mother explained. "The Pict never honored agreements."

I learned that there had been several different war leaders in each clan. Pict culture was a matrilineal society. They lived in small clan camps in the highlands. They built their dwellings from rock and sod on the mainland coasts that they used for winter camps. Inland stockade camps were used in the milder seasons. They also built a few fortresses on the Orkney Islands that have come to be known as '*broch*s.

"When the war leader in the camp died, replacement was left up to warriors who saw themselves eligible. It was eventually taken by the man with the best fighting skills and the most victories. Unlike their kings who received that right by means of lineage of their mothers, war leaders came from the most skilled among them. Older war leaders held no distinction among their number. They retired from fighting when they lost their fighting skills."

"When the Picts were organized centuries later by the Dal Riata Kings, they continued to follow matriarchal blood lines. Mother explained that the women of the Pictish people, held themselves as producers of the miracle of life. That, they believed, justified their position as heads of family clans.

In the olden times, clans had issues with other clans over property, territory or other matters that kept them isolated and independent. A Pictish warrior, named Maelchon, saw stubborn independence as a possible weakness. Others argued that their independence favored their use of guerrilla war tactics.

"Rome was frustrated with the native population. While the people south of the River Clyde settled in as part of the Roman Empire, the Pict refused to surrender, despite occasional heavy losses of their numbers. Rome finally had to admit that bringing the Pict into their Empire was hopeless," she said.

Chapter IX

"I must have been the center of talk in camp," Mother said. It seemed that everything that I did brought attention to me. Your Father found that it was impossible to keep me out of sight."

"I did not care for their ways or their constant references of how they did things in Rome. This was not Rome," Mother claimed.

"I considered the possibility that the real reason for their failure in Britannia was that they saw this region through the eyes of Rome. Other regions of their empire were organized under a central leader. Caledonia had no such leader. That difference never seemed to occur to your Father or the Empire in Rome."

"I relished my time in those early days in camp. Causing problems among the officers came with great pleasure. I must admit, that I was flattered with all of the attention that I drew."

"Mother, tell me more about the times of the Romans and how you lived with them in Father's camp," I said.

"I must have been the ideal image of a woman for all of the officers, not just your Father's. They all stopped whatever they happened to be doing every time that I walked past them," she said.

"Yes Mother. I know about that part. But, how did the Pict people help bring about the collapse of their interests in Britannia?" I asked.

"Yes, well, you see Esther, I never really had respect for what the Romans were doing here. Given my roots to the lands that the Picts called home I did all I could to disrupt their plans," Mother said.

"The Romans were driven to dominate the world. They stopped at nothing to bring foreign lands under their control. They had no reason to include Britannia in their Empire, except that Britannia could not defend itself. Britannia was consumed by an army that could not be stopped. There was nothing here that the empire needed," Mother explained, "It was just easy pickings."

"Anyway, I used your Father. He was the mightiest man that I had seen up to that point in my life. I never really intended to stay with him any longer than it took to have him sire my first born."

"The Roman Empire controlled and abused people in lands from the Mediterranean to Britannia and I was pleased to help make things as difficult for them as I could. As it turned out, they did not realize that the people who inhabited the highlands were not part of a larger civilization. Each tribe would have to be defeated, individually," Mother explained. "Rome first tried to tame the Pict as a civilization. Then they tried to defeat them as if there were a central Pictish army, like their own. Their efforts were doomed from the beginning."

"When I first came to your Father's camp, I had just reached my twentieth season. It was all new to me and it took a while before I learned to be a little more subtle with it, I might say. Once I had better control of my skills, I learned to enjoy causing the havoc that I brought to your poor Father and the rest of them," she said.

"Once I saw the affect that I had on them, there was no stopping me. I learned very quickly how to draw a man's attention.

"I pampered myself by bathing in the nearby stream. Everything in camp came to a halt as Roman soldiers lined the banks of the stream, watching me in the water."

"Looking back to that time, I was nothing like most of the enlisted men had ever seen. They did not have access to court concubines like your Father and some of the other officers. Most had rarely seen a white woman. Even fewer had seen a white woman naked. I was leagues beyond their understanding of what a woman looked like," Mother boasted.

"After the first few days, I let some of the officers approach me as I bathed in the stream. Some of them actually took their uniforms off and stood naked with me. They soon became the laughing stock of the camp as their piers stood around the edge of the stream and watched some of their comrades try to impress me with their manliness," Mother said.

"Quintus had been particularly aggressive. Quintus was a handsome and powerfully built man. I seduced him and a few of the other officers who I selected. I took the more handsome among them and met them in the forest or in their tents. It helped pass the time and I knew that it would eventually cause grave disciplinary problems in the ranks."

"Just as I predicted, some of them kept their experiences with me a secret. Others used them against their comrades. It was from these seductions that I honed my skills in causing men to forget all of their worldly responsibilities for the possibility of fulfilling their fantasies with me," Mother said, unapologetically.

"There was a legion, named Otto, who harassed me daily. He was big, ugly and crude. He would not leave me be. He insisted on making crude remarks as I bathed in the stream. He insisted in pulling down his trousers to show me the source of his apparent pride and reputation. Despite his obvious assets, I found him repugnant and nasty. I tried to discourage him but he would not go away."

"I told him that he was the reason that there were so many lesbians in Rome. I thought that would insult him enough to back off, but the big, dumb dullard would not pull his pants up and leave. I was at a bit of a loss to figure out how to get rid of a man who would not respond to a woman's insults, without severely injuring him, that is " Mother recalled.

"What did you do, Mother?" I asked.

"I finally let him follow me off shore. He got in a small dinghy, as big as he was, I remind you. He started out to the rocks where I stood as if I awaited his arrival. When he came near the rocks, he stood in the little boat and pulled down his trousers to reacquaint me with his equipment, I suppose. Well, anyway, his boat became unstable with him standing in the middle and it dumped him in the water. I intended to lure him to the rock and take him under," Mother recalled.

"What happened to him Mother?" I asked.

"Well, as it turned out I did not have to lay a hand on him. The big ox could not swim, apparently. He flailed around awhile and then sank under the waves. Disgusting man!"

"A few days later, news ran through camp that big old Otto had washed ashore along with his dinghy. It was said that he was found with his trousers yanked down to his boots. I went down to the shore and joined those who stood near the body wondering what had happened to the big brute. It was an ugly sight, him lying there, exposed for all to see what was rumored to be. One of the Officers said, 'I wonder what happened to the man?'"

"They walked away trying to avoid the officers who wanted to form a party to carry Otto up to camp and burial. The poor man had lost his respect in his final act," Mother said.

"I had my favorites among the officers. The news of my involvement with some of them spread through the camp. Apparently no one ever told your Father," Mother explained. "I was resolved to do all that I could to bring chaos to your Father's plans to complete the wall."

"Once I became pregnant with you, I had no reason to hold back. I did not pass up an opportunity to bring embarrassment to him or his command. No one, at least that I know of, ever associated me with Otto's death. I am certain that many saw him approach me in the stream, but they had no idea what I was capable of, or what I had done with him."

"Quintus told me much more than he should have about their struggles with the Pict people. He told me that the fear that Pict warriors instilled in his soldiers had taken its toll on the camp. The sounds of the drums and pipes at night caused them to lie awake," Mother recalled.

"Quintus said that it was a considerable time before the camp actually saw another Pict warrior. Without seeing who, or what, made the strange sounds at night, fear hung over the camp," Mother said.

"Quintus tried several tactics to respond to the night attacks. The length of the wall made it difficult to protect all of it. He was unable to instill enough confidence in his soldiers to space them at intervals along the wall. They would not stay in small groups needed to cover the vast length that extended coast to coast. Their training had taught them to find strength in their numbers."

"In the beginning of my time in your Father's camp, he was admired and even envied, for his success in capturing me. That soon passed. It was replaced with belittling the General for his lack of oversight and inability to control his woman. His subordinates knew that I was different but they had no understanding of where I came from. They must have assumed that I was just a camp tramp. For all that they knew, I may have arrived on one the Empire's ships that frequented the pier.

"I had no use for either the Roman peplos or stollas," she went on. "Your Father had both types made for me. He tried his best to keep me covered. He had little time to follow me around to see that I kept them on."

"I did not care for the heavy, draping fashions of Rome. They were too restricting for me," she explained.

"I was never difficult to find in camp, for there was always a crowd of men who gathered around me."

"Soon after my arrival, I sensed the contempt that other camp women held for me. Most of them joined the camp as a means of supporting themselves and their children.

They were like pigeons eating crumbs and leftovers from legion's rations. They had no real association with Rome. They all tried to ingratiate themselves with a senior officer so that they could benefit from the better rations that officers received. If that failed, they worked their way down the ranks until they found a man to take her in and share his rations with her in exchange for her favors. Many found themselves ignored as they all were being judged with Mother as the standard. "

"There were a few native Pictish women who had been captured and used by the Romans as concubines or laborers. I used them to supply the Pict with inside information from the camp. They could travel quickly through the night to Pict settlements in the north, bringing news of Roman movements and intentions," Mother recalled.

"Roman Legions of that time were issued a ration of hard-tack and salted meat. They were responsible for the preparation of their own food. Little was wasted and even less was left around for the women who tried to support themselves by receiving hand-outs," Mother explained.

"In those times, I knew that the working group formed to complete construction on the Emperor's wall received even less rations than professional infantrymen who were used to long marches with thirty kilo packs on their backs, including a months ration. They were professionals and had been trained to sustain themselves on very little," she recalled.

"One afternoon, as I returned to camp," Mother said, "I was assailed by a pack of women who intended to beat me into ugliness or chase me away. As the first one grabbed my arm, I slung her over a pile of rocks. She landed with an audible thud. Then another tried to grab me from behind. She found herself hanging onto a she creature like she had never seen. My strength was unnatural for a petite person, like myself. They had no idea what I was capable of," Mother boasted.

"I had another camp wench still hanging around my neck. My roar must have penetrated the peace in camp as I grabbed another and slashed her in anger with my claws. They could not react fast enough to avoid standing before me as I was enraged and, I am afraid I began to rip my assailants apart. I, of course, showed no mercy for my assailants.

"In my anger I grabbed the startled woman still hanging around my neck. I lifted her over my head and tore her apart, limb by limb, slinging pieces at the rest of my assailants while they covered their faces at the horror that they had unleashed. Even I had never seen me in such rage. I was empowered by the strength of *Sidhe Lena Gig* and was somewhat surprised by my own strength. Finally, my attackers took advantage of escaping my grasp and disappeared into the trees."

"They all scurried away trying to avoid the wrath and my aim with large rocks that I hurtled towards them as they ran.

"When I finally returned to your Father's quarters, I had calmed and I tried to be the picture of pristine."

"Your father asked me if I heard the commotion in camp. I, of course told him that I had not. I said, No, I had not because I was bathing."

"To take his mind from the disruption, I began to massage his back. It was his favorite."

"Your Father's camp," Mother continued, "was located in the eastern section of Hadrian's Wall. He was responsible to complete the section from that point to the eastern shore."

"Covered in fire ash, native warriors attacked his legions guarding the wall at night and the auxiliary workers who worked on it during the day. The Pict attackers were nearly impossible to see in the night. They tore down newly completed sections of the stone wall. In the beginning they climbed through the opening to travel south towards Britannia villages," Mother explained.

"The Pict carried swords, battle axes and bows. They were experts in the use of each of them. They were no match for a professional Roman soldier equipped with superior weapons, but the Pict avoided head-on confrontations where the Romans would have that weapon advantage."

"The Pict were masters at guerrilla warfare. Their triumphs were small and short lived in the beginning but they never ceased harassing the camp with small scale attacks. They knew their strengths and used them expertly."

"In the cover of night, they swarmed over the wall, hacked guards to death with their axes and knives. The devastation that they caused in the turrets along the wall began to take its toll early on. Not a night went by when the construction crews were allowed to rest from their work without fear of being attacked."

"Your Father knew that he was faced with a monumental challenge. Completing the wall while the Pict attacked at night and terrorized his construction crews, was to be a monumental task. " Mother said.

"He told me that he was warned about the Pict when he first arrived in Britannia. He doubted that a band of crude, untrained fighters could hold back progress. He failed to see how a few warriors could cause so much fear when his workers were guarded by thousands of trained infantry men. He later admitted that he had fatally underestimated their ability to interfere."

"The Pict people continued to terrorize the Roman guards who were left to protect the wall during the night, when work had ceased for the day. The legions and auxiliary workers were faced with the *'guerriero espirito,'* ghost fighters, who came upon them without being detected by the guards who were there to protect them."

"The haunting sounds of drums and pipes were heard in the forests and surrounding hills before an attack. The night sounds of jackals, owls and other night creatures were said to be ghosts assembling in the dark. Quintus tried to intervene with attempts to build confidence among the men, but the terror was impossible to overcome. It only worsened over time," Mother recalled.

"Quintus doubled and redoubled the guards to protect the worker's camp. He said that he often stayed awake through the night in his effort to instill confidence among them, but he could not stop the eerie and persistent sounds that echoed through the hills."

"The brutality that they inflicted in the dark of night became visible each morning when daylight exposed the slaughter that was left behind. Legions were not simply killed in battle. They were dismembered, decapitated and disemboweled. It was a terrible sight. I witnessed it myself. Their heads were almost always removed and placed on their own pikes. It was a gruesome demonstration that drove panic among his workers and the legions placed there to protect them," Mother continued.

"The haunting sound of 'Thump, thump, thump,' coming from the dark of night brought visions of death. The mourning sounds of the pipes in the valleys and hill crests north of the wall were unfamiliar to the Romans. I do not think that they ever saw the instrument that made the haunting frill.

The reality of facing ghosts wielding swords and axes came upon them. Roman officers were never able to reverse the fear that came in the night," Mother went on. "The Pict used their methods expertly and I could see the affects of their ways. If there had been somewhere the construction crews could escape, I am sure that many would have disserted their posts."

"The officers in camp did everything they could to return confidence, but words fell short when the haunting sounds of a night attack forewarned the arrival of night fighters who navigated their way in the dark, as if they were invisible. They came down upon the Romans with complete surprise. Before the legions could react, several heads would be severed and the assailants vanished in the dark of night. Your Father's officers were frustrated by these tactics. They had no idea how to mount a defense."

"Quintus's soldiers were trained to meet enemies head on. Never having to face these kinds of tactics, they had no experience to draw from."

"They were unable to form battalions of infantry, supported by cavalry and archers to face their enemy. Quintus' army of ten thousand was designed for field warfare where battles were won by the side that decimated the opponent's numbers. The Pict would not fight in a war of attrition. Their numbers were few. They learned to use methods in which the Roman's advantage of numbers would not come to play."

"The Pict launched arrows at the work line from hidden positions on the north side of the wall. By the time that the Romans had designed a response to meet the latest tactics, the natives changed their assaults, Mother explained."

"Your Father was enraged at Quintus' inability to protect his work crews. I saw the beginning of the end of times for the Roman army in Caledonia. It seemed to me that it was a simple matter of time when the will of the Pict people would outlast the Roman's patience for protecting their crews and the people of Britannia. They began to abandon their farms and flee to the city."

Chapter X

"The Roman Empire had long ago ceased their effort to bring the Pict tribes to peace," Mother explained

"I laid with Quintus one afternoon by the shore and listened to him talk about the problems that he faced. 'Constans has little time to finish the wall before the Empire calls him and the wall a failure,' Quintus told me. 'The empire has grown weary of the bad news coming from the camp,' he went on," Mother recalled. 'If we do not control the bad reports that make their way to Rome, Constans will be looked upon with as much disfavor as his wall,' Quintus continued," she continued.

"They should have realized the challenge of trying to stop an enemy with a simple wall. Again, the Romans used conventional methods to respond to an unconventional enemy," Mother explained. "It was doomed from the beginning. That could be seen easily from Britannia, but the central control of the Roman Empire kept them withdrawn from the reality of the frontier."

"The wall became a symbol of Rome's inability to influence tribes on the north side of it. Gone was the vision of including the highlands along with the region south of the River Clyde as part of the Roman Empire. During your Father's time in Caledonia, the concern for protecting southern Britannia was the issue," Mother went on.

"The Pict were locked in the highlands by the Britons and Romans from the south and west, and with Norsemen to the north. They carried on wars in all directions, refusing to give into anyone who attempted to civilize them. They were beginning to turn the tides of war with their stubborn and independent ways," she said.

"One night, while, Your Father and I lay sleeping," Mother continued, "A sergeant in Quintus' ranks kept his eyes focused on the clearing, south of one of the milecastles. The night storms of late evening made visibility poor and conditions uncomfortable for standing unprotected. Cold sheets of rain whipped down from the angry sky. The haunting sound of Pict pipes and drums reverberated through the thick, damp air of the night. The natives beat their war drums as they assembled in the dark. The realization that another attack was imminent," Mother said.

"Like the howl of wolves, the drums signaled a prelude to another night of fighting an enemy that was seen by no living witnesses." Mother went on.

"Quintus told me that his guards were unable to understand how their enemy could possibly assemble an attack while stinging rain and disabling wind gusts confronted them," she said. "Quintus recalled that his guards stood outside, in the driving rain, looking at each other in disbelief."

"Quintus learned later that a small band of Pict fighters had positioned themselves near a rock outcropping, down hill from a milecastle," Mother explained.

"The Pict were under the experienced leadership of a warrior from the north who they called, 'Odenn.' "Looking towards the shelter for an opportunity to launch his sneak attack, Odenn had his fighters lay low and quiet, as he anticipated the opportunity to begin his assault. Finally the storm drove renewed gusts of wind and rain on the wall."

"With their swords and knives drawn, they ran towards the wall ready to take advantage of the rapidly declining visibility. Odenn and two of his fighters began to crawl along the foot of the wall, out of sight of the unsuspecting soldiers huddled inside their milecastle shelter. On to the southern side of the wall, Odenn sent three over and down hill from the shelter. His intention was to surround the enemy on two sides."

"The Pict were covered in soot, mixed with rendered animal fat. They were nearly invisible. The cold, driving rain worked as camouflage for hitting the Romans with swift and silent force. Crawling along the wall, Odenn's raiders progressed steadily towards the guard house, now, from both sides of the wall. Their bare feet made no sound as they labored slowly, across the rocky surface towards their target."

"With the call of a night bird, Odenn sent his fighters forward, onto the guard house. He closed the distance from the north side of the wall at the same time," Mother explained.

"They sprang upon the guards without warning," Mother went on. "While they arose from their seats, they must have realized that their pikes were gathered in a corner on the other side of the room. Quintus said his soldiers could not arm themselves fast enough to react to the surprise attack. They had allowed themselves to become separated from their weapons. The scene left for the officer in the light of morning showed that the legions were killed with their own weapons

Odenn's fighters struck mercilessly. The attack surprised the guards who fell fallen into Odenn's trap. Their attention had diverted away from a possible attack by their own fear."

"Odenn rushed past two guards, nearest the door, to drive his sword deep into the chest of a guard who stood towards the back of the room, as far from the wind and rain as he could get. The other two reacted to the assault by turning their backs to the doorway to bring aid to their comrade. Two of Odenn's fighters grabbed the opportunity by attacking from behind. They lopped the heads off with a swift sword. The heads hit the stone floor with a mute 'thump.'"

"The Pict dispatched the rest of the guards with swords to the torso or took their heads off in a single lethal draw of the knife," Mother said. "All heads were skewered on the blunt ends of the abandoned pikes and driven into the ground. Their bodies had been disemboweled and taken out for the jackals to feed on."

"When they were finished with the guards, they descended on the crowd of unarmed workers, who from their attackers. The Pict intended to leave no witnesses and they didn't. The laborers were shown no mercy."

"Without ceremony, Odenn's warriors left the milecastle fortress and trotted back to their village."

"This had been a raid to deliver a message and having left it for all to see, they disappeared into the night and the highland storm that masked their path home," Mother explained.

"That message was quite clear to Quintus. It would take two guards or more for every worker to keep them safe," Mother said.

"When the morning replacement troops arrived, they came upon the grizzly sight of heads stuck on the end of pikes. There were no signs of a fight or struggle within the fortress, but the events of the previous night were clearly evident. They had been attacked and killed without warning or struggle. Three headless corpses were found a few meters away. They had been ravaged by jackals and other creatures of the night."

"When the officers were told of the breach along the wall, the General was advised that his troops had been taken without a struggle. 'Idiots,' he yelled. 'They were huddled together in the warmth of their shelter. Why do their assailants need for the same comforts?' he asked. 'I have lost eighty of my construction crews and forty of the legions who were supposed to be watching over them,' he yelled."

"Your Father was livid. I sat on a bench nearby and listened to him berate his officers over their inability to protect his workers," Mother said. "I let me silk gown drop off of my shoulders. The further it slipped, the more I was able to divert their eyes from the General towards me. All eyes were on me as I sat back on my bench and watched your Father belittle his officers.

"Are you people listening?' he asked.

"These people are natives," he went on. "They have crude weapons and they have no training,' your Father said. 'We outnumber them one hundred to one,' he yelled," Mother recalled.

"His officers stood before him, with their heads bowed. They found themselves without need to respond to the obvious."

"If you can not keep your troops alert while they bask in the comfort of their shelter, then perhaps we should tear them down and make them endure the same conditions that seemingly have no effect on their enemies,' he yelled. 'Idiots! These, so called, ghost fighters, have your troops in complete withdrawal from their training and disruption of the discipline that you are so proud of,' he continued."

"These natives are hardened beyond any point that we can understand,' one of the officers mistakenly blundered. 'They live like wolves. These severe weather conditions do not bother them,' he blundered on, trying to fill the awkward silence brought on by the menacing stance, legs wide and arms crossed in disbelief of his officer's audacity to make excuses for his incompetence."

"Then perhaps you and your subordinates need to learn to live like they do. Have your troops stay out of the fortresses shelters' your Father ordered. 'They will learn to live in the rain and wind like the enemy that has killed so many of your legion.' he said."

"The officers returned to their tents and declared Constan's directive. 'By order of the General, all guards will remain along the wall, outside of the guard houses, regardless of discomfort caused by snow, rain or storms,' they reported."

"The orders worked their way down to the sergeants and their subordinates with total resignation disbelief of their predicament," Mother explained. The fear that Odenn's night fighters caused among Constan's legions had taken its toll.

"Odenn and his fighters waited until the next storm to bring on another attack," Mother remembered. "I knew that they were coming and I am sure that everyone else did as well. We could sense the tension and anxiety in the thick, night air. One of the camp concubines had informed Odenn of the disruption among the troops. They were to stand out in the rain, regardless of conditions, their General had commanded."

"Odenn and his five raiders gathered in the same place, near the rock outcropping, down hill from their target. Two went over the wall while Odenn and two more crawled along the foot of the wall to a position close to the milecastle, from the north side. The rain and lightening crashed down in driving sheets laced with ice pellets. Odenn's men on the south side of the wall could see the troops standing in the rain as they had been ordered," she said.

"Quintus said, 'the wind swept down on them while the glare of the lightening exposed the guards' positions. We stood still, as lightening lit up the night sky. The rain poured onto their heads and blinded our vision,' Quintus told me. With the call of a night bird, they were attacked from both sides of the guard's stand," Mother recalled.

"As before, they were dispatched with swift swipes from Pict swords. Again, Odenn had his men staked the pikes with the heads stuck upon them. The bodies were drug inside, this time, in Odenn's attempt at bringing further disorder and weakened morale to his enemies. Harassment was Odenn's purpose."

"Odenn and his small band of patriots disappeared into the night. They trotted home, leaving another grizzly message for Roman officers," Mother said.

"When the guards were found in the morning, the bodies were inside the guard house, one sitting on the bench and the others against a wall. Their heads were skewered as before. By all appearances the guards had been attacked while they sat in the shelter of the milecastle, without sign of a fight, The message eventually made its way to Constans. 'They have disobeyed my order, and took shelter from the storm. It cost them their lives,' he told them."

"With Odenn's tactics in full swing, morale within Quintus' camp was at an all time low. The message from Constans was seen as, 'Your lives are not important to the Empire.' Senior soldiers did not need to be given that message. They had known that from the beginning. Sacrificing your life for the Empire was the duty of a foot soldier in Rome's infantry."

"'To others, the message was clear, but it seemed particularly without regard to the troops' responsibility. 'The *guerriero della norte'*, could not be beaten with their employment of guerrilla tactics. Roman guards would continue to be killed in the night. Their officers had no solution to the troop's noticeable decline in number. Replacement troops were on their way, the officers promised."

I came to appreciate Mother's pride in her native people's war skills. She had lived off shore from the old *Caledonii* tribes for many years and had gained great respect for their ways. Her dislike for the ways of the Romans grew out of her condemnation of the invasion of the lands of peace loving people who had no need or reason to be a part of the Roman Empire.

Their imperialist ways had taken in lands across the Euro continent and to the Isles of the Hebrides. Unlike the Norse people, Romans had no intention to assimilate into the native culture. They sought only to possess it, and Mother had no further need for them.

Father must have found it difficult to conduct the business of repelling his enemies and maintaining morale with his troops while returning Mother to her tent every time she walked naked through the camp. Escaping her noisy desires in the morning caused Father to be the subject of ridicule. It was at the base of their growing disrespect of Constans and his officers, along with heir seeming disregard for the enemy that they faced at night.

"It was not all about my lovers in camp, I was very passionate with your father," Mother explained. "I am afraid that I was loud in my demands and he was uncomfortable with the sounds of my passion carrying through the camp."

"To your Father's embarrassment, our love making was heard each morning before he reassembled himself and took his position in the officer tent. Little did he know that the camp was very familiar with those sounds."

"According to camp gossip, I emerged from the tent each morning after several forays of lovemaking, with a smile on my face and a song in my voice. The General was losing his grip on his command. I loved walking disheveled and naked, down to the stream and lounge in the comfort of the cool spring while I recomposed myself and refreshed my appearance after our morning sessions."

My Father must have been aware that his privileges as a General were not known to the common infantryman. He knew that he was entitled to a few comforts that were not available to his rank and file, but he must have seen that Sarah's behavior and his lack of concentration to his duties were causing noticeable damage.

I think this was the beginning of the end for Mother's time in Father's camp. Frankly, I suspect that she did not care. She must have known that she carried me in her womb and therefore, had gotten what she needed. As she put it later, "Anything else that I did was just for the sake of harassment," she said.

Even when the nights were clear, the guards were attacked and their body parts were found scattered about, the following morning. While the enemy did not inflict great losses in numbers, their tactics had Father's troops imagining ghosts in the night.

Mother said, "Then one night, Odenn and twenty of his fighters slipped around the wall and decapitated the guards as usual. They displayed the heads on pikes as they had in the past, but they did not stop there. They continued with an approach to the down hill and western side of the Roman encampment," she explained.

"While the rain had the legions huddled inside of their tents, Odenn's men approached them on the outer perimeter. Odenn quietly sliced through the tent wall and beheaded the two troops within. They killed many others in the same manner."

"They continued to work the outer perimeter of the tent rows without being discovered. Finally, the sound of death pierced the night when one soldier was disemboweled, he screamed before his assailant was able to take his head off."

"Odenn and his men sneaked back out of the encampment in the confusion and panic that was caused they found their comrades dead in their own beds. This caused a new wave of panic in camp," Mother said. "Now they were not even safe in their own beds."

"Odenn's men approached the wall, on their way out of camp, like waves take the shore. With Odenn stopping at the foot of the wall, his warriors ran upon him, placing a foot in his gathered hands and catapulted onto the crest of the wall in a single motion. The others followed one at a time, without breaking a stride onto Fenn's hands and over the wall. The last one stayed on the top and hoisted Odenn over. They trotted back to their village to the beat of their drums and the cadence of the pipes."

"These tactics continued for several more nights against Quintus' soldiers," Mother went on. "The troops were nervous and your Father was beside himself. Officers were being outwitted by a band of six men."

"'Trotting?' your Father screamed. 'A few men disrupt a camp of a nine thousand trained and disciplined soldiers and just trot off into the night and get away?"

"Your Father was irate. He could not stop screaming at his officers who stood at the foot of our bed where he had been informed of the latest attack. I sat up in the bed without making an effort to cover my nakedness. Nor did I display any anger at the three officers who gathered at the foot of my bed. I leaned back on my elbows with the covers below my knees, for all to see what they would."

"The intruders stood, gawking at me and paid little attention to your father's scolding. I later considered this as one of crowning moments. I secretly despised what your Father's troops were doing to our peaceful people of the highlands. I knew that my time in camp was nearing an end. Your Father had reached the end of his wits, and frankly, he had lost some of 'his punch,' if you know what I mean."

Mother was pregnant with me. She had what she wanted and began to plan her departure.

"Your Father tried to cover me and continue his rebuke of the officers, but it was too little, too late. I listened to Constans try to collect himself after the embarrassment that I had caused. Finally, 'Place guards on the out perimeter of the south side of the encampment! That is where they attacked from, is it not?' he asked. 'Double the night guards and get out of my sight!" he commanded," Mother recalled.

"Three nights later, as the rain drove down upon the highlands, Odenn told his fighters, 'Tonight, we pay the General and his lady a visit.' Odenn had no idea that I was relishing the havoc that I caused on behalf of the Picts. Without further planning or discussion, they left the shelter of their village and began their trek towards the Roman encampment. They scaled the wall as before, dispatched the guards and made their way, slowly, towards the north side of the camp."

"They worked their way from the first row through several others while they slept, killing their occupants in total silence. Now Odenn and his son Fenn stood on the outside our quarters. It was a tall, wall-tent with a large entrance on the west side. It was guarded by two troops who stood in the rain, pikes in hand," Mother explained.

Odenn slit an opening in the north wall of the tent. He, Fenn and two of his fighters slipped in through the opening, into the expanse of the large tent. They made their way towards the front flap and quietly beheaded the two troops guarding the entrance.

I watched quietly, as their heads were placed on the blunt end of their pikes and the spear end driven into the ground. They put one on each side of the entry, just as the guards had been before they met their swift death. Their bodies were carried in, one each placed in two chairs at your Father's desk."

"Fenn must have felt my eyes on his every move inside the tent. He glanced at the bed and saw me staring at him. I did not speak. Later, I considered the possibility that either Fenn had been among the party that carried the remains of the Pict warrior from camp months before. I was certain that he had been among them or that I had been described to him by one of the party. He kept eye contact with me as if he were trying to determine why I did not scream or try to escape."

"I sat up in bed and watched Odenn's crew. Fenn was not alarmed as he saw me watching. He motioned to Odenn to look in my direction as if he was unsure about what should be done with me. I made no attempt to awaken the General as Odenn made eye contact with me. We looked each other in the eyes. He finally gave me a nod of recognition and led Fenn away. They left your the tent, with me still watching them from the bed."

"Odenn and his fighters slipped back through the tent opening. They neared the wall when they heard the first scream. They lost no time looking back towards the camp, as they scaled the wall and disappeared into the night."

"Your Father finally awoke. He rose in the bed and saw his two guards sitting at his desk. "Guards!" he yelled. He wrapped himself in a toga and ran to the guards sitting in the dim candle light. 'Guards! 'he yelled. Neither rose to his command. He took the candle sticks towards the desk and saw that his guards were in chairs, headless.

"Guards!" He yelled. Damn it!"

"He ran to the entry and saw the heads on their pikes. Finally, an officer came to his side. They went inside and found the opening in the wall where the assailants had entered."

"Your Father was livid, engorged with rage. He felt like his officer's incompetence was going to cost all of them their lives. Your Father's included."

Towards the end of their relationship, the warring Picts were causing havoc along the wall and my Father could no longer give Mother the attention that she demanded.

I was born in the Spring of that first year. Mother told me later that I was a child of remarkable beauty. I was born with pitch black hair that shined with a blue tint in the light of the sun. Like all Mur'uchs my eyes were black and weepy. Mother said that I never let her out of my sight from the beginning. I guess that I knew that I was not among my own kind and wanted to make sure that I did not get left. If I would have known Mother's possessive attitude towards me, I would not have had any reason for concern.

Father prized Mother's attention even though it came at a price. The men and women of the camp, including soldiers, avoided her since the last disturbance outside of camp. He was never told what his men suspected, but he was sure that it had something to do with Mother.

Before Father fell asleep one night he placed Mother's purple and sealskin hat near the bed where she could find it. In the morning, she and I were gone.

Mother had caused enough disruption in Father's camp. They were months behind in finishing the section in Hadrian's Wall and his officers, troops and auxiliary were in disarray. Between the Pict night assaults and Mother's disruption around camp, Father was begging to return to Rome.

"I never saw him again," Mother said.

"I came to learn later that he returned to Rome, disgraced by his inability to protect Britannia."

Chapter XI

Mother took me and disappeared into the harbor before dawn. She had received what she intended from Father and did not need to remain in his custody any longer.

I did not know at the time that Mother's next intended mate would be a Pict war leader. She had reasoned that the seed of a Pict chief would provide the beginning for another daughter. Before time for that move came, Mother would spend all of the time she needed to care for me.

When we left the eastern shores after escaping the Romans, we traveled north, looking for a quiet inlet to settle in.

Near the opening of a small harbor, we found a wind shelter among the rocks. I loved to play around the rocks with the seals that shared our little rock outcropping off shore. The seals made space for us and we found comfort among them.

Mother allowed the seals to teach me water skills and trusted me in their care. I took to my new environment from the beginning. I had never known life in Father's camp, so this was really my beginning. I quickly learned to swim and dart around the rocks with my powerful tail as if I were one of the seals myself. My hair grew down my back and flowed smoothly behind me, like a wing, as I rolled and breached above the shallow waves with my new play mates.

As time went by, Mother watched small boats and canoes go by the rocks. With me at her side, she avoided contact with humans who stopped to watch. She had no intention of letting anything interfere with my needs. She knew that she would have plenty of time to settle with the villagers later. For now, she remained unavailable to men of the village who watched us from the shore and from boats as they rowed by.

Mother collected scallops, barnacles and clams around the rocks and broke them open for me. I continued to grow and reveled in my play with the seals.

When the wind blew storms onto shore, Mother and I escaped under the rocks, using them as a buffer as the seals did.

Several Pict warriors tried to approach Mother while I was still young. They came close to the rocks and stared at Mother. She allowed them to look all that they wanted. She always loved a man's attention. It would serve her well when she began to select a mate among the Pict.

She did not scold or threaten onlookers. She enjoyed drawing them close before we slipped into the surf and disappeared below. It became a game with me. When they got too close, I slipped into the water first with Mother not too far behind me. We always watched them looking around to see if we would return. We seldom did.

At that time she was content to keep me safe. I was to be the beginning of her dynasty of Mur'uch Princesses, and she was not going to let anything happen to me.

With me growing steadily at her side, she spent hours telling me about the people that my Father and other Romans called, "The Pict."

When I came of age and the time was right, Mother took her place upon the rock. It was time to begin the search for another mortal mate and more young. We waited for the leader of the nearby village to come investigate. Mother would have no other than Maelchon, war leader of the Wolf Clan and former King of the Roman dominated people of Wales.

I asked Mother to tell me more about our early days in the land of the Pict as we sat together on the rocks, offshore from where Fathers encampment had been hundreds of years ago.

"There were Pict clans from regions north of the Clyde," she said, "including the adjoining highlands and the isles of the north. The Pict were always fierce fighters and defenders of their independence from the Romans."

"My next mate was to be Maelchon, the war chief of one of the clans of the northern region. He must have heard about the beautiful sea maiden who raised her young on the rocks of the inlet. He had seen me several times as he passed by in his boat," Mother said.

"Maelchon was an independent minded man. He found little reason for loyalty to some of the old ways of Pict clans. He faced difficulty trying to convince them to change their war practices in ways that he thought might ensure their future. To Maelchon's concern, the Pict were fiercely independent and had not seen any benefit of banding together to chase away the Roman legions."

"I learned later that Maelchon saw stubborn independence as their weakness. The Pict refused to combine their clans and work together to keep their independence," Mother explained.

"Many of the women of Maelchon's clan were related to his mother and her sister, Wolfstan. He saw no reason to take one of these women to provide the care that his wife provided before she died," Mother explained.

"Maelchon was sure that changes needed to be made if they were to succeed against the foreigner invasion of their land. To demonstrate the need to change, he decided to approach the sea maiden who sunned on the rocks off shore from his village on the bluffs. His mother and aunts had spoken of the tales of Mur'uchs, Merrows and Selkies since he was a child in Wales and he was familiar with the lore and legend of 'sea maidens,'" Mother recalled.

I remember the day that Maelchon approached us as we sat off shore.

"'What do you seek, Warrior King?' I asked when he came within voice range. He approached the rock towards me, with you at my side," Mother recalled.

"'I come for you, Sea Maiden,' Maelchon said. 'I come for a woman to keep me warm on winter's night,' he answered. 'I seek a loving woman who I can sleep next to with both of my eyes closed.'"

"I want a Mur'uch to help me rear my son in the manner that you are famed for," Maelchon told mother. "I have a young son and I want him raised with the influence of your supernatural powers. Our women are good mothers as well, but they think in the old Pryten way. My son will need to be able to stand on his own and take the Pryten people forward into a changing world," Maelchon declared. "Your beautiful young daughter will be a perfect companion to learn the care and attention of a woman as he grows."

"I look for a woman companion, of my own, who is soft in her beauty and kind in her speech. I seek a woman who I can lie with and soothe my pains from battle. I saw her in a dream recently. She was tall, soft and graceful. She was quiet and earnest in her work and had no will to fight with men or other village women,' Maelchon told me."

I thought it a bit strange when Mother recalled this later. Does he know who he is talking to? I love my Mother, but she was so full of herself that she had little room for anyone in her space.

"You have women in your camp, take one of them," Mother tested. "Do you not find your own kind fair enough for your needs?" she asked.

"Maelchon was a big, handsome man," Mother explained.

"He was powerful in his build and he approached with an air of confidence. He was clothed with only a decorated leather sword scabbard that crossed one should and cross his chest to his right side. Unlike the Romans, he was without armor or uniform," Mother said.

"He said, 'as I said, they come with too much history and they are vengeful in their quest for power and dominance among the other village women. I would not be able to sleep with my eyes closed,' Maelchon told Mother.

"I am the war leader of my village and do not care to lie with one of them. They are as hardened as any of my warriors, and most are at least as fierce," Maelchon claimed. I do not want a wife and do not intend to take one. I only ask that you stay with me until my son is grown. If you chose to leave then, you may do so," Maelchon offered.

"Are you not Sarah, Queen Mur'uch of the North Seas?' Maelchon asked me. 'It is she, I seek," he said.

"Then you know the legend of the Mur'uch?" I asked. 'Yes. I know the legend from my Mother's sister and the old story teller, Finnbar,' he answered. 'She can provide me with the woman I saw in my dream. I plan to have she and her daughter raise my son. He is without a mother and needs the influence of a caring woman. I know that the legend says that your kind are caring mothers. I want to see him grow among our people with the advantage that I received from my mother. The women of my clan want me to sire their children and leave my son to his own. I will not do that to him,' Maelchon told her.

"Yes, I am Sarah. Come, Warrior King and tell me more of what you desire," Mother said.

"Maelchon said, 'I seek a fair skinned maiden with ample meat on her bones, with heavy bosom and butt to keep my mind off of cold nights. I do not wish for a white haired woman of the far north, or the black of the Romans, nor the red heads of our own kind. I desire a woman who can soothe my pains and who is soft to lie with. I look for a woman who will nurture my son,' Maelchon said, finishing his description of the partner he sought."

"Come closer, sweet prince," Mother told him. "Let me see the woman you imagine in your mind's eye," she said.

I remember being surprised at Mother's changed behavior. I did not know then that Mur'uchs could adapt their demeanor, much in the same way that we can change our appearance while luring a victim.

As Father's concubine, Mother was a spicy vixen with no care for anything but caring for her own beauty. She seemed to have changed to fit Maelchon's needs and I was taken aback by her adjustment at first.

I was looking from behind the rocks when Maelchon approached us and sat down on our rock. Mother gazed deep into his eyes and held his focus. He took the hat from her head and placed it in his coat pocket. She did not object nor try to take it back.

"Maelchon must have also known of the magic of sea maiden's and their hats," Mother recalled. "He made sure that he took control of it from the beginning. With my hat gone I began to take on the features of the woman he saw in his dreams and that he had just described to me."

"My lips spoke his native language. I was soft spoken and modest. I shyly looked down on to her lap as he watched her transformation taking place before his eyes," Mother said.

I remember watching Mother's hair change to a soft, auburn brown. Her eyes turned to amber gold and her skin became light tan. She tied her hair away from her face with a delicate braid that she braided in two stands from front to back. Her legs that appeared from within the bundled sea maiden tail were long, tanned and shapely.

Maelchon sat next to Mother, testing the softness of her thighs and belly. They were smooth to his touch. He ran his hand over her calf, past her knee and onto her inner thigh and soft belly. She was perfect in his eyes and to his touch."

Mother stood upon the rocks. Her torso was long and sleek. Maelchon took her in his arms and touched the soft, fleshy mounds of her backside. She was in full control of her powers of attraction.

"You will be fit for those cold winter nights in my village," he said. 'You are strong and well built. You will not see my son as an intrusion into her life. Your nurturing powers are very strong,' Maelchon said."

"As you see, I have a daughter of my own," Mother, told him. "I will care for her needs while I oversee the welfare of your son," Mother said. "Is that not a good trade?" she asked. "They will grow together and perhaps they will find each other for their own needs. Your son will need a mate of his own, someday."

"Yes, perhaps," Maelchon said.

I stood with Mother on my own two legs and held her hand. I must have still needed reassurance that I was not going to get left behind in this bargain.

Maelchon lead Mother and I to his boat. We sat on the floor, on a bundle of furs and skins. I came along, holding Maelchon's hand as we walked toward the. Mother and I sat still on our way to the settlement that would be our home for many years to come. Little did we know that these would be the years that we chose to recall above all of the others.

We said nothing as he rowed his small round boat towards shore and into the small protected harbor. Maelchon helped us out of the beached boat and onto the rocky shore.

Mother turned to look at me. I had never taken human form before. My little round butt was as different to me as my two new legs. I was pleased and finally assured that Mother had my welfare in mind along with her own. I must have been ashamed to think that she might not, for she always put me first.

We walked together, up the incline towards his village at the crest of the high bluffs that stood over the sea. I could not see huts or shelters as we walked up the steep incline. I wondered where we were being taken.

Chapter XII

As we finally reached the top of the bluff, I saw free standing stones with intricate designs etched into the surface. Mother saw them, as well and asked, "what are these symbols?"

"They are symbols of our identity as a clan of highlanders of the Pryten people, Maelchon finally said, filling in the awkward silence.

"This one is the Pryten clan of wolf, and this stone tells that. The wolf clan is part of *Sidhe Lena Gig* and her realm of all things natural, and all things supernatural, like you and your beautiful daughter. She oversees all things for mothers and daughters in your world and in mine. They say these stones were carved by ancient warrior and have been here since the ancient times, Maelchon explained."

Mother already knew that. She was being coy.

Maelchon led us towards an entrance of the winter village. It led down a stone lined path and steps that descended below the heavy turf that covered our heads.

At the bottom, another stone path led through rock lined tunnels and into a large, open chamber. None of rooms in the shelter or the stone tunnels that tied them together were visible from the outside. The entire habitat was under the cover of the sod above.

"Maelchon took us into the room in the center. It was a large, expanded, circular space that appeared at the end of the tunneled hallway. A center support pole and radial roof supports extended off of it like the spokes of a wheel. The room was lined with benches of stone, covered with furs and hides. Ambers from the fire pit near the center of the room glowed. Whale oil lamps on the support poles and near the entrance partially lit the room," Mother continued telling about our early times with the Pict.

I remember seeing eyes peering through fur, hide flaps that covered other entrances and tunnels as Maelchon walked us out of the center room. No one came out. They stayed behind their door cover and watched the Warrior king escort his woman to his private chamber.

Maelchon pushed the door flap aside and took us inside a smaller space off of the big room. We waited a moment for our eyes to adjust to the dark and smoke filled interior. A fire pit burned slowly. Its smoke rose slowly towards an opening in the conical, peaked ceiling.

Maelchon showed us to the heather stuffed covered, stone bench along the far side wall. He pulled his cover from Mother. She was truly beautiful in her human form.

I found a space on the other fur covered sleeping bench along the far wall.

Our skin was much different in appearance than the Pict women. Not only was it absent the tattoo markings, our skin appeared to be as young as one of their children.

"The Pict women wore nothing that would identify them as women. Their markings, ornaments and stone jewelry were similar in every way to their male comrades. They carried the same weapons as men and performed many of the same duties. The women carried themselves with the same noticeable self assurance as the men," Mother recalled.

"Maelchon's red brown hair was shaggy and wild. The dyed headband tried to contain the unruly hair. His face had a bluish tint, being covered with swirling patterns etched into his skin. Every space of muscle on his body was covered in the same way. He wore no clothing, only the sheath that contained his sword. He was a striking, powerful figure," Mother remembered.

"The thing that I remember the most about Maelchon, despite all of the tattoos on his face, was the kindness that shined through it all," she recalled.

Maelchon provided no clothing for Mother and me. We would remain without clothing during the warmer months, just as the Pryten natives did. During the colder seasons, we wore a fur wrap over our shoulder.

I liked Maelchon from the beginning. I began to understand why Mother adopted a submissive way for him. Her attitude had changed dramatically since her time in the Roman camp. She no longer boasted over her dominance of the men. She was quiet and dutiful in her chores in the settlement.

Maelchon's position and war experience among the Pict warranted respect from Mother and she showed it to him. In return, Maelchon showed kindness to both of us and his young son, Breidi.

Mother tied a carved stone icon of her matron, *Sidhe Lena Gig* around her neck. It was the only item of decoration on her body.

"You wear the symbol of our protective matron" Maelchon said.

"She is our matron protector. She was given to me by my mother many years ago," Mother said.

"Come then, we will take our midday meal in the clan room," Maelchon said.

When we reentered the room at the center of the complex, we saw a woman, with a small black haired boy standing by her side. He watched us intensely.

I looked towards the young boy and motioned for him to come sit by me. He reluctantly rose and walked towards me, cautious with every step. He finally sat beside me and looked me over.

Aethlgifu worked on preparing the meal. She placed slices of seal blubber and red meat on a hot stone that spanned a corner of the open, fire pit. Smoke rose to the ceiling as the fat sizzled on the hot stone and drifted to the ceiling where it escaped through an opening in the center. It smelled good, filling the shelter with the savory smell of cooked meat.

A flat loaf of dough rose on the other stone placed near the fire on the opposite side. Aethlgifu flipped the loaf to its other side as it began to brown and rise with steam coming through the small vent that Aethlgifu knifed in it top surface.

"What is the boy's name?" Mother asked.

"This is my son, Breidi," Maelchon said

"This is Aethlgifu," Maelchon said. "She prepares many of the meals for our small clan and cares for Breidi while I am away. She can be trusted. She is without child and a mate. She wet nursed Breidi after her own child died at birth. Her husband died in battle several months ago and she will join another when her mourning time ends.

"Aethlgifu is as her name says, 'a gift,' to Breidi and I. She and Breidi's Mother were childhood friends. She pays her respects for her passing by caring for my son."

Aethlgifu did not speak. She went about her work while watching Breidi who sat contently with me.

The youngster's hazel eyes took in everything. He leaned against my thigh as he stood between my legs. I gave him a hug and I held him close as he inspected me.

Breidi examined me carefully. I must have been different for he looked me over and ran his hands over my shoulders and arms, testing the softness of my skin. He touched my face and lips. It was not that I was without clothing. Pict women wore no clothes, so I was no different. It must have been the absence of markings that he must was used to seeing on Pryten men and women.

Breidi stood closer to me now that he felt safe in my arms. He placed his head in the valley between my bare breasts and remained there with his small arms around my waist.

"This is Esther," Mother said to Aethlgifu. The young woman looked over towards me. She neither smiled nor acknowledged my presence. She must have known where Mother and I came from and was uncertain what to do in the beginning.

"We eat together. Our hunters bring in meat and fish and we share in their bounty. Aethlgifu and other women prepare our meals and bake the bread," Maelchon said.

He filled two cups from a bag that hung in the corner of the room. "This is heather ale," he said. "Drink," he said. "It will keep your belly warm and help fill it when meat is scarce."

"What of Breidi's Mother?" Mother asked.

"She died during the birth," Maelchon said. "It was a difficult winter season and she did not have enough of life's energy to sustain the child and herself."

I watched as Maelchon lifted the cup and splashed a small portion on the stone floor. He then took a piece of bread and tossed it in the same direction after raising it over his head. The dogs from the unlit side of the room rose and sped towards Maelchon and the crumbs of bread that he discarded. Maelchon motioned them back to their places. They lowered their heads and tails and returned to their space in the dark corner.

Maelchon took a piece of the sizzling meat from the stone, holding it between his fingers with two small bites of bread. He raised it over his head and tossed it near the bread crumbs. The dogs rose again, with more aggression this time, before Maelchon told them to stay away.

As I watched Maelchon perform this strange practice, he said, "These, we offer to the gods that protect us and look over our clan," Maelchon said.

Maelchon lifted his cup to his mouth and took a slow drink of the hot ale, a bite of the meat and bread. He motioned for Aethlgifu, Mother and I to join him. We all broke off a piece of bread and used it to break off a portion of the meat.

Aethlgifu let me help Breidi do the same. Breidi puckered his lips and blew on the sizzling meat before he allowed me to raise it to his mouth. He held my hand and ate around my fingers rather than holding the hot morsel himself.

I took a drink from the cup as a woman entered the room. The women stepped back and made room for her as she entered. She did not sit, but stood over Mother. She looked towards me as if she had an objection to our being in the room.

Maelchon rose from his stool and stood between the woman and Mother. "Sarah, this is Wolfstan. She is the matron of the Wolf Clan,

Maelchon said, as were her ancestors before her. In the way of the Pryten clans, she is the leader of our village," Maelchon said.

Before Maelchon could speak another word, Wolfstan said, 'Who are these intruders that you have brought to the center of our clan? Why are these two women here?"

"The Mother is to be my mate," Maelchon told her.

"Why do you bring in a foreign woman and her black eyed whelp? Why do you not take one of the clan women?" Wolfstan growled. "They would all have you."

"Because I am the war chief of the Wolf Clan, and I will take the woman who pleases me," Maelchon answered.

"I do not need your permission to take a woman of my choice. You have turned the women of the Wolf Clan into she wolves with your unkind dominance. They scurry about and around you like they beg for the crumbs of life that only come to them through you. I would never trust a woman to raise Breidi who was only focused on their own welfare," he said.

"Wolfstan crossed her arms across her chest in clear refusal of Maelchon's reasoning. I could see it and so could Mother."

"I do ask for your acceptance of Sarah and her daughter. I expect you to give them the freedom that they deserve as my woman and my family," Maelchon demanded.

Having had enough of this woman hovering over her, Mother stood up to face her.

"She is Sarah,' Maelchon said."

"Where do you come from woman?' Wolfstan asked. 'Speak to me woman,' Wolfstan demanded. Without warning, she reached out to raise Mother's chin with her coarse hand. That aggression did not settle well with Mother. She grasped the old woman's arm when she raised it towards her and forcefully bent it away. Wolfstan's expression reflected the surprise and the piercing pain of Mother's hold.

Mother's eyes met her aggressor's, and a low, throaty growl came from her chest. Wolfstan realized her error and tried to free her hand from Mother's grip. Mother held it firmly, with even more force.

Wolfstan winced with the pain. Mother applied an even stronger grip when her tormentor tried to free her arm. Wolfstan's eyes focused on Mother's deep stare. The faint, graveled growl continued as Mother held the woman's arm in her grasp.

Mother finally released her arm when she saw that Maelchon saw her aggression towards his tribal mistress. Wolfstan took a step back and gave Mother the space required of respect.

"I am Sarah. I am the daughter of Estella, Queen of all shores of the north lands," Mother proclaimed. "You know well who I am and where I come from. Do not pretend that you are ignorant of the forces around you."

"Wolfstan saw the stone icon of *Sidhe Lena Gig* hanging from a leather string on Mother's neck. She asked, "Why do you wear the symbol of our matron?"

"Why do you asked such questions? You know the power of this symbol. It is etched on a stone near your door and you know she is my matron as well as your own," Mother said. "She gives me the freedom to influence the lives of mortals of these highlands and northern isles for their good, as I see fit. I am sure that you already know that. I intend no harm to you or your people," Mother explained. "Should you ever attempt to bring harm to my family you will be punished with a force that you have yet to imagine."

"There will be no need for that," Maelchon said. "Wolfstan is trying to defend her clan against a power that she has not previously met," he said.

Wolfstan and Mother stood silent as they returned each other's glare. Wolfstan gazed into Mother's amber gold eyes and then looked down and stepped away.

"As you would have it, Maelchon," she finally said.

Chapter XIII

From the beginning of our time with the Wolf Clan, I gave care to Breidi. Mother served his Father. Neither of us interfered in the organization of duties around Maelchon's shelter and we left plenty of space for the brooding Wolfstan.

We enjoyed our time with the people of the Wolf Clan. They lived comfortably inside the winter shelter of their dug out settlement. The winds from the sea were buffered by the bluffs and the sod cover of their burrowed complex of rooms. Fish from the shore and game from the hills filled our pots and warmed their bellies as they were cooked over an open hearth near the center of a large common area."

Mother and I cared for Breidi, feeding him warmed goat's milk, pieces of wheat cake and spoons of ground barley porridge.

My quiet assured nature was pleasing to Breidi and he relished my attention. When I sat, Breidi came to me and stood against me in the space between my knees and folded arms. His stare revealed his inquisitive nature and his little hands were always exploring around my neck and my chest. He was curious about the two women who had come into his life and did not hesitate to investigate what we were all about.

Breidi traced his youthful fingers across my face, near my eyes. He moved his hands over the tops of my thighs as if amazed by the smoothness of my skin and then moved on to my chest. He studied my eyes for the longest time. His curiosity searched for my thoughts that he must have perceived were hidden behind my unfamiliar, black eyes. I had the unfamiliar sense that Breidi had taken possession of me for his own and it was he who would look after my welfare rather than I watching over his.

Wolfstan complained to Maelchon later about Mother and I and how he would not be able to depend upon Mother to care for Breidi.

"I was alone with my son before she arrived," Maelchon objected. "Until she leaves, I have a warm woman for my bed and my son has a full time play mate to help him as he matures. I can finally sleep with my eyes closed and I have time to plan defense of our lands from the foreigners. They insist on pushing north to settle new land. I have too much to concern me without having to deal with a wife, jealous of the time that I spend away. You and Esther will do well with Breidi. I see that he has taken a liking to Esther already. Who could blame him? She is a beautiful creature."

During the following night, Maelchon and Mother lay in their bed, warmed by the small fire while Breidi and I slept on Breidi's cushion of fur covers. I held him close while we shared each other's warmth.

On the coldest nights, Pict villagers kept themselves warm by sharing each other's body warmth under a cover of fur around our shoulders as Breidi and I did in our bed.

Breidi slept in my arms from the first night on. During the coldest nights before Mother and I arrived, he must have found warmth in his father's bed. From this night on, he slept with his head on my chest and shoulder. I laid on my back with my arm under his head, holding him close. He began to sleep with his arm over my belly and breasts with his head lying between them. We kept each other warm under the soft furs. He never slept alone again.

"Wolfstan bothers you, about me?" I heard Mother ask one night.

"Yes she does, but that is her nature. She has overseen this clan for many years and she is jealously possessive and suspicious of outsiders,' Maelchon said. 'Don't worry over her," Mother recalled.

"All that I want is a child by you and a peaceful place for Esther to grow up," Mother said. "Esther and I are well treated here and I am in no hurry to leave. Someday, you will give me a daughter."

"How do you know it will be a daughter?" he asked.

"I know. Believe me," she said. "A beautiful daughter, at that," she told him.

We settled in with life among the Pict as their ways became routine for us. They were quiet and reserved.

We learned to fit into their ways of doing things. They were a happy, peaceful people who took joy in the small things that they did around the village. They found peace with what life in the highlands provided them and kept their needs simple. Wolfstan took care of all issues that arose between clans. She dealt with these things while they were minor issues, never allowing bad behavior to get out of hand.

The settlement was a peaceful place. Few things arose that caused a disruption to that peace. We had game meat and root vegetables to eat and we occasionally slaughtered one of the pigs that were pinned near the grain storage building.

Members of Wolfstan's clan left Mother and I on our own. They knew what we were and did not dare cross us.

As the first winter passed, we began to look forward to moving to the summer settlement in the valley. Maelchon had Mother and I help Aethlgifu store the flour and grain in the stone grain building near the grist mill. We kept grain in preparation for the following cold season. Breidi was at our side as we filled the room with sacks of grain and ground flour before we closed and sealed the door.

"When are we leaving for the Summer village?" Breidi asked me.

"I don't know," I told him. "This is new to me too," I answered.

The herders took the sheep, cows and pigs to the Summer village early one morning. That set off a frenzy of domestic activities. It was a time of excitement and endless questions from Breidi. "Come Breidi," Maelchon said. "It is time to load the horses with supplies. We will leave soon, but first we need to eat."

Breidi took my hand and lead me to the fire. We sat down near the stone oven that Aethlgifu used for baking bread. She pulled a piece of hot bread from the flat loaf and gave Breidi and I a piece to eat with honey and berries.

We finished loading one of the horses with household goods and waited outside while the metal smith and Maelchon loaded another horse with arrows, axe heads and other weapons that he placed in two large baskets strapped on the horse.

"Father has many horses," Breidi said. I watched Maelchon place a blanket across one of the mares and gave Breidi a foot up. He helped me swing my leg over and take my place behind him.

Mother rode on another horse that Maelchon led as we left the village and began the trek to the valley where I was told we would find the summer village. We passed over the hills near the shore as we moved inland. Our horse was tethered to Maelchon's mare as we walked along the path, pulling a travois of bedding wrapped in a fur bundle that Maelchon strapped to the travois frame.

"Look!" Breidi yelled. "It is our summer village."

The outline of the village walls became clear as we moved down the slope and into a wide valley of green grasses and a stream that flowed nearby. The small settlement sat next to the stream. The buildings were simple shelters of open, three sided huts with sleeping benches towards the rear and a small fire pit under an overhang in the front. The pit was smaller than one in the winter settlement.

When we arrived, Maelchon opened the gate and led the pack horses towards the center of the village. Breidi took my hand and led me to one of the wood frame huts, lined along the inside of the stockade wall. There were pens for the animals along the walls and garden plots laid out in the center. The herders and farmers had arrived before us and placed the garden plots in the center of the open yard. Villagers were working in the gardens when we arrived as we arrived.

I remember those early days in the late spring and summer when we walked through the valley and along the streams near the settlement. Aethlgifu fished the large stream near the village for trout and salmon as the settlement leaped into the warm season with activity everywhere. The smoke house was filled with Aethlgifu's fresh fish and the gardens came to life with young sprouts coming from the rich soil.

Evenings were passed with settlers sitting around a fire pit near the central yard. The village sage told stories of Faeries as we met around the fire during the cool evenings.

Once the work was done, Mother and I were free to take Breidi to the river to bathe and swim. Breidi clung to Mother and I as we waded into the swift, cold current toward a quiet pool near the bank on the far side of the stream. We sat for hours in the coolness of the water, soaking in the warm sun.

Mother took Breidi to hunt birds in the fields and pastures nearby. Her skill with the sling and stones became the talk of the village. She could down water fowl and stop a rabbit in its' track with a well place stone.

Mother was beautiful. Her skin tanned in the summer sun.

Breidi watched as Mother loaded a stone from her bag and placed it in the pouch of her leather sling. She wound it around, over her head and then let it fly by releasing the end of one of the strands. The projectile rocketed out of the sling pouch towards the target. We relaxed on the banks of the river and felt the radiance of the warm summer.

Maelchon loved game birds with herb seasoning stewed in Aethlgifu's pot or grilled on a flat stone near the fire. Flat bread baked in the outdoor oven and the aroma of Aethlgifu's bake goods. Aethlgifu watched closely and learned new ways as Mother helped prepare the meals. She used herbs from the fields that added flavor to Aethlgifu's stews and roasted birds.

"I learned this from those who served foreigners," Mother said. "It is a good thing to learn things new, even from our enemies."

We added deer meat to Aethlgifu's pot. Hunters stayed and sat around the outdoor fire pit and watched Aethlgifu and Mother prepare meals. They were simple but hardy. I wondered at the time if the hunters stayed to watch Mother cook or to be near she and I. We were so different from the other women.

Aethlgifu's stew pot was a constant fixture of the hearth. The warm, savory smell coming from the pot filled the air. We added meat and vegetables everyday and kept the supply of its hot contents ready to be ladled out at any time of the day.

We cleaned and salted fish and took them to the smoke house for the long winter season to come. We all helped in preparation for the times when fresh meat would be a precious commodity.

The ice lodged between Mother and Wolfstan did not thaw as we prepared food stores for the long cold season. I do not think that Wolfstan ever trusted Mother. Wolfstan surely was no stranger to the world of the supernatural and she must have been versed in the legends and lore of the natural forces that surrounded her world.

As the leader of the clan, Wolfstan knew the forces that came under the encompassing grace of *Sidhe Lena Gig*. The presence of two Mur'uchs in her village may have been her closest encounter with our kind, but she could not have performed her protective duties without knowing the ways of the Mur'uch. Mother did little to aggravate the envy Wolfstan held for us as villagers began to accept Mother and I into their clan.

"Wolfstan had ruled the Wolf Clan nearly all of her life," Mother explained. She remained fiercely possessive of all things in the village. Perhaps she sensed the other world influence and was not sure what she was to do with us so close to her daily life. We stayed apart from Wolfstan and did not cause conflict with her responsibilities within the clan.

Wolfstan's appearance was as rough as her behavior towards us. I always thought that her short, stocky frame was almost masculine. She stood with her feet spread wide, her powerful short arms crossed over her sagging breasts as she watched us. Her skin was adorned with black and blue markings of the clan and her knotted hair was braided with wooden and stone ornaments. They must have held some importance. I never saw her without them," Mother said.

"There were no more confrontations with Wolfstan. It appeared that we agreed to stay out of each other's way," Mother explained later.

The village worked during the growing season collecting root vegetables and grain that we stored in bags after it was dried.

Time at the summer settlement passed too quickly. We would soon gather the horses that grazed in the open valley near the stream, and begin packing them up for the return in the fall.

Chapter XIV

We moved back to the winter village after the harvest season of that year. Mother delivered a black haired infant before the cold season set upon our winter village. She was my first half sister. Her eyes were like my own, as black as night. Mother and I watched the baby that she named "Asta," play on the gravel floor near the central fire pit.

Breidi helped me take grain to the village grist mill where we watched the big mill stone crush it into flour. We swept the flour from the stone table into our bowl. Breidi was always at my side. The two of us were always together in the early times of our years with the Pict people. He seldom let me out of his sight.

We collected root vegetables and berries for winter storage with Breidi stayed at our side. We filled the basket that he carried for us with wild onions and selected greens from the forest floor. Aethlgifu was fond of placing onions and the bitter tasting nettles and fiddle ferns in her pot with meat and root vegetables.

I took a few berries and put them on top of a piece of Aethlgifu's warm bread, drizzled honey on top and handed it to Breidi. He stood between my knees as he ate the sweet treat, and licked the honey from his fingers

The cold winter winds soon came upon us. They blasted against the bluffs and over our earth covered stronghold. With little fire wood to spare over the long winter we made do with blocks of dried pea blocks from the bogs that villagers collected and dried for use during the coldest times when fire wood would be difficult to collect.

I heard the winds during the quiet of night, blowing over our underground rooms. The aroma of Aethlgifu's stew and the musty, earthy smell of burning peat filled the rooms where we kept warm under fur covers.

The entry to our sod covered village was on the leeward side of the hill. The passage that turned away from the entrance helped keep the wind driven cold out of our shelter. Settled into our small private sleeping quarters, off from the center common space, Maelchon, Mother, Breidi, Asta and I stayed covered in the thick fur covers of our beds. We ate salted fish, preserved from the Harvest Season and dried venison and hard biscuits of wheat cakes which we dipped in honey. The winter winds whistled over the smoke vents in the ceiling.

As the winter wore on, Maelchon heard about the attacks against the Roman encampment and the foreigner's wall. Maelchon said that a man, named Fenn had early success with his father, Odenn, in harassing Roman soldiers stationed along the wall.

Maelchon sent a messenger to Fenn's village to learn something of his tactics. Bad news from those who watched the foreigner's encampment persisted with the long winter season. Plans were being made to push the Roman frontier further north. A second wall, north of the original was being discussed by Septimus, at Emperor Arcola's bidding.

Days later, Fenn entered the village of the Wolf and came to sit by the fire in the center of the lodge. Fenn and Maelchon drank cups of heather ale and sat by the comfort of the fire. A long period of silence preceded their discussion.

Mother told me that relationships between clans in these times were strained over territorial hunting rights, stealing prospective wives and the general unease of being too near each other's settlements. It was said that the sons of a Cruithne Queen separated after their arrival on the island and formed independent clans that lived apart and had little to do with each other. Separation and independence were courtesies that they all understood and followed. In those times, the Pict Clans were nothing if not fiercely independent.

"Before the Romans arrived and tried to tame the Pict in the ways of the southern Britons, clans seldom encountered each other. There was nothing to share or to depend on from any of the other villages except when looking for mates. They farmed their own lands and raised a few heads of live stock without a need or reason to seek the presence of one of the other clans. Like Wolfstan's clan the others were comprised of a few interrelated families," Mother explained.

During our time with the Pict, the only interchange among the ten villages occurred as men looked outside of his own extended family for a mate. Mother told me that fathers sometimes visited neighboring clans looking for a mate for a daughter.

Fenn was still a young man when we first met him. His hands were big and strong and heavy as the war club that he carried in his stout grip. His stocky body sat over short, stout legs. His face carried the markings of a fighter and leader among his clan. They extended down his neck onto the broad chest. His legs were like a trunk of a mighty tree. He carried a fine sword, sheathed in deer skin. It was connected to a belt that extended over his shoulder and down his left side.

There were few possessions among the Prytens that were not made of the very rock that formed their beloved highlands or the minerals that came from them. Swords and knives were among the few personal items that the Pryten owned.

Centuries ago, the use of metals for making spears and arrow tips came from iron ore sources that were jealously guarded. Relationships were sometimes strained over the ore that they kept secret.

Trust developed very slowly for the Pryten people who scrounged for everything that they possessed and tended to be stingy about sharing them. There was no waste to be created in anything that they did.

When Fenn had his belly warmed with stew and bread, Maelchon said," I am told of your success in raiding the camp of foreigners. I am interested in your tactics and what you have found as I am fearful that the foreigners will want to advance their position northward, towards our settlements. I believe clans must come together as a force if we are to turn them back to the south."

Fenn said nothing for a long moment. Sensing Fenn's reluctance, Maelchon said, "Your success in harassing our enemy may lead to the awakening of a great bear that has found new determination to take down the pests that annoy him."

"That is possibly so," Fenn finally said. "Our attacks are aimed at more than disturbing the great bear. We aim to demoralize it and chase it away and strike terror into our enemy. It is true that we take the enemy in small numbers. It is also true that we have killed hundreds of them for each one of our own that has fallen. "

"How so, brother?" Maelchon asked.

"We never allow a survivor to see us. We attack swiftly and quietly, leaving no one to tell about their attackers. We leave messages with our ways of killing. We come out of the night and attack swiftly and then we leave the same way we came in,' Fenn told Maelchon. 'We do not kill thousands as they might if they caught us unaware. Our tactics bring fear to them. That is our way," Fenn told Maelchon.

"You do well, brother. I have heard of your tactics and you are to be commended for your success," Maelchon said. "I intend no disrespect to your methods, for you have stricken our common enemy with fear. Our allies in their camp tell us of the fear that you have planted in their numbers. They say that your warriors are the fiercest that they have ever met."

"Ummh," Fenn grunted, as if he had just made the neighbor war leader understand that they had not awakened the great bear for no good reason. 'It is true that we take few enemies with each attack. We are few. We can take twice, maybe three or four times our number without being seen," Fenn continued. "We seek to frighten the foreigners into losing their advantage. They are trained in the use of their fine weapons and many in number. To attack them head on would be the end."

"That is true brave neighbor. I see your reason and we of the Wolf Clan think that you are wise," Maelchon said. "My concern is that such tactics would not succeed if our enemy ever leaves his place behind the wall and comes out to attack us in full force."

"We are joined by the Scotti people of Dal Riata on many of our raids. They have come from the southwest after they lived in the old times in the big island that the Romans call Hibernia," Fenn told Maelchon. "Their numbers are few but their help is sorely needed, "he said."

"In the spring, we wish to band together with your clan. Perhaps we can strike even more fear into them," Maelchon said. "I fear that they will be unstoppable if their legions march north into the highlands. It is best if we can keep them busy along the wall. Perhaps you can convince your Celtic people to join us."

"Perhaps," Fenn said. "We should not wait until the season of new growth, however. Foreigners are disturbed by the forces of our winds, snow and rain. They huddle together in their tents and shelters to stay warm. We have them at a great disadvantage. There is no reason to wait," Fenn said.

"First, we shall have a friendly competition between our fighters. Competition is a good thing and it will serve to lower distrust and suspicion between our bands," Maelchon proposed.

"Good," Fenn grumbled. "Three days time, in my village," Fenn proposed.

"Done," Maelchon said.

"I remember Fenn and Maelchon were distracted when Mother came out of our quarters and walked towards them. Maelchon was alarmed because he knew that she did not understand that warring was a man's domain. Even in a clan where the mother's blood determined who shall reign king, some things were left to men," Mother explained.

"I saw my mistake and stopped short of Fenn and Maelchon," Mother remembered.

I remembered this as well. Mother's skin was soft in color and unblemished as she glowed orange near the fire's reflection that flickered on her soft, pale skin.

"Sarah," I remember Maelchon saying.

Fenn looked up and watched Mother. She wore the ornaments of the Pict around her neck. It hung between her young breasts that swung free and heavy with mother's milk for the infant that she held, suckling, in her arms.

The sensual image of a heavy breasted Pryten mother and nursing infant held Fenn's mind. He did not look away. Mother must have been the perfect image for the peace loving Fenn. Her presence surely evoked the long sought peaceful home with a young fertile wife that Fenn had not yet been able to experience.

I remember the connection that she made with Fenn that evening, as Maelchon rose from his seat and introduced Fenn to her. "Sarah, this is Fenn of the Jackal village," he said.

Mother approached Fenn and kept eye contact with him as she took his arm in greeting. Her pale skin glowed by the fire and her eyes reflected the orange flicker in the black pools of her eyes. He held her arm for an instant too long and realized his lapse in judgment.

"Forgive me, Sarah, Maelchon," he said. "I feel that the paths of this beautiful creature and I have crossed before, years ago."

"Yes," Mother said, "I believe that they have." Silence held the moment after Mother spoke those simple words. Fenn was held in silence.

"Don't worry neighbor," Maelchon said. "She is beautiful. Is she not?" he asked.

"Yes," Fenn said. 'She is breathtaking. I would never forget meeting her. And this beautiful, young creature is her daughter?" Fenn asked.

"Yes. This is Esther. She has her Mother's beauty," he said.

"She certainly does. Come, Esther. Let me see you in the firelight beside your Mother," Fenn said.

Fenn extended his hand and helped me from my seat. "She is remarkable as well, Maelchon. She will soon be a fine mate for one of your people. I congratulate you on your beautiful family and your fine son."

Mother and I stood by each other. She placed her arm around my waist and gave me an affectionate squeeze. We were the same height and looked more like sisters than we did mother and daughter.

"This is my daughter, Esther," Mother confirmed. "She is my first. Esther is the daughter of Constans the Roman General charged with building their impotent wall across the lowlands."

"Constans?" Fenn asked. "Yes, I remember him well. He was a notable foe and I see traces of his olive skin in your beautiful daughter."

Fenn took lifted my chin and looked me in the eyes. "Yes, you have your Mother's eyes. With them, there can be no doubt that you come from our ancient legend of the Mur'uch. You are beautiful creatures, both of you," he said. I returned to my seat next to Breidi, who grabbed me jealously.

Breidi wrapped his arms around my waist as I resumed my seat. He placed his head below my chin. His hand found a free breast and fondled it in his palm as if to lay claim on me as his own. He must have felt the tension of the introduction and the silence that followed. He clung to me with his head on my chest.

"Sarah lived among the Romans," Maelchon told Fenn. "I believe that she is a special gift to our people, and we must learn to use the powers of her insight." Maelchon said.

"Her presence here has not been entirely welcomed by the women of our village, but that is easily understood. I believe that these times call for extraordinary forces to withstand the force of the Romans.

"Yes, I remember Sarah, from many years ago. Father and I attacked the officer's tents in the Roman camp. We came upon Sarah as we entered the General's tent," Fenn said. "I would never forget those eyes and her natural beauty."

"You were a very young man," Mother said. "I remember you as well. I also remember another time when you and your Father came into camp to recover the remains of one of your warriors."

"Yes. We did not want to leave our brother for the Romans to display and gawk at," Fenn said. "I do not remember seeing you that night."

"I stayed behind a tent to cover my presence. I did not want to alarm you," Mother recalled.

"So you have seen the results of Fenn and Odenn's night attacks?" Maelchon asked."

"Yes, I have. Forgive me for not speaking of this before" Mother apologized.

"Your tactics have always been troublesome for the Romans. They never recovered from the sense of doom that you brought to their camp in the early years of my stay with them. The fear that you brought to the Romans with your night attacks remains with them. They have no defense for your tactics, and you have frustrated every effort they have made to meet your assaults," Mother said.

"Then you agree that out night tactics have been successful," Fenn said.

"Yes. I do," Mother said. "I have seen the disruption that your night raids causes in the Roman camp. Romans call your warriors, 'ghost fighters.'"

"Forgive me Maelchon, Sarah. I must ask for your wisdom on the matter of our future strategy to defeat the Romans. The women of our villages are wise and have always provided guidance in times of need. This is, perhaps, one of those times," Fenn said. "You have special insight on this matter. You also have a natural bond with our Pryten clans as your native subjects and therefore would not hesitate to give us the advantage of your insight."

"Yes I do," Mother said. "The Pryten people of the highlands are the roots of our legends. Our kind has lived among the natives of these shores since your arrival, in the early times," Mother said.

"With your permission, Maelchon, I would like to hear Sarah speak about how we might proceed into the future," Fenn said.

"Speak, Sarah. You are free to tell what you know about our struggle with the Romans. We would be foolish not to listen to you, and we would be even more foolish not to recognize the gift that the great spirit *of Sidhe Lena Gig* has brought to our camp," Maelchon said.

"You are wise to continue with your night attacks," Mother began. "From the beginning, Roman officers have been unable to explain the force that has brought so much devastation to the camp at night. Roman legions have no quarrel with the natives of this land and their officers have been unable to demonstrate the importance of taking this land as part of the empire," Mother went on. "The Roman legions still believe that your warriors are spirit driven. That is to your advantage. A soldier can not defend himself against a force that he feels is supernatural or possesses special powers over them."

"Roman legions are professional warriors and it is not their place to ask, why. Your night tactics have caused them to resist their superiors," Mother continued. "There are also thousands of stone masons and carpenters who are not professional soldiers. Their officers have been unable to provide protection for them while they build and maintain the wall. Your tactics have slowed their progress and have driven fear into their ranks."

"Your strength is in Pryten independence," Mother said.

"How is that so?" Maelchon asked.

"The previous enemies of the Roman Empire were led by a single and united force. Treaties, surrenders and defeat have always come from a single leader from their opposition. Since your clans are only loosely united and no single leader speaks for all Pryten, your people can not be defeated. Even if they eliminate an entire village, two villages, or even three or four, there are many others who will live on as if nothing happened," Mother explained.

"You strength is in attacking and harassing the camp as individual forces rather than as a united front. The constant changing of tactics confuses the Romans. They have been unable to develop a defense strategy. Your methods change with each attack," Mother explained. "They have no experience or training in fighting a force that refuses to meet them in open field combat."

"They have already tired of trying to bring the people and settlements of the highlands into their empire. After all, that is the reason the wall was erected, Mother said."

"In time," Mother continued, "they will tire from fighting an enemy that they can not see, yet kills hundreds of their numbers at will. It is my vision that they will leave Britannia and return to their land. As long as they can not defeat a united enemy, they will never know victory. Britannia is at the far reach of the Roman Empire and will be the first that they abandon," Mother predicted.

"While it may be important for the Pryten to unite for other reasons, fighting the Romans with unconventional and independent tactics will outlast their patience. Time is on our side," Mother went on.

"So, we continue in our ways?" Fenn asked.

"Yes. I see Pryten peace and Roman removal from our lands as costly, but inevitable. I also see that your methods are the only means of defeating the Roman will. A long as your attacks remain relentless, their determination to defeat your forces will fall short in time to come. You are strong in your bravery. Now be strong in your resilience and patience and use the stubborn independence that you were born with to persevere," Mother said.

Mother's words made an impression that evening. Maelchon and Fenn listened to Mother and made no attempt at contradicting her. Mother knew the damage that Fenn and his Father brought to the Roman Camp and she was loyal to their cause. There was no reason to think less of her vision. She was their sole source of knowledge of the Roman occupation of southern Britannia. She alone knew the Roman mind and the mood of the empire.

I watched Fenn as he listened to Mother's reasoning. He was clearly taken with her insight. I was sure that this would not be the only time that he would come for Mother's counsel. That meant that Fenn would have frequent visits to our settlement.

I began to consider the possibility that Fenn might try to take me as his mate and thereby attach his clan to ours. I knew that his previous mate was dead. I could plainly see that he looked at me with a measure of curiosity and desire.

Mother possessed a special feminine nature in the way that she presented herself. She was always sensuously female, above all things. She had the very essence of all things woman. She had a natural attraction that drew a man's attention to her like bees to honey

The mix of her natural essence and the scents of the sea were more than men could ignore. Some came from the far corners of the highlands to be in Mother's presence. They feasted their eyes on Mother's smooth, unmarked skin and the essence of her physical, feminine being.

I had never been with a man and was not experienced with their desires. Even though I was coming of age, I was reluctant to consider Fenn as a possible mate. My place was with Breidi and I was willing to wait until he matured.

I also recall thinking that I had to keep myself away from the attention of other eligible men if I was to wait until Breidi matures to my age. He was still a youngster but I anticipated a time when he would see me as more of a companion than a source of warmth.

Fenn rose to leave at the end of Mother's talk. He said, "We shall meet in three days time." He left the lodge with his three escorts and returned home.

"I am sorry husband, I did not know that you had a visitor. Please forgive my intrusion," Mother said. Maelchon leaned down and took his young son and lifted him for a big bear hug."

"Do not worry Sarah. You and Esther have a natural way of causing men to stammer and lose track of our thoughts. It is not your intentional doing," Maelchon said.

"It is a part of who you are. Breidi and I are very fortunate men to have you both here. Right Breidi?" he said. "And we appreciate the special wisdom that you brought to Fenn and I tonight. I should have considered asking you to speak about your experience in the Roman camp before. Fenn was wise to ask for it."

Dropping the subject and looking at Breidi, he said, "how does a bear go, Breidi?" Maelchon asked, dismissing the conversation.

"He goes, grrrrrrr! Papa," Breidi said.

"Grrr," little Asta said, mocking her big brother.

Maelchon took young Asta in one arm while he hugged Breidi with the other. He gave them both a nuzzle of affection on their cheeks. Asta's eyes shined in the candle light of the lodge. With the exception of her hair, she had all of the appearance of her mother and would undoubtedly take her special place in the world when she became of age.

Maelchon was a kind hearted man. It was his nature and it showed in all things that he did. The Picts that Mother and I came to know were held together by small family units that persevered through all challenges. Mother said that she believed that they came by that trait from the trials of their ancestor's past. They were peace loving, but it seemed that it was in their nature to live without it. In some way they were settled to live without it.

Maelchon handed Asta back to Mother. She sat down by the fire and sang a song to us.

The clan meeting in Fenn's village was held with great success. Once the competitions began, any resistance between the people of the two clans was overcome. There were competitions with bow, spear and throwing axe. The fighters from the two groups were closely matched. Fenn's fighters had an advantage from the skills that came from their repeated attacks on the wall of the foreigners.

Mother took Breidi, Asta and I to the shore to mingle among the seals that gathered around us. Mother brought shell fish back to the settlement to be grilled on the hot stone in the way of the Picts. She also took us bird hunting.

We looked forward to eating her quarry. We enjoyed watching her use her sling and stone to kill game birds. We watched as she took a stone and placed it in the pouch of her sling and spun it over her head for a brief moment before she released it. She downed a bird with nearly every attempt.

We brought the birds back to the settlement and gave it to Aethlgifu. She seasoned the bird with herbs from the fields and placed it on her grilling stone.

"I learned this from a cook in the enemy camp," Mother said. "We can even learn thing or two from an enemy," she said. She showed Aethlgifu how to roast the birds on a spit, suspended over the fire pit. They roasted brown, as Mother brushed sage branches and sea salt on them."

Asta tagged along everywhere Breidi and I went. We never complained about holding the child's hand and taking her along as we explored the settlement from the inside and up the stone steps to play in the shallow sod covering their home.

Maelchon began to teach Breidi how to use a bow at the beginning of his fifth year. He made a sturdy miniature of his own weapon and even supplied Breidi with blunt tipped arrows that he used for target practice.

Mother introduced Breidi to the sling weapon. She made a miniature of hers for him to sling stones at targets. Maelchon was not familiar with Sarah's weapon, but it intrigued him. "How did you learn to use this sling," he asked.

"It is used by the Romans. It comes from a part of their empire that they call the Mediterranean. It is favored by countrymen more than professional Roman soldiers," Mother said. "It is an ancient weapon, favored by village people," she said.

"Show me how it works, Sarah," Maelchon said.

She took a small, rounded stone from a small bag at her waist and placed it in the pouch in the center of the sling. "The stone goes there," she said. "Then, I circle the sling over my head, to gain power. When I have enough speed built up, I release the stone at my target," Mother explained.

"Show me," Maelchon said.

"Pick a target," she challenged.

"The tree, there," he pointed.

Mother put a stone in the pouch as she had explained, whirled it over her head before she released it. It flew directly to the tree and struck with a "whack."

"Let me try that thing," Maelchon said. "This can not be all that difficult," he claimed. He loaded his stone and began to circle the sling over his head. When he released the stone, it fell, harmlessly to the ground in front of him.

"This must be another one of your powers," Maelchon said. "This can not be learned by mere mortals," he teased.

Over the next few days, Breidi played with the sling until he learned to load a small stone and sling it a few meters. His early attempts were clumsy, but I could see that he would eventually learn the skill. He was determined to learn. His short arms lacked the energy in the sling that Mother generated, but it was soon apparent that he would not quit until he learned to use it properly.

The sling was foreign to Maelchon's villagers and it never became a common weapon while we were with the Picts.

The Romans had learned the skill from their enemies in a foreign land. This weapon was foreign and few imagined its' power. Learning another weapon as an adult was too much of a challenge for most people of the Wolf Clan but they all marveled at Mother's ability to hit either a stationary or even a moving target. She could sling a stone fifty meters and hit her target with consistency.

"Let me try, Mother," young Breidi said. "I can hit it. Watch me," he said. Mother showed him how to select a round, smooth stone from the shore. "I can hit those seals," Breidi bragged.

"No, you must not hurt the seals. They are our friends," I said. "Pick another target."

The winter season arrived with fury. The winds coming off of the sea blew across the sod covered shelter with ferocity. The maze of rooms and hallways that existed beneath remained comfortably warm. Fire wood was a precious commodity in a wind swept land that supported few trees. Mother, Breidi and I gathered twigs and smaller limbs of bushes that lived between rock crevices on the bluffs.

One of the village families cut and dried peat sod into small, manageable blocks. They were dried in the room near the smith's furnace before they were used in the fire pit.

Chapter XV

Wolfstan's winter village had been home to her ancestors for many generations. In the beginning, the stone steps and stone lined hall led into a large, single room. Additional rooms were added as the clan grew with her extended family. The central space, which Wolfstan's village used as a lodge meeting place was kept the warmest of all of the spaces in our burrowed stronghold.

The village speaker lived in a corner of the settlement among the many elements of rock, plants, herbs and potions around her. She spent a good portion of her days wandering the hill sides, collecting nature's offerings and testing their potency after being brewed into the wicked tasting tea that she served up to her visitors. Breidi had encountered the old woman occasionally as they crossed paths in the valleys or the woods nearby.

The village called the old woman, Ottar. She, and her ancestors before her, had been brewers of remedies for many generations of the Picts. Breidi often sat with her, looking out over the broad expanse of the valley. They some times sat for hours in between conversations as Breidi reflected on the Pict future and Ottar recalled the past.

Breidi and Asta, along with the other young ones of the settlement, played near the warmth of the fire in the lodge room during the long winter. The floor was covered with flat stones worn smooth by more than fifty generations of Wolfstan's ancestors. Sand filled the spaces between the stones, helping keep the floor warm during the long winter season.

Breidi held Asta's hand as he walked her along the outer stone, stacked wall where she loved to play on the shelves and pockets of spaces that were used dressers and storage. Breidi stood on the stone bench near the dresser and held his arms over his head. "I am your war lord," he claimed.

"Me too," Asta said as she reached for his hand and a boost onto the bench.

"No," said Breidi. "Girls can be queens and mothers of our kings, but war leaders are men like Papa and I,"

"Me too," Asta repeated, undaunted by Breidi's attempt at rebuking his half sister.

Breidi had grown considerably since the time that Mother and I came to the Clan. I think that I knew, even then, that Breidi was someone special and that we had a connection with each other. I was near my twentieth season when Mother and I were taken in by Maelchon. If Breidi was to become my mate, I had to wait until he matured.

I learned all that I could from Aethlgifu and the other women. Mother insisted that I follow her example in personal care and not fall into the habits of others. My breasts were fully developed and I felt like a woman instead of a little girl

We often sat by the fire as the old story teller of the settlement sat in the center of the lodge and began telling stories about the old times in the highlands and the mysterious creatures of that had been spoken about for many generations. His story telling help pass time in the winter months and gave the settlement an opportunity to sit near the center hearth of the lodge.

"Faeries of the olden times of the highlands were sensitive creatures. Bad thoughts and lies hurt their feelings," old Finnbar began."

These creatures are called *sith (shee')* and come in many forms. When they are out at night, we can hear the melody coming from their hillocks. They are the People of Peace, the Pixies, Silent Moving Folks, the Wee Folk and Prowlies."

"Only our Sha'man can contact the *sith* of the Otherworld.

"Ashrays, are the faeries of the water," Finnbar continued. They are either man or woman and they keep the appearance of a twenty year old." Asta turned to see if her mother and I were listening.

"They are active at night, like many *sith*. If they remain out through the night and are touched by daylight of the morn, they turn into a pool of clear water. They are not seen as much in our times," Finnbar said. "They spend most of their lives in the underwater realm where they are safe from our approach."

"Often, the Ashrays, or sometimes called Mur'uchs by the people of the western isle of Dal Riata Kings, are seen with seals and the *Boobrie*,' he went on. They are great water birds. Come Asta," Finnbar said. "Come to me," he repeated. The toddler wobbled over to the old timer and stood by his knee. *Boobries* are almost as big as Asta, he said with his hand on top of her head.

"Sometimes, the *Boobrie* can shape change into a horse and run across the water. Sailors call them 'ghost horses.'"

"Tell us of the Brownies, Finnbar," Breidi said.

"Ah, *Brownies* are the benevolent faeries. They are the faeries often found in our homes. We call them "*Housebrownies*," like Asta here," he said as he returned his hand to the top of her head. We have our own *Brownie*."

"Tell us of the other *sith*," Breidi insisted.

"Well, there are the *Buachalleen* who appear as small men, often found around herds of sheep. There are the Dryads, who's element is air and the old *Gnomes*, and the *Gruagach* who is grotesque and lives alone," Finnbar continued.

"She has the same name as our god of the sun, *Gruagach*," Breidi interrupted.

"That is so, young one. Have you heard of *Gruagach*?," Finnbar asked.

"Yes," Breidi answered.

"What of *Merpeople*?" Breidi asked.

"Oh," Finnbar began. "They are faeries of the sea. The males are called Mermen or *Merrows*, and the females are *Mermaids or Mur'uchs* from the land of Dalriada. Some *Mermen* are called *Blue Men*. They cause storms and throw stones at ships as the pass by. They are protective of the home in the sea and detest anyone who brings harm to the sea or the creatures who live in it. They can be sent away by reciting a rhyme, as rhymes confuse them. The *Nucklelavees* are fierce faeries of the sea. They are mean and ill tempered and must be avoided. A child can escape them by crossing running water, like a stream or river."

As the young ones retreated to their beds, Finnbar joined Aadan near the warmth of the fire. They took a cup of mead from Aethlgifu and held their hands near the flames. "The foreigners have nearly finished their wall," Aadan said. "I fear that blocking us from treks to the southlands will not be the end of their intent.

"Ah," Finnbar mumbled. "In the beginning they had their wall, and now they have placed fortress like shelters along the length. I fear that they will not tolerate our night attacks without trying to move further north to fight us on our own grounds."

"That is true, Finnbar," Maelchon said. "I have seen preparations for a wall further north in a place that the Britons call Antoine."

"It is a sign of their dominance of our people," Finnbar offered.

"What if they continue to move their walls north until they have us pinned on Shetland and Orkney?" Maelchon said. "We can not bring defeat to the foreigners without collecting the will of other clans of the north lands. While we continue to disrupt their build of the long foreigner wall with Fenn's village, we need to bring our clans together and take them on in battle."

"You are the war leader, Maelchon. In my time, we believed that harassing the foreigners was our only choice. We strike, as Odenn of the Jackal clan did, to slow them or make them see that conquering our native lands is not worth the loss," Finnbar said. I fear that if gather the clans in a unified force, that the foreigners will come from behind their wall to confront us head-on. I do not see that as a wise choice, Maelchon. We do not want to allow them to fight us from the point of their strength. We will lose and we will cease to be," Finnbar said. "I fear that our best tactic is to approach them from our point f strength, and not allow them to assemble on the north side of their wall."

Maelchon looked into the fire. He said nothing more. After a short time, Finnbar rose and found his way to his chamber. "Finnbar is a wise man," Maelchon concluded.

Chapter XVI

During the spring season of Breidi's eleventh year we hunted among the rocks along the bluffs for game birds. In the valley, near our summer village, we watched deer and wild goats roam among the trees and practiced with the bow and his sling.

I concentrated on learning skills expected of a woman Pryten woman. Aethlgifu and Mother, tried teaching me domestic chores, but my thoughts were with Breidi. He was a skilled youngster, not given to periods of laziness, like some of his peers in the village. I thought, even back then, that he was destined to be a leader among his people.

Mother worked with him in the use of the sling. He could launch a stone at a stationery target fifty meters away and strike it regularly. He did not have enough power, generated by circling the sling over his head before releasing, but he improved his accuracy with steady progress. Someday the power will come on its own.

Maelchon was amazed with his son's development. Mother promised Maelchon that she would care for Breidi and she had done the job well.

"This is a good weapon," Maelchon said as he watched Breidi and Mother practice sling stones at targets.

Asta played among the wildflowers and patches of sweet smelling heather while Mother and Breidi practiced with the sling. Breidi's bow that he had used as a small child had been exchanged for one with more power.

Maelchon changed Breidi's dull tipped arrows with iron tips from Braun's metal smith shop.

Breidi was different than many of the boys of his village. He was quiet and sometimes inwardly reflective. I usually followed him around the settlement and on his treks in the countryside. The hills and valleys away from the village were abundant with rabbits and game birds.

Young men from the village took notice of me when we first arrived. As they approached the age when they needed to take a mate, they were very much aware of women outside of the village population.

I heard them when they gathered to compare their thoughts about me. Breidi had not yet shown any interest in me other than as a companion and a warm body to sleep next to. He was too busy learning the skills of war from his father and a bit young to take interest in me.

A few of the local boys approached me. I must have been pretty enough to draw their attention. I was different than young women of the clan. That caused them to back away and I was relieved that none of them tried to approach me. Most of this escaped, unnoticed by Breidi.

They considered me as an eligible woman and they must have had a problem understanding why I followed Breidi around the village. Breidi was too young to attract a potential mate. He was still more interested in hunting rabbits than my interest in him.

Men of the Pryten clans entered adulthood before their fourteenth year. Like young men from Viking villages in the north, few lived beyond their twentieth season. As they joined in attacks against the Romans by their twelfth year, the chances of meeting their death before age twenty increased significantly.

As Breidi and I returned from a walk one afternoon three of the village toughs met us near the tree line of the clearing near our village. They called to Breidi and teased him about being followed by two girls. He ignored their taunting and continued to walk away.

One of the village bullies yelled out, "Witch!" He threw a stone in my direction. It landed harmlessly at my feet. Then another threw a stone.

Breidi wanted to ignore them and walk away, but I could see that his anger was getting the best of him. Finally, having had enough of their threats and insults, he picked up the stone that they threw at my feet and placed it in the sling pouch. While the gang of thugs stood watching, Breidi began whirling the sling over his head.

The boys jeered at Breidi and his weapon. They continued the insults as Breidi prepared to release the stone from his sling.

One of the boys yelled, "What is that toy for, little boy? Bet you can't hit me, with your toy," another said. Breidi circled the loaded sling over his head twice more with increased speed and released it directly at the biggest among the gang of mischief makers.

The stone took an arched flight towards our hecklers and curved in to strike the biggest of the boys. It collided with his stomach and breast bone with a loud thump. He dropped to the ground, hacking, trying to get his breath.

Breidi reloaded his sling and launched another stone that struck a second in the back of the head as he tried to escape the same fate as his loud mentor.

The third hit one that tried to escape Breidi's attack. He ran towards the village. Before he could run beyond Breidi's range of accuracy, he was struck in the back. The three of them arose and walked away, rubbing their wounds. I did not see that any of them were seriously wounded but I wondered, from that day on, whether Breidi could have if he intended to.

We walked off together and never said another word about it. The boys may not have wanted the village to know of the incident. No one in the village said anything about it when we returned. The one certain thing was that they never taunted Breidi or myself again.

We visited Braun at his smith shop. He worked in a small stand-alone building close to the eastern entrance of our village. There, he worked his considerable skills as a weapons smith. He produced broad axe heads, swords, knives and arrow tips. The unique dagger that was carried in a leather sheath, that the men called a "dirk," was a specialty of Braun's shop.

He collected the pikes that our warriors brought back from raids on the Roman camp. He told us that the ore that the Romans used was superior to what we collected in the region around our village.

The furnace produced heat and smoke that rose up, through the vent in the ceiling of his shop. It mixed with the smoke from the lodge that carried smells of baking bread and sizzling meat. Neither fire was ever allowed to burn out during the night or during times between uses.

Braun used his son Tamhais as a helper. It was Tamhais who trekked through the valleys to collect heavy oak wood for coals in his father's fire. He also collected the thin wisps that he used for arrow shafts. Tamhais attached the iron tips from his father's hearth with twisted sinew and animal hair.

We brought back several branches for arrow shafts and gave them to Tamhais. He ignored Breidi and kept his eyes on me. I am sure that Tamhais would be an important man in the village when he replaced his father, but like a few other young men, I never considered any of them as potential mates.

Weapons makers and metal workers were among the most important tradesmen in the settlement. The clan was in constant need of arrows, spears and other weapons that Braun fabricated in his shop. Metal working was his specialty, just as other from the clan worked as farmers, or hunters. Allowing Braun to work his craft solely, allowed others to specialize in other crafts.

Braun showed us the uniquely ornamented sword that he made for Maelchon. The curved pommel was decorated with native symbols etched in silver. Maelchon's shield had similar designs, differentiating it from the more common weapons carried by his warriors.

It was the soot from Braun's furnace, mixed with rendered animal fat that camouflaged the ghost fighters.

Chapter XVII

By the following spring, the construction on the milecastles of the Roman wall picked up pace towards completion and so did our attacks. Maelchon and Fenn's night fighters were proven to be well matched and complimentary as they proved in the match near Fenn's village several years ago. They had been united in their attacks ever sense.

The combined forces of the two settlements made up a group of forty men and women and half as many youths that traveled along to be runners and messengers. Breidi was among those. He did not have a bow, sword or axe like his father's night fighters but he was never without his sling and a few choice stones that he carried with him for target practice or hunting hares at the edge of clearings.

The other clans in the neighboring hills had not seen it necessary to join with the Wolf and Jackal clans, initially. Jealousy over territory and ancient disputes and stubborn independence kept them on their own. Maelchon still kept Finnbar's words about the dangers of meeting the foreigners in a head-on confrontation played over in his head.

"Undoubtedly, the old sage had a point, but how else were they to fight the foreigners back or keep them from further advancement? Maelchon thought."

Maelchon and Fenn sat many hours trying to determine a way to unite the clan tribes. When heater ale was heated, and the steam collected with a copper hood and drain pipe, a more potent drink that Maelchon called *Uisge-beatha*, "the water of life," trickled out.

Aethlgifu brewed the prized drink for the wolf clan. "It warms the belly and makes everything agreeable," Maelchon said.

"Fenn, I hear news that a man that they call 'Patrick' has brought news of the new religion from the east," Maelchon said. Some refer to him as a saint. Can that be true?

"Yes, I have heard such news as well," Fenn said. "It is said that there was a profit from the east who they called Christ, who traveled with his teachings of peace." The Dal Riata people have taken to Patrick as a gifted teacher on the ways of the Christ, and spoke of his life in the ancient times of the land that Romans call, The Holy Land."

"Yes, I have heard the same news," Maelchon said. The teachings of Christ have circulated for hundreds of years. Many have been intermixed with our ancient traditions and those of Odin and Norsemen from the far north.

Chapter XVIII

In the first united attack of the Wolf and Jackal clans, Maelchon and Fenn led their warriors towards the foreigner's wall. We traveled along the low lying valleys as we approached the wall from the west. I followed Breidi's group at the rear of the column as we progressed southward. The heavy night air did not give away our position as we crept along the valley floor, being careful of our step.

We came upon the Stream and ran along it in a valley that led to the Roman camp. As we got closer, Fenn slowed our pace, making sure that we were not seen by soldiers or camp concubines who came to the stream to collect water. We stayed crouched until we were sure that we had not been seen.

The numbers of garrisons that the Romans used to protect the wall had expanded over the years since they completed construction. The wall now extended to both coasts. Unrelenting attacks from the Pict attacks took more men that had been used to construct it.

Maelchon said that he had learned Septimus' had the habit of slighting the fortresses nearest section to the coast in order to bolster the numbers towards the middle. Fenn used that bit of information to our advantage. Septimus must have reasoned that the center was where the strongest attacks would occur. Like my Father, he would soon learn that Pict attacks were not predictable.

Septimus was a veteran General from Rome who had many years of combat to his credit. His skills and military training were similar to my father's. They probably attended the same schooling and campaigns during their own time. Unfortunately for Father and his replacements since, most of their experience was in conventional, open field combat in an open field.

Fenn and Maelchon were well aware of the Roman's inexperience fighting against guerrilla tactics and schemed to take advantage of their shortcomings.

I was not skilled in combat. Other women of the two clans fought along side of the men. I should have stayed back, but I could not find it in me to remain behind in the village knowing that my future was at risk. So, I trotted along with the youngsters towards the end of the column as we neared our target.

Fenn and Maelchon had their fighters huddle at the limestone quarry. This site worked well in the past. The Romans dug tunnels and holes in the stone quarry for limestone blocks that they used in the wall's construction. Forty men and women along with twenty youngsters gathered and rested while we waited for dusk.

With Mother's words settled in their purpose we used the dark of night to our advantage over the thousands of Roman troops in the camp and in the garrisons along the wall. I could hear them talking as the cool, crisp air and the stone surface carried their voices in our direction.

It was a clear night. We could hear the Romans laughing. They were undoubtedly relieved that tonight would not bring an attack hidden by storms from the coast.

Fenn and Maelchon spoke softly, as they worked out the details of the attack. The rest of us readied ourselves to follow their lead in what would be a two sided attack.

As nightfall arrived, Breidi's group completed several simple ladders to be used in scaling the walls. Septimus must have reasoned that the higher walls, near the coast would discourage attacks.

Fenn and Maelchon worked out the details and advised us how to use the ladders to overcome Septimus' perceived advantage.

Our success tonight, like the others, would depend on the element of surprise. Working against Septimus' reasoning gave us the advantage. They would not be expecting an attack in this location and probably had not manned their defense for an assault.

As the dark of night arrived, Fenn and his fighters led off. They quickly scaled the wall and dropped down onto the south side. The ladders were pulled over the wall with the last man, and placed close to the wall on the south side where they would be ready for the escape.

Fenn signaled for Maelchon and his men to take their position. He led them to the north side of the targeted milecastle. They put the ladders in place and climbed to the top, where they remained crouched, waiting for Fenn's signal.

At the signal of a night bird, Fenn closed on the unsuspecting sentries and silenced them with quick swipes of their daggers across their throats. The remainder of the garrison was still inside the barracks, unaware of the impending attack.

All of the guards had been eliminated. Without warning a Roman officer came from the barracks and exited the milecastle. He saw the remains of his sentries and called for help.

The legions poured out of the barracks to respond to the officer's call and our warriors dropped down from their perch on the wall. The noise of the battle brought additional soldiers to the aide of their comrades. When a number came out of the barracks they were pounced on from above by Maelchon and his men.

Breidi and I climbed the ladders with a few of the other youths and readied the ladders to be passed down to the south side for the escape. We had an ideal look out for the action below.

The Pict were nearly invisible in the night. Their soot and dark skin markings covered their presence as they stepped into the dark shadows around the wall and the barracks. The glare of the moon reflected brightly off of the helmets and shoulder armor of the Romans, making them quite visible. With limited numbers of enemy and the element of surprise, the Pict warriors were nearly invincible. The naked warriors moved slowly and kept out of sight. They were in their element and had a clear advantage of the soldiers, penned inside the barracks

Fenn's group stayed low to the ground and in the moon shadow of the wall as troops poured out of the milecastle to join the fight. As they passed through the narrow doorway they were pounced upon by Fenn and his Jackals.

The Romans became confused by these tactics, just as Fenn predicted. They reacted poorly to the unconventional surprise attack. They could not adjust their eyes to coming out a lit space into the darkness quick enough to protect themselves from the danger that waited for them.

The Romans were destined to die, one by one. Maelchon's men held their daggers in their teeth as they jumped down on their enemies below. I saw several taken before they knew where their attackers came from. The barracks was surrounded and the single exit offered no alternative to dying as they came out. The barracks were not built in anticipation of an attack from the south side of the wall.

Breidi and I watched as the Romans were startled at the sight of the Picts coming over the wall. The fierce suddenness of our attack eliminated half of the garrison at the beginning of the battle. Maelchon's group finished the remainder as they came through the doorway.

The Jackals carried battle axes, swords. They hung their bows over their backs. They would not be used in close-in combat. Swords and axes were drawn in preparation to close combat. The Roman legions had yet another disadvantage. Their pikes, made for open field combat against an enemy line were unwieldy in close combat. Their length made them difficult to maneuver in defense against swinging sword blades and battle axes.

"Watch," Breidi whispered. We looked down from above at the legions trying to maneuver with the long pikes in close combat. "They are invisible," he said. "Like ghosts in the night, they can not see out fighters," Breidi said.

Maelchon's fighters collected a few of the pikes and passed them to a pair of young men still perched on the wall above and watched the action below. As more enemy approached from the milecastle, they were met with pikes thrown down by the pair. The heavy weapon heads crashed through the armor plates of the legion's uniforms with deadly force. From a distance of ten meters, a thrown pike from an elevated position was a deadly weapon.

He was right. The Romans were no match for the Pict's skills at close encounter, night attacks. Their defense was futile, even hopeless in these conditions. They fell two, three, four at a time, as Fenn's group jumped them from the dark. With swift lunges, they struck down on the enemy who jabbed and thrust their weapons hopelessly in the dark. Pict swords and axes worked swiftly on the clumsy thrusts from helmeted legions. Fenn's plan was executed swiftly. The estimated two hundred Romans would meet their end tonight.

Ailpen and his wife Cait fought side by side against reinforcements coming through the narrow door. They easily split the thin metal helmets with swift force. Ailpen lunged his spear at an officer coming through the door who suddenly found himself skewered and lodged between stones on the wall. Cait met a legion who swung his pike, passing over her head as she dropped to her knees and thrust upwards with her sword. Her blade passed under his chest armor and into the stomach.

Breidi and I watched the severity that the Prytens used to finish the Romans as they stumbled out of their shelter in single file. The attack was vicious and merciless. The natives killed most of the legions with surprising ease, and continued on to the next without hesitation.

Breidi saw a legion officer approach Fenn from the back. The officer drew his sword and moved quickly to close the distance between he and Fenn. He intended to bring the sword down on Fenn's head. A yell would have drawn attention to the youngsters on the wall and may interfere with the planned evacuation at the fight's end.

With a set of practiced moves, Breidi drew his sling, took a stone from his pouch, loaded his sling, whirled it over his head several times and launched it at the officer. It flew in a perfect line and hit the bare headed officer, square, between his eyes. He dropped to the ground, on his as if he had been struck by an axe to the same spot. The stone having done its damage, he collapsed.

Surprised at the close call from his flank, Fenn spun around to see Breidi standing on the wall with another stone loaded and ready in his sling. With more time to build speed for his weapon, he selected another officer coming out from the barracks. As the officer tried to secure his battle helmet on his head, Breidi released his stone and hit the man in the temple, just forward of his ears. He dropped at Fenn's feet, beside the first one.

Fenn stood, looking up at Breidi and laughed over the young man's accuracy with the sling. Finally Maelchon entered the barracks with two of his fighters. They met and killed three Roman legions who remained inside. Two hundred enemy soldiers had been killed without the loss of one Pryten.

Fenn took twenty of his men and made his way towards the outer perimeter of the camp. With surprising ease they slit the back sides of the tents and entered. As they entered each tent they grabbed the pikes and drove them through the soldiers and the bedding, staking them to the ground below their cots. A few awoke after being impaled only to find that they were unable to free themselves before they were mercifully dispatched with a sword.

Row by row, Maelchon and his fighters worked their way towards the center of the camp. They would have continued if they had no been seen. Alarm spread through the camp when one of the officers came out of his tent unexpectedly.

Then, Maelchon began the call for a retreat. They had eliminated the garrison without loss from their own numbers. The damage had been expertly inflicted by the grossly outnumbered guerrilla fighters and we were prepared to escape without loss of our own. Breidi and I could see them sneak towards the wall in the dark.

We lowered the ladders onto the south side of the wall and steadied them as the ghost fighters scaled to the top of the wall and dropped down on the north side. One by one, they came up the ladders. A few remained behind to keep watch for danger and provide ample time for the others to escape. A few at a time, the youths helped their seniors up the ladder and to the safety of the north side.

Fenn sent the last two up the ladder. Two Roman officers, with their swords drawn, came upon Fenn. Breidi pouched a stone and whirled it over his head. I saw that he would not be able to pouch another stone in time to save Fenn from the second officer.

Seeing the advantage that they had over Fenn, Breidi pouched another stone, and let it loose. It struck the Roman guard near the his mouth. Maelchon watched in amazement at Breidi's accuracy with the sling and stone. The Roman guard dropped to the ground, holding his mouth, writhing in pain. Fenn dispatched the broken mouthed Roman, leaving no witness to the carnage that had taken place.

I held a bow that one of Fenn's fighters passed to me on his way up the ladder. I hurriedly notched an arrow and drew the string back as far as I could before I let the arrow fly. Not having sufficient strength for the heavy bow, the arrow dipped down in flight towards my target. It struck the officer in the upper thigh. He stopped just long enough, writhing in pain from the placement of my misspent arrow, for Fenn to regain his balance and stab the poor soul in the gut.

Fenn looked up at me. I was standing with the bow still in my hands. He knew where the arrow had come from. Both Fenn and Breidi looked at me and laughed. Fenn scaled the ladder and dropped down on the far side. I found the owner of the bow and dropped it down to him before I came off of the wall myself. We collected our ladders and started our trot towards the village.

All were silent as we made our way towards the village.

When they arrived at Wolfstan's settlement, little was said. We laid down to rest for the night.

At the break of dawn, Fenn arrived to speak to Maelchon who sat by the fire with Sarah, Esther and Asta. Fenn came in and sat down on a stone bench next to the fire.

"I believe that you saw part of what Breidi did with his sling?" Fenn asked.

"I saw him strike the officer and a second man in the teeth," Maelchon said.

"Actually, there was another young hero from your crew," Fenn said. "While Breidi is deadly with his sling, the young woman called Esther is deadly quick with the a bow."

"Yes," Maelchon said, gesturing towards Mother as she sat by the fire with Asta and I. "Mother began teaching me the use of the sling when I was very young," Breidi said with pride. She learned it from a slave in the camp of Romans."

Mother said nothing until she was spoken to.

"Their youth's use them the same way that our young use a child size bow. Is that right, Sarah?" Maelchon asked.

"Yes, he has improved his skills with the sling. It was developed by civilizations near the area known as the Sea of Galilee and the holy land," Mother answered. She returned her attention to the children on her lap.

"Breidi is to be congratulated for his courage and his skill. He saved my life twice last night," Fenn said. We should also thank Esther for her quick thinking. They both saved my life," Fenn said. "And I thank you Sarah for having the forethought to teach this young man how to use the sling. It is a perfect weapon to learn while training with the bow."

"You have amazed us again. The Pryten people have been enriched by you and your daughter joining us," Fenn continued. "Your beauty and kindness brought attention to you and now your wisdom and skills will be known by all Pryten in the highlands."

"I will tell Breidi when he returns, neighbor. He and Esther are out hunting hare for our midday meal. You may stay, if you wish."

"No, I came to give my thanks to your son. He is courageous and skilled," Fenn said.

Before Fenn arose to leave, Breidi came in with three hare in a sling over his shoulder.

"Come son. Fenn has come to pay you honor for your courage and the skill which you took out three guards last night. I only saw two, but Fenn tells me that there was another," Maelchon said.

"It was my honor to play a part in the success of your well planned raid," Breidi said.

"I wish all of our young would have been raised with the skill of the sling," Fenn said. "You will be of age to take your place beside your father and I in battle, and we will welcome you, your courage and your beautiful young companion."

"Are you as adept with your bow, young man?" Fenn asked.

"Almost," Breidi said. "I have not used a full strength bow yet," Breidi admitted. "Some day, perhaps, Braun and Tamhais will craft one for me."

"Well, there is no need to wait for Esther to draw a bow, she works a man's bow with skill if not great aim," Fenn laughed.

"Please sit," Maelchon said to Fenn. "Sarah will put these rabbits on a stick and roast them over the fire. They are a special treat, thanks to our sharp eyed hunter, here," Maelchon said, as he patted his proud son on the shoulder.

I watched Breidi with special pride. It did my heart good to see him recognized for his bravery.

Breidi was nearing his fourteenth season and soon would be ready to take a mate. I was more than ready for a pairing with my young companion. His maturing could not happen soon enough to suit my needs.

I watched Breidi accept the gratitude of these great warriors and I felt his pride in my heart. He lifted his head and saw me looking at him. I folded my hands, quietly on my lap. Mother began to prepare the meat. The three rabbits were skewered on a green stick and placed on a rack over the coals of the fire pit.

Mother placed the meat on a stone plate and rose to take it to her guest. Fenn took a portion of the sizzling meat and placed it on a round, flat loaf that he used as a platter and a holder for the hot rabbit meat. I filled the heather ale cups and all took tastes of the roasted rabbit. When the meat was eaten, they folded the bread and enjoyed the drippings from the soak loaves.

Maelchon took a handful of sand from the floor and rubbed it between his hands before he embraced Fenn on his way through the door.

"Peace to you neighbor," Breidi said. "And to you son," Fenn said as he left.

Mother and I were pleased with Fenn's visit. Breidi had grown to take his responsibilities as a young man. It seemed but a short while ago that he was still a small child. When I first arrived, he learned to use my body heat to keep him warm at night. He was a small child then.

He had grown into a handsome young man and my own body had developed as well. Breidi never stopped pulling me close to him at night to share our warmth just as he had done as a child. We wrapped our arms and legs around each other and slept face to face. We had learned the comfort of each other's embrace.

Mother had been with Maelchon for ten seasons. I had been the object of attention by younger men in the clan but I had been fortunate enough to avoid a pairing with any of them. Mother noticed them gawking at me, but none dared approach me. I was sure that Mother and Maelchon had agreed that Breidi and I would join in a pairing when he matured and became eligible to take a mate.

I was different than their native young women and I grew concerned that I would not be able to take Breidi as my husband if we did not act soon.

Because of my special bloodline, as a crossover between the worlds of the immortal Mur'uch and as an adopted member of the Wolf Clan, Mother had not fully considered the impact of Breidi taking me as a mate and staying with the clan.

The time would come soon when Mother would have to make a decision over leaving the clan, taking Asta and I, and returning to our domain in the sea. I had already decided that I would stay with Breidi.

I knew about the alliance between his people and my world and I saw no reason to go elsewhere to find a mate to produce young. I could stay with Breidi and raise his children. As long as he was alive, I saw no reason to leave his clan, with or without Mother and Asta.

Mother was pleased with her place next to Maelchon. He had been good to her and her daughters and she had raised Breidi to the beginning of his manhood as Maelchon asked her to do. That was their agreement, years before, out on the rocks at the mouth of the harbor.

At the end of the day, we all returned to Maelchon's quarters and climbed onto the heather box beds. Maelchon and Sarah took theirs while Breidi and I, and little Asta climbed in together. As a Queen Mur'uch, Mother was demanding of her man. She often laid on top of Maelchon with her face under his chin. She kept him warm in that way, after they worked up enough body heat under the fur covers.

A ceremony, honoring Breidi's acceptance as a Pryten warrior lifted the village in celebration. A lamb was roasted and a stew of mutton and onions simmered in the pot. The aroma from the stew pot and Aethlgifu's fresh baked bread filled the room.

When the eating was done, it was time to honor Breidi with his first markings. A mixture of pigment and ash was worked into his skin with an instrument and a tapping stick that Finnbar used to work the mixture into Breidi's skin.

The form of a wolf came from Finnbar's work. Another design of interconnecting lines and swirls like a knot was etched on the other side of his chest.

I could see that this procedure was painful. Breidi did not complain of the pain. He lay still on the matted carpet until Finnbar had completed his work. Breidi stood next to his Father as villagers passed by, grasping Breidi's arm in the traditional way of the Pict.

When the ceremony was over, Mother washed the excess pigment from Breidi's skin. He now had a Pict marking on each side of his chest that identified him as a man and as a member of the Wolf Clan.

I took special pride in Breidi and his new place within the clan. I wanted to be close to him tonight. I crept over to his half of the bed. He rolled over to face me. wrapped my arms around him and held him close. When we were younger he laid on my body for warmth. Tonight, he pulled me onto his body and pulled me to him with his hands on my butt. We snuggled as we had done since our first night together, but tonight, he took my face in his hands and kissed my lips.

My natural instincts took over. I rubbed my hips in sensual movement as I laid on Breidi and returned his advances. I took him in my hand and felt the firmness of his young, virgin flesh. I wanted to take Breidi in and have him conceive our first child, but we could not. We must only imagine our love until we were officially bound in clan fashion.

Breidi held his hands to the arch of my back and on to my butt as we rolled over again. He pulled me to him until our bellies touched and a sensation rose as he rubbed himself against me in a sensuous motion.

I felt a new urgency in his body. His back muscles were rigid as he moved over me. He ran his hands over my bottom and held me close to him while we moved together.

I felt the movement of his hips and the tension of his back as he pressed our bellies together. His hand found my breast and he rose over me. He lowered his face to my chest and placed his lips between my breasts, taking in the scent of my body as he kissed around them.

I was excited with his touch and wanted to take him in and collect his seed. I was sure that we were both ready, but I could not. Not until the tribe recognized us as a *handfasted* pair.

We stopped short of spending ourselves while joined for the first time that night. He collapsed on top of me and held my breast in his hand and caressed me softly, experiencing the soft, smooth skin. Lying beside me he traced his fingers over my young breasts and belly. His hands were soft and smooth, with a gentle touch of my thighs and belly.

We wanted to kick the heavy covers off of us, but we dared not attract attention to our movements under their concealment. Our growing body heat made them unbearable as he lay quietly next to me.

We stayed close that night, exploring each other's bodies. This was the first time since we came to the village that I knew that he looked at me as a woman. The close caressing and movement of our bodies brought both of us to full arousal. That night, I knew that he was ready for a mate.

It was clear that I needed to have Mother and Maelchon to get it done quickly. Breidi experienced the thrill of bringing a woman to passion. I was not sure that I would be able to stop either of us after tonight.

After nuzzling my neck and chest with his face, he fell asleep in the comfort of a woman's arms. I felt the warmth of his youthful body close to me and we shared each other's warmth through the night. We held on to each other as the fire burned down, uncertain about our future but aware of our mutual dependence on each other for the first time.

Chapter XIX

One fateful evening as we all sat to take our meal we received word that the Romans had retaliated on the Hawk's nearby stronghold. The runner from the Jackal camp said that we probably could not arrive on time to save the camp.

Maelchon, Breidi and thirty others grabbed weapons and took off towards the Hawk camp. When we arrived the slaughter brought upon the peaceful camp became dreadfully apparent. Only a few Romans from a garrison remained in the camp finishing their plan to defile every woman and child in the camp.

The smoke billowing up from the burning lodge filled the air and hid the damage from view as we advanced upon them. There were ten or more Roman's who remained in the village to finish their grisly work. Six of them had forced themselves on three young women and were taking turns violating them when we arrived. We remained silent while we closed on the unsuspecting rapists. The violence that they forced on the young women was almost inhuman. They were so involved with their assault that they did not see us approach.

Ailpein took one of the nearby pikes and ran it up one of the rapist's back side. With a meter of the shaft remaining out of the shocked Roman new cavity, Cait took the end and rammed him into a nearby tree. That finished the soldier's screaming agony. He flailed about for a few moments trying to remove the pike blade from the tree trunk. His death came slowly.

The others were pulled away from the young women and held at sword point while we searched the burning village for survivors. The three young women who had been assaulted seemed to be the only survivors in the village. The scene was total devastation and mindless slaughter of an entire village. Bodies of men, women and children were strewn about the site in all directions.

The young women were nearly unable to tell us what had happened. "They came over the crest of the hill, from the south," she said. "There were fifty or sixty of them. They caught us inside the lodge as we ate our morning meal. After they killed all of the villagers, except the tree of us, they left,……….except for three of them who stayed behind to rape us," she said.

We did not press for more information. It was not necessary. We could easily see what had occurred and there was no need to make the women relive their torture.

We buried the dead behind stone walls inside the village council room and left with the seven Roman soldiers and the three young women. When we arrived back at the Wolf Clan we were greeted by our villagers. All were shocked by the news and became as enraged as we were with the atrocity of the attack.

The young women were in near state of shock when Maelchon and Breidi tried to determine what had happened and more of the details of the attack. I remember Mother taking the women to our council room where she and Aethlhgifu tried to attend to their wounds and shattered nerves.

The men stayed outside to discuss plans for a possible retaliation. We considered the meaning of this raid. Maelchon believed that the Romans had retaliated against the village, believing that they must have been involved in our attacks on the roman wall garrison.

We knew that the Hawk Clan had elected to remain apart from our harassment of the Roman camp. The Romans apparently did not know that, or if they did, they ignored it. The Hawk Clan was a peaceful community and had been caught by a surprise attack. Perhaps, we considered, the Roman's had seen our ranks with women fighting along side men as they always did and had decided not to spare them.

Much consideration was given to a plan for punishing the Romans for the outrageous attack on an innocent village. Breidi participated in the discussion. His views and weapon skills were taken as contribution and importance to the clan. He had received his incentive to more his skills as fast as he could. He wanted, desperately to be among those who would soon leave a certain message for the Romans.

The attack on the Hawk Clan had raised the necessity and tempo of our plans to take revenge for the unnecessarily brutal form of the attack.

The two Romans that we brought back to our village had been suspended and drawn between trees. The lines were as tight as the lines would hold. Their uniforms had been taken from their trembling bodies.

After three days without food and water their conditions deteriorated to a stage of semi consciousness. Suspended as they were, they were unable to touch the ground with their feet. Their extended limbs carried all of their weight. We waited for the three Hawk victims to come forward to begin punishing the rapists. On the forth day a Hawk woman, known as Berchan came out to face her enemies. The other two women remained hidden inside of our village.

With a stunned, determined and intensity Berchan approached the Roman legions. She took their male member in her hand. As if she were taking grapes from a wild vineyard she sliced them off, one at a time. She threw the severed parts on the ground.

They remained tied to the trees for another two days. Fenn arrived and they continued the discussion of how to return the message to the Romans. The two Romans had nearly expired from the loss of blood and picking of jackals and other carrion eaters.

Finally the day came that we would take vengeance to the Roman camp. Maelchon had spoken of an outer world speaker who warned the Pryten people that a battle entered in revenge was a battle that would provide losses for their remaining days. Being a peace loving community, the wisdom of that statement was not challenged nor did it keep Fenn and Maelchon from carrying out their own brand of justice.

Sixty men, women and young arrived at the meeting place, down hill from a mile castle. The ladders were retrieved from the storage in the nearby tree line. The details of the planned attack were never discussed or provided to all involved. With haste, they scaled the ladders and engaged the troops in the garrison house. They were left inside the small fortress while the youngsters gathered fire wood a pitch tar from the pines and firs.

The door was held shut with boulders while fire was set to the stack of wood and pine branches. Panic soon set in as the fire began to consume the building and the Romans left inside. As these preparations were made the sixty night fighters took positions on the perimeter of the encampment ready to spring to action once given the signal.

A line of Pryten fighters stood behind the tents on the outside perimeter of the camp. When the signal sounded, they opened the tents with their swords and quietly took the lives of everyone within each tent. When each tent attack was completed, they moved forward to the next line and decapitated their sleeping residents.

The Prytens were six or seven rows in before they left that part of the camp and made their way to the officer's quarters. The officers met their deaths, clinging to their slit throats. They tried to scream. Their efforts were in vain.

After we had killed three hundred or more Romans we scaled the walls by use of the ladders and gathered along the tree line. As we prepared to march back to the village the pipers began playing the mournful sounding pipes. The drums provided the rhythm to our march.

As they had done many years before, the remaining soldiers and officers awoke to the sound of the Pict pipes and drums. The surviving camp rose from their beds and prepared themselves for engagement with their enemy. They soon realized that it was too late. Over three hundred legion and construction auxiliary workers lay decapitated and disemboweled in their tents. Great damage had been done and not a single loss was taken by the Pict.

Breidi's sword skills had come along with muscle development needed to wield the heavy blade. His accuracy with the bow began to separate him from most of the other young men of the clan. He was tireless in his practice.

My emotional attachment to Breidi finally became evident to Maelchon and Mother. I cared for Breidi's needs in preparation of his meals and repairs of his clothing and other domestic chores that he required.

It became clear to others in the Wolf Clan that I cared for the young warrior. We spent time together in the fields and forests and in the valley where we gathered shoots for arrow shafts and animal sinew for bow strings. The sounds that we made from our bed must have alerted Mother and Maelchon.

After swimming and bathing in the valley stream, we lay in each others arms by the valley stream and continued the exploration of our bodies in the warmth of the mid day sun. Instinctively, we knew what we could do.

I was, after all, a creature of the realm with my own needs that did not necessarily develop in sequence with my human companion. I had stayed true to Mother's plan f raising Breidi and prepare him to place his seed in my womb for my own generation of young Mur'uch. I had been capable of conceiving many years ago. I only had to wait until Breidi was capable of mating with me. I had waited long enough.

Breidi was as anxious as I was to get on with it. We lay together for hours, entangled in each other's arms and legs by the bank of the quiet stream. He fondled and explored my body with his gentle hands. I leaned back on the bank with my feet angling in the water and enjoying the sun. Breidi stepped between my legs and laid on top of me. We kissed and giggled in the pleasure of the warm sun against our naked bodies.

My young lover was in front of me, between my legs I did not want to resist taking his seed any longer. Our petting had brought him to full arousal and we ached to join in passion. Our desire for each other's attention had brought us to the point of consummating our love for each other, but we always had to withdraw from petting because of the severity of clan sanctions against unwed couples.

His hungry eyes and kisses were prelude to his gentle but persistent movement as he stood between my thighs. I could not resist his advances any longer. I wanted his seed for my first born. Breidi was at the age when young Pryten people entered into *handfasting*. We were capable of caring for our young as Pryten custom dictated.

Knowing the seriousness of our violation, I held his rigid flesh in my hand guided him in. The sensation was unbelievable. Breidi arched his back and lunged forward in aggressive motion, unable to control his passion.

We could not hold back. I ached to have him continue. His petting had taken both of us beyond the point of stopping. He rolled over and placed me to a sitting position. I braced my hand on his chest. I reached between our bellies and took him in my hand once again. His back arched with my gentle stroke. He watched my eyes and saw how much I was enjoying this long awaited moment. His motion slowed and his movement became gentle and slow.

He pulled my face down and nuzzled my neck and then my breasts as they swung and bounced across his chest as he quickened his rhythm. Breidi took both of them in his hands and brought them to his face. He squeezed them firmly in his hands as our rhythm carried us beyond concern over anything. He brought my breasts to his lips and kissed them hungrily. I felt the sting of his kiss on my soft flesh and then his quick spasm and sudden release while holding Breidi's face to my breasts.

Breidi did not stop his rhythm nor pull away from me. He continued, looking into my eyes as he went on. He saw my back arch and slowed while I regained my desire for more.

Neither of us were experienced in the skills of lovemaking but nothing held us back as we met each other's thrusts with our own as if we had been instructed on how to please one another.

We lay together until our hearts quit pounding in our chests and we could talk without gasping.

I knew that we had just committed our lives to a certain future. I was pleased with that prospect but I needed to tell Mother and Maelchon to allow us to pair.

The Pryten people held the family unit as a bond between a man and a woman. Promiscuity was frowned upon and adultery always led to rejection from the clan.

All Pryten pairings were overseen by the clan matron.

Mating outside of her oversight was not done. I knew that those were the rules of the clan and there would be no further discussion about it.

During our time with the Pryten people, mates were always taken from other clans in the highlands. That was one of the few times that clan members visited other villages in the federation.

Mother told me about this practice. She said that the clan matron performed the oversight to avoid pairing with blood relatives. The custom of exchanging young men and women between the clans had existed long before the Celtic people came to Caledonia. Native clan members could not take mates from one of the other clan families. Clan matrons arranged for young prospective mates to meet other eligible members from a sister clan.

Mother also told me that Mur'uchs were not concerned over that issue since she and her daughters avoided our male counterparts. Each of Mother's daughters were sired by different, human males.

"This is just another reason for avoiding Merrows," Mother said. She was right about that matter, no doubt.

Mother and Maelchon must have seen the fulfillment of Breidi's interests in me. The lighthearted smile on his face and eagerness to get me under the covers at night would have been clue enough for nearly anyone, let alone, Mother. Her senses about people's emotions and thoughts were becoming the subject of legend. Since the time of the connection with the Jackal Clan, visiting between the two villages became an ordinary occurrence.

Many of Fenn's clan must have heard him tell about the two Mur'uchs that had been taken into the Wolf Clan. In the beginning, they came to see for themselves. "Tell us about the future of the Pryten people," they would ask.

"The future of the Pryten people of the highlands will always be what it is now," Mother began.

"We will be faced with challenge from every corner by invaders and immigrants, just as we have been. Our independence and loosely formed confederation of clans will be out strength and our downfall," Mother went on.

"How is that so?" another asked.

Mother had discussed this issue with Fenn and Maelchon many times before, but members of the confederation from around the highlands wanted to hear this from themselves. They had heard of the Mur'uch Queen living among the Pryten people of the Wolf Clan.

Villagers arrived in small groups to see Mother and I. We treated them with kindness and soft voices so that they would have no fear of us. They asked Mother about the future and her time in the Roman Camp that they had heard of. Mother fulfilled their curiosity and sent them on their way back to their camps.

"It is so because we live apart from each other and refuse to draw strength and reinforcement from other Pryten clans. As a united force, our warriors would be almost invincible," Mother told them. "Our stubborn independence will bring about our decline as a people."

"Then why would our independence be our strength?" another asked.

"Our guerrilla attacks on the foreigner's wall and our refusal to act as united people brings havoc to the Romans like they have never seen. Our independence will not permit one clan to form a truce that would bring about the decline of us all," Mother pronounced.

"Then how can we continue?" another asked.

"We do as we have done. We continue to fight the foreigners and keep them on their side of the wall. We attack at night from all directions and never agree to surrender as a people," she advised.

"The Roman's war with us because they want the highlands to join with the lowland dogs and their slaves of Britannia in their empire. We refuse so they try to defeat and force us into their numbers. The longer we refuse and fight for our independence the more likely that the Romans will give up and go home. We have already cost them much more that they planned to expend on bringing the Pryten people to peace."

"Good!" one said. "We will continue our ways," he said.

"The Romans have enemies in every direction. Some are even close to the home of their empire and they will not want to expend so much of their resources to the very edge of their empire. They have attackers trying to take their homeland and they will give up on the highlands and go home soon," Mother concluded.

The crowd rose from their seats and brandished their fists, swords and bows in the air, encouraged by Mother's words.

The men of Fenn's clan probably came for the same reason as their women. They both came to see the differences in our appearance and habits and listen to Mother speak about their future.

The men probably took home a different impression than their women. Mother always greeted the visitors with kindness. She wanted their acceptance of our presence among them. I was never certain that we were accepted as one of their own but they learned not to fear us.

Some of our own clan members stayed away from Mother and I. The knowledge of our immortality must have been cause for some concern, I am sure.

I remember one occasion, just after Fenn came for his first visit. Several families came with him from the Jackal Clan. Many of the villagers on both sides had not been among others. That only caused a temporary disruption.

The women approached Mother and I. She gave us a thorough inspection. They had heard of Mother's words about their future but they wanted to see her for their own.

Mother held her temper long enough for them to touch her hair and skin. They had been told by Fenn and others about the sea maidens who lived in Wolfstan's clan.

They came with the anticipation of investigating this story and did not hesitate to stand close and examine us. I could hear Mother's faint growl coming from deep in her throat as the women poked and prodded at us. They took a strand of Mother's hair and brought it to their noses, expecting to smell the scents of the sea.

One woman approached Mother and looked into her eyes and about her skin of her shoulders and arms. She reached in and took a breast in her hand and felt the smoothness of her skin and the heft of its weight. Her own were weather worn and covered in blotted markings that had become muted over the years. I thought that Mother was going to harm the woman. She took the woman's hand from her breast and squeezed the woman's fingers in her grip.

The woman bent as if she were going to come to her knees before Mother let her hand go. The woman straightened up and stepped back into the crowd.

When they looked into our faces, they usually stepped back to separate themselves from the startling appearance of our eyes. There was no mistaking the impact that our eyes had on humans. The dark, weepy pools that were our eyes were strange to humans and they looked at them with fascination.

We never reacted to their inspection or tried to interfere with their conclusions, whatever they may have been as long as their touch was gentle.

Mother and I were quite settled in our purpose with the Pryten people and little differences were not an issue with us. Mother was set on helping the Pryten people survive the difficult times brought on by the Roman presence in the south. She had no intentions of allowing anyone to interfere with her purpose.

I believe that the development of my interest in Breidi took some of the pressure off of Mother's own situation.

If Mother and Maelchon were to foster the pairing of Breidi and I, Mother could allow that to take its own course without her having to change her plans. I knew that she was happy living with the Pryten people and relished in her position as a council to their war but I also knew that she would return to her domain in the sea one day. With me becoming settled within the clan, she did not have to concern herself with me.

The raids on the Roman wall continued as Breidi worked his way in with the senior warriors. They welcomed his weaponry skills and his bravery. It became apparent to Maelchon and Sarah that Breidi may well find himself elevated to that of the War Chief in the Wolf Clan once Maelchon relinquished his duties.

Breidi's archery and the use of the ancient halberd had greatly improved over time. His use of the sling and stone were of less importance in hand to hand battle, but he enjoyed hunting game birds and rabbits with his sling. He kept his accuracy honed and ready for use.

Maelchon and Fenn had expanded their forces with another clan of Pryten people from the highlands as the Romans completed their wall.

The sign of the Roman Empire moving northward was alarming to native highlanders of the Jackal and wolf Clans. It was only a matter of time before the legions marched beyond their wall and attacking clan settlements in the north.

The Wolf Clan and the Jackal clan planned to continue their attacks on the Roman wall using night tactics as Mother had advised. Maelchon and Fenn tried to convince other clans to join in the fight against the invaders with their own attacks. They reasoned that more independent assaults on the wall would add to the Roman's confusion and frustration.

Maelchon and Fenn summoned other clans from the west, near Dumbarton and along the eastern coast. We were certain that the Romans intended to push native clans past the northern coast of the highlands and onto the Hebrides or even Ireland. Rome's vision of taming the Pict was at its peak.

"Father, why do our clans resist attacking the foreigners?" Are the Foreigners not moving north to take more of our lands?" Breidi asked.

"Yes they are, and your concern is well placed. We need to band together in a united cause. Our harassment will be much more difficult if we allow them to come through the wall and assemble their army on the other side," Maelchon told Breidi.

"Perhaps in your time the clans will take your direction. We need to convince our brother clans to join in the resistance of the Roman push northward. For now we have the stubborn traits of our kind that permits us to survive under difficult conditions, that prevents us from adapting to changing times. Our culture is ancient, son. We want to continue in the old ways that provided for us in the old times. We have not yet found the ability to adapt to changing social pressures."

"Why do we not hold council?" Breidi asked. "Why do we not propose change to the twelve clans and reason with them over the need to unify our cause?" Breidi said.

"I will propose a clan council to Fenn and ask for his aide in gathering the war chiefs of all clans," Maelchon said.

Fenn and Maelchon agreed that they would each address the proposed council with five neighboring clans. Maelchon and Breidi set out for a visit to the northern most clans in Caledonia. The first would be the clan of the Hawk. Their village settlement was to the northern most reach of the Isle of the Picts on the northern shore.

As Maelchon and Breidi approached the region that Aadan believed was home to the Hawk Clan they stood along the northern shore, out onto the sea towards the Hebrides Isle of Orkney. Breidi had never visited with the clan of this region and only had a general idea where their village was located.

"Breidi, you follow the shore in the direction of the morning sun and I will walk in the opposite direction. Meet me here in half a day's time."

Breidi followed the shore line as his father directed, looking out over the easterly horizon for signs of the Hawk village. Within a short time Breidi saw traces of smoke coming from an area, just inland of a large peninsula that reached out from the shore towards the Isle of Shetland.

As he walked in that direction he sensed that he was being watched from the heavy rocks on the bluff above the shore line. He continued until he saw the traces of smoke coming from a settlement on the northern bluffs. This village was built much like his own. He stood and watched for a while. He still sensed that he was being watched.

Breidi returned to the meeting place and found Aadan there waiting for him. "What did you find, Breidi?" Maelchon asked.

"I believe that I saw signs of the settlement along the shore. I did not press in closer towards the village because I sensed that I was being watched and did not want to alarm them."

Maelchon and Breidi began their walk towards the area where Breidi saw the smoke. "There, Father," Breidi said, "On the horizon."

"Yes, I see it," Maelchon said. "We are being watched. Let's continue and see if they come out from their cover."

They continued their approach towards the settlement. "We have a man following behind us," Breidi said.

"Yes, I see him, and I believe that there are others" Maelchon said.

As they continued, more men came out from hiding and followed them until they were within clear view of the settlement. The pillar of smoke rose clearly from the vent hole in the biggest mount. The stacked stone lined a pathway towards it and the smaller ones around it. Three men came from their burrowed village and stood at the wall, spears in hand.

"We come in peace brothers," Maelchon said. They walked slowly towards the men at the wall and stopped a few meters from them. "I am Maelchon, War Chief of the Wolf Clan, and I come to sit with the War Chief of the Hawk Clan," Maelchon said. "This is my son," Breidi, of the Wolf Clan.

The three men gestured for Maelchon and Breidi to approach. They turned and walked down the steps and along a stone entry to a central space, similar to their own. Breidi and Maelchon walked towards the hearth and stood for a moment warming, near the fire.

One of the three said, "Sit with us."

"What is the reason for your visit?" an elder among them said.

"We come to the Hawk Clan to advise your chief that the Jackal Clan and the Wolf Clan plan to hold a council of all twelve clans of the Pryten People.

No one spoke.

"The Jackal Clan and the Wolf Clan live closest to the wall of the foreigners and we come to advise our brothers of the Hawk Clan that their intent is to expand further north. We intend to confront them and stop them from expanding further," Maelchon said.

"I do not see the foreigners," the elder finally said. "Why should the Hawk Clan prepare to attack an enemy that has not been seen?"

"The foreigners completed their first wall. It is intended to keep our tribes from traveling south into land that the foreigners say is part of their empire. They have now completed a second wall, two days ride north of the first. It is clear that they intend to continue expanding until they push the Pryten to the shore," Maelchon continued.

"We are at that shore now and we are content with it," the elder said.

"That is true brother," Maelchon answered. "The Jackal and Wolf Clans will crowd your homelands in due time if we can not stop their advance. Your lives will change when that happens.

"Hmmm," the elder mumbled. "We will address that event when it comes. Until then we seek battle or conflict with no one, foreign or native."

"Will you sit with us and take a cup?" the elder said.

"No, brother, we have other villages to visit and we need to return to our own settlement for the council of Clans," Maelchon said. "Thank you for your hospitality."

"Breidi," Maelchon said. They rose and left the chamber.

"We have others to visit, son," Maelchon said. "Hopefully as we return close to home, our brothers of the other clans will be more accepting of our fate than those that live at the end of the Pryten realm. When we return and before we have our council with the other Pryten Clans, we must talk to Sarah and Esther about you beginning your own family with Esther."

"Father, I wish to take Esther as my mate. She pleases me. We should bring fine Pryten warriors to our clan. I look forward to that talk," Breidi said.

"I have interest in seeing the clans unite to turn back the foreigners," Breidi said. "We need to bring all Prytens together. Without a mutual interest in protecting our ways, I fear that we will perish."

"Yes son, I am sure that your mind is on these heavy matters, but consider this. You are of age to begin a family. She will make a good mate for you. She is sturdy in her hips and has ample breasts for suckling your baby. More important, she is strong willed and I believe that she is suited well for you," Maelchon said.

"She has a strong bloodline from the foreign empire that runs hot in her veins. She will bring a strong male child to the clan. She is like her mother though," Maelchon prompted.

"How is that Father?" Breidi asked?

"She has her Mother's beauty and you will have to get used to other men gazing at her," Maelchon warned. "Be wary, but be gentle. It will not be their intent to insult you or Esther. They can not help themselves. As Pryten leaders we must keep them from harming our people but we also need to protect them from aggressive curiosity. They are a treasure to us because of their wisdom and we need to keep them among us as long as we can."

"Yes, Father. It is a large burden, but some one has to do it," Breidi quipped.

"Ha," Maelchon roared in laughter. "Yes it is, but we will manage, will we not?"

"There is a season for all things. This is the season for you to take your mate and start a family. We do not live as long as they do and it is not good to wait too long to bring in young for them to care for. The mix of your seed and Esther's womb is a good match," Maelchon said.

"What of Sarah?" Breidi asked.

"Sarah is a wise woman. She has a split soul between our world and her realm of the sea. She must mind both, as does Esther. She tells me that she has seen Esther's affection for you and she believes that you will be a good match for Esther."

"Someday, when you and I are gone a new season will come for Sarah and Esther. For now, they want our blood to run in the veins of their young to pass on to future generations of Prytens," Maelchon explained. "That was Sarah's agreement with me from the beginning of our time together."

"Will they outlive us both?" Breidi asked.

"It is their fate," Maelchon said. "They will outlive humans. Their relationship with the mortals of this region is a strange one, Breidi. They are held by their tie with the great Mother of all things feminine and are charged with looking over our welfare. Yet, they seek to use our blood lines to better their own. We both benefit from the other."

"Enjoy your time with Esther. I have enjoyed mine with her Mother. They are beautiful and they are generous to our clan. What more could we ask? Sarah and I have heard the rustle of the covers at night, on your bed. We know that it is time to enter into a handfasting with Esther before the clan Mother gets word of your activities at night," Maelchon warned. "I am sure that you have already tested Esther's lovemaking skills. The Mur'uch are known for their demanding and sensual lovemaking. If you don't give her what she needs, there are many, many young men that would like to shove you clear from her. She is beautiful and will make a wonderful mother to your sons and daughters."

"When we return we will meet with Sarah and Esther and make plans for the pairing. You are young now son, but remember that the seasons will rush by towards the end of our time. We must make our mark while we can," Maelchon reasoned.

Chapter XX

Maelchon and Breidi began their walk back towards the Wolf Clan. On the way they had three other stops to make to enlist other clans in their plan to assault the Romans head on.

The Clan of the Falcon was a half day's walk from the Wolf Settlement. They were turned away without hope of participation from them. Their last stop, before reaching the Wolf settlement would be the Clan of the Salmon.

They too could see no benefit or reason to risk loss of their number in fighting the foreigners. Neither the Falcon nor the Salmon saw no reason to confront the foreigners, who they were convinced intended to stay behind their wall. "Why else would they build a wall," they reasoned.

Maelchon and Breidi returned to the Wolf settlement, down hearted and dejected by the lack of unity among their kind.

Fenn returned with word of the proposed council meeting. "Two of the four clans have agreed to meet," Fenn reported. The six other clans see no need to attend. Three of those are clans are from the far western shores. They do not have the same concern," Maelchon said.

The Council was set for the end of the next month.

"Come, let's talk with Sarah and Esther. Perhaps they see more benefit for joining forces than our brethren of the north," Maelchon jested.

By the light of the fire, Maelchon said, "Sarah and I have discussed our proposed pairing between Breidi and Esther. I have said, while they are still young, time will march on and so will our end of times."

"Yes," their time for pairing and providing the clan with their young has come," Sarah said, "I am pleased with this pairing."

"Maelchon, Esther has shown her affection for Breidi and we should consider that theirs is a good match. He is growing quickly and has already shown his maturity in the council and his ability to feed a family," Mother said. "We should not wait."

"Yes, that is true," Maelchon said. "Esther will make a beautiful mate for Breidi. What of her need to return to your world?" he asked.

"That is for Esther to decide. It is true. She has my blood and my heritage in her veins. Her future among my kind or yours is her choice. They will make great babies," Mother said. "I am pleased."

"Esther, Breidi, what have you to say?" Sarah asked.

"I am pleased with your choice," Esther said. "I will take Breidi and be his mate to the end of our time together, however long that is to be."

"And, Breidi, what have you to say?" Maelchon asked.

"It is good," Breidi said.

"Then I will get Wolfstan and tell her of the news. We will fulfill our plan tonight.

Maelchon left the council room and walked the hall towards Wolfstan's chamber. In short time Aadan returned with Wolfstan in tow. As usual, when she saw Mother and I, she had a scowl on her face.

"Wolfstan, we wish to conduct *handfasting* between my son Breidi and Sarah's daughter, Esther," Maelchon said. The old woman said nothing but she turned and walked away to gather her belongings for the ceremony.

I stood with Breidi at my side. I was still a head taller. He tried to stand on his toes to make up some of the difference, but after a while he could no longer sustain his attempted deceit. I laughed as quietly as I could. He stood down on his heels and smiled. We stood, unclothed in the Pryten way, facing the still scowling Wolfstan.

"Is this your wish?" Wolfstan asked Sarah.

"Yes, it is," Sarah said.

Mother placed a yellow and white pond flower in my hair. She kissed me on the forehead and squeezed my hand. She was pleased.

"Then, so it shall be," Wolfstan said. She took a leather lanyard from around her neck and held it over her head as Breidi and Esther stood by.

"Great *Sidhe Lena Gig*," Wolfstan began, "Mother of all things of our world, we join in the pairing of these two young clan members. We ask that you might be pleased with this pairing and will take them into your hands and under your care. Bring young to this special pairing and grant them a long life together if it so pleases your purpose with us," she said.

Wolfstan took the lanyard and joined Breidi's hands in the tradition of the ancient Nordic custom of *handfasting*. She wrapped the lanyard around our joined hands.

"As is our custom, Wolfstan continued, "As a joined couple, you will bring forth children of this pairing. At the end of one year's time, if the pairing has not placed a child in Esther's womb, then you may forfeit the pairing and go separate ways, if either chooses to do so. In our ways, a pairing without children is not a good match and should be ended. A pairing without children does not serve the purpose of our matron."

"May *Sidhe Lena Gig* bring healthy children to you," she said. Wolfstan actually smiled, bowed her head and backed away before returning to her chamber.

"We will begin the dig for a hall and entry to a new chamber as soon as possible," Maelchon said. "There you shall live as man and woman of the Wolf Clan. For now, you may keep the bed in my chamber that you have used these years.

"We will go out in this direction," Maelchon said pointing to a solid wall behind them. "We will have it ready by the harvest season, and you two have had time to couple and bring Sarah some of those babies that she is so fond of."

"Now it is time for heather ale, Maelchon declared. "This is good. Tomorrow, we begin planning for the council of clans."

Aethlgifu prepared a large feast to celebrate our handfasting ceremony. We at roast venison, waterfowl, rabbit, carrots, onions cabbage and yeast bread. The heather ale flowed through the crowd and everyone forgot the heavy matters that occupied our minds. The pipers played our old familiar tunes of celebration as we ate and danced into the night.

When everyone departed, Breidi and I finally crawled into bed. We clung together under the fur covers of our bed. Asta took to a pallet at the foot of Mother's bed.

Breidi was as passionate as I knew he would be that night. We never took time to talk about my separate worlds.

Breidi did not ask about my world in the supernatural realm and I never pressed him to learn or understand it. We had been together in the Wolf Clan for many years. Perhaps the question had already been answered to his satisfaction.

We were awakened twice by Breidi's arousal and we joined under the heavy cover with the sweet and urgent rocking motion of our hips, joined together. We rested during the short interludes of our love making, lying still without intrusion of thoughts about our differences or the dangers that faced the clan and the Pryten people.

Breidi pulled me towards him once again. My back was to his stomach while he kissed the back of my neck and pressed against me while his passion rose and he rubbed against me until I took him in. I held Breidi, firmly as we spent ourselves and fell asleep once again, still joined. Each time, during our first night, we awoke and I pumped him for his seed and took it as a gift. I remember anticipating the time when I would carry Breidi's child.

I heard Mother and Maelchon whispering under the covers of their bed. There was an occasional laugh that they tried to conceal as Breidi and I fulfilled our wedding night dreams. They were happy with our pairing and I was filled with plans for as many young as we could make together.

I felt as if I had been freed of some sort of constraint of my body and will. Each time I took Breidi in and he rocked me to passion during the night, I took the moment and stored it for my future memory. I must have known that these moments were times that I would want to recall in another time.

Mother and Maelchon slept near by, never showing signs of noticing what we were doing.

It was if we were playing a game. "How much passion can we release before we bring the attention of Mother and Maelchon?" We rocked together in synchronized motion, his hungry thrusts meeting my own. We looked over the covers to see if our passion and giggling might have stirred Mother and Maelchon. Mother laid on Maelchon's belly, her face nuzzled in the nape of his neck. Her eyes were open and she had a look of proud satisfaction on her lips.

Knowing Mother's ways, they probably were playing the same game. Breidi and I had both acted like we were asleep, during many nights when they brought each other to the peak of passion before we collapsed on each other.

We laughed later. It was like "pay-back" for the many times that Mother and Maelchon kept us awake.

Our early, blissful days passed quickly. We spent them in the fields and forest, in the valley lying together on the soft, green grass near the river. Now we swam and frolicked around the stream, exploring each other's bodies and caressing each other to arousal, coupling and releasing.

Unlike people in the Roman camps, we Pryten wore little clothing except for winter season. They would only have been encumbrances that restricted us. Exploring unknown frontiers of our bodies and spending our passion on each other was much easier because of it. We did not need clothing, except, maybe to hide Breidi's occasional arousal at an awkward or inappropriate time.

Breidi was a very passionate man. Now that we were paired, he did not want to take our youthful times together for granted.

Breidi could spend hours, lightly tracing his youthful fingers over my shoulders and down my body like a wind blown leaf of the harvest season, tumbling and skipping across the rocky earth, barely touching the surface. His touch brought chill bumps to my skin and caused my nipples to stand high in anticipation of the fulfillment to come.

I was certain that I was already holding Breidi's seed in my womb. I felt a strange sensation in my breasts and tummy. I said nothing of it, as I was not certain what caused the change. I just knew that something different was going on in my body, and I suspected that it was Breidi's child.

In those days, Mother was totally absorbed producing infants with Maelchon's blood. She was with child, once again, when Breidi and I stood united in our *handfasting*. Mother did not look complete without an infant suckling her while hanging from the cocoon sling that she used to carry her young. Asta had been nearly a permanent fixture attached to Mother. When she began to squeal from hunger, Mother was always nearby to deliver nourishment. Now she had another on its way.

We lay for hours in the warm sun as we drew moans from each other before we joined again in passion. Our hands performed their magical prelude. We tried every position that came to our minds. Breidi had no knowledge of any of this but he was never short of curiosity and willingness to learn.

We had watched Mother and Maelchon in their bed as they moved together in one motion like a small boat attaches to a large wave that rolls and lifts them at its crests before it relaxes and comes rhythmically ashore. As if in one motion, one rose while the other fell as they clung together. I had seen them at this and picked up on their methods.

Breidi apparently learned nothing of this matter from his father. I sensed that Mother knew that I was watching. She was obvious in her effort to provide a lesson.

Mother was forever aware of others around her. She had many more senses than a mortal woman and she employed them all. Like a great soaring bird watching movement below, she was keenly aware of all things in her presence including me watching she and Maelchon display their passion for each other. She knew I was watching and she also knew that I found her demonstration entertaining if not hysterically funny.

I giggled at her ways, trying to hide my amusement under the covers,.

Mother's choices that led to living among the Pryten people had worked out well for both of us. She was free to stay as long as she needed without concern for me. Mother had a wisdom about her that I never doubted. Her senses of timing and advantage were always honed and at play when it came to placing her young in the best environment. Mother's young were always foremost in her mind and action. We were not to be trifled with.

She had an almost inaudible growl that emitted from her chest and throat when she felt that one of us was at risk. Invariably, whoever or whatever it was, backed away when she uttered this sound.

The camp dogs that came in for the winter slept in a dark corner of the room, always avoiding Mother. They knew that there was something different about Mother and their extra sense told them to be aware. With a single look of her eyes in their direction, or the utterance of that nearly inaudible rumble, they slipped further into their dark corner.

I embraced the days among the Wolf Clan and planned to stay with Breidi for as long as possible. After all, I figured that I had no need to rush away. I have hundreds of years to be somewhere else, and I had a special passion for the young warrior that kept my bed warm at night.

Chapter XXI

Members of the three participating clans began to arrive for the council meeting. They arrived in small groups of three or four warriors and clan matriarchs as they took their places near the fire in the Wolf Clan chamber.

There were no representatives from the northern coastal clans.

Mother and I helped Aethlgifu prepare the meals for the council members. We worked silently, passing through the crowd with heather ale and mead pitchers and cups. Mother drew eyes in her direction and I caught a few following me as well.

Fenn rose from his position. "We of the Jackal Clan, the Wolf Clan along with our brothers from the Hawk and Otter Clans have come together for the first time to consider our future. New times in our land have brought new developments that we are certain can not be ignored or denied," Fenn went on.

I looked on from the corner of the room, watching Breidi sit among senior council members next to his father. This was unspoken recognition from Fenn and Maelchon that Breidi had come of age and had prepared himself well in the acquisition of warring skills and leadership. My heart was full of pride for him.

"Many of our Pryten people have not seen the developments in the south and see no need to come together in a united front to hold off the foreigners. That is our loss," Fenn went on. "Many years ago, the foreigners built the first wall, and then the garrison houses and fortresses were built along its length from the sea in the east to the sea in the west."

With each passing season, they advance northward, taking more of our land into their hold. I see no reason to believe that they will stop there," Breidi said. "They have brought in new garrisons of their guards to protect their investment in the south. Maelchon, our host and his son Breidi, of the Wolf Clan support the Jackal Clan in a vision of gathering our might. We plan to hold off further advance by the foreigners for as long as we can."

Maelchon rose as Fenn sat. "We of the Wolf Clan have watched our brothers of the Jackal fight the foreigners at their wall. Fenn and his father, Odenn, have harassed the foreigners for many years," Maelchon said. "While we praise Fenn and his father for their bravery and adept skills in night warfare the Romans make plans to push north. They have added more guards to protect the boundary to their empire. The Wolf and the Jackal can no longer stand alone in our night tactics. We must unite when they come from behind the wall and surge north. They will come into the Wolf and Jackal land and those who have not seen to join us here in council. We must stand together," Maelchon declared.

"What signs do we have that the foreigners move northward, as you say?" one asked.

"I will let my son, Breidi, of the Wolf Clan answer that question," Maelchon said. "We of the older times will soon be gone and it will be time to let Breidi and his peers begin to take the lead," Maelchon said.

Breidi rose, and so did my heart as he stood before the council fire.

"We have seen the foreigners build gates in their wall. We believe that there would be no reason for building a gate if all they intended to do was keep us out," Breidi said. He hesitated and let his listeners take in his words. "They intend pass through their gate and surge into the north. Secondly, the Romans have taken in lands to the west and south, as well as across the sea to the land of the Scotti in Dalriada. We of the Jackal and the Wolf Clans, being closest to the foreigner's wall, have the advantage of a clear vision of their will and their might," Breidi said. Again, he hesitated to let them take in his words.

"There is no reason to think that the foreigners will not continue in their ways. The Pryten woman in the Roman camp tell us that the reach of their empire goes from the land that they call, the Holy Land, around the great peninsula of our father's, and as far as the land of the Welsh, the Britons and along the coast and isles of the Hebrides," Breidi continued. The crowd at Breidi's feet mumbled. Some nodded their heads in acceptance of Breidi's claim while a few others continued to mumble.

"Then, what are your plans, young warrior? one asked."

"First we must make ready, and we must be aware of their intent. We plan to post observers to watch the wall and gate. The moment that they decide to pass, northward te we must know about it," Breidi said. Many nodded their heads in agreement. A few others sat with a scowl of denial on their brows.

"When they begin to come through their gates, we need to be planted in a position to restrict their passage through the gate and kill as many as we can with archers. The more restriction we place on those gates the more success we will have in keeping them off of our lands," Breidi said. "If we let them through, we will have a much more difficult time meeting them. Our future will be certain."

"Fenn and his fighters have observed that it would be foolish to allow them to assemble and prepare to meet us in a frontal confrontation. Their numbers are great. We can not afford to face them in the way that their enemies have fallen before them in the past," Breidi claimed. They are trained as a unit to face challengers in open field war. They are confused by Fenn's tactics and fear for their lives when left alone in the night."

There was visibly more support for Breidi's words as he recognized the strengths of the Pryten people.

"Under no circumstances, even if they break trough the jamb of their gate and flow out beyond, should we ever face them in battle," Breidi warned.

"If we are to succeed in stalling their advance, then we must not be baited into head-on confrontation," he continued. "Fenn and his clansmen have done well for many years using sneak attacks and night tactics. We have no future in meeting the Romans in an open field battle. We must continue those methods and adapt as the situation demands.

"Stall their advance," one man repeated. "Is that the extent of our vision with the Romans, to 'stall their advance?'" he asked.

Maelchon rose from his seat and stood next to Breidi.

"Yes," Breidi said. The crowd began to talk among themselves. As Breidi let them go on, their talk got louder.

"Do you agree?" one of the crowd asked Maelchon.

"Yes," Maelchon said. Then Fenn stood with his two allies.

"I agree," Fenn said. "Our only hope is to delay their advance long enough for them to decide that it is not worth sacrificing more of their number, to gain more of our land. If we can not do that, then it is only a matter of time before they push us north," Fenn said.

"You ask us to watch our clan die for a cause that is hopeless," one said. "That is too much to ask peace loving people," he continued.

"It is much to ask, brother," Fenn said. "We are asking that you sacrifice some of your peace for the sake of freedom. It appears to us that we can not have them both. Peace will be freedom's price," he concluded.

The mumbling continued as I watched from the corner. I began to realize how fragile the Pryten people's ancient ways were. Like the Britons and Welsh of the south, they too would fall to the Romans unless they can weaken the empire's will.

"You ask too much," a member of the Hawk Clan said. He was immediately joined by others. "We will return to our ways in the north and live as we have for as long as we can," he said. "We will not put our warriors to slaughter for a hopeless cause."

They gathered their swords, bows and quivers and filed out of the room. There were four men and their matriarch remaining.

"We of the Otter Clan, will join with the Wolf and the Jackal to keep the foreigners behind their wall," one said.

The woman of the Otter Clan stepped towards Wolfstan and they began to talk between themselves. I could not hear what they said. The small crowd waited for them to finish.

"We of the Wolf and Jackals Clans, concur with the council. We must fight for our land before we are forced to flee. We only hope that there will be enough of us to gather if the Roman advance can not be stopped," Wolfstan said.

I was surprised by Wolfstan's decision. She had not given Maelchon support for his views in the past. Here, she agreed to sacrifice many of our clan if necessary in the cause of freedom of the Pryten people.

As the new year came, we celebrated two events. Mother delivered a new daughter who she named Fierra. The second event was Breidi's seed was growing in my womb.

Breidi was a full status warrior in his fourteenth year. Maelchon was nearing the end of his time and some thought that Breidi was most likely to take his place.

Chapter XXII

As promised, Fenn and Maelchon had look-outs posted near the gate in my Father's old section of the wall. Neither clan had made night raids on the wall. When reports that a Roman movement was imminent reached Maelchon he sent a runner to the Jackal Clan to ask for Fenn to prepare his fighters to meet with the Wolf Clan.

Soon, word came that the Romans were gathering south of the gate. Fighters from the Jackal, Wolf and the Otter Clans met below the gate. I wanted to go along, but Mother would not hear of it. With a child in my womb, she insisted that it was too risky. I stayed behind and Breidi, Aadan and ten more men and women left our village to meet Fenn.

The argument over whether or not the Picts should awake the great bear was a moot point by this time. They were no longer huddled behind their walls. They had increased their number at the order of Emperor Agricola and they were preparing to march northward.

Not able to stay behind and wonder how the battle progressed, I sneaked out through the village and walked at a distance behind our fighters. No one acted like they saw me as I crouched low, near a clearing, overlooking the gate. I could not see our fighters but I was certain that they would appear at the right moment.

I could see the Romans forming brigades behind the wall. They gathered near the gate and looked like they had finished preparations to begin their march. I saw two runners advance towards the wall on the downhill side from the gate and take positions where they could signal their comrades waiting behind a rock outcropping.

The march began with the sound of drums coming from the rear of the columns. Great trumpets sounded with the rhythm of the drums. Banners soon became visible as they came over the crest of the hill. The runners signaled for Fenn and Maelchon. They ran towards the wall, took positions on either side of the gate and waited for the Romans to advance to the gate.

"Hold your arrows until I signal. We will wait until they approach the gate," Fenn said. They waited. I could hear the sound of the march as Roman feet rumbled over the rocky soil. The rumbling sound of their leather sandals marching in unison was unmistakable. I watched with anticipation as the Romans approached the gate.

Fenn gave his sign to attack. The unsuspecting Romans began to fall near the entry to the gate as Picts archers shot arrows into their columns. As others approached the gate, the Jackals struck them down. They were hopelessly jammed at the gate by the force of the legions marching on to them from behind as they fell atop their comrades at the gate.

I watched as an officer came to the gate to investigate the calamity. As he prepared to dismount his horse, I saw Breidi notch an arrow and place it through the Roman's helmet visor. Panic continued to take over the legion as they continued to march into the foray taking place at the gate. The other Pryten must have seen the confusion that was caused among the Romans when their officer was taken down. They would watch for others as they came forward to direct the march.

The Romans could not see where the attack was coming from and there were no officers in the front columns to stop the march or make a decision to stop the columns. Soldiers and their pikes throttled the flow through the gate. Some began to turn back, but they found themselves overtaken at the gate.

Breidi's tactic was brilliant. The size and unwieldy nature of the Roman army worked against itself. The gate was narrow and it sat between two tall sections of the wall where they could not see beyond, to the other side. I could see no injuries on the north side of the wall. Volley after volley of arrows flew towards their targets and found their marks. The drums ceased. The trumpets became silent and the march stopped.

Fenn motioned for our fighters to retreat back to the rocks. I could see Roman officers making their way forward over the mass of bodies jammed at the gate By the time the first officer peered through the gate and around the edge of the wall, we had retreated and were out of sight.

From my vantage point I could see that confusion and chaos had taken over the Roman army. They were scuttled at the gate and it appeared that it would take a considerable amount of time for them to figure out what had happened.

Our fighters began their trek home. Two were left behind to relay any information on developments, back to hideout behind the rocks.

There had been no losses suffered by the Pryten People. By the fire that night, Breidi and Maelchon guessed that they may have downed nearly eighty Romans. The tactic of choking their passage through the gate had been a good one. We used the wall to our favor in a way that surprised the Romans. The wall became a hazard, but neither Breidi nor Maelchon knew if they could rely on it again.

One of the messengers came down the hill to our position late that day to advise Maelchon and Fenn that the Romans had cleared their dead from the gate and prepared for another advance. "I suspect that they will not try coming through the gate until daylight tomorrow," Maelchon said.

"We can stall their advance and frustrate them as long as we can use the wall and the gate against them," Fenn said. "Tonight, we build a barricade of fir trees across the opening. That will hold them for another day and give time for us to develop other plans. Eventually they will over take the gate and we need to be prepared to meet them when they do," Fenn said.

I came into camp that afternoon and found Breidi and Maelchon resting behind the large rocks that were strewn around the area. They used no fires and sat in absolute silence.

"Esther," Breidi said. "What are you doing here?" he asked.

"I had to come. I can not sit in the village and wait for news," I said. "I must return tonight. Mother will be upset with my absence, but I had to see you."

"What can I do?" I asked. "Is there something from the village that is needed here?" I asked.

"We need arrows," Breidi said. "Have Tamhais make up all of the arrows that he can. Bring them back before dawn. Also, have them make up several fire arrows, wrapped in pine tar."

"I will see you at dawn then," I said, and I trotted off towards the village. When I returned, mother was livid. Her objection to my disappearance was the risk that I took for myself and my unborn child. She was so fiercely protective that she hated to have me out of her sight.

I got to Braun and Tamhais and had them work on arrows through the night. I slept for a while next to mother and finally rose before dawn. Braun and Tamhais had a large batch of arrows which I wrapped in a bundle and put over my shoulder. The longer, fire arrows were sticky with pine gum. I kept them separate by bundling them in a piece of deer skin. I set off for the camp among the rocks.

I arrived before dawn and gave the arrows to Breidi. He held me, sheltered from the cool of night and rubbed my newly swollen tummy where our child grew steadily in my womb.

At dawn, I retuned to my vantage point on the hill and waited to see what would happen. I could see the barricade of pine trees and limbs that were placed across the gate. I could also see the small fire near the rocks where the fighters gathered and waited for the action to begin.

As Romans lined up at the gate, an officer ordered the first few soldiers in the garrison to remove the pine that became visible with the beginning of sunlight.

Our archers lit their fire arrows and sent them sailing to the obstruction in front of the Roman columns. In an instant the pile erupted in fire. The pine limbs caught fire immediately, sending large plumes of black smoke over their heads.

Our fighters gathered along the wall and scaled the rocks. They remained on top of the wall where they lay flat and motionless. One by one they sent arrows into the Roman flank, forcing them to push towards the middle of their assembly while they stood, unable to take cover or return fire.

As I watched the developments at the gate, movement along the wall to the far west alerted me to a garrison of Romans advancing towards our position. Breidi and the clan chiefs were not aware of this development. They could not see the advancing Romans from their position.

I climbed down from my vantage and ran towards Maelchon and Fenn. "The Romans have passed through the gate to the west and are advancing toward you," I said.

Fenn placed his hand on my shoulder in a gesture of thanks and sent me on my way back up the hill and to my lookout, vantage point.

I could see Fenn and Maelchon from my position and I watched with interest to see what they would do to address the latest counter move of the Romans. Maelchon moved his fighters to a position, downhill facing the oncoming Romans. Fenn took his fighters and moved out towards the north. They would sweep around the Roman left flank. Breidi and his fighters remained on the wall, harassing the main unit on the south side of the wall.

After a short while, I saw Fenn and his men move in behind the Romans. They marched like wooden soldiers, down hill and closing on Maelchon. I waved to Fenn. He could not see Aadan and did not have any way to know how close to Maelchon the Romans were. I motioned for Fenn to continue following the Romans until they were within sight of Maelchon's position.

As the Romans came upon Maelchon, the arrows flew from our fighters straight into the pack. Fenn's men moved in closer until they were within easy arrow range, and they loosed their arrows from behind the Romans. They were penned between the two Pryten units.

The legions began to break formation in panic. Trapped in close formation, they returned fire at Maelchon's position. Fenn continued the pressure and pushed the Romans up against their wall, where they were trapped by their own device and unable to flee. They raised their shields trying to block the onslaught of arrows being launched at them from two sides.

In panic, they tried to move uphill towards Fenn and escape Maelchon's men. This exposed their back side and lead to their final defeat. I watched in amazement as the Pryten fighters worked to eliminate every last Roman soldier.

Almost in detachment from the slaughter that they inflicted on their enemy, they continued until the last one was killed. Even when the Roman position was completely indefensible, and they stood like sheep as the Prytens poured arrows into their huddled mass, Fenn, Maelchon and their squad of fighters unmercifully launched volley after volley of arrows at the trapped foreigners. They made no attempt to change the Roman formation to take advantage of their panic and entrapment. Instead, they held their ground and notched arrow after arrow, sending them into the mass of their enemy.

I remembered something that Mother had told me several years ago about the Pryten mindset and why they fight with the ferocity that they do. Mother told me that the Pryten people had faced invaders in their lands since the days on the Eurasian continent, in times when then Mongols raided their villages and tried to kill their kind.

Eliminating invaders was part of the Pryten culture. Invaders had to be eliminated, not just chased away so that they could fight another day. They were to be killed, down to the last one standing. Before they would have themselves pushed off of their land, as they were when they fled to the Western Euro coast and boarded boats to escape, they would stand their ground and kill their assailants, one by one.

When the fighting subsided, scores of Romans lay where they had once stood. They had all been killed and were lying together on the ground. Their ill fated attempt at trapping their attackers had failed and it cost them their lives.

Among Maelchon's group, three of our fighters were killed. Maelchon, himself, was struck with an arrow to his chest and he was bleeding badly when I came to his aid. I held his head off of the hard ground while I looked to see how bad his injury was. Fenn kneeled down by us and placed his hand on Maelchon's forehead, brushing his unruly hair away from his face.

Maelchon passed as we held his head off of the rocky surface. I looked at Fenn and saw that his eyes began to swell with emotion at the loss of his neighbor and close friend. The only relationship of cooperation between two Pict War chiefs had vanished. Breidi would have to fill the void or the alliance would probably vanish with Maelchon.

In time, Breidi and his men retreated from their wall position and came down to the meeting point. He found his father lying, dead with a Roman arrow to his chest. He leaned down and took his Father's head in his arms. There was nothing to be said.

The loss of Maelchon was deeply felt. Breidi's father had died in combat in a manner that he surely preferred to dying of old age or disease, but nonetheless, Breidi was without his mentor and greatest ally. Maelchon would be sorely missed.

Breidi and two others hoisted Maelchon's body and we began our long, silent trek back to the village.

Mother stood at the entrance to our settlement as we approached. She saw us coming with Maelchon's body being carried by stretcher of green branches on the shoulders of his fighters. She approached us and kissed the warrior on the forehead. She took him from the bearers in her arms. Fenn's men looked in amazement as mother carried Maelchon's body away without assistance. She no longer cared to disguise her strength. Her reason for staying with the Wolf Clan had come to a violent end.

Wolfstan helped Mother conduct a cleansing of Maelchon's body and wrapped him in a woolen blanket. He was placed on the funeral stand. The fire was lit under it and his spirit soared away from his earthly trappings. In the way of the Pryten People and the ancient Greeks, the funeral pyre consumed Maelchon's worldly form and sent him on the wisps of hot ashes rising up towards the heavens.

Chapter XXIII

I was certain that Mother would not stay with the Prytens without Maelchon. I spoke to her in the evening as we sat together and ate game stew that Aethlgifu prepared over the hearth.

"It is time for me to leave, Esther," Mother said. "I have two young ones to rear and I need to attend to them in my way," she continued. "What of you, Esther?" she asked.

"As long as Breidi is here, I will stay with him and the Wolf Clan. We have a child in my womb and I want to be among Breidi's people when it comes," I said.

"Then we will meet again," Mother said.

I do not believe that Breidi heard any of my conversation with Mother. He sat nearby looking into the hearth. The tactics and strategies to face the Romans had been placed on his young shoulders. Doing nothing was not an option. It seemed that we needed to stand and fight or move to the northern highlands.

Breidi and I never spoke at length about Maelchon's death. I knew Breidi saw his passing as a natural event in the life of his people. Maelchon was nearing his thirtieth season and was near the later end of an expected life span of the Prytens of that time. Maelchon died in defense of his land

and people, and there was no reason to mourn the passing of a hero warrior, beyond recognizing the cause that he died for.

I knew that we had entered a difficult time with the Romans. Fenn and Breidi had nearly sixty fighters in their collective band. They would eventually face Roman garrisons that numbered nearly ten thousand. The odds and the eventual outcome were starkly apparent. But, there would be no stopping Breidi now. As time advanced towards the inevitable, the more I realized that Breidi's end was self evident. His deep concentration told me that he intended to finish what Fenn and Maelchon started. The Pryten people must unite as a cooperative front or vanish under the push of the Romans. They would not be chased from their land again.

With Maelchon's death, Breidi became the War chief of the Wolf Clan. I never heard anyone discussing the matter. Breidi was the only suitable replacement. The other men in the clan were less skilled in the ways of warfare and did not have Breidi's vision of the Pryten future.

Breidi and Fenn spent many nights sitting by the fire and discussing strategy for holding the Romans behind their wall. I even recall them discussing closing off the opening in the wall and holding it as a line of defense against the Romans. The irony in that option seemed to have escaped the two, but I can remember the stories Mother told about Father and his men putting the wall up to protect the lands in the south from invasion from the Pryten people in the north. To think that the Prytens would use the same wall to hold the Romans in, seemed a logical solution to me, even if it was less than a long term answer.

When I woke, the second morning after Maelchon's funeral rite, Mother, Asta and Fierra were gone. There were no signs of her having taken anything with them. She and her infants had returned to the sea. Mother would continue her quest to increase the number of Mur'uch. I was not saddened by her departure, for I knew that our parting was only temporary. I would see her later in a different place and time.

The council among the three clans defending their land against Roman advance continued for days. "We must avoid head-on confrontation with them, at all cost," Fenn said. "Their numbers are great and we would fall with little loss to our enemy."

"Yes," Breidi said. "We will continue with our night attacks, harassing them every time they stop and make camp. Our greatest ally is their great number. Hopefully we will continue fighting until they realize that we can not be had, and, that what we protect is not valuable enough for them to continue trying to chase us from it," Breidi concluded.

"Agreed," Fenn said. "I will send a runner to the wall while we make plans to greet them at their most likely overnight camp sites."

The war chiefs and Queens of the Pryten Clans needed a leader to help them look into the future. Had this occurred to them in Maelchon's life time, we were all sure that he would have been their choice. Without Maelchon, choosing Breidi seemed just a natural.

Fenn arose at the council and spoke to the small gathering. "We of the Pryten Clans see that the future of each of our villages has the same ending. We all face the invaders from the south and whether we like it or not we have a common outcome in our future. To help us make the most of our time we have decided that Breidi, of the Wolf Clan shall be our King. In the ways of our people, he is a descendant of Maelchon, former King of Wales and his sister-in-law Wolfstan, Queen of the Wolf Clan. He is our future."

"If there are those who think otherwise, let them speak now," Fenn continued. No one rose and no one spoke.

"We serve you," Fenn said to Breidi.

My belly had expanded to its maximum. The baby began to kick me, signaling that time neared.

We lay together on the bed as Breidi ran his hand over my swollen belly. It was as round as the moon. I treasured those nights with Breidi. He was young and strong, and he possessed the power of persuasion that great leaders need to lead people towards difficult tasks. I look to our child's future with pride. It would inherit those strong traits and move the Pryten people towards the peace that they so desperately wanted. In their case, they would never have both freedom and peace. They would only have one.

Without Maelchon, Breidi took charge of the Wolf Clan fighters and the other clans united to fight the Romans.

Prytens had never been unified. They were prideful, independent people who generally saw no need to act as a group. That notion began to change as news of the Romans continued to come to us.

"The foreigners will soon come from behind their wall and we must be prepared," Breidi told them. "They will soon be upon us and we must be ready. We must make preparations for a speedy escape if it becomes necessary."

Breidi spent several days visiting clans to the north to advise them of the past battle and the planned advance of the Romans. He returned frustrated with the mindset of his people. Never having mixed among their own kind for any reason in the past, the Pryten people did not see themselves as part of a greater population. It appeared that Maelchon's dream of unifying the clans would never be.

We learned later that Fenn had been working on his own to unify all Pryten people under Breidi's leadership. That would not happen until we met the Roman's surge.

The plan was finally drawn. Figuring the distance the Roman could move their massive army in a day's time, Fenn and Breidi plotted out the likely places where they would seek shelter for night camps. There, they would improvise attacks aimed at harassing the invaders and striking fear in their numbers.

Finally, the anticipated event arrived. The Romans crossed through their gate and began their march north. With their huge number, pulling supplies and support groups along with them, Fenn believed that they could clear ten Roman miles a day.

Fenn's runners watched closely as the Romans began their advance. The nearest Pryten settlement was believed to be twenty Roman miles from the wall. That was Fenn's Jackal village. Breidi scratched a quick map on the floor of the council room, showing the wall, the Pryten village and what lay between them.

"We hope to trap them in the valleys, if possible, where we have the advantage from above. That is not a plan that we can count on. They would be wise to stay to the high ground," Fenn said.

Fenn's runners returned with information on the movement.

"There are as many legion as ten milecastles hold," the runner said. They come up through the valley now. They take a route along the valley floor," he reported.

"We need to move quickly then, Breidi. You take the West side of the crest and I will attack from the East," Fenn said. "As long as we can keep them in the valley, we have an advantage."

Fenn's group waited for Breidi to cross ahead of the Romans and take his position on the west side of the valley. With a signal, they loosed their arrows at the Romans who walked in formation along the valley floor. Unable to escape the Romans they took several losses in their first skirmish outside of the confines of their wall. Fenn's men were not able to hold them as they climbed the slope towards his position. Still taking losses, the Romans continued forward until they took the crest of the hill and forced Fenn's men from it.

Breidi had his men advance toward the spot where he believed the Romans would make camp. I watched as he took a position and prepared to wait for the Roman column moving northward. As predicted, the Romans made their camp in an open meadow close to a stream.

During the night, Fenn's fighters attacked from the east side of their encampment and Breidi came at them from the west. We shot fire arrows, rubbed with pine tar into the camp. Few among them were killed with our tactics. Terror was our only ally.

Stopping the march of the Roman army was beyond our hopes. With each day, they steadily moved northward until they near our village.

Amid the uncertainty of battle being waged against the Romans, I delivered our first born in the Spring. Breidi named our son, Robb. Mother would never let me rest over my failure to produce a daughter. That was never my intention. Breidi needed a son and the Pryten people needed a successor.

I explained much later that it was important for Breidi to have a son to continue his work in unifying the clans, and I told her that there was no danger of Robb becoming a Merrow, as she feared. Hopefully, she would eventually give up harping at me over Robb.

Breidi was proud of his son. From the beginning, he made plans for Robb to join his small band. Breidi talked to Robb for hours, telling the amused infant about the responsibilities that would be his someday. "You must unite the clans, son," he told him. "We will perish if we live apart."

The Romans were working to complete the new wall, north of the Wolf Clan village. It was being hastily put together with a stone foundation, but unlike Hadrian's more substantial wall, the wall they called "Antonine's" was built with turf on the stone base behind a deep ditch. Breidi's village would have been entrapped by the wall. They had no choice but to pack up and leave their village.

With little on their backs they left the Wolf Clan village and began their trek north. Fortunately, their granary was near empty after the long hard winter. They would have time to construct a new one and plant a new crop of barley before the harvest season. Living without a granary during the cold season would be nearly impossible.

Not having a choice, we moved towards the rugged highlands. As we approached a garrison of auxiliary workers building the new wall, being watched over by legion regulars, we took cover until dark.

As the sun set and the workers retired for the day, we crossed the newly dug ditch in the night and continued on until dawn. Not wanting to risk being seen by Roman patrols, we settled in for the day.

At the end of the second night, we came upon the lake region and settled near a peaceful stream and Loch we called Tay. Here, we decided to start a new beginning in the highlands. We would call this lake region, home.

The first order of business was planting the barley fields. Wolfstan's clan thought that they would be free from the Roman invaders, and live a peaceful existence. The area had good sources of water and high hillsides on which to build our homes.

Breidi built our home, like the others. He dug into a small hillside and burrowed into the rock and sod as far as he could. He leveled the interior floor, and lined the walls with the plentiful rock, strewn about the ground. The downward slope would help create a run-off from our shelter and keep it dry in the rainy seasons. He covered the roof with sod and built a rock hearth.

Within a few days we had most of the homes completed and we began to work on completing the granary for the harvest.

There were out buildings used for the metal smith and the malturer along with a common longhouse that we would use for clan meetings and councils.

Each home was built with a center support and braces that supported the roof as we had in the old clan village. The long house had two supports in mid floor, but was otherwise constructed in the same manner. Rock boxes were built to hold the heather branches that we slept on. Te long house had benches around the inside perimeter for sitting and another set in the center near the hearth that we would use for group meals.

A man named Brun was in charge of the stone building to store our barley grain harvest. He was also the old village malturer. He mixed his fermented malt with spring water and let it age in oak casks for a season or more. The resulting whisky was fast replacing the heather ale as the preferred spirit.

The news from the south was never good. The foreigners completed their northern wall and continued to push northward. With each passing moon, the Romans pressed northward.

Fenn's, Jackal Clan built their homes in our village. They would share the crop that we planted jointly and draw from the granary over the winter. As a larger population, Breidi thought that we would have a better chance of survive in the event of an incursion from the south.

In the first council meeting of the highland people, Fenn and the matriarchs joined Wolfstan and crowned Breidi, King of the Pict people. The Romans still called Breidi's people "Pict." I never heard that word used by a Pryten.

A Christian missionary who had followed the Scotti people to the land of the Pict joined our council. I remember him as a funny appearing man. The fact that he was the only one in the room with clothes on, probably added to my impression. He was obviously uncomfortable with a room full of naked clansmen, women and children. He called himself, Columba.

We had all heard of the Christian movement. Mother certainly was exposed to it when she lived with my father in the Roman camp. There were even missionaries who accompanied the camp. Among the Pryten people, the blessings of an almighty were all around us and we recognized them. If we had had a god of peace it might have been more recognized. But we did not.

Fenn's clan had taken many of the teachings of the Christians into his settlement, many years ago. Now, Columba had come to Breidi's stronghold to perform a rite that Columba called "baptism." It seemed like a strange ceremony, but I am sure that Columba had known of my beginnings he would have been much more uncomfortable.

The missionary went through the crowd gathered in the council room and performed the rite for several others. Wolfstan and I abstained.

We sat by the fire pit in the village center. Robb played at his father's feet in the rubble that covered the ground. Fenn and Breidi both resented having to move our peaceful village away enemy reach. Neither had the mindset to retreat, but they had the welfare of their villages to keep in mind.

In that short time of peace, we lived a good life in the new village. Breidi made Robb a sling, like his own. It looked like the one that Mother had used to teach him how to hurl stones at game birds, Romans and our own clan members who heckled us when we were young.

Robb enjoyed playing with the sling and stone. Breidi showed Robb how to select a few suitable stones to be kept in his pouch for later use. "A good stone is one that will fly straight, so it should be nearly round," Breidi told Robb as we sat in a field by the stream. Breidi and I used to while away hours wondering about our future in this same spot.

Breidi was especially fond of the river stones that had been rounded with time. We selected a few for Robb to test and saved a few to place in his pouch.

"These rocks have changed with the passing of time," Breidi told Robb. "Unlike the Pryten people, these stones have adapted to their environment by rounding off their stubborn features," Breidi told Robb. "Maybe that is a thing that you will teach our people when you become War Chief and King f your people."

"Now, let's see you sling that stone," he told Robb. He took a nice rounded stone from his leather pouch on his belt, whirled the sling over his head and let the stone loose. "With practice, you will have that weapon to depend on for hare and game birds. Good job, son," Breidi said.

Chapter XXIV

"What news from the south, Fenn?" Breidi asked as they sat by the hearth watching Aethlgifu roast the rabbit.

"We hear from the Otter Clan that the earthen wall is nearly completed and that the Romans have moved their garrisons north to defend it," Fenn said. "If they continue the northern movement we may see them in the highlands by next Spring."

"We have a difficult decision if that happens, neighbor," Breidi said. "We can not continue to allow them to push us further north."

"Our young ones want to stand and fight," and we may have to join them," Fenn said. "I am getting too old to run away from the Romans. My bones will not take any more rock house building. It may be easier to stand and fight than to pull up and move again," Fenn jested.

"My son, Karl has been to the new earthen wall with his men. At night they attack in the old ways. They have lost few among them with those tactics and it may continue to give the Romans the sign that we are not going to be swallowed up like the Britons of the south did many years ago," Fenn said.

"I have heard one among Karl's numbers that the Otter Clan looks to move north and settle with us," Breidi said. "They fear being overtaken."

Robb grew through the winter season. We gathered around the fire in our hut and watched him fight ghosts with the wooden sword that Breidi made him. He whacked the center supports with his toy and growled at his invisible enemy to, "stand off."

"He has his father's brave heart," I said.

"Yes, I am afraid that his generation may know less peace than we have now," Breidi said.

"What did Fenn say? Is their news of further advance?" I asked.

"No," Breidi answered. "But, it is just a matter of time. They intend to settle all of our land and may not stop until they push us to Orkney."

"Robb's years will be difficult years for our people. He will need all of the skills that he can muster," He said.

"Come husband," I said. "Come join me. The winter wind is cold and we have another seed to plant for harvest."

Breidi crawled under the covers with me and we kept each other warm while the brisk winds buffeted the back side of the little hill that protected us from the north wind. Robb slept in the opening in the wall that we used to store our clothes and bed covers. He had become accustomed to sleeping there after Breidi convinced him that he needed to keep an eye for the enemy approach from the south. Robb's wooden sword, still in his hand, dangled to the floor, still firmly in his grip.

"Karl, what are your plans for another attack on the northern wall?" Breidi asked as we all sat and ate mutton stew and flat bread. "We need to keep pressure against their forward progress if we are ever to hope to turn them back."

"We leave at dawn," Karl said. "We take twenty from our village and twenty from Fenn's. We will arrive near the wall before dusk and make preparations for a late night attack."

I walked along behind Fenn and Breidi's fighters who trotted south towards the Roman encampment. I held young Robb's hand as we walked along. Our second child was safe in my womb. I could not remain in the village. I felt compelled to be with Breidi.

We gathered at the edge of the clearing watching the Roman camp come alive in the morning. Many came to the stream that ran between our position and their camp. Fenn motioned to his best archers. They took four Romans as they bent to splash the cool stream water on their faces. They uttered no sound as they collapsed face first into the stream.

Fenn motioned for his fighters to circle around to the right and come in behind the camp. There were only a few moments before the sun rose and the cover of night would be lost. Breidi came in towards the camp from the opposite side of Fenn. With the stealth of night, both clans moved in to attack the Romans where they lay. From the perimeter they worked their way in towards the center of the camp and ran their spears and pikes through their enemy, still sleeping under their capes.

Fenn and Breidi made their way towards the officer tent, still undetected. One by one, they quietly slit openings in the backs of the tents and dispatched the officers.

As Fenn worked on opening the last tent, the officer inside was alarmed by the noise. He cried out before Fenn finally plunged his dirk, deep into the man's chest.

I watched as Breidi saw the struggle and came to Fenn's aid. He came upon Fenn just as two legions ran for the officer's tent. Breidi killed the one closest to Fenn as he raised his sword to strike. The second came upon Breidi and ran him through with his pike. I saw Breidi collapse to the ground. After taking the second soldier out, Fenn leaned over Breidi for a moment before he picked his comrade up from the ground and escaped into the cover of the woods where we had assembled earlier.

Breidi was struggling to cling to life by the time that Fenn brought him to me. I leaned over him and he took my hands and brought them to his mouth for a last kiss. He placed his hand on my belly to feel the young one I carried in my womb. With one last embrace of Robb he passed on into the dream world.

We hurriedly gathered Breidi and Robb and trotted back to the village.

The following morning, Fenn, Wolfstan and many of the villagers gathered to perform Breidi's last rite. In the way of his father and the Pryten people Breidi's ashes swirled above the pyre and disappeared.

Fenn's life had been saved again by Breidi. That fact did not escape Fenn. He was deeply moved by Breidi's bravery and disregard for his own life in saving another.

Fenn and I never spoke about it but I am sure that he knew that I would not remain with the Wolf Clan long after his passing. Robb was a Pryten bred warrior and I knew that he would not become part of the world of the Mur'uch, Merrow and Selkies. His place was here, with the Pryten.

Two moons went by when Fenn came to tell us that the Romans had given up the sod covered wall and had began to evacuate their encampment behind the emperor's wall. We could not believe the break in our fortune. Could it be that the Romans had finally realized that they could not tame the Pryten people?

Several days later, Fenn's runner came to the village with the news that the Romans had finally moved out. He said that the word from the emperor's wall was that the Romans had been instructed to return to Rome. There were wars with others in their homeland that required their presence. They were said to have told the Britons, "You will have to handle the ghost warriors from the North on your own."

There was great celebration in the village. Aethlgifu prepared a large stag with root vegetables and flat bread. Brun produced several casks of whisky. We ate and drank through the night.

Fenn rose from the crowd with his cup and toasted Breidi. "He never achieved getting the Pryten clans to unify as he wished, but he did get the foreigners to leave our land which was a far greater accomplishment. We will hold our cups high for Maelchon and Breidi, forever. They shall dwell in our legends forever," Fenn said. He sat down next to Aethlgifu and took some more of her stag and bread. She beamed with pride as he ate the morsel.

The following morning, I placed Robb, still wrapped in his fur cover near the bed where Aethlgifu and Fenn had spent the night together. "This is a good match," I said to myself as I slipped away into the early morning. "Robb will be the bond that will hold them together."

I spent several days near the rocks offshore and watched for Fenn and Robb. "This is sweet parting, Robb, I hope that we meet again," I said to console myself, as I fought back my motherly instincts.

Chapter XXV

I met Mother on the coastal rocks near the Shetland Islands in the Northern Hebrides.

Norsemen had moved in with the natives of Hebrides Isles over the last several generations and had lived in peace with the mixed breed of Pict, Hibernii and Norse inhabitants of the rustic shores.

Nordic crews used Shetland and Orkney as re-supply bases for expeditions south west of Caledonia. To the far West, the Hibernian isles of the old Dal Riata kingdom were settled as well.

The need to resettle in lands that supported their numbers became critical to the Viking people. The tidal islands of Scandinavia were overcrowded. Farming and hunting were limited from the beginning. Increasing populations made the issue even more immediate. Small crops of barley were planted on Shetland. From that they produced bread and whisky, and used the remainder as revenue in the good seasons.

Nordic crews were restless sailors and explorers by their very nature. They saw expeditions of lands within their expanding reach as critical to the survival of their culture. The need to relocate became more critical over the last few years. Invasions of lands on the big isle of the Britons became regular events.

The advent of the teacher prophet called, Christ, had passed several centuries ago. Norsemen began to take in some of the teachings of Christians, but they were reticent to drop their ancient pagan beliefs. There was no pressure in this region for them to change their ways, so they took a little from both traditions. In that way they thought that they had less risk of offending either.

Mother was keen to select her next mate in a succession of mortals who sired her daughters. We now populated the eastern shores of the isles of Britons, the isles of the Hebrides and the eastern shore of the land of the ancient Picts as far south as the mouth of the River Clyde.

During the first spring on Shetland, Mother stayed close to the rocky shores at the mouth of a small harbor that protected the inlet to the largest Shetland Isle. Ships passed by Sarah as they arrived and departed Shetland and re-stocked their ships.

The Shetland population lived, for the most part in a small village of sod covered lodges of homes and outbuildings that supported their community.

There were livestock pens, surrounded by short rock walls, an iron smith shop and baker's shop. A weaver and a hide tanning shop filled out the remainder of the community that mirrored the cultures used in the tidal islands of Gotland and others along the Scandinavian coasts.

The Norse people shared many of the same village life that the Pryten people of the highlands. They had a dedicated iron smith, who made spears, arrow heads, battle axes, helmets and shields. A weaver salvaged old discarded clothes from the men and fitted the material for children and women. She also used wool from her flock to fabricate covers, capes and clothing.

There were livestock pens where they kept highland cattle, poultry and pork. It was located next to a tall smokehouse where workers smoked fish and meat for winter use.

The leader of the Norse community on Shetland was a man that they called Olaf. Mother had her mind set on him from the first time that she laid her eyes on him. Olaf was a large, strapping character with a barrel chest, short powerful legs and arms like the limbs of oak trees, and he had a mighty voice that could be heard from good distances as he roared and laughed his way through each day.

I learned later from Mother that Olaf wanted to find a settlement that would support his village population. As Shetland was so close to Norway, Olaf came ashore, but did not leave as he had intended to. Originally, according to Mother, Olaf was going to use the island that he called "Unst'" as a stop off for further expeditions on the Caledonia mainland or beyond.

"Olaf left Norway with several crews to avoid the increased taxation of the Norwegian King, Haraldr, 'The Fair Haired.' Already strapped with more taxes than they could pay, Olaf set out to find a new home," Mother said.

She said that Olaf decided to stay in Shetland as his home base. Olaf's wife had remained behind. His duties in Shetland kept him away for much of the time. He finally decided that he needed to relocate. He left his lieutenant, a man named Omar, behind to tend to the village. Over the last difficult winter in the north, Olaf's wife died of the coughing sickness.

Olaf told his crewmen that he had seen the mistress among the rocks. "She has been in the area since the end of the long cold season of the north. She is a captivating creature, I can easily see."

Olaf decided that he wanted to investigate the Mur'uch maiden who watched ships come and go from the harbor. On a sun drenched day, feeling the need for the rewards of the Season of Renewal, he took his skiff and rowed his way towards Sarah and a youngster at her side.

I was with Mother as the powerful man sat in his skiff and rowed towards the rocks. He was a massive man. His powerful arms and shoulders powered the small boat across the water with ease.

I was carrying Breidi's second child in my womb and would not be ready for any further mates until the child was born and could live on her own.

When I arrived, Mother said, "Where is your first child?"

"He is with Fenn and Aethlgifu, among the Pryten's," I said.

"He?" Mother blurted.

"Yes, his name is Robb and he will remain with the Pryten for as long as he wishes. He is welcomed there and appreciated for the bravery of his grandfather and father, who gave their lives for the village. He will surely rise up to meet his destiny among the Pryten people," I said.

"Hmm!" Mother said. "A Merrow."

"No!" I yelled. "He is not a Merrow. He lives as a Pryten and will remain a Pryten to take his place among them as his Father and Grandfather did before him."

"Where is such a big powerful man going in such a little boat?' Mother yelled to Olaf.

"I am in the mood for the good things that happen in the renewal season, following a cold and miserable Winter," he replied. "You remind me of the newly appearing wildflowers inland, sweet maiden, and I desire to see my share of such good things."

"Ahh. Come then warrior, let me see what you have in mind," she said.

We saw the huge, muscular man handling the boat and the waves around the rocks with assurance. He pulled his skiff up, onto the rocks and approached Mother. I slipped into the water and stayed near the rocks so I could watch Mother do her thing.

"Where have you been in your travels?" she asked.

"I have been as far as the great Peninsula of the Iberians, and on to Rome," where a man can be treated like a king for the price of supporting a wench of his choice," he said. "I have been around the coast of these isles of the Hebrides to the shores of Hibernia and down the west coast of the isle of the Britons to the land of Wales," he continued.

"Well then sailor, you must know your mind in the details of your wishes," Mother said, playing off of the big man's assertive manner. She was really practiced at this courting ritual, if we can call it that.

Olaf looked Mother over, as I watched from below.

"He is not bashful or backwards," she thought. "That is good," she uttered quietly. Mother's hold on the minds eye of this big man revealed his preference for a darker skinned, black haired woman from his memory of the Mediterranean and the courts of Rome.

Olaf must have been satisfied with the back hair, olive skinned maiden. He stooped to sit with Sarah. What of the children?" Olaf asked as he looked at Asta and Fierra, sitting by her mother. She sat silently, unconcerned with the man talking to her mother. No man, or thing, would dare try to harm a child of Mother's and I was sure that the big Norsemen knew the legends of Mur'uchs well. He came from the shores of Estella, where my Grandmother lived up to the tales and lore among the Norse people.

Mother placed her hat near her hips as she combed her black-blue hair away from her face. Olaf eyes widened and his imagination soared with the image of him lying with this beautiful woman.

"I will be the envy of all who come to trade in my village, once they see what I possess," I heard him say.

"You have all that I desire, maiden," he said. "An amply round and soft backside for keeping my belly warm during cold nights and a full bosom to keep my hands warm as well," Olaf declared.

"Good," he said. He picked up the hat from the rock and placed it in his chest pouch. He rose and offered a hand to Mother. She and Asta stood and walked with the big Norseman to his skiff. Mother wasted no time with this one.

As chief of his Viking band, Olaf lived in the big stone, circular building that they called a *broch*. I came ashore, following Mother, Asta, Fierra and Olaf and watched them enter the great stone structure. It stood out from the more ordinary, one story stone and sod homes around it.

"He the building over from the previous occupants just a few months ago," Mother said. "As chief, he demanded the biggest and best home in the village."

Olaf's new home was an ancient structure that must have belonged to an Pryten King or Queen. It was constructed for comfort and convenience. The time and materials that it took to construct the building eliminated the possibility that it was built for anyone other than the village's most important person.

"They were erected as defensive forts many generations ago by the early Pictish people," Mother said when I asked her more about it. "The leader of the clan would have had this built for her and her family. This one may also have been used as a place to gather," she said.

This building was much bigger than what we had lived in with the Wolf Clan. It was several stories high, with a narrow stairway that ran between the outer wall and the inner chamber wall. Olaf had a staff of people who maintained his household. Most were Nordic women.

Livestock was kept on the ground floor with a separated entrance through the outer wall and accessed through a single opening from the lower side of the building. The first, second and third floors were accessed through an opening on the up hill side.

"The upper two floors of the house were reached with the use of the outer stairway," she said. The vent in the center emitted a sweet smelling smoke from a fire that must have been in use preparing a meal for the chief."

After Mother settled in with Olaf, she came outside and found me near the backside of the house. "How is it Mother?" I asked.

"How is what?" she returned, testily.

"How is it going to be for you and Asta and Fierra" I said.

"We will see. He is so big, I fear he will roll over on me during the night and squash us," she said.

Chapter XXVI

I remained in the village during the time that I carried Breidi's second child. I wanted to see how Mother fared with the Norsemen and, frankly, I was intrigued by the exuberant life style of these big affable Norsemen.

The village inn was always busy with visiting sailors from Scandinavia. They arrived in the harbor, loaded their ships with supplies, took on warm food and drink and left as they had come, rowdy and life loving.

They filled the village with treasures from expeditions as far as the Roman Empire, Iceland, Greenland and a new territory in the far west that they called Newfoundland. Furs, gold and silver filled their loot bags. They came ashore to trade for the goods and services at Shetland that they could not get in Norway or for their journey.

There were few Vikings on Shetland that came from lands other than Norway, The Fin and Danish Vikings tended to travel east from their villages, where they established settlements deep into the Baltic Sea.

Shetland was within easy reach of Norway and her natives depended upon supplies coming through the port on Orkney's main island. Trade was the center of a robust Shetland economy as ships arrived ad brought their goods ashore for sale or trade. I watched ships coming ashore from the south and the west bringing in loot and trade goods while others came from Norway to pick up grain and food supplies to take back home.

Norsemen were a fierce looking lot. They bundled themselves with furs and leather gear that kept them warm on the sea. Their cargo ships and war ships were open boats. They wore heavy seal skin boots that their villagers or the boot man here on Shetland. He used leather, seal skin and fox fur, jackals and other mammal hides that cargo ships provided.

Vikings adorned their clothing with small metal shields and other ornaments that they sewed to their vests and sashes as a means of indicating their importance within their crews.

I found Norse wear somewhat strange after living with the Pryten people. I had not worn clothing except in the coldest times of the winter season. Prytens had no need for clothing except for what was used to cover and protect their genitals. Their chests and legs were nearly always bare.

I had to get used to wearing clothes. Mother fixed an outfit for me with the help of one of Olaf's house maidens. I wore a big, loose fitting shirt with an open front under a vest and long skirt. Wool leggins covered the lower part of my legs and feet. I wore laced fur skin boots. I refused to wear anything under the skirt.

I watched the Norsemen as they caroused around the village. They were very different from Pryten men. Norsemen were big and boisterous. They always seemed to have a woman's entertainment on their minds. Pryten men were nearly always naked and were much more reserved about their needs. I came to learn other differences in the two cultures as I stayed on in Shetland's village.

The innkeeper kept several women in a house and barn near the inn. They were available as servants and entertainment for his guests. They made their rounds inside the taverns where they served as hostesses while they were not occupied taking care of a Viking seaman's needs.

The tavern was usually full of rowdy crewmen. They drank their fill of the Norse, honey fermented drink that they called "mead." They drank large quantities of the brew with every meal. The inn keeper had barrels of mead fermenting in a cool storage room at the back of the tavern. It had an earthy, sour smell that filled the tavern.

I watched Mother as she made her way around the village. She was already known as a Mur'uch matron from a Pict clan of the highlands.

Villagers on this Shetland isle had lived near the sea all of their lives and they knew the stories of Mur'uchs, Merrows and Selkies. We were known as *havfine* in their native language. We have lived among Scandinavians for many centuries and we seldom drew much attention among citizens of sea side villages even though our hair and skin colors were much different than their own.

There were a number of Nordic tales about small, black haired children who dwelled near seaside villages. They were sometimes seen in the company of our cousins the Selkies. Villagers believed that they were part of our history.

Olaf had several people who helped him keep the village longhouse. Mother preferred to perform some of the duties herself. Olaf and his crews sailed to the shores of the southern Britons, Wales and the old kingdom of the Dal Riata looking for treasures and plundering villages and monasteries.

Olaf came back to Shetland only long enough to restock his ships and set sail again. Olaf was restless while so many crews were at sea, all looking for new settlements. He feared that he would be left out of the profits from discoveries. With so much activity, ports and sea side villages along the east coast of Caledonia and Britannia kept watch for serpent headed ships from the north.

Romans in southern Britannia had all but disappeared when they left to defend their home land against their own invaders who were attempting to retake some of the lands that the Romans occupied. Raids on the northern highlands, isles and villages were unheard of at this time. Britons had a much bigger concern. Norsemen were raiding their monasteries and villages at an alarming rate. Fear spread up and down the coast of Britannia as castles and estates of Anglo Lords were pillaged.

Without the Roman army to defend them, walls and fortresses were erected to keep the ruling family safe from Viking raiders.

Olaf was a menace to any village near any shore. Either he or another of his crews plundered villages from the land of the Saxons and their capitol of Paris, around to a city that Olaf took possession as a stopover, that they called Duiblinn. It had been a Christian ecclesiastical settlement named after the black tide pools that were prominent in the area.

I learned that the expanse of Norsemen reach was lengthened significantly by the use of stop over points in the Hebrides Isles and the town that Olaf found that came to be called Dublin. I also learned that they were restless travelers, due in part by the lack of sustainable villages in their far north lands. The need to relieve their land of the increasing burden was crucial to their survival.

While Olaf was out on one of his frequent expeditions, I often stayed with Mother and the other women who worked and lived in the longhouse. We sat in her quarters on the top floor. The warmth from the hearth on the first floor came up the stairway into her chamber. There was a great view of the village and the surrounding sea from the small, slit openings in the wall.

"They are still looking for a place to settle. They needed settlements that would support their numbers," Mother told me one evening as we sat near the hearth on the first floor with Asta and Fierra. "King Haraldr" has chased them out of Norway with his greedy tax increases. For now, it appears that Olaf will stay here in Shetland," Mother told me. "He has become wealthy from the trade that comes through the village."

"He had better be careful with his talk. I fear that Haraldr will hear of his intended treason. The distance between Shetland the Haraldr is much too short for such boisterous talk," she said.

We spoke quietly as we were in the company of a couple of village women who were busy sweeping the stone floor of the big hall. They busily avoided our presence by pretending to be engaged in sweeping their brooms across the floor.

Asta was a beautiful dark headed child. Her black eyes darted about the room, taking in everything that moved or made a noise. Mother had her hair tied back from her impish face in the way that she did in the times of the Roman encampment with my father. She held a big honey jar on her lap. She dipped a spoon into the jar, searching for the sweet treat inside. She drizzled some of the golden sweet on the small smoked herring that she got from the fish jar. She ate the fish and reached for another. She held the herring by the tail and dipped it into the honey jar. When she lifted it out, the fish was covered with a drizzling coat of honey. Mother did not try to help her or scold her as she held the fish above her mouth and chewed off the head while dripping a mass of honey on her face, her clothing and the bench.

I always believed that allowing her children to do what they could do for themselves was one of Mother's ways of raising independent minded women. Asta showed plenty signs of that eventual result.

Asta's small, dark green, apron skirt hung to her seal skin boots. She was a striking child. Her black hair and deep, mysterious black eyes inquisitively absorbed everything about me as she chewed her fish.

Fierra stayed close to Mother, as she too kept her eyes on me.

Asta looked at me with open contempt and disdain. I watched her sizing me up, calculating what she might lose as a result of my presence while she continued to dip for honey with a piece of herring.

Asta released a nearly inaudible hissing sound as our eyes met and remained fixed on each other. Neither of us was willing to be the one to look away from the challenge. Her hands stopped moving above the honey jar as I watched them develop short, but quite pointed talons. The spoon no longer seemed to fit in her grip and she momentarily lost interests in the sweet treat.

"It is alright Asta," Mother said. "Esther means no harm to you or to Fierra."

Fierra mocked her sister's mood. She stopped leaning on Mother's leg and stood erect when Asta released a deeper hiss.

Fierra had Asta's deep black eyes and inquisitive stare at all things unfamiliar, including me. But, her hair was the color of Shetland's barley crop in the harvest season. It was a golden, flaxen blonde. Mother had it tied behind her head in a manner that mortal mothers might arrange their daughter's hair. "The resemblance certainly stopped there," I thought. "This is no ones little girl."

Fierra had a menacing scowl on her face that was anything but innocent or little girl like.

I had no intent of being chased off by these two little, hissing brats. "They would not threaten me with my own game," I thought.

They both jumped backwards and took cover as I released my own, matured version of their puny little hiss. Even Mother jumped uneasily on her bench as the deep, guttural lizard like sound came from my mouth, aimed at the two little imps at her feet. My face tightened and stretched as my lizard-like mouth opened wide to release my assault on the little brats who dared show their displeasure with me, a senior among our kind. My tongue flicked in their direction, where they cowered behind a table and benches. I saw them peering from around one of the table legs, trying to see if I was to continue my attack.

The two house maidens dropped their brooms and nearly knocked each other over as they escaped from the disturbing sounds that filled the room. They rushed through the open doorway with their hands over their ears, never looking back for the source of the unfamiliar and disturbing sound.

Asta had dropped her honey jar and Fierra scurried away, across the floor. Both released a much more muted hiss from the assumed safety of the new space they created between us.

"There was no need for that," Mother said.

"Keep your little Brats out of my face," I demanded. "I will not be threatened by your little she bitches. Why don't you try to teach them some respect for their elders?" I asked.

"We do not need to get into to that," Mother said.

"Well, we do during the few times that we are in each other's presence. I am not here to take the little brat's space or to cause them harm. They need to understand the difference," I said.

Mother hesitated. She said nothing for what seemed like a much longer time than it must have been. Then she said, dismissively, "what are your plans, Esther?"

"I plan to stay in the region until Breidi's child is born. From that point, I will go west to my realm in the North Irish Sea, I suppose. Is that not your intention?" I asked.

"Yes. It is my intention that you take the West coast of Caledonia, the Sudry Isles and Ireland as yours. You know that," she said.

"Yes, I assumed that this was still your plan for me, but with these two," I looked over at Asta and Fierra looking on from across the hearth and flicked my tongue at them again. "I just was not sure," I said.

"Their future is not your concern," she said.

"Then I will stay, here on Shetland, until my child is born," I said. "Then I will move on to my own domain," I said.

"Come Asta. Come Fierra. This is your older sister and she means you no harm," Mother explained to the two little she brats.

"Esther will be with us only for a short while," she told them.

"Short while, my fluke," I thought. "I will stay as long as I wish."

Chapter XXVII

I intended to stay in the village for the remainder of my pregnancy. I became interested in learning more about the Scandinavian culture. I needed to learn more about their ways for the time when I would go on to my own domain.

Most of the men that I to encounter in these times would be Nordic chiefs like Olaf. They were the prominent men throughout this region and their successes in defeating challengers for their realm showed that they were the dominant culture of the time.

Vikings plundered new villages and often moved in with local populations and intermarried native, Celtic women. Their will was often pressed on locals when they assumed leadership roles in their adopted village. They often filled a void in farming villages where local men worked in the feudal system. This was occurring from the northern borders of Caledonia, The Hebrides and the big island that locals began to call Ireland.

In the mean time, I needed to stay independent while I waited out my pregnancy.

I worked as a servant in the village inn, refilling mead cups for the rowdy crowd that frequented the place. I knew that I could get to learn the Viking ways in the more relaxed environment of the inn.

I made sure that my pregnancy showed through the apron and bib. We laced the leather top to fit snuggly under our boobs. It lifted them up like a pair of yeast rolls put up on a shelf for rising.

Helga unlaced part of her vest and shirt so that her famous assets would be more prominently displayed. She had children that she had to care for on her own. Her husband had died at sea and she needed all of the coins that she could collect and was certainly not bashful about using her good looks for profit.

Life for an unmarried woman was rough. She needed a steady source of income. Taking coins for sexual favors was expected in places like Shetland. In view of the short life span and even narrower time of attraction as a young woman, Helga and the others had to get what they could in any way possible.

I certainly found no fault with Helga. We actually became close as we watched out for each other while we worked together.

Helga's husband had been a crewman on Hagar's ship. He was an active seaman, traveling as far as the Mediterranean Sea in search of new villages to pillage. "They brought young maidens from that part of the world to sell as slaves," Helga told me one night. "They collected beautiful, young women that would bring the most profit. Hagar also ran a house where he sold the favors of some of his young maidens before they were spoken for in a sale."

Since I would not offer the services that Helga specialized in and was not competition for Helga, she and I learned to watch out for each other. Most of the other women avoided me. Helga was not intimidated by me or my kind. Her husband told her about mermaids of the Mediterranean.

Along the coasts of the Roman Empire, they called them Sirene or Sirena. They were famous for their siren song. Sailors were said to be helpless in resisting their call. I took to Helga immediately. I found her frank lack of fear or concern of my kind a welcome relief. She had plenty of challenges in her life and seemed to have developed a sense of strength in meeting them. That suited me just fine.

"My husband, Aiden, was familiar with Sea Maidens and their skills," Helga said. "I suspect that he had been lured to the side of more than one sirene during his travels."

Some of the taverns patrons did not let my present condition interfere with their invitations to "roll in the hay," as they put it. "Where are you from lass?" was a question that I heard asked most frequently. I may have looked younger than the other ladies of the tavern.

The tavern was on the ground floor of one of the larger buildings in the village. The entry was three steps down from street level. The ceiling was only two meters above the stone floor. Cups, tankards and other drinking vessels hung on pegs on the second story floor supports. They were an annoyance for many of the taller patrons in the crowded space of the tavern. It was heated by a full crowd of warm bodies and a fire at one end of the room.

The confined space and the lack of fresh air was a bit of a problem for me. I often felt "shut in" when the room was full of drinking, rowdy patrons. The fermented stench of mead filled the heavy air. I had trouble breathing the stagnate air but I decided to stay with the job because I wanted to know more about Nordic men. There were few places where it was on display more than Sven's inn and tavern.

I had to take frequent breaks to step out into the open air to clear my head and escape the confinement of the crowded room.

I watched several anxious crewmen carry their choice of available hostesses up a narrow stairway attached to the wall on one end of the tavern. There was also a ladder that extended down from an opening in the floor above. Few used it, as it was difficult to negotiate with a screaming, kicking hostess on their shoulder.

The second floor used for guest sleeping and entertaining tavern hostesses, was nothing more than a loft of hay and dried grasses.

I tried to stay away from the second floor and the ladder. I had seen several women, surprised by a large crewman who grabbed them around the waist and carried them up the ladder.

I would not risk the injury of my unborn child with these oversized brutes who lightheartedly bullied their way around the inn. They were mostly good natured men but they were so big and loud. I figured that a gang of men just back from pillaging and killing innocent villagers could hardly be expected to show composure when they were full of heather ale and mead. They were ready to entertain women in any way that they could imagine. They were fueled by endless quantities of mead, ale, whisky and prodigious lust for all things female. It seemed no mystery to me that they had no intention to behave themselves.

In my time on Shetland I learned that Nordic crewmen knew that their lives were short lived. Many young men and women of their native villages died before their fifteenth birthday. Most caused by either cold, winter diseases or as a result of injuries in battles and raids. I knew that they and many villagers at home anticipated their own deaths before their twentieth birthday. By the time that they reached twenty five years of age, they understood that they were living on borrowed time. If they lived to see thirty, they knew that they had to live for every moment.

If I considered their fate, I could understand the reason for their rowdy, life loving behavior in the tavern. Who could question a man who believed that his death was overdue? This question helped me face the crowd in the tavern with new understanding and at least some appreciation for their point of view. As an immortal, I saw them as characters passing by as if I stood by on a road side watching revelers pass by in a celebratory parade.

"Don't be harsh on these men," I told myself. "They have but one life to live and they have to get it all in before they become thirty years old."

I kept busy with my mead pitcher and tried to escape the frequent invasion of big, rough hands seeking to reach up my skirt to fondle my butt. They seldom stopped there. They usually moved their inquisitive touch to my belly and the soft tuft below. Some released me when their hands reached my pregnant, extended belly. Sometimes, even that would not stop them. I would grip their hand in my own and squeeze it until it brought tears to their eyes if they did not remove their hand from my skirt when I asked them to.

I wore an apron over the long skirts that hung down to the top of my shoes and a leather vest that fit under my breasts and a linen, loose neck top. Our dresses were designed to accentuate our bosoms which spilled over the leather and linen top when we stooped to fill our mead pitchers or place meat trays on the tables. Trying to keep temptation under control, I tried to keep my boobs hidden under the loose fitting top as best as I could. For the most part that was a losing battle since they came out each time I stooped.

Our outfits were all part of the recreation of the tavern. Crews were hungry and lustful after weeks at sea. The tavern owner prided himself over the women that he hired to serve his guests. It was all part of the enjoyment of the place. I might have enjoyed it more had I not been pregnant at the time.

So, I was willing to give these men a measure of enjoyment, considering their short, action packed lives. A little touch on the butt would not hurt me. I gave them that much. I saw their aggressive and curious behavior as a flash in time. These men would grow old and pass on to make room for more curious generations to follow.

Mother and I made our way in the world by virtue of our attractiveness. Attracting mortal men was a virtue and strength that we exploited. How could we take exception to men who followed their curiosity and punish them for their reaction to it?

I could usually persuade them to remove their hands by making eye contact. Some were more stubborn than others and took a stronger message when they pushed the limit of my patience and understanding.

"Where are you from little wench?" one said, while he ran his hand up the back side of my skirt. "Your little arse is smoother than a baby's butt." I sat on his lap, wrapped my arm around his massive neck and looked him in the eyes. His free hand moved to pet me between my thighs and what the Viking friends, here, call *fitte*.

"Oh no you don't" I said."Get away from there!"

His mood changed when I released a bit of Mother's, cat-like growl that came from deep in my throat and chest. He took his hands out of my skirt and allowed me to stand and walk away.

"Did you see that one?" he said to a table mate. "That little wench is gorgeous and her belly and thighs are as smooth as baby skin, but something's not right with her. She growled at me, the little wench."

The crowd watching us laughed at their shipmate in a raucous roar. I went to the kitchen and returned to his table with a platter of meat and root vegetables. I laid the platter down and hugged the good natured warrior and kissed his head. They laughed at him as he sat with his arms folded across his lap like a scolded schoolboy.

I got a lot of attention at the tavern. They knew that I was different and many more knew the legend of my kind. My reputation and the knowledge of the ways of a Mur'uch among frequent patrons allowed me to avoid being mauled too often. Those who knew the legend enjoyed flirting with me in their own good natured way.

The more knowledgeable among them called me their "little herring," or hollered, "here fishy, fishy." Others were not as sure about themselves, or me. Legends of supernatural forces of the sea were quite common topics for conversation in the tavern.

Chapter XXVIII

One huge man, named Fain, came into the tavern nearly every evening. He came in for a hot meal and a few cups of mead. He usually sat quietly, by himself, by the corner fire place where he took his meal and mead. Fain was the village metal smith and weapons maker. He was a huge man and probably older than most of the young crewmen in the tavern by ten years or better.

I sensed that few would risk tangling with Fain. His hands were as big as smoked hams and his arms were as thick and heavy as oak logs. Few bothered him as he sat in the corner where he attended to the fire.

I learned that whenever I felt threatened, I could go to Fain and sit on his broad lap like children finding a safe place when playing tag.

I learned from Fain that he had lived on the Shetland Islands since he was a small child.

"My Father was a metal smith as well. That is where I learned the trade," he told me one night.

"Father made swords and shields for crews. He also made other, more simple objects like door and window hinges and the like. But, Father's real skill was his sword craft. He was the most skilled craftsman in the Hebrides," Fain said.

"You see this dagger?" he asked. He pulled a huge knife from his boot and proudly laid it on the table for me to inspect. It was longer than my fore arm. The hilt, handle and pommel were adorned with heat fasted silver and brass ornament.

"Father crafted this many years ago. It is one of his best. He left it for me to treasure. I have had huge purses offered for this knife but I will never let it go."

Fain lifted the knife, demonstrated its balance and slammed the point into the old wooden table. The broad blade drove into the wood with a resounding thud. The reaction from the crowd was like that of a covey of game birds, chirping and chatting away before an instantaneous and complete pause when they sensed an owl or hawk overhead. As if by one voice, the tavern noise stopped, instantly.

They all looked in Fain's direction. They knew exactly where the noise came from and they checked to make sure that the giant posed no harm before they returned to their entertainment.

I became known as "Fain's Wench," as some called me. We reasoned at the time that we both benefited from that perspective. He got a woman for company and I received protection without having to demonstrate my own capabilities of dealing with aggression.

He was a kind hearted man, mellowed by his age and the rigor of his occupation. Fain would have been a good mate for a woman who needed shelter and food, for he was one of the few wealthy men in the village.

Fain sat in the corner by the peat fire place and tended the fire. The dim light in the corner of the room was washed away by the orange glow from the fire. Fain's chair was a place of honor and it strained to hold the weight of the big metal smith.

In addition to his gentle nature, his craft demanded high prices in fur, silver and jewels from the Mediterranean. He would have been a good catch.

"Who is it this time Esther?" he would ask. I sometimes pointed to my problem patron, and said "him." More times than not, Fain would rise from his seat, put me down and walk casually toward the problem. The sight of seeing him coming was usually enough to get men to leave the tavern. The more stubborn were thrown through the door.

Fain was a crowd pleaser. He was becoming known for grabbing crewmen by the back of their pants and throwing him a few meters through the door and out, onto the street. That always brought a cheer from the rowdy crowd.

In the beginning, I spent a lot of time on Fain's lap. Too many wanted to test the rumor of my origin and the uncommon softness of my skin. I allowed them some leniency unless they became violent or demanding with me. I enjoyed a man's attention but I did not intend to allow them to maul me.

Many of my regulars offered a few coins when I took especially good care of them. They enjoyed placing their coins in the cleavage of my breasts, lifted by the tight leather bodice. I allowed them this little pleasure. By the end of most night I had collected enough silver and copper to fill a mead cup.

I had no use for money and normally kept my collections for Helga. She could always use extra income.

"How is my favorite mermaid?" Fain would ask. He let me sit on his lap. I wrapped an arm around his neck and gave him a kiss. That caused a few good natured jeers from the crowd. It also let the others new arrivals know that I was Fain's girl.

Fain patted my bottom when I stood beside him or sat on his lap. His big hand moved in gentle rotation on the cheeks of my butt, never groping or poking. His touch was kind and gentle. I sensed an appreciation in him and did not mind his demonstration of our familiarity. I grew to enjoy the touch of is broad hand on my butt. His familiar touch gave me comfort and confidence.

"I am fine," I answered. I felt like a child, being defended by this giant.

Through my time at the tavern, I learned that Norsemen were rowdy and exuberant about everything that they did.

From the brutal scene that I witnessed at Lindisfarne to the loud and boisterous display in the tavern, they lived with an intensity that I had never seen in other cultures. When compared to the quiet demeanor of Pryten men these men met life with a lot of excitement.

I finally met Olaf a few days after my last visit to Mother in his big house. He was a massive man like Fain but had a more boisterous, fun loving demeanor.

"This is my oldest daughter," Mother said, as he came to our side by the hearth. "Esther, this is Olaf, the village chieftain."

"Ahhhhh! Another daughter," the giant said. He seemed so big, at least compared to Breidi, Maelchon and many of the men of the Pryten people.

"I have seen you at the inn," Olaf said. "You work for Sven, the inn keeper?"

"Yes," I said.

"You are Fain's girl," he said.

"Yes. Fain keeps me safe and out of trouble with the other patrons," I answered.

"Fain is a good man," he said. "You could do a lot worse, my dear. He lived here with his Father and Mother and learned the metal smith trade. The fortunate among us have one of his swords, or the even more treasured swords that his Father crafted."

"Here, this is one of Fain's. He drew a sword nearly a meter long. It gleamed in the light of the fire. Few of our men have these," he claimed.

"Most of our crews carry a battle axe. These swords are too expensive for the most crewmen. Fain makes a fine battle axe and so did his father," Olaf said.

He raised the sword over his head. I heard the whipping sound of the blade as it cut through the air. "It is a combination of the strength of the blade and its light weight. That is the mark of Fain's blades."

"So, another daughter, Sarah he repeated. "Have you no son's?" he asked Mother.

"No," she said. There was a moment of silence.

"What about you Esther? Have you no sons?"

"Yes," I have one son," I said. "He lives among the Pryten people in the highlands."

"The Prytens" Olaf said. "The natives that the Romans called, "The Pict," are among our friends. That was not always so," he continued. "The Pryten are an independent minded people. Their warriors are fierce.

Norsemen faced them many times before we settled in their villages, here in the Shetlands, on Orkney and on the mainland," Olaf explained.

"We have respect for the Pryten. They are industrious farmers and staunch defenders of their way of life. Unlike the lackeys that live south of the emperor's wall, they defend their ways and refuse to be taken over by outsiders. Their spirit is kin to ours, I would say."

"My son is Robb, of the Wolf Clan in the central highlands," I said.

"I do not know individual clans of their people, nor have I ever seen the interior of the highlands. Many of the people, here on Shetland, have Pryten blood. We live with them in peace as we have for several generations. Clans of the highlands are much more independent minded and have not taken us in," Olaf said.

"I believe we took these islands from the Pryten many of centuries ago," Olaf said. "They have lived on these islands for hundreds of years."

"Robb is the son of a King of the Pict. His name was Breidi. Some call him "Brude," in the old language. Robb is also the grandson of the great War Chief, Maelchon," I said.

"Robb now lives with Fenn in a combined stronghold in the lake region. His Father and Grandfather were both killed fighting the Romans."

"The Romans have returned to their homeland to defend it against their own invaders, "he said. "Good riddance. The people of Britannia and Caledonia can finally return to self rule."

I said nothing of my own Father, Constans. I looked at Mother. She took my message in silence. Neither of us intended to tell Olaf about our lives, many, many years ago.

"You have your Mother's beauty, Esther," Olaf said. "You look like sisters, rather than mother and daughter."

"Perhaps, you are aware that we do not age like mortal women," I said.

"Yes," he said. "I know the legend of Sea Maidens from our Motherland. It is your Grandmother Estella's domain. All Scandinavian people are familiar with Estella. She is both ageless and ancient."

"Yes, well," Mother interrupted. "Olaf, come sit and have some stew and bread. Let me fill your mead cup."

"Where have you just returned from?" I asked.

"I came from the coast of the Francs," Olaf said. "We still look for a place to settle our people. They are starving in the motherland. They have no fields to grow crops or forests to hunt game. We live off of the shore and from our invasions of the Francs and Anglos. Our motherland is overwhelmed. We must move on."

"I am confident that Nordic people will find their way," I said.

I said my goodbyes and left the longhouse for the inn. Sven would be waiting for me. I had become a favorite with his most frequent customers. Even though I did not let them carry me up the stairs, they still enjoyed my company and Sven benefited from the increase in business.

When I arrived, I helped Jettie finish roasting the mutton carcass hanging over the large kitchen hearth. The outer flesh was nearly done. We began slicing from the carcass to feed the hungry mob that began to fill the tavern. The deeper flesh would cook sooner as we carved away the outside.

The smokehouse had salmon, goat and game birds ready. I prepared platters and carried them into the tavern. The savory aroma of the sizzling meat filled my senses. I held the platters over my head to avoid taking in too much of the smell of animal grease.

The big loaves of flat bread came from a village baker's shop. They were taken into the tavern with the other food. The crowd grew restless as we neared dinner hour in hopes of a hot meal and the smell of fresh baked bread added to their anticipation. They looked towards the kitchen and waited for the food to come to their table.

The tavern filled quickly at dinner time. We only brought food to patrons sitting at tables. Those left standing would have to wait until bench space became available. The standing crowd grew anxious with the anticipation of a meal. We brought platters after platters of roasted meat, vegetables and bread to the tables. The smell of the roasted meat circulated with the smoke that drifted through the candle lit tavern.

The crews came into the inn to eat, drink and carouse. Sleep would come to them later. The rigors of a long voyage at sea would help them sleep once their bellies were full and their lust sated.

They kept themselves nourished with hard bread and smoked meat while at sea. There was little room to stow food supplies on board. When they finally came ashore in the Shetlands, they were ready for fresh, hot food and cool drink.

I dipped the pitcher into the large barrel of mead that we kept out back. Sven had two men who helped him keep a ready supply of mead, heather ale and the highland, barley malted whisky.

There was no room for storage inside the kitchen and it would not last long if it were left in the tavern. I took six wooden tankards and made my way past a sea of groping hands, expectant faces and growling demands. This would go on until Sven and Jettie served all of the prepared food and most of the mead and whisky.

"Esther," one hollered, "come sit on my lap and let me tell you a story about a wee, tiny, little man." The crowd roared with raucous laughter at the man's crude and self deprecating suggestion. Their moods were relaxed while drinking mead and highland whisky. Some would drink until they passed out, face first on the table. Sven was not big enough to throw them out. That chore was occasionally taken on by Jettie with the help of a couple of her regulars.

Jettie was a big woman, broad at the shoulders and hips. I enjoyed the protection that she and Fain provided me. The crowd knew that I was favored by the odd pair who looked after me.

"You are full of stories, Luther," another answered. "She needs something real. Bring yourself and your platter over here, *Liebchen*. I need a woman like you," another called. Sixty pairs of hungry, lusting eyes fixed on me as I struggled past out stretched arms and groping hands as I made my way through the crowd standing by for a table.

I held two platters of hot, greasy mutton high over my head as I worked my way to the far side of the crowded room. As I went through, they grabbed at my flanks or my top trying to take advantage of my occupied hands. It made passing through the crowd all that much more difficult. I learned early on, from the house matron, Jettie, not to let them get away with any unwanted groping or physical mistreatment.

Despite my intentional tolerance of a few exploratory hands, I knew that I had to interrupt the intentions of a man who may not stop at a few touches.

"Nip it, while their memories are fresh," Jettie had said.

Jettie would know about such things. Sven is her Uncle and she had worked in the tavern since she was a child. The years showed on her face and on her frame where fat and muscle from hoisting the heavy platters had filled the space in between her top and her belly, making it all the same, rounded figure. When she walked through the crowd with platters or pitchers over her head, she swung her generous butt into the crowd and cleared them from her path. She would turn to take advantage of the opening in the crowd as she cleared it with her elbows, knees or backside. Sometimes she lifted the platters over her heads and charged, front first through the aisle. Her massive boobs and belly worked well at clearing a path as well. Through the crowd she went with her massive bosom working like a battering ram, pushing the meek and unprepared aside.

No one dared grab one of Jettie's boobs. That would be an open invitation to a tongue lashing and swift kick in the *balle*.

Despite her rough exterior, Jettie was a likeable woman. She stood near the kitchen with her arms crossed over her mountainous chest, overseeing the progress of her domain. She had little patience for some of the nonsense that hampered her duties at getting meals served and the mead and spirits sold. She was the serving boss and no one ever challenged her claim or tried to interrupt her progress.

I never heard of Jettie's beginnings. Many families sent their daughters and sons to extended family members to begin learning a skill at an early age.

It was common practice in a culture where children never had a childhood and life was abruptly ended before they reached their late teens.

Jettie had probably been loaned out to Sven by her parents. No one knew what had become of them. "She has always been here," was all of an answer that one could get when discussing Jettie's beginnings.

I tried to work my way through the crowd when one of the more lubricated nit wits grabbed my butt with his greasy hand. I carried two platters of sizzling meat over my head. He leaned into me and reached inside my top to grope my breasts with his lamb grease laden hands.

There I was, standing there with my grease slimed boobs completely out of my top while I had two platters of meat over my head. The big oaf took unusual pleasure in my predicament and awkward stance while he fondled and squeezed away at my *titta*. I had no intention of letting this violation pass without some appropriate punishment.

I remembered Jettie's words and decided to make a spectacular example out of this man's errant behavior.

He still has a hold on my tits and they are completely out of my blouse. My patience was about expended. The unwelcome exposition of my bosom and his rough treatment were more than I needed to forgive at this point and he showed no sign of releasing them.

I growled at him and told him to let go, but he refused. His lamb greased hands held my tits over the top of my bodice as he took way too much pleasure in demonstrating their suppleness.

I said, "enough," when he began to draw the attention and envy of his tablemates as he began lifting and bouncing me around with apparent forgiveness on my part. This was more than I chose to allow.

Jettie looked on as I gave up on civil means to get him to take his hands away from my top.

"Here," I said, and I handed the imbecile one of the platters of meat that I had been holding over my head. He reluctantly let go of my top and looked at me in surprise. While he held the first platter, I dumped the contents of the second one, onto it. He held the now heavy, hot platter in his hands and looked up at me, his face still reflecting his utter surprise.

His expression changed when I brought the newly emptied platter down on his balding head. "Whomp!" the heavy oak platter sounded as it met his thick skull. His eyes rolled back to the back of his head and his mouth came open. He collapsed forward, landing face first onto the table and the overloaded platter still in his grip.

His table mates roared. "Ha!" one said.

"Did you see that? She knocked Peter colder than a cod with that platter."

One of Peter's mates lifted his face from their steaming evening meal and pulled the platter back onto the center of the table.

Jettie watched the entire event from her usual spot near the doorway to the kitchen. Her arms stoically crossed. She was in total control of her domain and showed little reaction to my aggressive reaction from having my tits mauled by this parading showman, imbecile. This was one of the few times when I was really pissed and apparently I showed it.

Letting these boys have a touch here and there is one thing and I have learned to let most of it pass, but allowing this seagoing numskull to play, 'hide the pea,' with my tits was a different matter. I cower to think what Mother would have done had she been faced with this violation. She probably would have brought an end to this beast's miserable existence.

I recovered myself back into my blouse and walked back towards the kitchen. The crowd was broken up with laughter at the treatment of the poor soul still splayed across the table.

When I returned for another load of food, I asked Jettie, "did I do alright?"

Jettie said, simply, "that should do it."

When I returned from the kitchen with two more platters, "pass this on," I told the man at the near end of the table.

"No lass. This is for me." He took a hand full of meat and placed it on a portion of hot bread. As he lifted it to his mouth, the man next to him took a portion and began eating before the platter made its way to another. I carried platter after platter and pitcher after pitcher. The other women did the same. It did not stop until every crewman was occupied with food and drink.

I learned from Jettie, "once that you deliver the platter to the table, stay out of any ruckus that takes place over dividing portions. They need to work that out on their own."

As the night progressed, the crowd grew louder. They roared in their boisterous play. The grunting sound of satisfaction mixed with even louder demands of the crowd fell away from me, meaningless and unanswered. No single voice could be heard through the crowd noise. I communicated with eye contact and tried to meet their demands the best that I could.

Few evenings in the tavern passed without a fight involving ten or more patrons. Their good natured fun usually ended with several men sleeping face first, on the table where they had eaten and drank themselves into forced rest. Discretion was always the first victim of a night of drinking and lusting.

"*Winchan!*," One yelled. That was one word that I could single out in the background noise. I hated that word. In the beginning of my time at the tavern, I took it as a personal insult. Jettie provided some wisdom on that matter as well.

"They call us 'wenches' because that fills the lustful image of their loin heavy minds. Most of them would be drunk and passed out before they could ever fulfill their own imagination with us," she said.

I still did not like the word, but I could not let them see that it bothered me.

It was a common term that I came to learn at the tavern. It was from their native Germanic language, meaning "totter, waver, stagger, or "as one does when drunk" in their unflattering Germanic version. Most, who used that word to attract my attention, I am sure, thought that I was no more than another unfortunate target of their lust filled intentions like all of the other tavern women.

They had not intended the term to be flattering. If Fain was around when someone called me a wench, there was usually trouble to follow. I would search him out while I struggled to maintain a better temperament.

Chapter XXIX

There were many nights at the tavern when Fain came to my rescue. Most times, I could fend for myself. The crowd didn't know that I could read their minds. Times might have been more peaceful for me, and Fain, had I not been able to see what they were thinking. Their less than innocent imaginings about me occasionally brought out the worst of me. I was in a difficult spot with these brutes. I could easily dispatch them from their miserable lives with a well placed slit of a fingernail, or broken their bulbous necks with a good twist of their heads but I could not do that and live among them.

I had to find a more human response to deal with their indiscretions. Knees to their groins, platters over their heads or a well placed swing of a heavy mead tankard became part of my repertoire. My regular guests came to anticipate one of those reactions and even seemed to enjoy the buildup to one of my defensive retaliations.

Like a Pict drum, sounding in the distant. The anticipation increased as the expected attack neared. Many knew that I did not strike out over a simple pinch or pat on my butt. It was for those who did not stop there, or listen to my warning, that they watched for my retaliation.

Mother was much more practiced at deciphering a man's intentions than I was, but I was learning. Reading minds was, after all, an endless source of entertainment and a well practiced defense against ill intentions of all kinds.

Each environment was loaded with unique temptations for Viking crews. With only a day on land before they sailed off on another voyage, they tried to pack each hour with release of their pent up desires and needs of their stomachs.

Night and day, their seemingly inexhaustible energy for raucous behavior continued. They used the far wall of the tavern to wager on throwing their belt knives.

The sound of the heavy blades thumping into the wall was constant. One looked around the room for a target and finally settled on a hat from the head of a young crew mate and pinned it to the wall with a serving knife. While he made his way back to the table, knives whistled over his head and struck the wall near the hat. "Thump!" the sound came as the broad bladed knives stuck in the log wall.

I recall one evening, when I first encountered my gentle giant. Fain asked me to fill his cup. While I poured, he looked into my eyes. I saw a faint smile cross his lips that came from the familiarity and contentment between us. I looked back into his eyes and I saw that he knew of my origin and was not threatened or alarmed by it.

Fain later explained that he had seen other sea maidens in the past and his familiarity allowed him to enjoy our company without threatening us or putting himself in danger. It was a peace with the nature of our kind that I had not seen since Maelchon brought Mother and I to his settlement.

I recall, he said, "Sweet Esther, you are such a beautiful creature. I enjoy your company." He spoke quietly so that those around him could not hear. I put my ear close to his face, and felt his warm breath.

He said, "I believe that I have met your Mother. She is nearly as beautiful as you."

The roar of the crowd disappeared into the background as I listened closely to the gentle man. The crowd was still rowdy, demanding of my attention, but I was held by Fain's kind thoughts and words and I blocked the noise from my thoughts. I could not linger long, for I felt Jettie's eyes fixed on me. She would be demanding that I continue my serving duties if I stayed with Fain too long.

"I have seen your Mother in the village and in the ports of the islands of Orkney," he said. "You are even more beautiful than she. I see kindness in your deep, weeping eyes. Your peaceful nature comes through them."

"For those of us who have made our living on the sea, your kind has always filled our imagination with gentle caresses on a sun drenched shore, far from home," Fain said. "We all imagine lying nude on our backs on the warmth of the summer sand with a beautiful sea maiden draped over us while we nuzzled the sweet skin of your neck and shoulders and enjoyed the moist warmth of your fluke bound hips across our laps," he went on.

I needed to return to my duties but I found it difficult to ignore his kind words. I had never been spoken to in that way and hearing it in the sometimes hostile tavern crowd made it seem all the more appreciated.

Fain's lack of fear or personal judgment took me by surprise at first. I was not expecting such sentiment from such a large, imposing man. I became absorbed in his gentle nature and kind intentions. The crowd continued to roar behind me, throwing insults and demands in my direction, but I focused on Fain's soft approach.

I rose from his lap to see Jettie looking directly at me. Her heavy arms crossed over her massive chest in the stance that we all came to know her for. She smiled as I rose. She and Fain must have been old acquaintances of the past.

I found it difficult to pull myself away from him, but I needed to move on. His eyes had told me that he looked upon me as a woman, appealing to his senses. There were no reservations attached to his vision of me as a mermaid or a tavern wench.

"I would gladly keep you in my house," he said. "You are to be savored. For many Viking crewmen your kind keeps us alive and vital while we are away from home. But, I have never seen another whose presence is as fresh as yours."

Fain was a kind man, even kind to a fault. Some mistook his tender side of his demeanor as a weakness. That could prove to be a fatal nearly error in some. For me, there was no need to take exception to his innocent intentions.

Fain was a different sort. He was older than most of the crowd, by many years, I would judge. His red beard had taken on the gray of aging.

A man of his age would be looking to retire from the demands of crewing a ship and fighting for a living. He was at peace with the later phase of his life and his touch across my butt was an adoring acknowledgment of his acceptance of my kind. I enjoyed sitting across his lap while he rubbed my aching back and bottom. His touch was soothing and undemanding.

Fain's best hunting and carousing years were behind him. While he enjoyed the company of some of the younger crews that frequented the tavern, he was not lust driven like many of them. He enjoyed the food and drink provided in the tavern and tolerated the noise that came with it.

I placed my hand on his bearded cheek. The roar of the crowd was muffled as I concentrated on his words.

"You will always have a place in my home, sweet creature," he said. "If you need a safe place to stay while you are in the village, seek me out. I would welcome your company."

I heard, "Fain, stop hogging the wench's time. Send her over here and let me get some of her." The words bounced off of me as if they were intended for someone else.

I went on about my business of filling cups and serving hot platters of meat and bread. I checked back with Fain every few minutes. As I pushed through the crowd, I placed my hand on his shoulder and kissed his brow.

"Send her over here," I heard.

"Fain. If you can't handle the wench, send her over here and let me have her."

I continued my rounds with the pitchers. I placed the empty tankards down, on a table and began to fill them. As I poured, a new patron ran his hand up the back of my skirt. When he reached my butt, he gave me a familiar pinch and a less than gentle pat. His hand remained up my skirt and he showed no signs of releasing me. It was much too familiar to let this big thug get away with. I needed to discourage him and his tablemates from trying that again.

Jettie's advice was still fresh in my mind as I swung an empty tankard in my left hand and struck the poor man's face with a swift backhanded swing. He fell backwards, off of the bench seat. In trying to regain his balance with a hand on the bench seat, he pulled his three bench mates over with him.

They fell in succession, as they lost their balance and crashed, backwards, onto the floor. Boom, boom, boom, they went as they landed on their backs with their feet in the air. The crowd roared with laughter.

I looked over to Fain. He simply sat there with a smile on his face. He shook his head in amazement, and then laughed with the rest of the crowd. It was a funny sight. That was for sure. Four big, husky warriors, lying on their backs with their spilled tankards and food emptied on the floor and all over their clothing and their feet flailing in the air.

The poor fellow rubbed his cheek where the tankard landed. That would surely swell and may leave a mark to remember me by. He uttered something unintelligible. The crowd roared at the sight of the four of them lying on their backs.

The crowd yelled and hollered insults at the foursome as they attempted to right themselves. I am sure that the gist of their insults had something to do with a wench taking out four husky Vikings with one strike.

We all laughed. Good natured Norsemen were always ready for a raucous, good time. Fighting and horseplay and carousing after women were all part of their short lived, existence in the northlands, away from home.

Jettie stood in her corner with her arms crossed over her chest as usual. When she saw the foursome tip over backwards, off of their bench, she bent over, slapped her knee and began to laugh and shake her head. "That's a good one," I heard her say. Ha!"

My victims finally got up to recapture their injured pride. The crowd around the table laughed at them to the point where they finally abandoned their attempt at reclaiming their pride.

As the owner of the curious hand reclaimed his seat, I patted the big brute on the head and he carefully patted my bottom. He flinched at another attack of the tankard as I reached back with it in my hand, as if were going to clobber him with another volley. The crowd all laughed at the poor man. He turned out to be a good natured victim of my need to demonstrate what might happen to others who reached into my skirt. I almost wish that I would have picked another to illustrate my message and allowed this poor soul his indiscretion.

I found that Norsemen were gregarious people and meant no real harm to any of us. They were rowdy from confinement of their long voyage. They intended to spend the night carousing at the tavern. In a different place and time, they came over the sides of their ships using the same level of intensity attacking villages and monasteries.

These men were big, rough mannered fighters, dressed for the cold winds of the sea. Most wore a funnel cut cap with the pointed end dropped over their brows or ears. Most wore leather vests or battle gear decorated with metal discs and patches of fur. Their leggings extended from their boots, on up, under the open bottom of their outer garment. Their dress was designed for function and freedom of movement. A few metallic or wooden ornaments sewn onto their vests or hats provided the only points of uniqueness or custom made design.

When I returned to the table with another wooden platter of roasted meat, sitting on loaves of flat bread, one reached in and began tearing pieces of bread away with a few morsels of the juicy meat. Helga sat on a man's lap with her arm around his shoulder. She had the poor man all worked up. He looked ready to empty his coin purse for a few moments of her favor.

Helga kissed his forehead while he fondled her boobs with his greased hand and crumb infested beard. She spilled generously over her square necked linen shirt and apron top. His hand left a grease smear across her bosom where he had fondled her. The base emotion of lust drove his actions. He finally gave up trying to fill his belly with warm food and arose from the table with Helga in his arms. He carried her up the ladder to sate a different sort of hunger.

Helga waived to the crowd as they cheered and yelled insults at the pair before they disappeared onto the hay loft above. Helga was draped across the man's shoulder as he negotiated the ladder, spilling Helga's abundant bosom out of her top.

The rest of the crowd ate hungrily, not stopping until they had cleaned the platter with bread. They swiped it across the platter to get every bit of remaining mutton juice and crumbs.

I returned with platters of roasted water fowl and another with ladles of juicy stew meat over bread. All were consumed by taking chunks of meat between their fingers with bread. I refilled their tankards three times before they shoved the empty platters away.

The next table I served in the same manner. Emma slaved over the hot fire in the back, ladling portions of stew on top of large loaves of bread. This went on until every last portion was delivered by me or one of the other servants. There were still platters of smoked fish for those who had missed the main serving.

By early morning, the tavern held the odor of mead and barley spirits, mutton and the strong stench of body odor. I usually needed some fresh air after a few hours in the tavern.

Chapter XXX

I found Fain sitting in his chair by the fire, dreaming quietly as he watched the flames lick the peat blocks that he added to the fire. The smoke from the earthy fuel rose slowly towards a vent hole in the ceiling.

I had enough of the noisy crowd, but I did not want to return to Olaf's house. I approached Fain from behind and placed my hand on his shoulder. He jerked slightly, somewhat surprised with my touch and interruption of his deep thoughts.

"Fain," I said. "I am ready for a bath for my aching back and a warm bed for my head. Is your offer of welcome still good?" I asked.

"Yes, of course," he said.

We walked down the narrow street between rows of shops. Owner's quarters were on the second floor, over the owner's shops where lights had been put out for the night. The drizzle and heavy air of the night kept the peat smoke from roof vents close to the street.

We walked out through the door, up the street lined with closed vendors, towards the houses at the village edge. Most shops were closed and their doors were locked for the night, except for one at the end of the street.

"This is Anders shop," Fain said. "He is the village malturer," Fain explained. "The barley grain that he buys is fermented in barrels and boiled in a copper and brass contraption. He drips his malt whisky into containers over there," he pointed.

Anders opened the shutters on his shop window to wish us a good night. "He does most of his work at night," Fain explained.

"Good night, Fain," he called.

We walked on through the street and finally came to a single hut at the end.

. Fain's house was a small, one room over his metal smith shop. It was apparent that this was a home of a single man. It was no bigger than a single fire could warm and there was no sign of a woman's touch.

The fire pit carried the same earthy smell as the larger one in the tavern. There was a single box bed of straw, covered with furs of all kinds. A table and bench made up the furnishings in the room. Both table and chair were made custom to hold Fain's huge frame. I could not sit on the bench and touch the floor with my feet.

Fain hung his hat and leather vest on wooden pegs driven into the vertical supports for the walls. A huge helmet, sword and shield hung together while a few winter fur wraps hung from another.

Fain used rendered fat for fuel for the lanterns hanging from two posts. They filled the room with a warm, orange glow, revealing some of the simple details of his home.

Fain walked through the door and down the stairs carrying two empty wooden buckets. I stood by the warm fire and took in the peaceful surroundings. It was quiet. There were no loud patrons demanding my attention or trying to drag me up the ladder. I stood still, enjoying the peace and serenity of the undemanding surroundings of the gentle man's home.

Fain returned with two buckets of water and poured them into a large iron pot next to the fire. We sat quietly until the flames produced steam bubbles in the pot.

"Come," he said.

I loosened my skirt and let it drop to the floor while Fain held my hand for support. It fell around my bare feet and ankles. Fain looked on in a gentle, yet appreciative way. I began to unlace the leather string from my bodice.

Fain said, "allow me," and he began loosening the leathers. As the bodice came loose, he took it away and placed it on the floor beside my skirt. I stood with my hands up as Fain looked on. His eyes shined in the candle light as he looked at me in the shear cotton shirt. With a trace of impatient, trembling hands, he unbuttoned the shirt and let it hang open for a moment before he let it fall from my shoulders, onto the bend of my elbows.

I stood for a moment and watched Fain fill his eyes. He took my hand and held it while stepped into the tub of steaming, relaxing comfort of the fresh bath water around my feet.

I removed my linen shirt. Fain took a small pail and dipped warm water from the pot and gently poured it over my shoulders. The warm water tickled as it ran down my backside.

He gave me a small piece of lambskin. I used it to wash myself as he poured more warm water over me while I stood in the big caldron pot. Another pale was poured over my head. I stood still while he took the lambskin washcloth, wetted it and began to wash my backside.

"That feels so good," I said. "It has been a while since I have had the luxury of a warm bath." He rewetted the cloth with warm water and washed up and down the back of my legs. The warm water felt good against my back. His hands moved in circular motions around the small of my back and the round cheeks of my bottom.

"Where did you live last?" Fain asked.

"Mother and I lived with the Pryten, a few miles north of the Roman wall," I said. "Mother's mate was Maelchon," the War Chief of the Wolf Clan and I was the mate of Breidi, Maelchon's son."

"I have heard the name Breidi, or Brude, as some have referred to him," Fain said. "Didn't he rise to be the first King of the Pict?"

"Yes. He was a remarkable young man," I said.

"Your skin is soft and has the shades of an olive skinned maiden from the Mediterranean," he said. He twirled a strand of my hair on his finger and brought it to his face.

"I have seen a few of your kind in the village and around neighboring ports, but you are by far, the most beautiful creature among them," he said.

I found a sense of peace in his familiarity with my kind. I decided that I would stay with Fain, if he allowed me. I knew that I could relax here.

"You are a remarkable young creature. You are beautiful beyond a mortal man's words," he said softly.

He gently rubbed the lambskin over my back. "You make me wish I was twenty, or even ten years younger. Now, all that I can do is look at you, enjoy the softness of your skin, your sensuous curves and wish that my body could perform what my mind imagines." He held me by the cheeks of my butt in both hands and gently pulled me towards him. His hands covered my butt. He gently lifted my milk laden breasts as he placed a knowing kiss on my swollen belly.

I laughed at his jesting. "You aren't as old as you think," I offered.

I was still a bit surprised by the big man's ability to be so tender with his words and kind with his actions. "I held his upturned face between my swollen breasts and kissed his brow. "You are a sweet and gentle man, Fain and it has nothing to do with your age. Once we have brought this young one into the world, perhaps we will have time to see how much energy you have left in you. After all, I am at least three hundred years older than you are," I jested. Fain squeezed my butt cheeks even harder between his massive hands.

"Ouch!" I protested. "Easy." We laughed together.

"I remember hearing about your Mother from some of the crews that have passed through the village. I had no idea that she had such a beautiful daughter," he said.

"The legend of the *hovfine* of our culture tells us about beautiful sea creatures that live off shore from our villages. Much is said about them luring men from the village and causing their disappearance. I have heard these stories for as long as I can remember but I never imagined that a creature like you would be so human-like.

I have seen other sea maidens from the shore or while in a boat as we passed their rock but I had never been this close. Even the ones that we have all seen come ashore in the Shetlands did not have your gentle ways," Fain said.

"Mother has her own ways of dealing with mortals and we tend to live by them," I began to explain. "She and her Mother have perfected a system in which we mate with the more notable men of local culture, as Mother did with my Father. She receives the benefit of the best sires for her children and they enjoy us as their mates. We do not try to destroy humans that come to us," I went on.

"So your beauty comes from your Mother and the bloodline of a Roman General?" Fain asked. "I wish that I could keep you forever, Esther."

"Well, you can keep me for now," I said. "I owe you for your protection and hospitality in your home. Who knows what the future will bring? I have no intention to leave you now," I said. "Maybe we can work off some of those hindrances of age that you worry so much about," I said.

"Well, if anyone could do it, you could," he said. "You make my imagination run wild."

"We will take care of that soon," I said.

"My child comes from Breidi, of the Pictish culture. Mother has had many more than I. Each one has a special bloodline that gives them an advantage over many humans."

"Mother and I lived with the Pryten, or the Pict, as the Romans called them." He continued to wash my backside with the warm water, circling the warm cloth around my bottom in continuous circles. I did not complain at first. His touch was nearly as gentle as his voice.

"You knew the Romans?" Fain asked.

"Yes, I knew about them when we lived with the Pryten. My Father was, Constans. He was the General of the Roman Army charged with building the wall. "That was a long time ago. I said."

"I did not know that your history went back that far," Fain said. "But now I know where you get the rich color of you skin. Your Latin blood shows through. There is no mistaking a Latin woman's deep beauty. I see it in the tone of your skin and the rich luster of your hair."

"Mother took my Father as her first mate. We lived in their camp until I was born. She took me away and remained off shore from the Pryten camp until I was of age."

"So you did know something of our nature?" I asked. "You knew that we live among mortals and produce our offspring from them," I said.

"Sure. Most of us have been told about the legend of the Mur'uch," Fain said. "Like I told you, I remember seeing your Mother years ago, but I have never been in close contact with your kind.

There have been a few who have come on land in the isles, but most stay offshore. Their intentions are not as pure as yours, or your Mother's."

Fain continued washing my backside, going over and over my butt until I thought that he was going to rub the skin off of it. "Fain," I whispered, "That side is clean enough. Come around and scrub my front."

I giggled and he smiled at my jesting as I turned around in the pot and faced him.

He wet the cloth and rubbed it gently over my shoulders. I held my arms over my head and let him follow his imagination. I sensed his mind darting from thought after thought as he took in the details of my figure. The cloth went over my shoulders and onto my chest. He lingered there while he gently tested the firmness with his cloth.

My arms remained, crossed over my head as I let him follow his eyes with the soft lamb fur, tracing around and over the nipples of my breasts, across my ribs and down over my extended belly. He was in deep thought about a man whose youth had escaped him. He pushed the thought from his mind and attended to the pleasure that stood before him.

Fain squeezed the water bound cloth on my belly and by watched the stream of water run down, between my legs. He dipped into the water again and squeezed more of the warm water from the cloth.

I watched Fain's eyes widen as his mind took him back to memories of another time when he was more confident of his abilities. He kept returning to that same thought.

He wetted the cloth and wiped the warm water over my belly and down to my thighs. His touch was gentle and I found myself closing my eyes and enjoying the sensation of his touch.

His lambskin traced over my extended belly in wide circles as he squeezed some of the warm water from his cloth. I felt the trickle as it rolled over my belly and down between my thighs. He moved the lambskin to the lower side of my belly and onto the soft inner sides of my thighs.

"Oh," I whispered. "Your touch is soft but sure," I said. He remained silent as he rubbed the cloth from one inner thigh, over the soft tuft where the other thigh joined it. That was the most sensuous touch that I had ever felt in my life. I began to ache, and imagine what it would be like to lie with the gentle giant.

Mother had told me, when I was much younger that a man's touch at the point where our legs met was a weak spot in "our armor."

My condition would keep that thought as a mere imagining but it did not keep me from enjoying the gentle pleasure of the light touch of the fur across the most sensitive part of my body. I allowed Fain room to wash my inner thighs and legs as I stood still in the warm water. His gentle stroke moved from the top of my feet to the top of my inner thighs. His ability to keep his touch soft and gentle amazed me.

He interrupted that private thought with, "forgive and old man," he said.

"You must be cold. I am enjoying this too much. You are the perfect picture that a man holds in his mind when he dreams of a beautiful woman. I have forgotten myself."

He pulled a large lamb skin wool cover from the bed and brought it to me. He placed it around my shoulders and patted the water from my skin.

He stood before me and looked me in the eyes. Before he could make another apology for his age and his supposed inabilities to please a woman, I pulled him close, placed my hands behind his head and warmly kissed his lips. .

The lambskin was still wrapped around me. He carried me to the bed and laid me gently on the deep, rich pile of furs that lay across it.

I had never seen so many furs. There were skins that looked like bear, as well highland cattle and goat.

"Do you like them?" he asked. "I get them in payment from hunters and trappers who come through Shetland. I replace their knives and arrow tips and they give me these in exchange."

"Oh, yes," I said. "They are beautiful!"

He must have seen me eyeing the fox furs. He took a red fox cover and replaced the wool still wrapped around me. Then he took the white, winter fox blanket and covered me with it.

"Oh," I murmured. "These are beautiful."

"They are fox," Fain said. "The white one is the arctic, winter fur."

I wrapped myself in them and buried my body under the richness of their touch and sheen against my naked skin. The tallow lamps glowed gold in the room. I felt the sensation of the warm, soft furs against my sensitive skin. I have never felt anything as luxurious as these furs. The touch against my bare skin was sensual.

The memory of Breidi passed through my mind. The times when we took our passion to its peak on the furs of his bed removed me from the present surroundings. We made love under the cover of furs, not quite as luxurious as these. We would kick them off of us as our body heat built under the insulation of the furs.

"There are many times that I long for his gentle touch and the passion of Breidi's youth," I thought.

Breidi and I slept together from the time that he was a small boy until he died. My memory recalled the times when I snuggled him in my arms and kept him warm during the winter nights of our early times together. He enjoyed cold nights when we laid together, on our sides facing each other. His hands cupped my breasts and he scooted down until he could place his face in the space between them. There, he would remain, falling asleep in total comfort.

Fain undressed himself and washed in the warmth of my bath water. He came to bed and kneeled over me. "You are a firm man for the age that you claim," I said. I ran my fingers over his flat stomach and watched his body respond to my petting.

I reached out from the pile of furs. I took Fain's hand and pulled him onto the bed. He kneeled on the bed beside me as I looked over his strong body. His chest was broad and strong, his arms hung at his sides like powerful tree limbs.

I lifted the cover of fur and he crawled under the covers. The warm glow of the lanterns and the luxury of the fox furs against my skin lifted my spirits and filled my mind with peace. My back pain had eased and my mind was relaxed. Fain had performed his soothing touch and made me feel much better.

We fondled each other while we lay, side by side. Our touch took each other to new heights before relaxing and beginning anew. There was nothing about the gentle man that would have kept us from joining had I been willing to, in my condition. For tonight, we would enjoy what we could.

Fain took me to a new height with a small piece of mink. He stroked it along my neck and across my shoulders. I lifted the covers and he pulled the mink between my breasts and over my sensitive nipples.

"Ahhharrg!" I screamed over the ecstasy of the fur's sensation. I caught myself from another outburst and laughed as he took it over my swollen tummy and around my belly button. It tickled, running nerve reflex up and down my spine. "Ahhharrg," I screamed again.

The touch of the mink on my belly produced chicken bumps on my arms and a warm yearning for his touch.

Fain pulled the fur across my inner thighs. The mink traveled back up, on the inside of my legs, across to the other and down. He continued this motion until I took his wrist and begged him to stop. The sensation of the soft fur between my outspread thighs and the warm bath cleared my mind and prepared me for a good night's sleep.

"I can't believe that this is happening to me," he whispered. He rubbed the fur over my face, near my eyes and spoke softly in my ear. "I will always remember the kindness that you showed an old man tonight."

"No one deserves the closeness of a woman more than you do," I said. "A woman looks for the luxury of a man's kindness, not the youthful violence of inexperience."

"Tell me more about your life, Esther. I have heard all of the tales of story tellers, but I have never held the company of a maiden," Fain said.

While he began to tell me his story I ran my hand under the cover and over his belly. I lifted the covers away and began to massage him with a slow even touch. I was attracted to this gentle giant and wanted to relieve him of his self doubt over his abilities to satisfy a woman.

"Well, I began my life at the end of the time that the Christians call, 'the second century.' As I told you, Mother took a Roman General as my Father. She wanted his seed to begin her line of mermaid daughters with the blood of the most powerful mortals of this region. While she was in his camp," I went on. "She did everything that she could to disrupt peace in his camp and stall the erection of the wall. Nothing was going to stop their work, even thought the early Prytens harassed the Romans while it was under construction," I went on.

"What about the Pryten? The Pict?" he asked.

"Maelchon was Mother's second. He was a kind man. Mother and I have many fond memories of living with our native people. We consider the Pryten as our own. Our history in this region originated with them. We lived among them until Maelchon and Breidi were killed, fighting the Romans.

Mother's experience with Pryten attacks on the Romans while she was in their camp helped the Pryten people learn to defeat their foe. The Pryten are a great, peace loving people who have never known peace," I said. "We fear that their decline is near. They will soon be absorbed into the Norse culture and will lose their individual identity, we fear."

"Where will you go next?" he asked.

"Someday, once my child is born, I may return to the western shores of Caledonia or the islands of the Irish Sea," I said. "For now, I will remain here, in the Shetland Islands with you. I thank you for your hospitality and kindness."

I laid my head on Fain's broad chest. My swollen belly lay safe, close to his hips.

I took his hand away from my butt and lifted it to my belly and swollen breasts. Fain's body was warm and comforting.

We lay beside each other as I told him about Breidi, Mother and our lives. He knew about Grandmother, as most Norsemen would.

"She has been seen along the coast of Norway," he said. "Stories about Estella and Norsemen go back for several centuries of seducing men to her rocks where they never returned. Our lore tells us that she took them below to live among sea creatures of the deep sea."

"Not a good place for a human," I volunteered.

"No, they were never seen again."

I nuzzled the nape of his neck with my face and fell into a deep sleep in his arms.

Most of the nights in the Shetlands continued the same routine. We spent many nights enjoying a warm bath and sitting on furs in front of his fire after we left the tavern.

Chapter XXXI

I enjoyed the peaceful surroundings of my host's home. It was confining in its small, one room space but I was able to finish my pregnancy in these peaceful surroundings.

"Tell me about your youth, Fain," I said.

"I was born, here, in the village. My Father was a weapons smith known for his sword craft. His blades are still prized today. Mother worked in her bake shop. She made the high rising yeast loaves that the tavern uses today."

"Those times were more peaceful than today. The pressure on families to find new settlements has increased over the last several years. Their King has levied new taxes that most of them cannot pay and so they slip off into the night and look for new settlement sites. It is a difficult time for natives in Norway. Some have joined Swedes and Danish crews who have sailed east of the Baltic to find sites," he continued.

"Father came here years before I was born. He set up his shop and began to take advantage of the iron and carbon steel that he could get through trading. He made stronger steel in his forge and began to craft the long narrow swords that we see today."

"A crew brought the old marble stone that I have today from the Mediterranean. It has a fine grain .that works with the new steel that I use today. None of these things would have been available in Norway. Too much of their energy is spent trying to feed themselves and survive the long winters. They have little time for crafts like metal fabrication. Those things they have to trade for here and on Orkney," he explained.

Father made swords for Rognvald Vysteinssen and others. Today, I cannot take the time that is involved in making ornamental swords and axes. The demand is too great. Now, crews sail the coast of Britannia pillaging villages looking for trade goods. They need weapons more suitable for their use.

"What about the village? Fain. Has it always been this busy?"

"No. In the beginning there were only a few trade shops. The village did not grow until the demand for supplies going to Norway began to grow."

We laid still, late into the night as he told me about his village and his work. I fell into a deep peaceful sleep in the comfort and safety of the big man's arms.

Fain arranged for a midwife to attend to me when my time came. The birthing went well. I named the child, "Gretchen."

Fain had a house built next to his shop. We had outgrown the one room place. It had space for Gretchen and ample room for our bed, the fireplace and hearth and room for a table and benches. Gretchen liked to spend her days with Fain and I in the shop. She returned to the house when the noise of the clanking metal disturbed her. The noise of the hammer and heavy anvil was more than either of us could be around.

Nights in the tavern passed quickly. Most of the patrons were in a good mood while at the tavern. Few looked for a reason to complain.

I worked my way through the tables carrying double fists of cups, tankards and pitchers performing my serving chores. Tonight, as most nights, the crowd got louder as the night moved on. Eventually their minds turned to the other pursuits that they came to Sven's Inn for. They wanted to "roll in the hay."

Other women took time from their hostess duties to take one of the crewmen upstairs. They returned a short while later, looking as if they had been on a short stroll around the village, dragged by their hair. The girl's partners seldom returned to the tavern floor, having fallen asleep in the hay.

The rest tipped their tankards and drank their mead, ate their portions of smoked fish and mutton, usually spilling large quantities of both on their vests and laps. Nothing interrupted their zeal towards enjoying their few nights on land. At dawn, there were several crewmen remaining in the tavern, slumped onto their plates, tankards still in hand.

They lived like each day was going to be their last. No words were left unspoken, no hunger unfulfilled and no imaginations left untold.

I learned a lot from the Norsemen who came through the village on Shetland and visited Sven's tavern. They were men made coarse and hardened by days and nights on the open seas and the unrelenting, harsh elements of their lives in their homeland. Years later, I often wondered what they would have been like had they lived in a better time or another place. I mused what would have been had the Norsemen of Shetland been allowed to live among the court of my Father's Rome.

Nordic people would become known to be some of the most inventive and organized people of the Euro continent and the isles of Britannia.

Mother said that Finn and Danish sailors had settled near many of the ports in the Baltic Sea. They brought improvements to the populations that they adopted as their own. Harsh times and difficult conditions made them search near and far for better lives. Those that tried to stop them would meet even worse treatment.

News of Olaf's intended take over of Haraldr's kingdom was frequent fare in the tavern. I warned him that his intentions were being repeated in the tavern. He dismissed the matter too easily, I thought. Haraldr's reputation as a brutal king was also spoken freely in the tavern.

"Mother," I said. "You must tell Olaf that words of his plans for overtaking Haraldr's kingdom are spoken freely in the tavern." She did not seem to care what might come of Olaf if Haraldr got wind of his treasonous ways.

The traffic coming from the port, carrying trade goods never ceased. Furs, leather and valuables of all kinds came into the village where they were taken in by merchants and put up for sale or trade. Merchants, craftsmen and artisans of all trades were constantly busy making and selling goods to be sold on Shetland. Much of it went to Nordic crews to be used on expeditions and raids on villages of Briton. They paid for much of these goods with pillaged loot.

The Pictish people of the Shetland village were engaged in more menial labor. Trees were scarce except for a few traces of shrubs in the crags and valleys near the shore, so the village depended on peat to burn and cook. Centuries of felling trees for firewood had deforested Shetland. There were few tree stands within reach of the village. Locals were using dried pet from bogs on the Caledonian mainland for fires as they had for years.

The Pict did the cutting, stacking and drying of the heavy sod fuel. They also did most of the growing and field tending of farm crops. They stayed off to themselves, infrequently coming into one of the merchant stores and shops.

There were several craftsmen with shops near the docks that made replacement oars, sails, sail masts and a host of other seagoing products like fishing nets, harpoon spears points and rope.

Carts were pushed up the hill from shore loading with goods of all kinds and uses. Shetland was a busy place, kept on the move by Nordic ship crews coming and going on a constant basis. Fain's blacksmith business kept him busy, making and repairing weapons and armor. He took two youngsters from the village to help him in the shop.

His large smith shop was an open front enterprise. He worked near the furnace and anvil that stood just inside the overhead cover of the building.

Fain's self doubt did not last long. I sat across his wide hips and watched him enjoy pleasures that he probably had forgotten about. He never failed to respond to my touch. We played like newlywed youngsters until late into the morning.

We laid in the fur covers at night after we satisfied his growing appetite for lovemaking.

I watched him work swords and battle axe heads as his helpers produced hinges, oar locks and other domestic metal products. The assault on my sensitive ears from the clanking and banging noises was nearly as much I could stand.

I enjoyed Fain's company and benefited from his generous offer to keep me while I was still pregnant, but I could not stay long. The noise was too much for my ears. Smoke and suet filled the air around his shop. I found it difficult to breathe and unpleasant on my skin.

I saw Fain's helpers as I visited him for his mid day meal. Both youngsters stayed away from me when I came around. Fain had not told them about me. Their inexperience did not supply them with enough answers to make them comfortable around me, I supposed.

Great quantities of whale blubber came ashore in huge chunks from whaling ships. It was cut up in smaller portions and dumped into the large cauldron at the oil merchants shed. He rendered the smelly fat into oil that we all used for lamps. Another merchant made lamps out of brass or copper and his wife made wicks from wool rope.

Most of the shop keepers, merchants and tradesmen had wives who lived with them in the village. I noticed that children, especially boys, began working with their parents at a very early age. In the way of Norse villages, boys were often apprenticed to their uncle or another family member to learn a skill. That was the method that brought Fain's two helpers.

Nordic girls occasionally worked with a baker or weaver but most of what they needed to learn would be taught in the home by their mothers and aunts. They were often married to the son of a family friend and remained in the extended family by the time they reached their twelfth birthday. Many died during the ordeal of their first child birth.

Among the Pryten, life was much simpler. The variety of goods and services of the Shetland village were not available in their home settlements.

There was more leisure time and children were not used as apprentices in their stores. Life was difficult for Nordic people and I came to respect their need to explore the world looking for more hospitable settlements for their families. There was no time for a child to roam the fields and shores as Breidi and I had done. Nordic children did not have a childhood of any sort.

I heard more mention of Olaf's planned treason. I spoke to him one evening.

"Olaf," I said. "Your men boast about your intentions to dethrone Haraldr. You need to tell them to abandon such talk. It could easily make its way back to Norway by way of anyone willing to take money from Haraldr in exchange for news about you. They speak too frequently about your intentions in the tavern. It is common knowledge."

Olaf would not pay much attention to my warning. I heard several people in the tavern talk about being recruited to join Olaf in a planned invasion of his capitol. I thought that such talk was ill advised and I continued to warn Olaf as time went on.

I was approaching my time of delivery of Breidi's second child. Each day brought me closer. I stayed in Fain's house as my delivery time neared. Mother insisted that I remain close by and make my needs known to the women who tended to Olaf and his house. I decided to stay away from Mother's two daughters.

Chapter XXXII

After Gretchen's birth, I remained in the comfort and company of Fain's house. I felt safe with him and I owed a great deal to him. I sensed that I needed a powerful man to protect me from village curiosity and rumors that were told about Mother and I. He was always there to protect me.

Mother had the village chief to watch over her. I knew that Fain would do the same for me.

Fain was a wise and seasoned man. His wisdom provided a peaceful existence on the Shetlands. He knew how to avoid problems with villagers and crewmen by minding to his own and avoiding trouble. He was at peace with his age and position in the community. I sensed that he had nothing to prove to anyone and he found peace in that.

Olaf did not seem to mind having a few more women around his house. He encouraged me to remain in his house, but I had no intention to stay with him while his treasonous plans were common talk around the village. I felt that I might expose Gretchen to harms way if I was a known resident in his house.

He never quite got over how Mother and I looked the same age. Since we do not age past our twentieth year, his perception was actually accurate.

I tried not to enter the big house if Olaf were home. I did not feel comfortable around him. His carousing ways kept me alert and I found it difficult to rest while his mind sought new opportunities of conquest whether it be a new woman or a King's realm. The images that I saw in his mind told me that his curiosity could lead to trouble.

Fain was happy to let Gretchen and I stay with him. His love of the little black eyed infant showed through his smile, partially obscured behind his thick red beard. We spent hours, by the warmth of the fire as he bounced Gretchen on his knee and swung her over his head.

Harbor traffic in the Shetland port was heavy with ship traffic. The heavy Viking cargo ships that they called a "*knarr*," came through the port with loads of pillaged goods from the coasts of Britannia, Wales and Ireland. I watched them arrive in port, loaded with lumber, iron, flower and other goods as well as the loot that they pillaged from monasteries and villages.

Fain took Gretchen and I to the port one day to meet a cargo ship that made the Shetland harbor the day before.

"You will meet my old friend Othar," he said.

When we arrived Othar's crew was unloading giant sacks of flour and barley from the bog knar. I had seen as many of these cargo vessels as I had the warships that they called the *drakkar*. This ship was nearly twenty meters long and much wider than the smaller warship. Its sides were higher and there were more oars and a bigger mast.

They loaded the grain on a horse drawn cart in preparation for the haul up hill to the village and the dry market. I held Gretchen in my arms as we watched the activity around the port.

"Othar! Fain said. "Welcome to Shetland. I see Odenn has kept you safe, old friend."

"Yes he has Master, Fain. And who are these beautiful creatures?" he asked. "Is the little one a product of my old friend's loins?"

"I wish she were," Fain said. "I would be glad to have such a beautiful child to cherish in late season of my years. She is a beautiful one, is she not, friend?"

"Oh yes. And this must be her Mother."

"This is Esther," Othar, and her young daughter, Gretchen. Esther has been with me for the last few years and I have cherished her company and that of her young one," Fain said.

"Well, I will say that I have not seen you so young at heart and lean as a rail since we were kids in Gotland," Othar said. "She must be keeping you young, you old tyrant," Othar said.

"What a beautiful, black eyed creature you are," Othar said to me. No wonder no one has heard from my old friend. You have been lying in your bed with this beautiful creature and who could blame you."

"Othar took my hand and brought it to his lips. Then he took Gretchen's hand and kissed it, as well. You can certainly pick them, old friend. They are beautiful."

"So, you are Esther?" Othar asked.

"Yes, I am the daughter of Sarah and granddaughter of Estella of your Scandinavian shores," I said.

"Ahhhh, I see the resemblance now. I saw your grandmother many months ago as we left port where she was sitting, protecting our port from her perch on the rocks near the harbor," Othar said. "I knew that you were not one of the native women of Shetland. You are much too fair. Don't tell your Mother, but you are even more beautiful than she is."

Othar took Gretchen's hand and bent to kiss it. Gretchen hissed and tried to withdraw her hand. She looked at me for guidance. I smiled and said, "Gretchen, this is a friend of Fain's. It is OK, he just wants to kiss your hand."

Gretchen relaxed and Othar kissed her tiny hand and smiled. Gretchen smiled at the funny man who wanted to kiss her hand. It became a game. She began to tease Othar by offering her hand and then withdrawing it as he tried to kiss her hand.

"She is a beautiful child. Who is her sire?" he asked.

"She is the daughter of Breidi, the late King of the Highland Pryten people," I said.

"Breidi is a son of Maelchon, the former King of Wales, is he not?" Othar asked.

"Yes. That is true. Maelchon and Breidi both gave their lives fighting off the Romans," I said.

"My good friend Fain is a fortunate man," he said.

"Fain, you haven't found a beautiful maiden for me, have you?" Othar asked.

"No friend. I am afraid I could only find one for myself. Perhaps you can hold on for a few years and see if young Gretchen would be interested in entertaining an old man," Fain jested.

Othar told us that he had traveled to the Iberian Peninsula and the north African coast. "A good day's sail is one hundred and fifty Roman miles," Othar said. "We load the *knarr* to the gunwales with cargo and make the long trip to *Dubhlinn*, where we have made an outpost on the River Poddle."

"In Dubhlinn?" Fain asked.

"Yes, friend. The fighting is nearly over with the native people around the port at the mouth of the River Poddle and we have built a settlement for trade. I usually unload at Dubhlinn and return to Iberia or the southern shores of Britannia. The fleet in Orkney makes the trip from Dubhlinn to Orkney or the Shetlands.

"Come, Othar. Join Esther, Gretchen and I for a tankard at the inn. We can sit and listen to you tell your tall, impossible tales of your stealth and bravery while we supp," Fain said.

"We walked up the hill towards the inn as Othar's crew finished unloading. He reached for Gretchen. She recoiled away from his reach. "It is good," I said. Gretchen let the big Captain take her from me but she did not take her eyes off of me as we entered the tavern.

"You are a beautiful babe, young Gretchen. I fear I grow too old to hold much hope of waiting until you mature," he jested. "Do you have an older sister, *meine liebchen?*

Gretchen looked at me. I shook my head, "No." She turned to Othar and shook her head, and said, "No,"

"Ahhh! By the eyes of Odenn, I cannot bare such bad news," he jested. Gretchen laughed at his teasing and crawled back up on his lap, where she stayed content while we visited with Othar. She insisted that Othar hold her tiny hand and bring it to his cheek when she demanded.

"So how does it go in Dubhlinn and the southern shores?" Fain asked.

"Dubhlinn allows us to shuttle our commerce back and forth to the isles without having to travel the entire distance on our own. The Britannic King can not defend his shores. We have our way with his shores and monasteries along the coast. I fear that we have nearly drained them of their value, now, but at one time we took what we wanted without a fight. We have returned to Dubhlinn with young maidens from Maelchon's old domain and the southern shores of Britannia. We get a good return for the wenches, if we can get them there without having them mauled by our own crews," Othar laughed.

"The gold and silver are gone, but even Britannia produces a new crop of young wenches every year," he laughed.

"What about the Mediterranean and African shores. I believe that those kingdoms are rich in gold and silver," Fain asked.

"That is true, old friend. Both have loads of gold coins for the taking, the problem is that, unlike the lackeys of Britannia, they fight to keep them. With a large raid, of many ships, we could not take gold from either the Roman Empire or the African coast," he explained.

"For now, I am relegated to hauling grain to Dubhlinn and the western coast of Caledonia, near the mouth of the River Clyde. We trade grain for distilled spirits at Dumbarton. We get a good trade in the south for it. Seems we can not get enough of the distilled spirits on board to satisfy the trade in the south," Othar said.

"How is trade in the village?" Othar asked.

"I have more trade for knives and swords than I can possibly meet. I have three apprentices in the shop making knives and axe blades. That allows me to tend to the sword business. I simply can not meet the need," Fain explained.

"Olaf takes most of my trade for knives and axes with him when he sails south, along the eastern coast and across the channel to the coast of the Franks, near the mouth of the River Seine. He returns with ample loads of goods from the Franks. He brings back goat skin bags of wine and the dry spirit that they call, 'sack,' Fain explained.

"Seems the world is out to make us a bunch of lazy drunks," Fain jested.

"T'is true, old friend. "If we could make enough wine, barley spirit and mead, we could be wealthy men," Fain said.

"That is true as well, friend, assuming that we did not drink it all ourselves, that is. There is little trade for our old swill, mead in southern markets," Othar said. "They have wine from the Franks and barley spirits from the highlands of Caledonia and the old Dal Riata Empire. No one wants to drink the slop that we have survived on for so many generations."

"I remember being told of a Sea Maiden and child off of the shores, adjacent to the Roman camp, many, many years back," Othar said. "I believe that it must have been your Mother that they speak of," Othar said.

"They tell a tale of a Sea Maiden, named Sarah, who was part of the Pictish legend from the old times along the Roman wall," Othar continued. "Was that your Mother, Sarah?" he asked.

"Yes. Mother lived with the Roman General charged with constructing the wall. He was my Father," I explained. "Mother worked against the General's interest in building the wall and their attempts of driving the Pictish people away."

"She has become part of the Pictish legend," he said. "She left the General and we moved in with Maelchon in one of the Pict strongholds of the eastern highlands, I believe," Othar said.

"You are familiar with our kind, I see," I said.

"Of course. We have lived along the shores for many generations. You and your Mother are legends in these isles."

"Where will you spend the night, old friend?" Fain asked.

"That depends if I can find one of Esther's sisters," Othar jested.

I raised my hand and waved at Helga and gestured for her to come to the table.

"This is Helga, Othar. She is as close to a sister as I can get, unless you wanted to roll in the hay with our Mistress, Jettie, over there," I said.

"No, thank you," Othar said.

He turned his attention to Helga. He looked her up and down like he was buying a horse instead of entertainment for one night. "Helga, are you, sweet *Liebchen*?"

"Yes. That is me," Helga said.

I leaned my back against Fain's chest and pulled his arm around me and I watched. Othar stood to face Helga while he continued to check her over. He gave her a hug while reaching around behind her to grab her backside and pull her in to him.

"She will do just fine," he said. Othar took her hand and led her up the ladder to the loft. "More cushion for the pushin'," he said as he lead Helga up to the loft.

My nights were spent in the gentle man's arms, under the luxurious fur covers of his bed. Gretchen slept on a pallet of furs that Fain made for her in the corner of the room.

I took great pride in rewarding the gentle giant for his hospitality, protection and his patience while I carried Gretchen. I had grown quite fond of Fain.

We made love and I listened to his stories about his Father, the Shetland Islands and the Nordic way of life.

Fain had more life left in him than he first believed. He was a tender mate. Like his fellow Norsemen, he must have recognized that he too was living on borrowed time and if he was to experiment in new pursuits, he needed to get on with it. We laughed and rolled on the bed until late each morning. By the time we had been together for a few seasons Fain had forgotten the apologies that he had made about his old age.

He did not seem to mind being late at his shop. Most of the village knew about us and I thought that they may have allowed Fain some leeway at this point in his life.

Gretchen stayed by our side. She laughed when we laughed. Her first years were spent in the peaceful confines of Fain's small home. She was protected and cared for and that was all that I cared about for the time being. I wish that I had met Fain a generation or two ago. I would have been glad to have taken his seed in my womb and produced a fine son to take his role as sword smith.

Most of the village women avoided us. Some of the women in the tavern let me be, however, the wives of other tradesmen were not so willing to give us freedom to move around the village. Women avoided speaking to us. We always caught their eye, but we were never engaged in conversation with them.

"We are bred to attract the most eligible men," Mother had told me, long ago. "How could we do that if we looked our ages? We would not have our choice if we looked like most of these village women," she had explained. "We do not need the care of mortal females. We only want the seed of their best men. They will have to do with the left overs."

"Between us, we have taken the village chieftain and the most eligible bachelor around. They surely can not be expected to take that sitting down," Mother reasoned

Mother has to be six, maybe seven hundred years old. Even Olaf wouldn't have taken Mother's bait if she looked her age. We are immortal, and so is our youth.

Anyway, Olaf was physically attracted to both of us, and I knew that I would not be able to continue living with Mother as long as Olaf could not seem to resist coming near me. That was all the more reason to stay with Fain.

Mother never caught on to Olaf's roaming attention. At least she did not catch on that I know of. Perhaps it did not matter to her. She had what she wanted.

She was more involved with Asta and Fierra, and spent very little time entertaining Olaf. However, she became pregnant, again after we arrived in Olaf's village. She probably felt that she had what she needed from Olaf and did not need to attend to his needs any further. She may not have cared if he did find his way to my bed, but that was not in my plans.

Aside from his constant carousing and wandering attention, Olaf was a good man. He took good care of Mother and her brats. They never wanted for anything. They had the biggest and by far, the warmest living space in the village. The women, below, kept the peat fires burning. The heat rising from the fires drifted upward and kept her chamber warm and comfortable.

Life with Olaf was good for Mother and my sisters for a while. Then, it turned very bad, very quickly.

Chapter XXXIII

One early morning, a fleet of twenty warships came ashore while Mother and I visited. A hundred or more warriors poured overboard onto the beach and up the hill towards the village. Screaming warriors, carrying battle axes and broad swords descended upon us as we lounged in the morning.

Leading the band, was none other than King Haraldr. Being a peaceful village, lead by a Viking chieftain, some would never have expected to see this. I had.

Within a short time, villagers were chased inside their shops or away from the village. Haraldr and his men pounded on Olaf's door until they broke in. Olaf arose from his bed and ran down the stairs in his night shirt only to come face to face with Haraldr.

I watched from the vantage point of the upper chamber doorway as two warriors took Olaf by the arms and held him in front of their fair haired ruler.

"I, King Haraldr, charge you, Olaf with tax evasion and treason of my kingdom," the King said.

"You and your villagers owe back taxes. I have come to collect," he said.

"We owe you nothing," Olaf declared.

"The Shetland Isles are part of my kingdom, as is the old village on our mainland to which you have avoided paying taxes. You cannot flee from your responsibilities by sailing into the night and taking root elsewhere," Haraldr went on.

"If you refuse to pay your back taxes, I shall have no alternative but to invoke punishment for your tax oversight and your plans to rebel against me," Haraldr said.

"Further, news of your planned rebellion against me has reached my kingdom. Punishment for treason is death to the traitor."

"You hear the tales of fools," Olaf said.

"You are the fool, to think that you can refuse to pay your due. I am told that you plan an uprising against me," Haraldr said. "What do you say to these charges?" Haraldr asked.

I saw, Olaf trying to escape the grasp of the two warriors that held him. I ran to Mother's bed. "They are going to take Olaf," I said. "We need to escape, if we can," I said.

Having only the single stairway that led from our top floor room, we had no way of avoiding Haraldr and his men. They stood at the bottom of the stairs, blocking our only way out.

"Here they come," I said. Mother and I watched from the top of the stairs. Three soldiers entered our chamber and found us all huddled around the doorway. I rushed back to gather Gretchen.

"Take them," one ordered.

I was so upset at being caught up in Olaf's business. I had anticipated this raid but I had not been careful enough to avoid becoming involved. I should have remained in Fain's home. I knew that I had made a big mistake. Now, all we could do is fight our way out and escape the King and his guards.

"One took Mother by the arm, and another took me as I held Gretchen in my arms. Asta and Fierra clung to Mother's night shirt. They were making a god awful racket.

The leader of the two soldiers reached for Asta. She released a shrill that caused him to step back. The little she devil attacked his leg with her talons and teeth. Then she ripped his leggings open and tore his boots as she worked her way up his leg and onto his mid section with her teeth and claws. She ripped away strips of fabric with her talons and finally sunk her teeth into the man's thigh. He screamed while he saw the child ripping into his leg.

I was still being held by one of the soldiers. While I considered my escape options the leader of the guards tried to pull Asta off of his chest. She lashed out and clawed him, sinking her teeth into his arm. Fierra hissed and growled at his feet while taking bites out of his toes. He became so agitated and alarmed at the pair of she creatures that he began to yell for help. He kicked his leg and launched Fierra against the wall. She crumpled to the floor and began to hiss like an abused cat.

Mother became enraged with the treatment of her whelp. She easily broke loose from the grasp of her captor. Neither one of us could have been held by a single man. We had remained calm and were content in trying to escape without killing one of the King's guards. After the mistreatment of her young, Mother had seen enough to bring her full force to play on the unfortunate trio.

Out of the relative normal appearing woman being restrained by the guards came an enraged she monster. She stood menacingly over her quarry slashing her talons as she began to retaliate. The monster roared, bearing her shark teeth while she grabbed the first guard. Her movements were sure and quick as she lashed out. She cut her abductors to shreds and slammed them against the stone block walls like rotten melons.

She pushed another backwards. He struck the wall with the back of his head. He thought he had Mother restrained. She struck him with a sickening thud and popping sound of broken bone and torn cartilage. He slid down the wall to the floor where he remained silent. The trail of blood smeared down the wall made it clear that he would not be a further problem.

I heard the other soldier utter something in his native tongue. I did not understand his garbled words, but his meaning was clear. It was shock. The monster in Mother had him suspended from the floor, lashing at him with her teeth.

Mother held him by the throat, just under his chin and held him off of the floor. I was still being held by the third man whose grasp weakened as he saw his comrades being molested by a force that he had never witnessed before.

Mother walked to the doorway, still holding the big warrior from the floor by a grip of his throat. She released a shrill that surely was heard by the entire village as she pulled the man's head from his shoulders and threw both pieces down the spiral stairway.

My captor let me loose and tried to squeeze by Mother at the door. She took him by the head and tried to cram him into the narrow archer slit opening in the wall. It was not wide enough, but it did not stop Mother from shoving most of him into the hole anyway.

We gathered Gretchen, Asta and Fierra and began our escape down the narrow stairway. Asta and Fierra were still hissing and growling.

Olaf, the King and two others stood at the base of the stairway. Haraldr stood in shock. Haraldr released Olaf but he stood in the King's face, laughing at him. Olaf continued sticking his big red finger in the King's face, laughing over the expression on the King's face. Olaf's guests had made a mess of the King's men and he was in near shock.

I saw the King draw his sword as if he was about to face Mother. She went down the stairs. Mother released another of her shrills. The King dropped his sword as he placed his hands over his ears to muffle the shriek of Mother's call.

Olaf laugh all the harder. He stuck his finger in Haraldr's face once again and laughed at the exasperated King who stood terrified. He held his hands over his ears. Haraldr could take the insult no longer.

Haraldr drew his dagger and plunged it deep into Olaf's round belly. Olaf coughed and spurted blood in the King's face before he let out his last laugh. The big Viking chief crumpled to the floor at the King's feet.

We watched from the outside entry as the King fled through the door and down, through the village.

Chapter XXXIV

Not having further reason to remain on Shetland, Mother slipped away to the shore and began her way towards the Orkney Islands. There was no reason for Mother and her young to remain on the Shetlands. She now carried Olaf's child. She had what she wanted and did not want to risk her young in the event of a fall out over Olaf's attack on the King.

Gretchen was big enough to survive our escape but I could not want to leave Fain without expressing my gratitude for the gentle years that we spent together.

The entire village must have been witness to a sight that many were not capable of understanding. Mother's identity had surely been made by most. It was time for her to leave and let Haraldr have Shetland.

I intended to stay a night or two with Fain to see what disruption Mother's battle had caused in the village. I had not planned on leaving Fain. I did not want to run off before I had a chance to thank the big hearted giant for his hospitality and protection.

I waited in Fain's home for the remainder of the day. I did not want to chance being seen or involve Fain by appearing in his shop on the first floor. As dusk arrived, Fain came through the door.

"Ah," he said as he saw me sitting by the fire. "I heard about the ruckus at Olaf's place. I was afraid that you were involved in it."

"I am afraid that I could not have avoided it. I went to Olaf's house this morning to visit with Mother when Haraldr crashed through the door and tried to arrest all of us. They killed Olaf. Mother and her daughters have fled south west towards Orkney. I can not stay much longer. I need to leave the Shetlands as well," I said.

He had a piece of mutton and some bread that he brought home. He offered a piece to me, but I was not really a mutton fan. The grease upset my stomach. I seldom ate meat.

After Fain finished his meal I took my shirt and outfit off. I threw them in the fire. I would not need them and I did not want to compromise Fain in my involvement in Mother's treatment of Haraldr's men. I washed the suet and grime off of Fain, using water from the pot as he had done for me the first night. When I finished, he took his turn and bathed me with the lamb wool cloth.

When we were finished I crawled under his fur covers and put Gretchen in the corner on a pile of furs of her own. Fain joined me in bed. I held the big man and kissed his broad face.

He pulled the white fox fur from the bed and wrapped it over my back. "This is for you to remember me by," he said. The fur was luxurious in its softness. I would treasure it forever.

I took his arm away and crawled on top of him once more. My face nuzzled against his neck. His heavy arms spread across my back, penning my chest to his face. I struggled under the weight of his arms. Finally I rose to my accustomed sitting position. He smiled as I guided him to my moist acceptance between my thighs. Gently, we began a rocking motion. I watched the expression of uninhibited pleasure cross his face.

He took my breasts in his hands and pulled them to his face as we put a rhythm to our anxious movement, meeting each other at the peak of our thrusts until we were spent.

As we lay beside each other, laughing about our physical appetites, he said, "I am going to miss you greatly, sweet Esther of the sea. You have brought new life to my late years and I will pass on someday with a smile on my face that was place there by your love," he said.

When we were both spent, I started to tell Fain how he had been there for us, he had fallen into a deep sleep before I had a chance. A broad smile stayed on his lips as he drifted away.

After several minutes, I, too, finally came to a deep slumber.

I awoke during the night. Gretchen was still in the corner sitting upon on the pile of covers. I picked her up from her pallet and wrapped her in the winter fox fur that Fain had given us and we slipped out through the door. I was not happy leaving Fain but I needed to protect the three of us by moving on. Villagers would be pressed to report us to Haraldr if we remained in the village.

I had no intention in getting Fain involved. We slipped out through the dense night air and began our journey.

Gretchen and I arrived in Orkney and found Mother and her brats on the rocks off of the shore from a village on an Orkney isle. She was settled safely from the events in Shetland that the rocks off shore from Orkney provided.

Mother had two daughters to rear and another in her womb. I needed time to raise Gretchen, so we settled among the rocks and basked in our momentary independence. I would have enjoyed several more years with Fain had the circumstances been different. He would have made a good and proud sire for a child had he been younger. I enjoyed my time with him and forced myself to remember him in the setting that we were given.

The years in the tavern with Fain looking over me from his corner seat by the fire were among my most treasured memories. I will settle with that.

The years that followed were uneventful for us, once we escaped the problem with Haraldr. Those same years were riddled with turmoil for the Pictish people. A succession of one king after another tried to unite the Picts, the Dal Riata kingdom and the Scotti people. No man seemed to be able to address the separate issues of the Picts, the Irish and the Scots so that they could live peacefully in a collective kingdom.

As a creature who lived off of the strengths of mortal leaders, it certainly was a good time for Mother to concentrate on her young and not on those who struggled for power on shore. Nothing seemed certain at that time and no one leader stood out with the strengths of Father,

Maelchon and Breidi. That did not stop Mother from taking men from the village on the big Isle of The Orkneys.

She had her time with the village Mayor and a few of the crewmen who came to Orkney to do business. There were several Pictish families who lived on Orkney. Their sod covered, stone houses were similar to the winter settlement used by the Wolf Clan. With the single doorway on the leeward side of the house, the winter winds whipped over the mound without reaching the inhabitants.

Orkney operated a lot like Shetland. The era of the Vikings was in full bloom at this time. The coastal villages of the Briton, Scotti, Irish, the Francs and several others all lived in fearful anticipation of marauding Vikings coming ashore to loot and kill at random.

The Pict of Orkney had lived through a period of fear of Viking war ships long ago. They no longer suffered from such invasions, but lived in peace with the crews who shared their islands.

The village tavern and inn was quite similar to the one on Shetland. It was operated by a single innkeeper and overseen by a matron who tried to keep her girls moving among the tables of flesh hungry patrons.

The Viking rage at this time was boundless. As new kingdoms took in the expanse of Dal Riata and rose and fell in the region, the Vikings found themselves having to fight battles for lands and settlements that they had already won under the previous rulers. Things were not going well for Vikings, at all while Dal Riata was in a constant state of flux as its King asserted influence of his own.

Orkney held villages of Picts who aimed to flee the turmoil in the Caledonia highlands being generated by Vikings warring with Alpin and his son Kenneth Mac Alpin, the successor to the new King of Scotland.

Kenneth Mac Alpin led the Scots of Dal Riata to free themselves from Pictish domination. Mother kept a keen eye on Mac Alpin who was being accused of shameful deeds against the Picts as he followed his Father's lead. The younger Alpin struggled to take Caledonia out of the hands of resident Pict leaders and take them into his wider plans for a combined Dal Riata. He intended to erase the Pictish culture and eliminate the Christian Pictish Church both led by Oengus II, the source of Alin's rebellion.

The power struggle that followed took what little peace and freedom that the Pict had gained since the death of Breidi and the evacuation of the Roman Empire and its army from the highlands.

Mac Alpin's intention was set Dal Riata free from Pictish Oengus's domination and establish his Scottish own rule over the Picts. The Pict, once again were stretched too thin with rebellions of Scots in the south and Viking incursions in the North.

The port on the main Orkney Isle was active with Viking war ships teamed with Captains and crews anxious to fight for lands that they had once held without challenge.

Village merchants tried to flow merchandise through Orkney like it had on Shetland.

Viking ships arrived with loads of cargo for trading and departed nearly empty. They brought pillaged goods to Orkney to trade for weapons that they needed to fight Mac Alpin. There was little being produced on the island at the time. Merchants were too busy feeding fabricated goods to Vikings who kept the harbor humming with activity.

The strong arm of Haraldr had extended all of the way to Orkney in his time. Taxes for doing business in Orkney continued, beyond his time and into the reign of his son, to be too burdensome for most merchants. Blacksmith goods, livestock, grain, fabric and furs were all taxed heavily.

Native Orkney Islanders resented the intrusion from Norway, but were not in a position to demand anything. They did not see themselves as Norwegian subjects and did all that they could to avoid charging and paying taxes.

We watched from afar as Viking war ships arrived in Orkney following raiding expeditions in England, France or southern Scotland. They offloaded large bags containing loot that they carried into the village.

The period that would be called the Viking era by future kings of the Franco and Anglo Empire, was in full swing. It was a time when the whole of the Euro continent and the Isles lived in fear of the sight of sleek ships coming to shore, gorged with warriors carrying axes, spears and broadswords.

I often left Gretchen with Mother so that I could visit the village and learn more about what went on in Orkney. I did not work as a servant in one of the many inns and taverns in the village like I had on Shetland. I was no longer pregnant and did not have much of an excuse to avoid entertaining men in the hay lofts above the taverns. The constant turmoil of events in Scotland kept Viking crews agitated like a nest of enraged hornets. Most had lost their free living exuberance to the alarming events of the time.

I watched many of the Viking crews bring their loot into one of the inns and trade it for coins. There was never an exchange of taxes and this enterprise was operated out of sight of the Norway's new King, Hakon, "The Good," the younger son of Haraldr, the first King of a united Norway. Hakon needed income to man and supply his army and the vast expanse f his early empire.

In the early days of our time near Orkney, much of the loot being traded came from Monasteries along the coasts or in the land of the Francs. There were ornamental challises, plates, cups, crosses in gold or silver being traded for coins as well as goods and supplies. Viking crews were on a rampage. Agitated by the events in Scotland and the Scots of the south, Mother and I knew that we needed to move on. The calamity of everyday life on Orkney was no place to raise our young.

All villages and monasteries along the coasts of western Europe became eventual targets for Viking crews. I heard them talking to merchants and inn keepers, out of sight of Hakon's men, about their benefit of their shallow draft boats being able to navigate rivers and streams, far into the Euro continent. No village was safe from their aggravated, plundering reach.

Gretchen grew up in the midst of this activity near the shore of Orkney with Asta and Fierra. We watched the ships coming and going and tried to bask on the sun drenched rocks during the short Summer seasons. Asta was nearing her twentieth season and was ready to begin her life among the mortals. Gretchen and Fierra watched as she sang the ballads of another time to crews who entered the harbor.

Gretchen and I began to anticipate the day when we would leave Orkney and find a new home, away from the chaos that had taken over this once peaceful Pictish isle. I often longed for the days with Fain in Shetland.

As Asta tried to absorb the over zealous instructions from Mother, Gretchen and I knew that Asta would be left to ply her magic on Orkney when Mother took Fierra and returned to the Eastern coast.

Gretchen and I moved on towards Dumbartonshire and the castle on the rock.

Near the mouth of the River Clyde stood a huge rock with a small fortress at its base. This was the castle of the Strathclyde Governor's domain. There was a village of Scotti-Pictish people who lived their lives in the shadow of Strathclyde and his foreboding castle.

He had defended his land against Roman invaders and Viking plunder by using the rock as an escape route. When danger came, the Governor and his subjects scaled the steep rock face and took refuge on its relative safety.

The diligent population of the village that they called Dumbartonshire worked like protective ants around the grounds, in the nearby village and up the River Clyde toward the village of Glasgow.

We spent months on end near the friendly harbor and passed the time watching the busy traffic of a life built around shipping and the making of Scottish barley malt whisky. I knew that we would not linger long but my plans were move forward significantly, when, one day I spotted a Merrow, sitting on an outcropping of rocks near the shore.

I took Gretchen to meet her first Merrow. We approached the merman as he sat and drank from a bottle of the fine local whisky. There was a case of bottles hidden in a crevice. Half of them appeared to be empty. It took no imagination to see why the fat he-creature found comfort in Dumbartonshire.

"Good day, Merrow," I said.

"And to you Miss," he said. "And to you young Princess," he said to Gretchen, who took up position behind my back.

"What is your name, sweet Princess," he asked Gretchen.

"Gretchen," she answered from the safety of her place at the base of my fluke.

"What is your name?" Gretchen asked.

"Why, I am Marvin the Merrow, Prince of the western shores and the River Clyde, at your service," he said. He dipped his funnel hat and tried to bend at what should have been his waist.

"Marvin, is it?" I asked.

"Yes, Miss, the name is Marvin. I have been near these shores for many generations. I do well here. The villagers feed me and we get along just fine," he said.

"Do you intend to stay in this region, then?" I asked, fully expecting to be told that he was. "Why would he leave?" I asked myself.

"Yes. I have no reason to leave. Like I said, they take care of me and I bring fortune to them during the fishing season. It must be an even exchange, or they would not encourage me to remain," he said.

I thought, "They feed you and keep you drunk so that you do not, somehow, wander ashore and molest their daughters." I immediately regretted thinking that because I soon realized that he had read my mind, as Merrows sometimes do.

They may be lazy and slovenly but their minds are often at least as keen as our own. I knew that I had stepped into a barnyard full of smelly cow piles. "Step lightly," I told myself.

"As for your concern about their daughters, I have my own harem and have no need for mortal women," he said. "Come, my dears," he said.

Three of the worst ugly smitten faces that I have ever seen, appeared on mermaids who came upon the rock behind Marvin. "These are my three Princesses of the deep," he said.

They were extremely homely. Gretchen retook her position, behind me. I placed a reassuring hand on her shoulder. The forms of Marvin's three maidens were grossly misshapen and more closely resembled barley bloated highland cattle than they did semi-humans. They all had his mead and whisky distended bellies from over-libation.

One came closer to him and sat by his side, drooling in anticipation of his attention. He raised his slimy nose and whiffed the air like a highland bull in search of his favorite cow in estrus.

That was enough. We needed to escape this assault on our senses. "Well, yes, nice to have met you Marvin," I said. "Enjoy," I said, and was not sure why I did. Enjoy what?

Chapter XXXV

Gretchen and I soon left the shores off of Dumbarton and leisurely made our way, west, towards the big island between the Isle of the Pict and the land of the old Scotti people.

It was here that we spent our days while Gretchen grew into her own. We spent hours while I told her the stories of my beginnings with Mother in the times of the Romans.

We were near this isle when Mother asked me to come back to the east coast of Caledonia and find the Viking Chief Rollo. After a looting Lindisfarne and stopping in the Shetlands they arrived here. I had left Gretchen here to watch the settlement as I followed Mother's wish.

A month after I saw the ship pass my rock and sail back to Norway to advise the old village that Rollo had found a location for a new settlement, Gretchen saw a fleet of four ships in the far distance make their way to Rollo's small harbor.

Gretchen and I watched as the ships passed us and made their way into the small protective harbor that Rollo had found weeks before.

Women with small children, men carrying tools and supplies all came off of the transport ships moments after they ran their crafts up on the shore. We watched as Rollo came to the shore and greeted them. Many stood near the shore taking in the beauty of their new land.

The hills were covered with lush green grasses, the waves broke on the rocks of shore and drifted their way into the harbor and washed upon the shore in a gentle, repetitive rhythm.

While I watched the people, Gretchen had her eye on a young man that walked proudly beside Rollo. "Mother," Gretchen said, "Who is the young man with Rollo? I have watched him while you were away. I like his smile and eagerness to learn from his master."

"That is Knut," I said. "I met him in Shetland. He was assigned to watch the ships while Rollo went into the village for food and lodging. He is a handsome young man, isn't he?" I asked.

"Yes, he is," Gretchen answered.

"He is a fine young man and will do well as he grows under the care of his Prince," I said. "He is a little bit young for too much interest," I said.

Rollo put his workers to the tasks at hand. New rock homes went up in a circle around a larger center longhouse. A smoke house for meats and fish, a metal smith's shed, a weaver and a few other building went up in a short time.

I watched with interest as Rollo led his villagers towards completing their tasks. He was a fine specimen of a man and I began to take an interest in him. He was bigger than most men I had ever seen, except for Fain and maybe Olaf.

It was time to find a new mate and I had my mind set on this gentle giant. Time was wasting.

Gretchen would do well on her own. I suspected that she would take Knut as her first mate. I was not overly concerned. I knew that Knut would take good care of her.

Small fishing boats passed our rock during the following days. Fishermen brought in catches of cod as well as herring that they netted off shore. In the beginning, we slipped under the rocks when they went by. As time past, we made our presence known. We lowered our heads in the bashful way of a supposedly innocent sea maiden as they went by. They saw us and it was not long before Rollo was sent out to investigate.

Gretchen and I watched the big chief, leave Knut on the shore while he climbed into a boat and rowed out to meet us.

"Fair maidens," he called. "May I approach?" he asked.

"Yes, mighty warrior. Come," I said.

Rollo pulled the boat up on the rocks and came to sit near us. "I am Rollo, son of Rognvald of the Vysteinssen clan of Norway," he said. "We met in Shetland."

"Yes, we did," I said. "I am Esther, daughter of Sarah and granddaughter of Estella of your Nordic coastlands. Yes, we did once meet in Shetland. Mother sent me to follow you and your crew to see where you would settle. I was with you on Lindisfarne and followed you to Shetland and on to this isle," I said.

"Yes, I remember that you sat with Knut, on the shore," he said.

"I meant no harm Prince Rollo, and I am sure that Knut told me nothing that he should not have," I assured him. "We have made a habit of following the progress of the notable from the region. Knut would not tell me as much about your intentions as I wanted."

"This is my daughter Gretchen," I said. "Gretchen stayed behind watching over your new settlement while I was away. She has eyes for young Knut," I said.

"Knut is a fine young warrior. He will be a good catch for any woman someday," he said. He watched Gretchen climb up on the rock and take her place beside me.

She was a petite picture of beauty. Her striking black hair and weepy eyes made her soft pale skin seem even lighter and more delicate. I knew that she would never have a problem attracting any man that she desired or fit her purpose. She liked to dress in purple satin. Her pale skin and black hair contrasted with the deep hues of her satin dress. A purple and seal skin head band finished her dress and kept her silky hair from her face.

I considered, many years later, that Mother's plan of selecting 'the mighty' for mates produced quite satisfactory results. As annoyed as I get with her self centered bigotry, she knows what she is talking about and has results to prove it.

I took the hat from my head and placed it on the rock between us. I saw Rollo look at it, but he made no immediate attempt to take it.

He had bright hazel eyes and red-brown hair that peaked through from under his cap. His trimmed beard made him look all the more grand. His dark green shirt and brown vest were worn but clean, as were the golden leggings that were attached to his powerful legs with leather strings.

"I come for a maiden to live with me. My mate died the past winter from the coughing sickness and I have no prospects in this small village. I will insure that you want for nothing if you will come and attend to my needs," he said.

"What about young Gretchen?" I asked.

"Oh!" he said. "Wait until Knut sees her. You can see that he still stands on the shore, where I left him. See him there," Rollo pointed off to the shore in the distance. "He looks out here at us, seeing what I am doing. He will be beside himself when he sees that Gretchen comes ashore with you."

"What is your plan for Gretchen?" I asked.

"I would like to meet Knut and live with his people," she answered for Rollo, with an anxious smile on her lips.

Rollo took my hat and slipped it under his shirt and stood with his hand extended to help me up. His mind never wondered about my appearance and how he might want it changed to meet his preference, and I did not ask about it.

I gave Gretchen a hand as we stood. Gretchen took a shirt from Rollo and wrapped it around her shoulders and buttoned it. I was cloaked in the white fox fur cape that Fain gave me.

We followed Rollo off of the rocks and into his boat. We set off for shore, towards a tiny speck in the distance, pacing anxiously, anticipating our arrival.

"Where did you get the fox fur?" Rollo asked.

"A friend in the Shetlands gave it to me," I answered. I thought that would be the end of that conversation, but Rollo said, "that wouldn't have come from my friend, Fain, the blacksmith on Shetland?"

"Yes. I did not realize that you knew Fain," I said. "Forgive me."

"Sure. Fain collects furs of that quality in payment for his weapon making skills. He is a fine man and a great friend. How is the old boy?" Rollo asked.

"He was doing well when Gretchen and I left him," I said.

"I am sure that he was. Fain is an old timer with many memories of your kind when Shetland was a remote frontier.

As we approached, Knut stood, suddenly unable to move. His eyes were locked on Gretchen.

"Knut, the line," Rollo called as he pitched it at him. The line hit him on the face and dropped to the ground as he kept his eyes on Gretchen.

"Knut this is Esther and her daughter, Gretchen," Rollo said.

"Fetch some blankets and bring them here, would you?" Rollo asked. "Knut! Did you hear me?" Rollo said. Knut turned and ran up the hill. He soon returned with two blankets. He gave one to Esther and the other to me.

As we walked up the hill, we drew attention from a group of bystanders. Most people were busy working on their homes or at another trade.

Knut walked around behind Rollo and I, and unabashedly placed the blanket around Gretchen's shoulders. He took Gretchen's hand and walked with her up the hill towards the longhouse.

Knut turned to look at me. "I believe that we met in Orkney, didn't we?" he asked.

"Yes we did," I said.

"I knew that it was you. I would never forget that face," he said. I always hoped that you would come back for Rollo. Now you have brought an even better surprise," he said. "Now I have my own sea maiden." Knut looked up at Gretchen and marched her up the hill, preparing to show her off to the villagers.

Knut was still holding Gretchen's hand as we entered the longhouse. There were three village women inside, tending to their domestic duties around the Captains house. They stepped out as we came in.

The longhouse was wide, supported by two vertical poles that suspended the roof a great distance over our heads. I had never been in a Viking longhouse before.

There were rough cut tables, chairs, and benches along the walls and near the hearth in the middle of the room. Stone boxes crammed with fresh cut straw served as beds. They each had fur and leather skins that covered them.

"Rosemarie," Rollo called. "Would you find Martha and ask her to make up some clothing for Esther and Gretchen?"

"Yes, of course," she said, and left the room.

"This will be your home," Rollo said.

"We use this as a meeting hall and a place to celebrate. So, you will see people come and go. Do not be alarmed by the lack of privacy. It is important that the villagers see this lodge as part of their own home. They come during the evening to drink mead and whisky with us. You will have to get used to the interruptions. It is the Viking way. Their loyalty is rewarded by the chief's support and protection," he explained.

I learned more about the longhouse and how it functioned in the community as our first few days passed.

"Gretchen, "have you been watching the ways of these people?' I asked.

"No Mother, I have not," she answered.

"Watch them," I said. "I have never seen such industrious people. I seldom see them relax. I believe that their work ethic is what has made them so important, in this time. They will soon become the dominant people of theses coasts," I said. "I am confident of it."

"You were once among the Pict, were you not?" he asked.

"Yes. Mother and I lived among them many years ago," I said.

"There is a story that the Pict tell about two sea maidens who came onto their land and lived in one of their villages along the eastern shores of Caledonia," he began. "This was years ago, in the times of the Roman occupation."

"Yes," I said.

"They lived with the Pict in a time when they warred against the Romans who wanted to keep them away from the Britons in lower Britannia. Their legend says that one of the maids paired with Maelchon, a King of Wales, while the daughter *handfasted* with Brude."

"Yes, I knew him as Breidi, as he was called by his Father."

"What else does the legend say?" I asked. I had not heard our legend told and was anxious to hear it out.

"The legend goes on, that Brude helped Maelchon and village neighbors hold back the Romans as they marched north and tried to conquer the independent minded Pict," Rollo recalled. "The Mother, who they call, 'The Legend of the Pict,' lived with one of the Roman Generals sent from Rome to erect the wall in northern Britannia.

"They say that she undermined the General and caused disruption in his camp while the Pict scaled their wall and killed soldiers by the hundreds. The legend says that she was a beautiful siren who could not be resisted by the Roman. They go on to tell that she was the reason that the Romans did not finish construction of the wall so that it would be affective in keeping the Pict warriors in the highlands."

"They also say the Mother was skilled in the use of the ancient sling and stone from the Holy Lands," he said. "The daughter *handfasted* with Brude and produced a future Pictish King, named Robb."

I could not control my emotions. Mother would be ashamed of me if she saw me weeping over the story of my son, but I could not hold back the tears of the joy of that this news brought.

"I am sorry, if I have offended you," Rollo said. "I was sure who you were after we met in Orkney. I did not mean to cause you pain."

"No. I am very pleased to have you recall Robb's story," I said. "I am overwhelmed by the recollection of his life. I have not been told his story before."

"He was a fine King of the Pict. He preceded Oengus and the Alpin Kings who have followed," Rollo said. "

"Your Mother is a revered figure in the legends and lore of the early highland people," Rollo went on. "She was a mysterious figure to many of the early settlements of the highlands. But, they see her, now, as a source of miracles in a civilization that held the power of women above all things."

The new settlement on the isle had become home to ten families when we first moved in. Each had their own home that they constructed out of stone and lumber and they often had a separate structure that they used for their crafts and trades, nearby. The baker, weaver, weapons smith, wheelwright, cooper all had their own shops.

"You may help the women prepare the meal for tonight's celebration, if you wish. That might help you learn some of our ways. " Rollo said one morning after we had been in the village for a few days. "We celebrate our new settlement and ask for Odin's blessings tonight," he said, while we sat to eat the morning meal of wheat cakes, porridge and honey.

Gretchen and I were not much help in preparing the first meal in the new longhouse. The women of the village made the preparations and did not ask for much from Gretchen and I.

They brought in smoked fish and large quantities of flat bread, and sourdough yeast bread, butter and honey. The ever present stew pot hung near the fire, where it had been since we arrived. They added morsels of meat, white carrots and another king of root vegetable that I did not recognize. The anticipation of the crowd grew in anticipation of the feast to come.

When the village was gathered in the longhouse, a village elder stood and began speaking. I remember such customs from the village in the lake region after Breidi converted to Christianity.

The elder praised Odin for the safety and security of the village. He then asked for Christ's blessing for the sustenance that the food brought to their bodies and their household. Gretchen and I stood aside while the elder spoke, not wanting to interfere with something that had nothing to do with either of us.

Gretchen and I watched as the women ladled stew over loaves of flat, birch tree flour bread. Their cups were filled with ale or the fermented mead.

Gretchen and I watched the progress of the meal. The women took their smaller portions and extra for their children. The smaller children shared the stew with their mothers. They broke off small pieces of bread from around the edges. They used the pieces to take morsels of meat and vegetables.

Gretchen filled Knut's plate and poured a cup of ale. Gretchen began to take in the ways of the village from the very beginning. Knut seldom let her out of his sight. She was quick to tend to anticipate his needs.

When the meal was eaten, the cups were emptied, they all went back to their homes and left us in peace. Rollo and I slept in a larger bed while Knut and Gretchen took a smaller bed, nearby.

I learned that among Norse, hospitality was a matter of honor. I think this celebration had done Rollo proud.

The Sudry Isle was a peaceful place, I thought. The village came alive in the morning as fires were rekindled. The smells and sounds of morning activities came from the homes and shops. I enjoyed the busy mornings in the village when the fires carried the aromas of baking and cooking through the village.

"Porridge," I said as I handed Rollo a bowl of the meal and a serving of butter and honey, as he liked it. I filled his cup with mead and found a nearly fresh loaf of bread for him to eat it with. Rollo ate in peace. He had the welfare and future of the village on his mind. Those matters kept him working towards getting the settlement functioning.

The village grew to fourteen families and eventually twenty over the remainder of the summer. Rollo had a pier built for securing the village fleet. Trade ships began arriving by the fall season.

They brought in grains and food supplies that the village had not yet been able to produce for themselves. They were exchanged for iron smith goods, fabric products from the weaver as well as raw and combed wool fleece.

Crews were sent off to the south and further west the isle that people began to cal Ireland. They all brought back loads of goods that they proudly dumped on the big table in the longhouse. "You have done well," Rollo said to a crew that emptied their bag of loot in front of him. "Where did this come from?" Rollo asked.

"From the south, in the land that they call 'Wales," one answered. "The villages are small and they don't have the big church houses of the Anglos of the East," he explained. "We brought a few carpenters and stone masons with us. They can be used to help finish building before the Winter season," he said.

"Good, we can use them. Did you find women for our crews?" Rollo asked. "There are still a few without women."

"No, we didn't Rollo," he said. "Perhaps we will go west to the shores of the Ireland and bring back a few maidens."

"Do that," Rollo said. "They will provide young ones in the Spring. We need to get them for our crewmen before winter."

The crew left the goods on the table and walked out. Knut took a few pieces of silver and stored them under the floor boards with the other loot for safe keeping.

By the time that November arrived, fire had been collected and prepared for our first winter. Fish had been smoked and stored in the cool of the earthen and stone store house.

Oats, rye, barley and wheat were stored in barrels and casks prepared by the village cooper, along with aging barley malt whisky for next years supply. Pork was rubbed, dried and stored with mutton and goat that we slaughtered during the time that Vikings called the "Blood Month," when domestic animals were slaughtered and put up for the long cold season.

Crews had returned with several Irish maidens to be distributed to single men and those who intended to keep a second woman. Many of Rollo's men had taken women from other ports and villages. Some wanted to add another.

As Viking crews were at sea most months of the year, it was not uncommon in our time to find Vikings that had a home in every port where they supported a woman and children.

Rollo had an order in place that he used to recognize his crewmen. Some had distinguished themselves in battle and held a senior designation among his crews. Those would take their choice before junior ranking crewmen were allowed to pick a woman from the line-up after they brought the women to the village. That took place in the longhouse and went on as other crews brought Irish women, until all men had at least one woman for his house.

Gretchen and I watched the continuous parade that went on, day after day. The women from the Irish coast were young. Crewmen brought back women of child bearing age. It appeared that there were very few that were beyond their fifteenth season. Neither Rollo nor Knut showed any interest in the process.

"Rollo, I do not understand the need to bring in women from foreign lands. Why not bring women from your villages in Scandinavia?" I asked as he held me close under the heavy fur cover of the bed.

"Hmmh," Rollo grunted. "There are many reasons," he said. "Which one do you want to hear first?" he said.

"I don't know, Master," tell them all," I answered.

"Hmmh," he grunted, again. I realized that he would just as soon gone to sleep as explain the domestic ways of the Vikings, but I wanted to understand.

"First, most of the women from our villages die before their fifteenth birthday. Usually the coughing sickness takes them. We desperately need to establish new lands with women who have longer life expectancies. Our villages in Norway were too small and too distant to ensure that we did not needlessly multiply the exposure to such diseases."

"Secondly, why fill our ships from the village with women, when we can carry needed cargo for use in the settlement?" he asked. "We have always been successful in finding women for our crews in whatever land that we visit. In a way, the mix blood that we get from adding new people from other cultures helps us learn new ways. We make use of all of them. They also improve our chance of avoiding common diseases from Norway," as I just said.

"Third," he said, "I could see the end of his patience in having to list the reasons for their ways. "It is good to bring in new blood," he said.

"My Father told me long ago that our practice of bringing in new blood has its own benefits. Men who select women within the confines of their own village will eventually marry their cousin," he said. "That is not good," he concluded. "People who marry their cousins will soon look like Englishmen. English nobles always marry their cousins so that they can retain their family wealth."

"Those cultures who live remotely and have no choice but to mate within their own family line will probably mate with several cousins as a matter of fact and will eventually rear runts," he explained, not so gently.

"Are there more?" I dared to ask. "Why have you not taken a woman?"

"I need to explore new settlements for my people. I have not burdened my self with a *handfasted* mate and children while I find it necessary to continue my search," he answered.

"I need a woman, like all men need women but I have not settled in one place long enough to begin a family."

"The people of Scandinavia are suffering in these difficult times," he went on. "As my Father did before me, I need to find new settlements for them. Our lands are blighted. They hold little grain and our forests are without game. There are too many people for the land to sustain."

I began to understand his reasoning. The one reason that I felt that he omitted was simple. They took young attractive women from villages throughout the extent of their considerable reach, because they could. I reasoned that this practice kept them with a young mate, even while they age themselves.

After the Romans returned to their own empire in the Mediterranean there was no one around who could stop them from doing as they pleased. Gretchen and I talked about my conversation with Rollo and the answers that he gave to my questions.

We recognized that, while his reasons held water, the truth of the matter seemed to be that Vikings were curious, restless and nomadic people of the sea. No one was capable of stopping them from taking what they wanted, including women to warm their beds and slave workers to build their villages and tend to their fields.

Chapter XXXVI

In the following days, Knut showed Gretchen how they dried and ground the inner bark of the birch tree that villagers used as flour. They found numbers of things that they could do together. Rollo and I watched from the fire as the pair played board games and passed the hours in the dark, cold season.

We heard the noises coming from their covers of their bed, across the room. Gretchen was ready for a mate and Knut would soon be ready himself. Gretchen was plenty capable of teaching him everything that he needed to know.

"With the settlement well established, I am looking towards a new expedition in the land of the Francs," Rollo told me. "In the early Spring I will take a few ships and depart for the Franco coast to see if there are suitable lands for our people still in Norway."

This village holds as many families as it can support already and we will need more.

Rollo and Knut left with a crew and traveled south east towards the Welsh coast to take loot for trading in Orkney in the spring. He planned to explore the land at the mouth of a river that the Franks called, the Seine. They said goodbye and left the shore one early morning.

We stayed in the village, making further preparations for winter. I could tell from the moment that they left that the mood of village women changed.

They made no attempt at including Gretchen or I in anything that they did. We stayed on our own. We had everything that we needed so we avoided reasons to mix with them.

"Why are they upset at us, Mother? We did nothing to them," Gretchen said.

"Well, yes we did. We took the most eligible bachelor in the village along with his young apprentice, away from them. We are not of their world and they resent our presence among them just like they did on Shetland where Mother and I took the most eligible men.

We seldom get along with mortal women for just that reason. We only take their best and leave the 'scraps' for them. I would not be happy with our kind either," I explained.

Rollo returned with Knut and several bags of loot. We held a celebration that night in which Rollo pulled treasures, one by one from the bags and awarded them to his worthy crew in recognition of their value to his crew and their village. Even Knut received a handsome silver plate for his work around the boat and camp.

Knut matured during the first few months that Gretchen and I were among his people. He was a handsome young man. Gretchen brought out the best in him. He was in his fourteenth season and was nearing an age when he would be taking a mate. I knew that Rollo had seen the same attachment between the two, but he had not said anything about it to me. He probably would wait until the time came and face the issue then. Their giggling at night reminded me of my early times with Breidi in the Pryten village. Remembering those days brought joy to my heart. I was not supposed to sense those feelings but I had been fortunate with Breidi and Fain. I would never forget either of them.

We stayed in the longhouse for most of the winter. Villagers came and left the longhouse as they pleased. Women brought their young in with them to give them room to roam during the cold months. Their own single room houses were no bigger than one fire hearth could heat. The body heat from the constant gathering along with two fires kept the longhouse warm.

The winter passed and spring arrived. We had plenty to eat and wood to keep us warm. Survival on the Sudry Isle was much improved with ample food stores and fuel for our hearths. Over the winter we discussed the spring expedition. "Gretchen and I do not wish to stay here when you are away on such a long journey," I said.

"Then you will both come with Knut and I on the voyage," Rollo concluded. We were both relieved with the prospect of accompanying Rollo on the voyage.

Gretchen was elated with the prospect of being with Knut. As expected, I had seen them take to one bed during most nights of the winter as I had once done with Breidi in the Pict settlement.

Preparations were underway for our expedition. Rollo sent men to Norway to enlist the help of several crews from the old village. They were to meet us near a small village at the mouth of the Seine, called Rouen. We, according to Rollo, would need the aide of several more crews.

Gretchen and I were not sure what to expect. The villages on the coast of the West Francs were unknown except for a few who had raided small villages along the shores.

The loot from winter raids was loaded into the ship and we set sail for Shetland. The ship glided over the rough seas with surprising ease as we headed north, along the coast and east passed Orkney and on to Shetland.

The seas never settled during the first part of our journey. Rollo mapped out his route with a chart of the stars and check point along the way to Shetland. After several days we entered the harbor and secured the ship to the shore.

Knut, Gretchen and I had several items that we need to purchase as we walked up the slope towards the village. Knut was relieved that he was not assigned the duty of staying with the ship. That duty was given to another camp boy.

Knut lead us towards the village with a bag of loot that we needed to trade for coins, before we visited merchants to secure the items that we would need for the remainder of the voyage and our camp near Rouen.

Knut took his platter and the few other items that Rollo had given him and began negotiations with a merchant. He haggled with the merchant for a while before he received his coins. We had grain, dried and smoked meat to get in the village. I saw the old tavern and inn where I spent nights on Shetland, many years ago. I did not bother telling Knut and Gretchen about that experience and I did not enter the inn to see what had changed.

Rollo joined us for a late supper at a tavern on the opposite end of the street after he sent a camp boy down to the ship with our purchases.

"Esther, I learned today that our Friend Fain passed away," he said.

"Oh, no! He was such a gentle and kind man," I said. "He protected Gretchen and I during our stay. He was there for us when we needed him," I said.

"Word is that a young woman from the village tavern kept him company and lifted his spirits over the last few years before he died. He must have taken an interest in her. Those that knew him said that they had never seen him happier."

"Thank you," I said.

As we ate our stew, bread, and drank our ale, I asked Knut and Gretchen, "have you two talked about your future? Are you anticipating a handfasting?"

"We have not openly talked about it, but I would very much like to take Gretchen as my *handfasting mate*," young Knut said, rather bluntly.

Gretchen did not answer. She looked at me and smiled. I took that as a sign of her willingness to join with Knut in handfasting if I thought it was the right decision.

"Well then," Rollo jumped in, "We will plan the *handfasting* after we land and get settled in Rouen. I would be pleased to have Gretchen join in our family as an in-law. Then it is done," Rollo commanded.

We finished our meal and listened to the performers put on their act in the tavern. They played the drums, a flute and a stringed instrument as they danced across the floor with the inn's maidens and servants. We all took our nights sleep on the hay, one floor up the ladder, while the musicians continued their song and dance.

Chapter XXXVII

In the morning we arose early and went to the shore where our ship was being readied by Rollo's new camp boy. Ten other ships from Rollo's old village in Norway had arrived during the night and put ashore next to our own.

There were warrior crews of thirty on each of the ten *drakkars*. I watched Rollo inspect the ships and count heads for his expedition. "Good!" Rollo said. He was pleased.

"We will leave for the Franco coast in due time. For now we will finalize what we expect and what we are to do there," Rollo said.

With the crew captains surrounding Rollo, he began to lay out the plan on the sand. "We will sail down the east coast of the isle of the Picts and south to the Britons. Then we will assemble and sail directly east towards the mouth of the River Seine. We will put in, in Rouen and camp overnight," he went on.

"The following morning we will sail up the Seine to the capitol and set siege to Paris and the King of the Francs, 'Charles the simple" he said. "Before we leave for Rouen, get what we need here on Shetland. The rest we will take from Rouen."

I was reminded of my first born, Robb while in Shetland. A series of kings were appointed over the years to lead the Pict, including Alpin and his son Kenneth Mac Alpin after Robb. They led the Pict while Robb was still among them. I had been told that Robb was the war chief among the Wolf Clan and later served under Alpin as an important military leader.

The Pict never surrendered their independence. They never knew freedom and they never knew peace. Their tribes were gradually absorbed into the Dal Riata Kingdoms and eventually became untraceable as a people.

Their legacies are the many monoliths engraved with their symbols, and a few broch buildings still standing on Shetland. But their biggest legacy is the frugal and stubborn nature of the Scottish people. I can say that I am sure that a good deal of the frugal and stubborn characteristics of Robb might well be attributed to Mother.

I was proud of Robb's contribution to their culture. He, his father and grandfather were all brilliant leaders and capable military generals. Mother never forgave me for giving birth to a male but I can easily see that Robb helped his father's people right to his end.

Rollo's crews met along a secluded shore, south of the city of Aberdeen. We set off together to arrive by early morning at the mouth of the River Seine.

Rollo's calculations of our course were brilliant. I marveled at the navigating abilities of Norse sailors. Before the time of instruments, they did it at night by following the stars and using them as reference points against physical features in route.

We arrived in Rouen before dawn, as planned. The anticipation of the action to come showed mightily on the faces of the crews. Their first sight of the Franco coast looked promising and they were anxious to get started.

This land was new to all of them. Rollo must have been given some instructions on the geography of the river and the village of Rouen. It was a significant distance from the coast. The shore line of the river was lined with prosperous appearing villages with fishing wharfs, green fields and vineyards.

As we approached the Rouen shore, villagers scattered to avoid confrontation with the well known Vikings.

Rollo and his men leaped over the sides of our ship and swept into the village. Knut was among them. They secured villagers in a pen to keep them safe and out of the way. They took food and supplies that they would need on their trip up the Seine.

The villagers were not injured or molested as Rollo had instructed. "Do not, in any way, harm villagers of Rouen. We will need them if our plans work out. The village women are to be kept prisoner in their own homes until we return," he ordered.

"We shall sail up the Seine later today. Get what we need for an overnight camp, outside of Paris. We leave as soon as preparations are complete," Rollo ordered. His men scurried off in different directions following his orders.

Some villagers were surprised by Viking warriors storming into their homes and shops. No one was injured while Rollo's men took what they needed. Gretchen and I walked along the shore and out into the fields of green crops in the midday sun.

"Mother, look at the shades of green," Gretchen said. "I have never seen so much greenery, even in the Sudrys."

Rollo told us that other crews had laid siege and were planning on capturing Paris and the lands to the north. King Charles, "The Simple," had sustained heavy losses but had held the Viking leader Sigfred at bay, at least temporarily.

None of the Viking chiefs believed that Charles could hold out much longer. Perhaps Rollo's attack would be timely, we thought. Charles was King of the West Francs, and did not have support of the total region.

Rollo became agitated and his aggression grew with the anticipation of the battle with the West Franco King. He looked around at the lush countryside of fields, forests and farmland. He was anxious with the prospect of taking this land for his people and himself. Rouen's shops and market were booming with food supplies and market goods. The little town square had shops offering even more goods and services than Orkney or Shetland.

Mother and I stood in the center of Rouen and look around us. "There are two bake shops, a green market and several places offering the local wine," Mother said. "The meat market has cuts of lamb, beef and several poultry items," I said as we swept the scene before us with our eyes. Most of the market workers were away from their shops. They fled when they saw us come ashore.

"This is a beautiful land," I said to Rollo as he stood near his ship, preparing to depart.

"Yes, we would be fortunate to live here, near these fields, vineyards and this river with access to the sea. Can you imagine?" he said. His voice reflected the emotion that he felt at the prospect of telling his father and others in Norway, about the lush countryside near the Franco coast that would become their home.

Rollo's agitated state had been hard to live with since we landed in Rouen. He was so anxious for his people to come to Rouen that he could not rest or eat.

"Yes, I can," I said. "Go safely, Rollo, and hurry back"

"Good," then it will be yours, if all goes well. Pick out a spot for a home for you and I. Tell Gretchen to find another site nearby for she and Knut. I will be back with Gretchen's chosen man in a few days time," Rollo said. He and Knut walked out together.

Rollo climbed over the side of the boat as it was pushed away from shore. His crew took to the oars. They glided along the placidly smooth river surface under the power of their oars until they caught the wind. The sail went up and the ship lifted from the wind that billowed the sail fabric.

Rollo was on his way. He needed to get this mission completed. If he failed, he would be a very difficult man to live with.

We whiled away our time in the village, investigating the lush vineyards and farms surrounding it. Some of the villagers came back into town to see if their homes and shops were still standing. They must have been relieved. We had not disturbed anything. We tried to make them feel at ease with our presence. That part would be more difficult.

Gretchen and I watched the villagers as they came back to their shops.

"These people are quite vulnerable," I said. "They have no real ability to defend themselves."

"Look around, Mother," Gretchen said. "Their lives are dedicated to operating their farms, running their markets and shops. They have not invested a single moment with concerns of defending themselves against aggression."

"This region is different from the north. There, they spend so much time and energy defending themselves that they have little time or resources to plant crops and operate markets. Rollo could learn a lot from these people," I said.

Several days later, word came that Rollo and his crews were on their way back to Rouen. We stood along the shore in anticipation of news.

Rollo gathered his crews together. He was about to speak when a crewman interrupted him with a message.

"A messenger from the King," the man yelled.

"Show him in," Rollo said.

A small man, perhaps an elder or a member of Charles' court was escorted in by a crewman with a large hand on the hood of his robe. The man looked like he was about to faint. "Do you have word from the King?" Rollo asked. "Speak!" he said.

"A message to the leader of the Vikings," he whispered, meekly.

"We are all leaders of the Vikings," Rollo roared, spreading his arm towards the crowd of his followers.

"The King wishes an audience with the Leader of the Vikings. He intends to offer a truce," the little man said.

"Ha! A truce, is it?" Rollo asked. The crowd of Viking warriors roared and boasted at the prospect of the King's offer. Rollo held his hand up, as a signal for silence.

The little man continued, "Yes. If you would be so kind to escort me safely back to Paris, I will take you to the King," he said.

Rollo and two of his biggest warriors, and the little man, got in a ship and sailed back to Paris.

"What is this about?" a crewman said.

We did not know what to do after Rollo, so abruptly left to return to Paris and the King. We went about our business as best we could. The anxiety increased. There would be no peace of mind for his crews until he returned.

Rollo and his men returned to Rouen, without the diminutive messenger. We could not wait to hear what the King wanted from Rollo. We all crammed into the new longhouse and waited for him to speak.

"The King of the West Francs has proposed a truce for our people," Rollo declared. "His capitol has been ravaged for years. He can not protect Paris and run his government. He has proposed to us that we protect Paris and the river, in exchange for the lands from Rouen to the coast," he announced.

"What does that mean, Prince?" one asked.

"He can not protect the capitol and its people against continuous raids from Nordic crews. He needs us to protect it against future invasions," Rollo explained.

"What does he ask from us?" Ruud asked. "We are to protect the King from our own people?"

"Yes, that is what he proposes. We will stop the Nordic crews from sailing up the Seine, to Paris with intentions to sack the city and the government," Rollo said.

"And this land is ours, to keep?" another yelled.

"Yes, that is true. But, let me say this. We can not live peacefully among the Francs if we do not treat them well. This is their village. We must live peacefully among them and let them see that we mean no harm," Rollo said. "Any crewman who mistreats a Franc in this region will have me to deal with," Rollo promised.

"Do you understand me?" he demanded.

"Aye," a few said.

Rollo's had difficulty understanding why a King would give up such valuable land, filled with forests, prime farmland, vineyards, river frontage and a coastland, as well.

"He only asks that we prevent other crews from sailing up the Seine and pillaging Paris. We will be the keepers of his kingdom and we will rule a portion of it for our own people," Rollo explained.

"We will take the coast lands where the River Seine flows into the sea, and inland to our camp, here in Rouen," Rollo repeated. He has named me 'as count' of the region as he intends that we settle in with the people."

"Tell them about the king's foot," one of the crewmen shouted.

"Oh, ha," Rollo roared. "The King's foot. Yes."

"The little wart demanded that I kiss his foot as sign of my acceptance of him as my king," Rollo said.

"What happened?" another shouted.

"Well, by Odenn's spear, I am not kissing any man's foot," Rollo exclaimed. The laughter in the crowd rose again.

"Did you tell him that you would kiss his foot if he would kiss your arse, Prince?"

The crowd erupted, again.

"No. I did not tell him that. I should have though," Rollo answered.

"So, what happened, then?" another asked.

"Well, I did not want his majesty to be upset by a simple matter of respect. I had Alfred, here, kiss the king's foot," Rollo declared.

There was more laughter from Rollo's audience. "Ha, Alfred kissed the King's foot!" they roared.

"Yes. Tell them what happened next," another yelled.

"Poor Alfred has never kissed a woman, let alone a king's foot," Rollo said. "He got a little excited." There was more laughter and good hearted pushing and shoving.

"Well, poor Alfred lifted the puny king's foot so high, trying to kiss it without subjecting himself to the humiliation of bending over, that he put the king on his back."

The crowd roared and shoved poor Alfred around, laughing at the poor man.

They continued their rowdy laughing, pushing Alfred and telling about the king that found himself on his back, before his court. Apparently the king was terribly embarrassed. He dismissed his court as Rollo and his party left the palace.

"Friends!" Rollo called, with his hand raised.

"Friends!" he repeated.

"Ruud, Knut, find the villagers of Rouen and ask them to return to their homes," Rollo directed, as the crowd settled down. "Tell them that they have nothing to fear from us. They may not believe us in the beginning but they will soon realize that we intend to do them no harm," Rollo said. "Remember what I said about mistreating these people."

"Also remember that we have a lot to learn from these villagers. They have lived and benefited from this land for many years. We need to learn how they do it," Rollo said.

Knut and Ruud walked off towards the village center to begin spreading the news. "This is wonderful news," I said to Rollo. "Finally, you have a place for your people."

"Yes. This land is fertile and its rivers are rich. Come, we have a handfasting ceremony to plan," he said.

"First, let me show you a site that I believe would be good for Knut's home and our own," I said.

We walked through the abandoned village towards the open fields on to the eastern side. Some of the shops were still abandoned. Rollo waived to the few shop keepers that looked through half closed doors as we walked along.

"We needed to find the villagers and have them return to their homes and their markets if we were to succeed in settling in with the locals," Rollo said.

"It will come in time," I said.

The eastern side of the village opened up onto rolling hills and wide pastures of grass, rolling down to the river's edge.

"This is it?" Rollo asked.

"Yes," I said. "What do you think of it?

He stood silently and looked out over the wide expanse of the river valley. His powerful arms folded over his chest, he declared, "By the eyes of Odin, this is more than any man could hope for."

We walked back through the village and found Knut and Ruud standing with a few villagers near the center market place. Knut was trying to explain to his French speaking audience that they could return to their homes without fear of being attacked. Rollo walked to Knut and took a place beside him.

"Come," he started. "This village is ours," he spread his arms out wide with his palms up to show them that they were free to resume their lives.

There were on going celebrations in the town center. The crews began drinking the local village wine from storage barrels, bread from the bakeries and meat and vegetable from the market. It would be a while before the crews settled down and got serious about settling into the local population.

Chapter XXXVIII

King Charles would not live quite long enough to see the significance of his settlement. Rollo took the offer so hastily that it should have occurred to him that maybe he sweetened the offer too well.

No one understood the potential of this treaty. The generations of French Kings and Dukes of Normandy to come would quarrel and fight over the lands that came to be known as Upper and Lower Normandy.

The richness of the countryside hills and farms was unmatched anywhere in the region. The strategic placement of the village that developed in the wide, natural harbor would change the future of the lands on both sides of the narrow sea between the Franco coast and the Isle of Britannia.

In the early times we were not sure that the villagers understood Rollo and Knut's attempt to welcome them back home. Rollo must have realized that if he left them alone, that they would eventually figure it out on their own.

Rollo put his hands on Knut and Ruud's shoulders as we turned to walk away, leaving Rouen's citizens to reclaim their village center on their own.

"Come," Rollo said to Knut. "We have houses to build."

Rollo called his people together to proceed with the *handfasting* rite for Knut and Gretchen. As the Pryten people had done many years earlier, their hands were bound and a blessing was spoken over them. An Elder asked for the pairing to bring young ones to the young Viking and his bride. Few knew that she was actually the daughter of the King of the Picts. She was already six hundred years old.

Rollo knew the history, and Fain would have known, if he had been able to join us. Gretchen and I were content staying with Rollo and his band for the time being. We intended to see how the Scandinavians would assimilate into the French population.

By the time that Knut and Rollo built our houses on the edge of town, several other Norse ships arrived with more families from the North. They scurried around the countryside, taking claim of lands near the village.

Rollo tried to temper their enthusiasm, but nothing would hold them from grabbing whatever they wanted to claim. "People," Rollo said. "Remember that the Francs have settled much of this land for themselves. Do not try to claim their lands as your own. Spread out to the countryside beyond the village and see what we can develop on our own" Rollo instructed.

Many of them did what Rollo instructed. There were land claim issues to straighten out for those who did not listen. Those matters were later taken to the village Mayor where he and Rollo presided over civic problems caused by Norse settlers.

Our houses were made of wood frame, with the walls covered with layers of river mud. We white washed the inner and outer walls and covered the floors with split green timbers, turned flat side up in the manner of the Franco people.

The roofs were supported with long timbers from the forest and covered with bundles of thatch grasses from the fields. The rolling hills yielded grain for bread and beer. The surrounding forests gave up deer, wild boar and game birds. The river was deep with fresh water fish and fowl. To Rollo's people, paradise had been found and claimed.

Rollo spent hours with the village Mayor. In some way they overcame the language barrier and began to understand each other's point of view. The Nordic people had much to learn from these peaceful villagers.

The villages of the far north had nothing resembling the resources enjoyed by the people of Rouen. Rollo was anxious to claim as much of it for his people and himself as he could without taking land from the people who had lived here for generations. He was driven to establish the Norse people in the region. Despite Rollo's instructions, locals were removed from their farms by land grabbing Norsemen in the frenzy of activity.

Rollo assigned regions of the Normandy coast and inland regions to men of his crew as rewards for their loyalty. They ruled the regions as their own and soon became absorbed in the French way of farming and raising farm stock.

The manner which they planted and harvested the expansive fields of grain, the vineyards that produced grapes that they depended on for their most common drink and the operation of trade shops, market and smith trades were all new to the Nordic people.

One of the early advantages that the Norsemen brought to Rouen was the erection of a longhouse to serve as a center to the village and a meeting place for councils. The French were slow to come to the longhouse, as they must have thought that it was only to be used by Norsemen. Such notions would take generations to overcome.

"Ruud, we must erect small fortresses along the river with a vantage point to look over the channel by the sea." Rollo said as we gathered in the longhouse. "Nordic crews have stopped here to trade with us and have not attempted to continue on to Paris. That does not mean that at some point they will attempt it. We need to be ready for them."

"I will take a crew of twenty and build towers near the river where enters the harbor. We will also need to begin a settlement near the harbor," Rouen said. "We will be ready," he promised.

Rollo listened to Ruud explain the need to develop a port at the mouth of the Seine, at the coast, using the natural harbor to anchor trade ships. Ruud's plan included shops of merchants and trade crafts to sell and trade goods brought down river from Paris to the port.

"We will build store houses to secure the goods as they come through the market. We can operate markets for trade like Shetland and Orkney, but we will do it better than they did," Ruud said.

"Good, Ruud," he said. "Go and get it started."

Rollo and Knut took crews up the Seine and onto some of the many branches that fed into the river. They found goods that would help the commerce that they planned for the port. Wine, pork, beef, lumber and an endless list of goods could be traded and sold it they could get the trust of French country settlers.

They were slow to trust Rollo and his crews. Fear of the sight of Viking ships coming up river towards their villages was so engrained in them that their guard was always heightened. It took months for them to realize that Knut and Ruud had no intentions to harm them.

Ruud began using a ship yard in the harbor, down stream of Rouen. He had crewmen set up facilities to build a fleet of merchant ships. They needed to be shallow draft cargo ships, capable of hauling large loads of products on shallow rivers and streams that lead off of the Seine and into the countryside.

Vikings were experts in ship building. Ruud involved locals to help in the yard that he had built to work on new vessels.

Chapter XXXIX

Rollo was a restless man these days. Nothing that I could say or do seemed to settle his frantic mind as the months went by. I came to understand that Rollo, like most Viking leaders could not settle down while there were expeditions to new regions that needed to be done.

I did not interfere with Rollo's plans. The settlement near Rouen was going well, without him. The more that we could keep him away, the quicker we could include the French. Rollo needed to travel and no one was going to get into is way.

He set out with a crew to investigate other regions of the area that was now being called, "Normandy." He traveled along the coast and up the Seine and the branches that fed the Seine, deep into the continent.

The news that we received was causing difficulty with the locals. Despite his agreement with the King, Rollo continued to raid villages and took what ever he wanted. Some of the crew found young maidens of their liking and brought them back to Rouen.

In the spring, the King recalled Rollo to Paris. We all went along to see the city and find out what the King had in mind. We were welcomed into the city and the palace by uniformed court guards who took us to Charles.

"The treaty has been drafted and you have been named as the Count of the lands that I understand you have called 'Normandy," the King said.

"You have honored our agreement and fulfilled your responsibilities to our land."

"The King's messengers must not have told him that Rollo never stopped pillaging and taking lands outside of the original agreement," I said to Knut.

"As a sign of your allegiance to the French people and myself," the King continued, "We ask that you be baptized and take the Christian name, 'Robert,'" he continued.

"Hmmh," was all that I heard from Rollo.

"This will be a sign of your commitment to my kingdom," Charles said.

"Hmmh, you have our allegiance but I am not inclined to change my identity," Rollo said. "Norsemen are proud of their heritage and will not be pleased to hear that their leader has become a French Christian," Rollo went on.

The silence in the room made us all nervous. Rollo stood before the King and said nothing to relieve it. He seemed unyielding to the King's proposal.

"It is a requirement of our agreement," Charles said. "You must lead your people into settling into the French country culture. You must be the first to release hold on your old ways and accept the future," the King pronounced with a note of overconfidence and reason.

"Hmmh," Rollo rumbled. He looked at me and then to Knut. We both nodded our agreement with the Kings demands.

"We must remain proud of our heritage," he said to us as we huddled to discuss the issue. "How can I be a Christian Franco? What does that mean to our people?" he asked. Frustration and doubt filled Rollo's face and composure.

"It is inevitable," Knut said. "Generations from now, our people will only meld into the countryside if we lead the way. We can not ask the French to become Norsemen," Knut said.

"Then, you will have it your way Charles," Rollo said. "I will be known to my subjects as 'Robert,' Count of Normandy."

"In return, I demand that my sons all be honored with the same title and hold the lands given to us by our agreement, for all time. They shall have independent authority over the lands that we possess," Rollo demanded.

"Further, all goods produced and sold from our principality shall be owned exclusively and controlled by the citizens of Normandy, without taxation."

"That is bold," we thought. The tension in the room rose while we waited for the King's response to this demand. It weighed heavily on his mind.

The King looked confused. He sought the advice of his court officials. They considered it for a moment and said, "So be it, Count," he blurted. His court advisers took the King aside. They demanded they he not make such an agreement.

Their efforts to stifle the king fell in vain.

I agree to your demands," he said. His courtiers stormed out of the room, leaving the King on his own.

Rollo was baptized with his Christian name and he signed the treaty. It was later named, 'Treaty Saint-Clair-sur-Epte, as the first ruler of the principality of Normandy.

We returned to Rouen. Rollo, now "Count Robert," called his people and the Mayor of Rouen in to advise them of the treaty.

"This land is our principality and we will live by its wealth. I call on all of our citizens to develop our independence from the French King by growing, cultivating and fabricating goods to be sent to Ruud at the port and sold in market that we will control.

"The King is simple and fragile," Rollo claimed.

"I believe that he has given away the richest region of his realm. I can see that his eventual successor will find fault with this agreement. We need to move quickly to capitalize on our position. Charles will soon lose support over this matter. It will take everything that we have to convince Charles' replacement to live by his word.

"Ruud, we will need ships and crews in ready."

"Knut, you will take charge of collecting goods and having them delivered to Ruud for sale and trade in port. I expect every artisan, craftsman and farmer to deliver one of ten of everything that they produce," Rollo commanded.

"They will resist but we need to prevail in this demand. They will see higher prices for their goods as a result," Rollo said." Go, we have work to do."

Chapter XL

Over time, French coastal citizens accepted the Nordic people. Rollo had ships built for use at the port. Ruud's market began to flourish. Most people did not seem to mind trading one in ten of their products in exchange for the security that Rollo and his people provided. They also saw the increase in value of their goods, as Rollo had promised.

They were accustomed to paying higher taxes to Charles and must have received less for it than what Rollo's plan gave them.

Word from Paris and Charles was not as positive. It was said that Charles' court advisers resented Rollo making a profit from the work of the French people without taxation support for his court. This did not settle well with Charles. His advisors must have finally convinced him that he had made an error in allowing Rollo to avoid paying taxes to the King's court.

Rollo paid little attention to the King. He had what he wanted and he had a plan in place to take advantage of it. "These first years will be difficult ones," he told the Mayor. "Our struggle will begin when his court throws him out, or when he dies and is replaced."

Knut traveled the Seine river valley from village to village over seeing the production of goods for the port. In time, he had ships traveling in both directions loaded with products for the countryside.

Grain, livestock and wine were all in demand. In the Summer of our first year in Normandy, I needed to find Mother and tell her about Rouen.

In order to demonstrate his acceptance of the culture, he took a wife from among the French. She was Popee, the daughter of Berengar of Clair. He had been the previous Count of the region that we now called Normandy.

I was pregnant with Rollo's child. I had what I needed and I was anxious to get away from the clamor around Rouen. I was ready to move on.

I left the village to find Mother and advise her of the settlement in Rouen. I saw Rollo's marriage as political alignment as much as anything and I found no fault with it. My time would come to leave Rollo and return to my world.

Gretchen stayed with Knut. The young Norseman played an important role in Rollo's scheme to enrich the region. Villagers often traveled Northeast on the Seine to visit Ruud's busy port. Knut ran cargo ships between the port and Rouen and others deeper into France on the Seine or one of its tributaries. He used Rouen as a collection point for ships to drop off the goods that were destined for the port. Before I left to see Mother, the river, Rouen and the Port boiled with life and new energy.

French farmers, vintners and craftsmen soon found the Rollo's scheme of operating a port for the collection of their goods worked in their favor. It opened new outlets to sell and trade their products from foreign visitors at the port.

I found Mother near her favorite rocks, on the coast where she met my Father nearly eight hundred years ago. As usual, I had to hear about Asta and Fierra before I was permitted to talk about Gretchen, Knut and Rollo.

"Asta has taken over the harbor at Orkney. She has produced three daughters with Norse chiefs who have made Orkneys their home," Mother said. "As you probably know, this has been a difficult time for people who live near shores, in reach of Viking raiders. People are terrorized with the prospect of seeing ships bearing down on them."

"Fierra has taken over Shetland. We have learned that for now, it is better to depend on the Vikings than it is to depend on those who await their attack," Mother claimed. "They all seem to think that it is just a matter of time before than are descended upon from the sea. Villages and Monasteries along the coasts of Briton and the Franco Empire have all been plundered," she continued.

"Well, the villages on the Seine River Valley have no reason for fear Vikings." I said, as I finally had an opening to speak. "Rollo is now the Count of Normandy and he has his hands on everything that happens in the region.

He has been charged with insuring that other crews not be allowed to come in through the harbor and sail up river. Rollo sees Normandy as his personal property and he is keen to make sure that no one else profits from it."

"He has developed a port in the harbor for trade where the big river empties into the sea," I hurried to say before Mother interrupted me again with more useless news about my two step sisters.

"Norsemen are settling into new villages around the port and on to Rouen. Their violent ways will end soon, I believe. They have what they have been looking for. There may be a few rogue crews who continue sacking monasteries and small towns, but they will soon be in the minority," I said.

"Knut and Gretchen are doing well. She is to deliver her first born this Spring. Knut is a busy young man and will provide a fine living for his young family."

"Has she followed my methods to avoid Merrows?" Mother asked, bluntly.

"She knows your procedure, Mother," I said. I began to see red."

"Whether she decides to use it or not is her decision. She may not take to our way of life," I answered, knowing that she would not let that statement remain unchallenged.

"She must!" Mother demanded.

"No!" I shouted back. "She will follow her heart and make the decision whether to follow our way or live among mortals. That is her decision and I have told her so."

"Hearts have nothing to do with our world. We do not live on love. We live to control the realm of the seas. She will end our reign if she remains apart for our ways," Mother claimed."

"Our way has endured on the Euro continent and the isles for over two thousand years. We can not allow her to end it with her own self indulgence," Mother spat.

Mother was enraged with my denial of her tradition and I was livid with her attitude towards Gretchen. Her narrow view would deny Gretchen's choice. The world of the Sea Maiden might decline if our offspring were given room for choice. She was right about that, but I refused to agree with her. It was her dominance that was causing the problem between us.

I knew the roots that Rollo began to nurture in Normandy would soon reach Britannia and the Euro continent. I had even considered the possibility that the kingdom of the Francs and that of Britannia would someday unite under one kingdom. Mother would never have accepted that kind of prediction, so I kept it to myself.

"You must not allow Gretchen to remain with the mortals," Mother demanded. "We have an opportunity to take the western lands of the Euro continent into our world and dominate the people who inhabit it."

"I wonder why I keep countering her demands," I thought. "I know that I will not be able to change her ways. They have been around for a thousand years. My hesitation to agree with her indicated my disagreement. She became quite disturbed with me."

"Leave my shores," she demanded. "I can take no more disrespect for our history and our future. Go live with your Duke."

"First you bring a Merrow into the world of the Pryten and now you have reared your daughter to abandon our ways, entirely. Leave!" she roared.

Her ways are inflexible. She raised Asta and Fierra to live the traditional lives of her world and they probably would never look beyond it. That is not the way that I saw for Gretchen's future or Rollo's that of the child in my womb. In some way, I needed to find a middle ground. I owed that much to Mother, if I continued to insist on differing with her about the matter.

The source of the problem, I came to realize, was rooted in my determination to let my descendants live with the mortal leaders of their time for as long as they felt that they made contributions to their welfare. I saw a connection between their welfare and our own, in that we benefited from their success in dealing with the challenges of their time.

Since my time with Breidi remained a pleasant and fulfilling memory in my mind, I could not reject the senses of the heart as easily as Mother could. Therein lay the difference.

Chapter XLI

I returned to Rouen and Gretchen. She brought a beautiful daughter into their household. Knut was proud of the child and began to teach her the ways of the citizens of Normandy. Many of the traditions of the Franco people and those of the Nordic people began to meld together into a unique region of its' own.

Knut stood alone in that vision within his own immediate sphere of family influence. Rollo was driven by gathering the resources and population of the region under his own influence. He maintained a separation between the French population and his Nordic citizenry in his mind. Perhaps unconsciously, but it existed, nonetheless.

In the beginning there was a language problem that separated the people. Few people spoke the Germanic Nordic tongue of the Vikings as well as the language of the Francs. That issue would self correct over time but it was a difficult obstacle in the beginning. The Franco population and their Nordic neighbors did little to interchange with each other unless forced by reason of commerce within the region.

I sat with Gretchen one day while Knut was away and told her about the confrontation with Mother. It certainly did not go as well as I had intended.

"My visit with Mother did not go well, Gretchen," I began.

"She would deny you your will to raise your children in the tradition that you choose," I said. "Asta and Fierra have remained loyal to the realm of the supernatural. Mother demands that you do the same," I said.

"I wish that you would not have confronted Grandmother about this. I will, as you said, make my own choices. I may have avoided a head-on confrontation with Grandmother. Now she is aware of our differences and will most likely not be willing to let it be. The time that she takes her vengeance out on our world may be unavoidable now," Gretchen said. "What if she decides to take the future of my Anne in her own hands? What if she storms in here one day and takes my child from me?"

"You may view your ability to resist Grandmother's powers greater than I. I do not dismiss her influence as easily as you do," Gretchen said.

"I did not think of it in that way. I am sorry. I think that you must be right," I said.

"We will see," Gretchen said.

"I could not stand by and allow her tell me how you will live your life," I offered. "Now I see that I should have avoided the entire conversation. I lost control of my temper when she demanded that all of us live as she lives."

I wish that I could have avoided telling Mother about Gretchen, after having to listen to Mother talk about Asta and Fierra. The way Mother sees it, we have no choice but to live a life that serves Mother and Grandmother.

Gretchen named her child "Anne." She had all of the physical traits of the sea maiden. Her big, shiny eyes darted around the room looking for her mother or father. Knut held her above his head and she laughed, filling the room with happiness and innocence.

Rouen had grown since Knut began using it as a trading stop on the river. New homes and merchants built in every direction. The town spread its width into the surrounding fields and across the river.

The vineyards expanded as local vintners worked new fields of their fruit and prepared it for processing in the village. Several families were involved in picking the harvest and bringing it into the village. Grape harvest time was a reason for celebration among the French population of Rouen. They dropped their own commerce and joined other as they picked and delivered the harvest to the town processing plant. Large vats of grapes were mashed by women who climbed into a large hopper that held the harvest and tromped around until the fruit juices were released. People from all over the village and the countryside joined in.

Popee had her first child by Rollo. They named him William. They both knew that he would take his Father's title as the Count of Normandy some day. I felt that it would come sooner than some might predict. Rollo had attained his goal for his people.

The question was, whether he would settle down and live a peaceful life after accomplishing this miraculous feat. I doubted that he would. That would lead to a problem with others who had designs on benefiting from the profits that came from Normandy even in its earliest times.

The huge miscalculation that Charles made over the potential value of Normandy began to play heavy on my mind as it caused disruption among members of his court. They said that Charles was a simple fool.

Rollo, Knut and Ruud had made the region work for him and produce huge profits. They were unhappy with Charles. Most began to anticipate a time when Charles would be replaced.

Rollo was too absorbed in the day to day issues to realize that he had created a source of jealousy and indifference. There were people within the King's inner circle who calculated ways to share or redirect the wealth being created under their noses.

Rollo remained restless after William was born. Unable to settle down and enjoy the fruit of his labor, he traveled the region and began plundering villages within his realm and beyond. With Rouen as his base on the Euro continent, he traveled deep into the country side and took whatever he wanted.

Knut had a falling out with Rollo over his interference with the supply to the port. He tried to convince Rollo that the people would never come to trust Nordic people if he continued raiding their villages and molesting citizens. Merchants along the river feared being attacked. With Rollo still on the prowl, there was good reason for concern.

"My crews are restless," Rollo told Knut. "They want to see where the rivers lead them and they want to travel the coast line into new regions.

Expecting my crews to suddenly become pacifist farmers is too much. Traveling is in their blood.

Everything that my people grow or make is my property. They have no say in this. By order of their own King, Normandy is mine."

"No one will trust us, Prince," Knut said. "Stealing from your own people will bring about a bad outcome."

Knut went about his business and neither he nor Rollo ever brought the matter up again, at least not that I know of. The port was booming with trade at this point and hopefully they could keep it going.

Merchants began to realize the benefits of Knut and Ruud's supply line. The riches of Normandy pulsed through the port. It would have been difficult to carry on this kind of activity without attracting the attention of those who would desire a piece of the action.

I remained concerned and told Knut that he should be aware of the spectacle that Normandy was fast becoming. "Knut, you and Ruud need to watch your backs," I said. "It would be naïve to think that those who were not included in the commerce of Normandy will sit on the sideline and watch the wealth flow for the benefit of a few. I see those in Charles's court to be among those that we need to be most concerned about."

"You have to realize that before Charles made this blunder, his court received taxes from the region. While they were miniscule compared to what the citizens of Normandy pay now, at least it was something. Today, they receive nothing, and are surely jealous of being cut out by the actions of their nit wit King," I warned.

"Charles is weak. He does not possess the power to hold his advisors at bay. They are the one's who are losing out."

"I see what you mean," Esther. "Rollo does not see this as an issue, I am sure," Knut said.

"No. He does not," I agreed. "Rollo is bound to be the target of contempt, just by the virtue of the tempest that he created when he was awarded Normandy."

"Normandy is the proverbial 'hot potato,' of our time," he said.

"I am afraid so."

Later, I heard Knut tell Ruud that they should begin escorting ships up and down the river to protect their merchants from rogue crews.

Chapter XLII

Word came to Rouen that two sea maidens had been seen on the rocks near the harbor and Ruud's port. I believed that it must be Asta and Fierra, but I left to find out what the rumor was about.

I left Rouen and traveled down the river on one of Knut's cargo ships. The river meandered its way through the countryside until it reached the large harbor. I walked along the piers and docks that Ruud had installed to receive cargo ships. There were several vessels from Scandinavia and a few from sea side villages on the Franco coast. At this point, the Britons were kept away by their own fear of Norse crews who sailed in and out of the harbor.

I soon found Asta and Fierra just where I thought that they would be. They sat at the entrance to the harbor causing a scene as ships sailed by.

"What are you doing here?" I asked.

"Mother sent us here," Fierra answered.

""You know that the Franco coast is my domain? Do you not?" I asked.

"All lands and seas of this region are Queen Sarah's realm," the arrogant little Asta said.

Her attempt at dismissing me got under my skin. I fought the urge to strike back at the little brat.

Instead, I stuck to my verbal assault. "Be gone, you two," I demanded. "You have plenty of ports in Shetland and Orkney as well as Ireland and the Sudry Isles. Leave and do not come back."

"But Mother gave you the Sudrys and Ireland, many years ago," Fierra wined. You can not have both," Asta said.

"Well, tell Mother that they are yours now. I claim the seas and shores of Normandy for my own. You can have the Sudrys and Hibernia," I said.

"Surely, you can not find fault with that?" I asked. "These ports and harbors I claim for Gretchen and myself. We have invested ourselves in the mortals who made Normandy what it is today."

"Go. Tell Mother what I have said," I told them.

As they left the shore, I looked at the progress that Ruud and Knut had made. Ships were tethered to the piers and they sat at anchor, deep into the harbor. If the two of them could ever convince the Britons to use the port, they would benefit from an enormous increase in their business.

My senses were torn between arguing for expansion of the port to add even more profit to the commerce and trying to stifle the attention that the robust port drew. I just knew that something calamitous was about to happen.

I decided that I needed to stay in the area. Rollo did not need me anymore. He had Popee and they had William, the heir to Rollo's title. They had plenty to keep their minds off of me.

When Knut and I returned to Rouen following our business near the port, Knut talked to Rollo about convincing the Britons and the Scots to use the port for trade.

"The Britons will not come to the harbor," Rollo predicted. "Perhaps the northern Scot people from Aberdeen might not fear of trading with us. It is too early to expect the Britons to approach Nordic settlements."

"If we stop pillaging the Briton's coast line, they might not fear us," Knut said.

"Perhaps, but I have no control over what crews do outside of Normandy and the coast," Rollo said.

I could feel the frustration Knut had with Rollo's short term

"Then I will sail for Aberdeen and speak to King Constantine's court," Knut said. "We will begin with them."

I accompanied Knut and Ruud to meet Malcolm.

We arrived at the port and waited to meet an official who would send a messenger to Constantine's court to announce our arrival and intent to visit. Word soon came via messenger who we followed back to the castle complex. We were admitted to Constantine's court. He sat with six advisors, all clamoring to get the closest seat to the Scottish King.

From the moment that I entered the chamber I sensed Constantine's eyes upon me. I watched his eyes and the expression on his face as he glared at me.

"We are messengers from the Duke of Normandy, your majesty. We come to discuss an opening of a trade agreement between the people of Normandy and the citizens of your realm," Knut began.

I could still sense Constantine's eyes.

"I see," Constantine said. We waited for him to continue. It was clear that he did not intend to say anything further until he had heard more about the reason for our visit.

"As you may have heard, your Majesty, we have developed a trading port, in the harbor, at the mouth of the River Seine. The port has become an important outlet for goods from Normandy and we are beginning to see products from other regions coming through the port," Knut went on.

"We see benefit for creating an expansion of our trade with the people of Scotland. We invite your consideration of bringing Scottish trade ships to Normandy where your Majesty's citizens can buy and sell goods with others who have already done so," Knut went on.

"And who might, those others be?" Constantine asked.

"We are limited at this time to traders along the French coast and those of Denmark, and Norway, at this time," Knut offered.

"I see," Constantine said.

"You expect the people of Scotland to trust those who have raided, plundered and killed their way along our coast?" Constantine asked. His contempt for our people was not hidden.

"Yes, your Majesty. That is our hope. The Duke has asked us to extend our hand in a peace offering," Knut began.

"Peace offering? His crews still patrol the coast of Scotland, threatening the lives of our people, stealing everything that they see and raping our women. Does the Duke's peace offering protect us from the slaughter that persists today?" Constantine asked.

"That is too much to ask at this time. When your murderous crews stop pirating our shores, perhaps then we might expect relaxing our guard. Today, I do not see that as a likely outcome," the King replied.

"And who is the beautiful young women that you have brought to my court?" he asked.

"I am Esther, your Majesty," I said.

"And where have we met?" Madam.

"Perhaps you are thinking of my Mother, Sarah," I said.

"Sarah? Do you speak of Sarah, Legend of the Pictish people of Caledonia?" he asked.

"Yes, your Majesty. Mother and I lived among the Pict of the highlands. She is the widow of Maelchon? Is she not?" he asked.

"Yes, your Majesty, and I am the widow of Breidi, King of the Pict," I said.

"But Brude, as we call him, has been dead for several hundred years."

"Yes your Majesty. That is true," I said.

"Come forward my dear," the King ordered. I approached his chair on the raised platform and knelt before him. "Come closer, my dear," he insisted. "Let me see the face of a six hundred year old widow.

I rose and took three steps toward the King.

He put his hand under my chin and raised my face to meet his eyes. He looked into my eyes and I sensed a relaxation of his guard, even an appreciation for our legend.

"You look marvelous for your age, my dear," Constantine spoke softly. "Is your Mother as beautiful as you?" he asked.

"Nearly," I said.

"Ha," he laughed. "What do you have to say to this proposal that these young men bring to your native people," he asked.

"Yes your Majesty, we must look to the future, when ships cross the narrow channel between Normandy and the shores of Briton. It is time for the Normans to bury their axes."

He bent over to whisper in my ear, "You need not call me 'your Majesty' my Queen. It is I who should be kneeling before you," he said.

I looked him in the eyes and smiled as his words came upon my face in the intimacy of the moment. I felt the slightest puff of air across my face as he spoke softly and so close. The intimacy of the moment reminded me that I needed to find another mate and a sire for my next daughter. The King of England might meet Mother's specifications, I mused. "We will see," I thought.

"Should we trust the words of these gentlemen?" he asked. "Do they have the authority to stop the raids of my villages and towns?"

"These two young men are honest in their intention, your Majesty, but they do not have the power to stop rouge crews from plundering your shores. You hesitance is wise, your Majesty," I said.

"Why have you come here?" he said softly. No one in the room could have heard our words.

"The population of Caledonia and the Hebrides Isles are my native people. Mother and I have lived among them in peace for, hundreds of years," I said hesitantly. "I care what happens to them," your Majesty.

"Stay with me, my dear. Tell me more," he said.

Constantine rose from his chair with my hand in his and lifted me from my kneeling position.

"Thank you, young Knut," he began. "We will consider your offer for we do know of the goods coming from Normandy. We, like others, could benefit from these products but we are hesitant at this time to place ourselves in the hands of those who have murdered so many of us. Go, tell your Duke that we prefer to wait and see how outsiders are treated in the den of wolves, before we wish to join them."

"Esther will stay with me so that we may talk further about the welfare of the people of our highlands," he said.

Knut and Ruud left the chamber. I remained behind. The King looked me in my eyes. I saw the appetite for beautiful women and the mystery of curiosity in his thoughts.

"Come my dear. We have much to discuss," Constantine said. He took my hand as we entered his private baths where we sat on a rose petal bench, lined with pillows. The view over the warm bath and through the bay window carried out through the palace grounds and onto the fields beyond.

There were attendants who came in to watch over Constantine as they took his robe and walked him down the three steps to the warm pool. They came to me and helped me to my feet. One lifted the tunic over my head while the other removed my slippers. They walked me down the stairs to the pool as they had Constantine. He watched me as I entered the pool. The water came up to the bottom of my butt. The water tickled on my bottom and between my thighs as I walked towards the King. I joined him on a water bench, notched into the side of the pool where we sat, side by side.

The water covered my lap and no more. He cupped his hands and brought warm water over my shoulders and watched it run over my shoulders and chest. His hands caressed my inner thighs as I leaned back and enjoyed the warm elegance of the water. "This King must be related to Fain," I mused as I let him massage me.

He rose and stepped between my knees. He splashed water over my belly and chest before he moved in and we joined in the warmth of the pool. We relaxed between two more sessions when we joined with our hips under water.

Finally, we returned to his bed and the shear privacy curtain that surrounded it and enjoyed the breeze coming through the court windows.

"The stories of your time among the ancient Pict are legend to Scottish people," Constantine said. "Tell me when it began."

"Her first was my Father, a Roman General assigned to build Emperor Haden's wall. She stayed with him in camp until I was born. We then moved off shore from a Pict village. Years later, we went into the village with Maelchon and his son, Brude. Mother had two daughters by Maelchon and I had two by Brude," I continued.

"Was Robb your son?" he asked.

"Yes. He was my first born. He stayed with the Pict, in the Wolf Clan. He grew up to become one of their early kings," I continued.

"My daughter Gretchen is Brude's daughter, as well. We left the Pict and lived in a Norse village in the Shetlands Islands for many years.

Mother was Olaf's woman. I lived with a blacksmith named Fain while Gretchen became of age."

"I moved on to The Isle of Man and joined Rollo, who now is Robert I, Duke of Normandy. Young Knut is my daughter's husband," I said. "We have been in Normandy since."

"History has not overstated the legends of the supernatural that have influenced our ancient clans," he said. "The people of our time are influenced more by Christian teachings than the old Pagan traditions, but I think that it is wise to remember our ancient people in the context of their time," Constantine said.

"You must bring your Mother to court. I would enjoy meeting her," he said.

Chapter XLIII

Young William grew into a handsome young man. It was clear to Knut and I that Rollo would soon feel the pressure of his age and take a more leisure attitude towards his responsibilities and the people of Normandy. At least, that was our hope.

It was apparent from the time that William began taking some of his Father's responsibilities that his loyalties were much more French than Danish or Norwegian. He spoke French, preferred French food, French wine and French women. The transition that I feared would take many generations actually began to appear in the second generation.

I went back to the harbor and left Knut and Gretchen to work out these matters. I was more concerned about Mother's threats than I was over Rollo.

I delivered Constantine's baby in a time known on the Christian calendar as 926AD. She was a bright infant and she brought me joy from the beginning. I had taken the rocks, off shore, where I found my two half sisters.

I began telling her stories about Mother and I and some of the people that we knew over the last eight hundred years or so. Before she was capable of understanding me, I am sure, I told her about my Father's time, the Pryten people and the Vikings of her era.

Our days were spent in leisure, watching the ships come and go through the harbor. Then one day, with no warning, Mother showed up. I had been dreading this since I ran her two brats away. I knew that things had been too peaceful.

"Asta and Fierra told me about your demands," She said, as soon as we were within speaking distance. "I do not appreciate you deciding who gets which part of my domain."

"As you wish, Mother," I said. "I have no plans to leave here, so do what you will."

"If you want to stay here, that is fine with me. This is new to all of us," She said. "Asta and Fierra can stay in the Hebrides and Ireland."

"Have you left the Viking?" she asked.

"Yes," he has children by a mortal. He is not doing well. The years of sailing on the cold, rough seas has him ill," I explained.

"I wish you no harm, Esther," she offered. "I treasure you, as my first, and no one will ever take your place. I let my temper get the best of me."

"Are you going to return to our world, then?" she asked.

"Yes, Gretchen is occupied with her life and I have this young one to look after," I said.

"What is her name?" she asked.

"Her name is Wendy," I said.

"Ahh! You named her after me," she chided.

"Yes, she is named after both of us," I said.

"We will see you again and you will not hear from my two, 'Brats,' as you call them. Mother left peacefully. She must have been more interested in gaining the region that I claimed as mine than she was squabbling over the territory that I left behind.

Word came that Rollo had turned his responsibilities over to his son, William. He became histories Second Duke of Normandy. He and his wife Sprota took over the region with a different approach than the way his father had ruled.

William, who they distinguished from other Williams at the time became known as "William Longsword."

William's ways soon showed him as more of a Franc than a Norsemen. Problems with Norsemen in the region developed into a near rebellion within the first few years of his reign. He soon became criticized as being too easy on his French subjects. Williams days were surely marked.

His Nordic citizens wanted William to continue dividing Normandy up among them as Rollo had done. Many had been given lands and villages by Rollo in exchange for their loyalty. William began to take those lands back. He became the subject of criticism and threats. This developed while Charles was imprisoned. His foes were among his court advisors who aw Charles as weak and stupid. He was known in those times as Charles, The Simple.

William seldom knew a moment of peace as he tried desperately to rule the French people of Normandy. He tried to use a measure of humanity while being challenged constantly by his Nordic subjects who refused to release their old ways. William was at a meeting with Arnulf of Flanders trying to settle their differences when he was killed.

This was a troubled time of the new French King, Louis who saw Charles' gift to Rollo and his descendants as a sign of his weakness was anxious o have the land returned to the crown.

Rollo should have predicted this development. He should have known that he had secured a valuable piece of France. Much more valuable than he should have received for the services that he provided.

William's son, Richard, Richard I, as history knew him, was called "The Fearless." He was a boy when his father was killed. He found himself at constant difference with the French King and his court.

The replacement of sons after fathers continued for many generations in a rapid succession in the years that Wendy and I stayed near the harbor. They died during rebellions or by assassination as their greedy relatives desired the riches that Ruud and Knut's harbor brought to the region many years before.

The danger in those times no longer came from Norsemen. The issues came from greed of those who wanted to replace those that operated the profitable port and harbor. The original Norse crewmen who settled into Rouen and the nearby countryside had passed on generations ago.

Knut and Ruud left their legacy to their sons and daughters. Gretchen returned with Wendy and I. The activity around the old port never slowed. After years of resistance, the people of Scotland began to trade in the harbor that became know as "Le' Havre."

I left Gretchen and Wendy to watch the harbor at Le Havre' while I returned to Constantine's court and his wonderful, warm baths. I would live well under his care and I looked forward to helping him overseeing the care of our ancient people of the highlands.

My prediction of the kingdoms of Britannia and the Francs uniting finally happened after William II (William The Conqueror). Even William II had trouble retaining control of Le Havre and Normandy. He was resisted and challenged for the entire period that he was King of England and France

Even then, Le' Havre continued to be fought over. The riches of the region that Rollo won many centuries before were desired by the English crown and the French Empire. It was responsible for the joining of the two kingdoms. All future Kings of England trace their lineage through Rollo, the first Duke of Normandy.

William held reign over Britannia and France after he took victory at the battle of Hastings. William did not bring peace to the combined regions either. His throne was constantly faced challenge.

As for Wendy, Gretchen, they spend some of their days with Mother near the Scottish coast and the remainder near the French harbor. I never saw Asta and Fierra again. I understand that they stayed on the western side of Britannia and Ireland.

Wendy enjoys hearing her grandmother tell about our lives with a Roman General, a Pict King and a Viking who changed the face of Europe.

Mother embellishes on the details of her life, but who could blame her? She had lived among the best of them.

Manufactured By: RR Donnelley
Momence, IL USA
June , 2010